Praise for the Capital Crimes Novels

"A dazzling series."
—*The Atlanta Journal-Constitution*

"Dead-on descriptions of Washington's most crack-ridden streets and exclusionary shindigs."
—*USA Today*
on *Murder at Ford's Theater*

"A satisfying tale . . . remarkably fresh in
its insights about politics, intrigue, money, and sex
in the city by the Potomac."
—*The News & Observer* (Raleigh, NC)
on *Murder on K Street*

MARGARET TRUMAN'S

INTERNSHIP IN MURDER

A CAPITAL CRIMES NOVEL

▸ DONALD BAIN ◂

FORGE®

A TOM DOHERTY ASSOCIATES BOOK | NEW YORK

MARGARET TRUMAN'S INTERNSHIP IN MURDER: A CAPITAL CRIMES NOVEL

Copyright © 2015 by Estate of Margaret Truman

A Forge Book
Published by Tom Doherty Associates, LLC
175 Fifth Avenue
New York, NY 10010

www.tor-forge.com

Forge® is a registered trademark of Tom Doherty Associates, LLC.

ISBN 978-0-7653-7051-8

Our books may be purchased in bulk for promotional, educational, or business use. Please contact your local bookseller or the Macmillan Corporate and Premium Sales Department at 1-800-221-7945, extension 5442, or by e-mail at MacmillanSpecialMarkets@macmillan.com.

First Edition: August 2015
First Mass Market Edition: June 2016

Printed in the United States of America

0 9 8 7 6 5 4 3 2

For Zach, Alex, Jake, Luke, Abigail, Sylvan, Ellie, and Gray.
I'm too young to have this many grandchildren.

PROLOGUE

Washington, D.C., had been good to Capac Lopez. Since arriving twelve years ago from Peru, he'd found the ethnically diverse city a fertile ground for realizing his dream of opening a Peruvian restaurant in the United States. He'd been brought up around restaurants. His father owned a popular café in Lima, and Capac had spent much of his youth washing dishes, prepping food, and accompanying his father to the markets in the early morning to choose fresh ingredients for the café's ambitious menu.

But at the age of thirty, and with a young wife and infant son, Capac made the wrenching decision to leave his parents and siblings to forge a new life in the United States. Now, eight years after a tearful farewell, he was the proud owner of a thriving restaurant in Washington's bustling Adams Morgan area of the city.

It was hard work, leaving Capac little time for recreation. But on many Sunday mornings he indulged in a favorite pastime, an early-morning hike through the woods of Washington's Rock Creek Park, twenty-one hundred acres that cut through the center of the nation's capital, America's oldest natural urban park.

Being outdoors provided Capac with a sense of freedom. He especially enjoyed the twisting trails in the southernmost section, not far from Adams Morgan and the National Zoo; on some days he could hear the lions roar. On this particular Sunday morning he'd left his house even earlier than usual, arriving at the park as the sun began to rise. It promised to be a lovely day, the city's notorious humidity having dropped to a more comfortable level, the brightening sky a harbinger of what Capac liked to say would be *el día gordo*—a fat day.

Capac loved to breathe in air that was fresher than in the city, observe small animals scurrying about, examine wildflowers, and splash cold, fresh water from streams on his face. Trash left behind by others angered him, and he quietly cursed them in Spanish as he balled up a plastic bag and shoved it in his pocket.

He was heading home when something—a piece of green cloth?—caught his eye. At first he ignored it; he couldn't pick up every bit of trash. Whatever it was had been partially obscured by a layer of leaves. After taking a few steps away, he returned and bent over to see better. He used his sneaker to kick away some leaves, revealing more of what had captured his attention. More leaves were wiped away. Now the cloth came into full view. It was one leg of a pair of green slacks. Capac straightened, afraid to go farther. But then, using his hand to brush off the debris, he briskly, desperately allowed dappled sunlight to fall on his discovery.

It was a body. A woman. Blond. Pretty? Hard to tell considering the shape her face was in.

Capac turned away and gave up his breakfast to the forest floor.

* * *

Homicide detective Jason Ewing had been with the Washington Metropolitan Police Department for eighteen years, one of more than two thousand African-American officers on the force. With him in a conference room at police headquarters on Judiciary Square was the department's superintendent of detectives, Ezekiel "Zeke" Borgeldt who, after a long career with the Federal Bureau of Investigation, had been recruited to take over the demoralized and understaffed detective division. The two men, along with Ewing's partner, Jack Morey, three years as a detective after eleven years in uniform, were meeting to discuss Capac Lopez's discovery.

"What do you think?" Ewing was asked by his superior.

"The conclusion the press and public will come to is that we've got a serial killer on our hands," Ewing said. "This is the second vic in the park in the past three months."

"But two homicides don't add up to serial killings," Morey put in.

Borgeldt looked down through half glasses on the tip of his bulbous nose as he read from the report. "This one's twenty-two years old. The previous one was twenty-seven. No obvious connection between them. The older victim had been reported missing by her husband two months ago. No one reported this new woman missing. The ME is still trying to come up with a name for her and where she came from."

"A hooker?" Morey asked.

"Who knows?" Borgeldt said, sighing. "Amazing how many people disappear and nobody even knows or cares that they're missing."

"Or maybe they're happy to see them gone," Morey quipped.

"Same MO," Borgeldt said, "same cause of death, blunt

force blows to the head, both bodies buried in a shallow grave covered with leaves."

"What I don't get," said Ewing, "is why whoever killed these women took the time to dig shallow graves. Those areas are popular with hikers, families with kids, lots of people. Sure, the graves are shallow, six inches deep at best, but it takes time to scrape away that much dirt and lay a blanket of leaves over the bodies."

Borgeldt pulled photographs from the file and fanned them out on the desk. "The ME estimates that this victim was killed within the past two weeks. Nobody walking in that area saw what this Lopez guy saw?"

"Hikers aren't looking for bodies," Ewing said. "Lopez was pretty far off the path when he discovered her."

"You ran a check on him?" Borgeldt asked.

"Sure," replied Ewing. "Family man, came here from Peru eight years ago, owns a popular Peruvian restaurant in Adams Morgan. I've eaten there a few times. Nice guy. Good food."

"What about that Russian guy women were complaining about, the one they say harassed them when they were hiking in the park?" Morey said.

Borgeldt shrugged. "Wouldn't hurt to bring him in again for questioning. Pick him up."

THE SEDUCTION

1

I'll have one of your patented Collins drinks," Congressman Harold "Hal" Gannon told party host Lucas Bennett.

"Tom or John?"

"What's the difference?"

"Bourbon or gin? Tom uses gin, John uses bourbon."

The congressman laughed. "Where did Florida's leading malpractice attorney learn so much about making drinks?"

"I bartended during law school, got interested in the subtler aspects of it. Besides, if doctors ever stop cutting off the wrong limb or leaving sutures inside patients, I might need a job behind a bar."

"Bourbon."

"One John Collins coming up. By the way, I only use Meyer lemons."

"As opposed to?"

"The usual lemons. Meyers have a deeper taste, a hint of orange," Bennett said as he prepared the drink behind the marble bar top in his posh waterfront home. "They were invented in China. Some guy tried to grow them in

California, but his trees had a virus that damn near wiped out every other citrus tree in the state. They eventually figured it out." He shook the bourbon, freshly squeezed lemon juice, sugar, and ice in a stainless shaker, poured the concoction into a glass, added club soda, garnished it with an orange slice, and handed it to the congressman.

Gannon took a small sip. "Wonderful," he said, smacking his lips. "I know some bars in Washington that could use you."

"I'll send my surrogate," Bennett said as his twenty-two-year-old daughter, Laura, joined him and accepted his embrace.

"She's a lot prettier than you are," Gannon said.

"Which means she'll get better tips."

Lucas Bennett was a big man in every sense. He was overweight, but the pounds were solidly packed on his six-foot-two frame. His flowing white hair gave him the look of an orator of yore. His ruddy face and ready smile belied a keen legal mind and a killer instinct when engaged in an adversarial situation with another attorney. Hal Gannon had been one of those lawyers who'd once felt the heft of Bennett's intellect and the sting of his silver tongue.

But that was before Gannon put his Tampa law practice into mothballs and successfully ran for the U.S. House of Representatives from Florida's Fourteenth Congressional District. He was in his fourth term. In an amusing irony, Lucas Bennett, his former opponent in court, had been one of his most generous backers, and Laura had worked as a volunteer on his most recent campaign.

"Has Laura acquired your skills, Luke, as a—what's it called?—as a mixologist?"

"I make a dynamite cosmopolitan," she said, "and I can pop a cap off a beer bottle in the wink of an eye."

Both men laughed as Bennett's wife, Grace, joined

them. "You have to get out from behind the bar, Luke," she said, "and mingle with our other guests."

Grace Bennett was reed-thin but not emaciated. A physical therapist at Tampa General Hospital, she was a workout fanatic, and her sinewy, muscular arms and chiseled face—not an ounce of excess flesh anywhere—testified to a lifetime spent in gyms and lifting paralyzed patients back into wheelchairs.

"I suppose I should," her husband said as he rinsed his hands in a small sink and dried them. Before he followed his wife to where their other guests were gathered on an expansive patio that led down to the water and the slip at which their small cabin cruiser was docked, he said to Gannon, "I know I've thanked you before for arranging Laura's internship in your Washington office, Hal, but I'll say it again."

"Looking forward to having her," Gannon said.

"Just make sure she doesn't fall in love with some knee-jerk Democrat," Bennett said jovially.

Gannon, a conservative Democrat, said, "Even if he's a Blue Dog?"

"Well, that might make a difference," said Bennett. "Enjoy your drink Hal. I'll be back in a few minutes to whip up another round."

Gannon's reference to Blue Dogs reflected his leadership in the House of Representatives' band of right-leaning Democrats who often sided with their Republican counterparts. They'd taken the name Blue Dogs to mock the Yellow Dog Democrats of the early 1900s who were branded with the nickname because it was said that they would vote for anything, even a yellow dog, rather than a Republican.

Gannon and Laura watched the Bennetts go through open French doors to the terrace.

"Your folks are great," Gannon said, placing his barely touched drink on the bar.

"You aren't drinking this?" Laura asked, picking up the glass.

"I don't drink much, just an occasional social sip. Didn't want to offend your dad."

Laura took a healthy swig and smacked her lips. "Yummy."

"I'll take your word for it."

Congressman Hal Gannon would be considered handsome by any standard. He had a shock of unruly black hair that defied taming, which could also be said about his earlier bachelor days in Tampa. He topped six feet in height, and even beneath his red-and-blue-striped sport shirt you could see that he was physically fit. Like Grace Bennett, Gannon was no stranger to gyms, both when he was home in Tampa and when in Congress, where he took full advantage of the House's workout facilities. His jaw was square, his green eyes probing, mouth always on the verge of breaking into a boyish grin. *The Washingtonian* magazine had named him one of the House of Representatives' handsomest men.

"Looking forward to coming to work for me?" he asked Laura, who took another sip of the drink.

"Are you sure I'll be *working* for you?" she said playfully. "When you work for someone, you usually get paid."

"We have rules about that in the House," he countered, "but maybe I can squeeze something out of the budget—if you're good."

"Good at what?" she asked, raising a nicely shaped eyebrow.

"Hal!"

Gannon looked through the open doors to where his wife, Charlene, waved at him.

"I'm being summoned," he said.

"Your wife is so beautiful," Laura said.

"She is, isn't she? Looking forward to when you arrive in D.C. The housing service landed you a prime spot, a two-bedroom on Capitol Hill, only a few blocks from the office, lots of space for you and your roommate. Roseann, my chief of staff, will help get you settled. Ace those final few exams before you come. I like my interns to be achievers and . . ."

"And?" she said playfully.

He shrugged. "Available, I suppose. Excuse me. See you in a month, Laura." He hesitated, came forward, kissed her cheek, and joined his wife.

Laura finished the drink her father had made for Gannon and placed it on a tray of dirty glasses behind the bar. She took in her image in the back-bar mirror. She was her mother's daughter, albeit more fleshy, more womanly. Her legs were long, her waist narrow. Unlike her mother, her bosom was large and amply occupied her pink silk blouse, its top buttons undone to reveal some cleavage. Both mother and daughter were brunettes, although Laura's hair had more of a copper tint to it; she wore it loose and shoulder length.

She turned her attention to the terrace, where what someone had said generated gales of laughter. It was a money crowd. Social gatherings at the house were always attended by her parents' wealthy friends, and Laura knew that she was fortunate to have been born into the Bennett family. She'd never wanted for anything and had been blatantly spoiled. She was in her senior year at the University of Southern Florida, majoring in health administration in its College of Public Health. She hadn't chosen that major. She would have preferred something more artistic, like acting or painting. But her father had convinced her that she should graduate with a usable degree, which wouldn't preclude her from pursuing artistic endeavors on the side. Law school? That's what Lucas Bennett really wanted for his only child.

Laura's attention went to Charlene Gannon, the

congressman's wife. No doubt about it, Charlene was a stunning woman—silver-blond hair, lovely figure, and perfectly painted oval face. She and her husband made a picture book couple. The media, always on the hunt for juicy stories about elected officials, pounced on every aspect of the Gannons' private life, focusing most recently on the fact that Charlene spent little time in D.C. with her husband.

"Why would anyone choose to run for office and open himself to such public scrutiny?" Laura once questioned her father after reading that the public's view of members of Congress ranked only slightly higher than serial rapists and below identity thieves.

"Ego," he replied, "pure, unadulterated ego."

Hal Gannon certainly had such an ego. Maybe "self-assuredness" was a better term. Laura smiled as she watched him break into a contagious laugh at something a woman said. If anyone had the right to be self-assured, she decided as she went to the patio and joined in the spirited conversation, it was Hal Gannon, successful attorney, popular member of the U.S. Congress, and movie-star handsome.

A real hunk.

In a month she would be leaving Tampa for Washington to become an intern in his office. Growing up in the opulence of the Bennett family had been wonderful, as carefully measured and nurtured as her father's favorite drink recipes.

But it was time to taste something new.

She couldn't wait.

2

Mackensie Smith had come full circle.

He'd been one of Washington's top criminal lawyers, a go-to guy when a case seemed hopeless. But after losing a son and his first wife to a drunk driver on the Beltway—and seeing the drunk get off with what Smith considered a slap on the wrist—he closed his office and accepted a professorship at the George Washington University School of Law, where he'd taught fledgling attorneys about the real world of law.

While his stint in academia had been satisfying, the call of the courtroom became too loud to ignore. After many long discussions with his wife, Annabel Reed-Smith—herself a former attorney, now owner of a pre-Columbian art gallery in Georgetown—and with her less-than-enthusiastic blessing, he resigned his post at the university and put out his shingle again: MACKENSIE SMITH, ATTORNEY-AT-LAW.

He'd spent most of the day taking depositions in a case involving the allegation that his client, a prosperous businessman, had bribed a government official in return for a lucrative contract. Mac was in the midst of reading the stenographer's transcript when his receptionist informed him that Mr. Brixton wanted to see him.

"Send him in, Doris."

How's my favorite private investigator?" Smith asked as Brixton entered the spacious office on Pennsylvania Avenue.

"Could be worse," Brixton said. "I could be on a long flight sitting next to a congressman."

Smith smiled. He'd never heard Brixton say he was good, or fine, or feeling great. His response always bordered on the negative.

Robert Brixton's decision to open his own private investigation agency in Washington, D.C., hadn't been easy. How could it have been? It seemed that nothing good had ever happened to him in the nation's capital.

Born in Brooklyn, he'd ventured south to where cops were being hired, and spent four years in Washington as a uniformed officer. He'd also met and married his now ex-wife there. The marriage hadn't been any more successful than his stint with the MPD had been. On the positive side were two precious daughters from his ill-fated, hormone-driven coupling with Marylee, and they'd grown into beautiful, albeit vastly different, young women.

But an event occurred many years later that led to the death of his younger daughter, Janet, during his second unpleasant stint in Washington. It drove a stake into his heart and sent him back to Brooklyn.

Washington, D.C.?

You could take it and shove it, as far as Robert Brixton was concerned.

But leaving D.C. for good following the tragedy of his daughter's death wasn't to be.

He could thank (or blame) Mackensie Smith for that.

* * *

"Have a seat, Robert. Drink?"

"Love one."

Smith opened a custom-built cherry cabinet and placed a glass on the drop-down shelf. "Gin?" he asked over his shoulder.

"Got any brandy, or cognac?" Brixton asked.

"Cognac," Smith said, pulling out a snifter, pouring two fingers of Hennessey into the glass, and handing it to Brixton.

"I'm drinking alone?" Brixton asked.

"Looks like it," said Smith. "I have a prospective client coming in an hour. How's that case you've been working the past few weeks?"

"Not too bad, but it barely covers the rent. I'm getting paid out of MPD's informant fund." Brixton sampled the drink. "Good stuff, Mac. About the case. I've had two sessions with the wife, who thinks she's talking to a hit man. The wire works, the cops are happy."

"She wants her husband killed," Smith said flatly. "Who was this fellow who put her in touch with you?"

"Name's Augie. He's a street guy I used to get information from when I was a cop on the force. He's older now but still a nut job, into drugs, petty theft, the usual. This wife meets him in a bar and starts talking about how she hates her husband and would like to see him gone. Can you imagine? This married lady who lives in a million-plus house, has kids, the works, tells a low-life like Augie, who she never met before, that she wants her hubby killed? Stupid, huh?"

"That's being kind."

"So Augie, who knows I've opened this agency, tells her that he's got a friend who might be able to help."

"He thought that *you* might be a hit man?" Smith said, chuckling.

"Do I look like a hit man?"

Mac raised his eyebrows.

"Don't answer that. Anyway, she calls me and we meet. She claims that her hubby beats her now and then. I think she's got a sweetie on the side and wants the old man out of the way so she can run off with the guy. 'Get a divorce,' I tell her. She says, 'He'll never give me one.' I say, 'Just leave.' She says, 'I'll be broke. He'll keep the bank accounts, the house, everything.' I ask her why she hates the guy so much that she wants him dead. She tells me that he's a moron who is cheap with money, is a lousy father, and his feet smell."

"His feet smell?"

Brixton joined in Smith's laughter. "I told her it'd be cheaper to buy him a lifetime supply of foot deodorant. That made her laugh. That's the key to setups like this, Mac, keep it light."

Smith shook his head. "She *is* a foolish woman," he said. "How much has she agreed to pay you?"

"Depends on what she decides she wants done. For a couple of broken knees and a messed-up face, twenty grand, double to get rid of him."

"So you went to the police."

"An old buddy of mine at MPD. He meets with his superior and they decide I should wear a wire and get her on the record paying me to have her husband killed. 'Wearing a wire.' That's old cop-speak, huh? I used to wear a wire when it was a bulky machine taped to your body. It was a Swiss recorder, a Nagra. The batteries generated heat, made you sweat, which wasn't good when the guy you were recording was suspicious. Man, I remember taking that damn thing off. You pulled the tape and your chest or groin hair came off with it. Not pleasant. The so-called wire I wear now is about the size of a dime, fits into a shirt button, sends the signal back digitally to the guys recording the feed. Big difference. Anyway, I balked at first when they asked me to record her, but they upped the ante so I said okay."

Smith shook his head. "What's her husband do for a living?"

"He owns a garbage collection company."

"Mob connections?"

"In Washington, D.C.? I thought J. Edgar claimed there was no Mafia in D.C."

"Hoover claimed a lot of things that weren't true."

"Mafia connections? I don't know, and I don't give a damn. His murderous Mrs. and I haven't gotten that chummy."

"What's the next step?"

"One more meet with her tonight, usual place, the parking lot in the Pentagon City Mall. They can't haul her in until she actually hands over the down payment and it's clear on the wire what it's for. She's supposed to have the cash with her tonight. After that, I'm done. They'll have her on tape, they'll arrest her, she'll get an attorney, and the legal circus begins."

"As long as she doesn't seek out *this* attorney," Smith said.

Brixton's relationship with Mackensie Smith and his wife, Annabel, had led to his decision to remain in Washington after the death of his daughter. Smith had announced that he was going back into private practice and assured Brixton that he could use his experience as a cop and private investigator, provided he became licensed in D.C. While he disliked Washington and its major industry—politics—he decided that Smith's offer was too good to pass up. Smith advanced him the $5,000 for his PI bond and took enough space in his law practice to include a small suite for Brixton's new agency. Brixton passed the mandatory FBI background check, renewed his license to carry a concealed weapon, his favorite Smith & Wesson 638 Airweight revolver, and settled into his office adjacent to Smith's: ROBERT BRIXTON, PRIVATE INVESTIGATOR.

Y ou have anything for me?" Brixton asked Smith.
   "Check in with me tomorrow."
   "You know how grateful I am for all you've done for me," Brixton said.
   "When both parties benefit, it's the definition of a good deal, Robert," Smith said. "Say hello to Flo."
   "Same to Annabel."
   Brixton returned to his office, where Flo, his receptionist and paramour, was up on a ladder painting a red horizontal stripe on the gray wall in the reception area, using painter's tape to define the line.
   "What are you doing?" Brixton asked.
   "Adding some color to this drab wall," she said.
   "It looked nice just the way it was."
   "It was dreary," she said, returning to her task.
   "If you say so," he said, and disappeared into his private office.
   A half hour later she poked her head in. "Finished!" she proclaimed. "It looks great."
   "Yeah, I'm sure it does, but maybe you could paint a stripe on the floor in the hallway to lead a couple of paying clients in here."
   "We're doing fine," she said. "Mac always has work for you, and you're developing your own list of clients. It's a lot better than it was in Savannah."
   "I know, I know. You're right. Anything new on me getting hired to perform background checks on new government employees?"
   "Just the e-mail that arrived yesterday saying that they want to meet with you."

The government had gone on a hiring spree and was taking bids from private agencies to catch up on its backlog of investigations.

"By the way, Will Sayers called. He wants to have dinner with you tonight."

Willis Sayers had been an editor and reporter on the *Savannah Morning News* when Brixton was on that city's police force, and he had been reassigned to D.C. to run the paper's Washington Bureau.

"No can do. I have to meet up again with that loving wife whose husband's feet smell."

"If that's true, she has every right to kill him. What time are you meeting her?"

"Eight. Shouldn't take more than a half hour. We'll have an early dinner, huh?"

Brixton and Flo Combes had met while he was with the Savannah, Georgia, police department. He put in twenty years as a cop in that quintessential Southern city, rising from patrolman to detective, the last six months tethered to a desk while his knee, which had taken a slug from a wanted felon, mended—sort of. He hadn't found Savannah any more to his liking than Washington had been—everyone talked funny—but it had had its virtues. Meeting and falling in love with Flo Combes topped the list.

Upon retirement from the Savannah PD he'd opened his private investigator agency there. But he had eventually had enough of the genteel South, and he and Flo hightailed it back to Brooklyn, where your worth wasn't determined by the family into which you were born, and where people didn't say "y'all" even if you were the only other person in the room.

Their retreat to Brooklyn didn't work out. Brixton fell into a cynical funk, which Flo found difficult to deal with. After a few volcanic blowups, she flipped him the bird and stormed out, leaving him alone, without much income, and lacking even her warm body to snuggle up against. But then he received the job offer from SITQUAL, a private agency augmenting State's security apparatus, and traveled south to the city that he'd grown to detest, or at best mistrust. Flo had softened by then and rejoined him in the nation's capital, where they were a couple again, lovers as well as colleagues.

They left the office at five, went to the Capitol Hill apartment that had been Brixton's and that they now shared, enjoyed the baked chicken thighs and salad that she'd whipped up, and watched TV, switching between MSNBC and Fox News. "Equal opportunity cynics" was how Brixton described their political leanings. As Brixton was about to leave to meet the unhappy wife, Chris Matthews on MSNBC interviewed two congressmen, a Republican from Arizona, and Hal Gannon, Florida Democrat, who had just cosponsored a bill in the House calling for a cut in funding for unemployment benefits.

"Who says there's no bipartisanship in government?" Brixton mumbled as he adjusted the miniature transmitter he would wear that night. "Between them they'll turn us into a banana republic."

"Congressman Gannon is gorgeous," Flo commented.

"Is he? I never noticed."

"His wife's a knockout, too," Flo said. "I've seen pictures."

"The beautiful people, huh? Guess that doesn't hurt when you run for office."

"Be careful, okay?" she said, walking him to the door.

"Piece a cake," he said.

"Just the same, be careful."

He kissed her, drove out of the apartment building's underground garage, and headed for the Pentagon City Mall in Arlington, Virginia, across the Potomac River from the District. He parked in a predetermined spot, away from most cars but not so far that they would stand out. An unmarked police van with two plain-clothes detectives was parked a hundred feet away. One manned a small camcorder with night vision through which he would document this, the final meeting between the wife and Brixton. Brixton's conversation with the wife would be recorded on a digital recorder operated by the other detective.

Ten minutes later she arrived in her metallic blue BMW and pulled into a spot next to Brixton. He gestured for her to get into his vehicle. She shook her head and motioned for him to get into her car. He shielded a smile. She was being cagey, didn't want to talk in his car. He got out and slid onto her front passenger seat.

"Hi," she said.

"Hi. Everything okay with you?"

"I'm fine. You?"

"I'm okay. So, we have a deal?"

She nodded.

His transmitter didn't record nods.

"You still want to go through with it?" he asked.

She hesitated, and he feared that he might have caused her to be suspicious. But she said, "That's right. I want the bastard six feet under."

"Okay," he said. "You brought the money?"

Another nod.

"How much did you bring?"

"Half, twenty thousand."

"So you want your husband gone, not just beat up. You want him dead."

"That's right. When will you do it?"

Brixton shrugged. "A coupla days. I've got what you gave me about him, the photos, his schedule."

"How will you do it?" she asked.

He forced a laugh. "Trade secret," he said.

"I don't want it to be too messy," she said. "There'll be the funeral and—"

"I'll try to be neat," he said. "Where'd you get the money?"

"My mother."

"Your—?"

"I told her it was for a business I want to start."

Brixton had to struggle to not say aloud what he was thinking: *You're not only stupid, you're vile.*

"Anything else you want to tell me?" he asked.

"No."

"Then we go our separate ways, never met each other, right, except when you pay me the second twenty grand?"

"Right."

"You leave first," he said. "I'll wait until you're gone."

It happened quickly. She leaned over, kissed him on the cheek, and her hand went to his crotch. "You're really a pretty nice guy," she said. "I mean, for somebody who does what you do for a living."

"Yeah, thanks," he said, removing her hand. "Let's keep it strictly business. You still have to pay me the rest of the money."

She laughed. "Whatever you say. Don't worry. The money will be there for you."

"I just don't want to get stiffed on the second payment."

"You won't be. Just kill the bastard."

"It'll be done just the way you want it. Good luck to you."

After she'd driven from the lot, he walked over to the police van.

"Got it all?" he asked one of the detectives, who replied with a thumbs-up.

Brixton removed his jacket and undid the transmitter, handed it to the detectives. "She's nailed to the cross on this," he said. He also handed them the money she'd given him.

"Nice job."

Brixton looked at him as though he'd just said something blasphemous. "I know what I'm doing," he said. "I'll come by tomorrow to give a written statement. You guys take care. It's been a pleasure doing business with you."

"Hᵒw did it go?" Flo asked when he returned home. "Good, smooth, real smooth. Never underestimate how dumb people can be. Drink?"

"Love one."

They toasted his success that evening.

"When will they arrest her?" Flo asked.

"Any day now. Her lawyer will claim entrapment. Lotsa luck. I never led her, never encouraged her to go through with it. The DA's got a solid case."

"Why didn't she just get a divorce?"

"Like I said, she's a moron. She came on to me, kissed my cheek and grabbed my crotch."

"Bitch!"

Brixton laughed. "She's not bad-looking."

She playfully swatted him with the back of her hand. "What's on tap for tomorrow?" she asked.

"A meeting about the background check contract, and I want to track down Augie. Augie's all right, but I want him to know that if he sends anybody else to me as a hit man, I'll put out a hit on *him*."

"You'll get paid."

"Not worth it. You know, lowlifes like Augie are

sometimes more trustworthy than so-called pillars of society. I learned that from the Mafia types back in Brooklyn. They're bad people, but when they promise you something you can pretty well count on it, not like the politicians who promise whatever you want to hear and then screw you. Let's watch a movie."

Before starting the movie on the TV, an old Bogart flick, they changed into pajamas, slippers, and robes, refreshed their drinks, made a bowl of popcorn, cuddled on the couch, and settled in for another evening of domestic bliss in the nation's capital, about which President Harry Truman once said, "If you want a friend in Washington, get a dog."

3

Florida Congressman Hal Gannon caught an early-morning flight to Tampa to attend a fund-raising luncheon hosted by attorney Lucas Bennett. It was held at the famous Columbia Restaurant, one of the oldest restaurants in the United States, a bastion of Cuban food in Ybor City, Tampa's Cuban neighborhood, which was once the world's cigar-manufacturing center.

The Red Room, one of fifteen dining rooms, was packed with Gannon supporters, many from the city's Cuban-American population. His success at straddling the political fence—a Democrat with right-wing leanings—had worked for him. Although his true political bent was conservative—he more often sided with his Republican House colleagues than with his Democratic caucus—people assumed that he represented true bipartisanship in wretchedly partisan Washington, a voice of reason, they said, a man who is able to put politics aside for the good of the nation.

His after-luncheon speech reinforced that image to the wealthy backers eager to add to his reelection coffers. Along with his bipartisan reputation, he was viewed as a family man with solid moral values. His stunning wife, Charlene, sat at the head table and beamed up at him as he told the crowd what it wanted to hear. At the end of the event, a number of men and women approached and pressed checks into his hand.

"Hey," Gannon said through a practiced smile, "you already paid plenty just to be here."

"That was for the food," a matronly woman said. "I want you to have more to carry on the good work you're doing for us in Washington."

As the fund-raiser broke up, Gannon was approached by an attractive young Cuban-American journalist who asked him for his views on lifting the embargo against Cuba.

"That's a complex issue," he replied, taking note of her cleavage. "I really don't have the time to get into it right now. I'm due back in D.C. for meetings. But anytime you want to stop by my congressional office, I'll be happy to discuss it with you in depth. Pick the right day and we can discuss it over dinner." They exchanged business cards.

"I would like that very much," she said.

"So would I," Gannon said.

Luke Bennett drove Gannon to the Tampa airport for his return flight to Washington.

"Nice speech," Bennett said from behind the wheel of his silver Lexus.

"Nice crowd, too. Thanks for putting it together, Luke."

"My pleasure. The Cuban-American community loves you."

Gannon laughed. "Some do, some don't," he replied. "The old-timers like it when I talk tough about Castro and Cuba. The younger crowd would just as soon see us send white doves of peace and give that Commie thug hugs and kisses." Another laugh. "Good thing they don't compare notes on what I say to each group."

"How's my girl?" Bennett asked as he exited the highway and navigated roads leading to the airport.

"Laura's doing fine," Gannon said. "She's a terrific gal, smart as hell."

"What do you have her doing?" her father asked.

"Working on constituent requests. Keeps her busy. Tip O'Neill was right. Good politics *is* local."

"She called last night. Grace got the feeling that she might not be crazy about her roommate."

"Oh? I hadn't sensed that. I'll ask her about it."

"You do know, Hal, that I'll be happy to rent her an apartment of her own while she's in D.C. working for you."

"I think it's better that she stay within the housing system for interns, Luke, but I'll follow up with her about the roommate situation. Thanks again for the luncheon and the ride."

"Anytime. Is Charlene staying in Tampa for a while?"

"Yeah. She prefers working on her paintings in the studio we built off the house to playing the role of a congressman's wife up north. Can't say that I blame her. But Charlene will be coming to D.C. for some events in a couple of weeks.

"How's your mom?" Bennett asked.

"The same. I visit her in the home whenever I'm here and can find the time. She doesn't even know who I am anymore."

"Best that she's in a good facility that takes care of her."

"I know. My sister gets to visit her more than I do, but with her three kids, she's busy. Life's strange, huh, Luke? It goes fast, and we'd better wring all we can out of it before it ends. I'll get back to you after I speak with Laura."

Bennett watched Gannon stride into the terminal and wondered at the sort of life he led in Washington as a member of Congress. Before Gannon had tossed his hat into the political ring in Tampa, Luke Bennett had been approached to run for the House seat that became vacant when its occupant died. He'd waved off that overture without thinking twice. The idea of being dropped into the squabbling circus that Congress had become was not appealing. Worse, having to run for the seat every two years seemed akin to being put on the rack. "Don't be silly," he told those who queried whether he'd consider running.

Hal Gannon had a different view of the opportunity. Back from his Tampa fund-raiser, Gannon took a taxi from Reagan National Airport to his one-bedroom apartment in the Adams Morgan section of the District, a vibrant, funky community of bars and restaurants, coffeehouses, art galleries, and bookstores catering to the city's young people, who flocked there after dark to take in its sometimes raucous nightlife. The center of Washington's Hispanic population, the area boasted more than thirty nationalities, the city's true melting pot. When Gannon chose to rent the apartment on busy Eighteenth Street, some of his colleagues raised their collective eyebrows. It was an unusual location for a member of Congress to rent a place in which to crash while the House was in session. Most congressmen and -women vied for apartments closer to the Capitol; when money was tight they doubled and tripled up to save. But Gannon had the resources to live where he wanted. He responded to Adams Morgan's vitality and youthful culture. It was there that he found the freedom that he'd longed for back in Tampa, the feeling of liberation that he'd enjoyed when he went off for his first year of college.

He'd been a high school track star in his hometown in Minnesota, was voted most likely to succeed, was president of his senior class, and excelled on the debate team as well as being the lead actor in student productions. He was a star, and he basked in the glory of it. There were plenty of girlfriends, enough money to keep his five-year-old car in gas, and lots of like-minded buddies with whom to share beers at the bars in town that didn't check ID. He was the clichéd big fish in a small pond, and it satisfied his adolescent need for acceptance and glory.

He used his treadmill in the apartment for a half hour before showering, and changed into casual clothing. He left the building at seven, drove across the Arlington Memorial Bridge, and pulled into a parking space a block from Café Papillon on Lee Highway. He sipped a glass of white wine at the bar while waiting for his dinner companion to arrive. He mused about how things would have turned out differently in his life if his parents and sister hadn't moved to Tampa as he was about to graduate from high school—and if he hadn't met Charlene.

"Sorry I'm late," Rachel Montgomery said, kissing his cheek, "but I got stuck in a meeting that seemed to go on forever." She aimed a stream of air at a stray strand of silver-blond hair on her forehead and muttered a four-letter word. "We're doing *Don Giovanni*," she said as she settled next to him. "The bitch playing Donna Anna—" She laughed. "I'd say pardon my French but we're in a French restaurant. The bitch is being the diva, 'get me this, I need that.'" She adopted a deep, dramatic voice. "'I simply cannot play that scene with him.' She hates the baritone playing Don Juan. God, what a nightmare!"

Gannon listened without bothering to hear what she'd said. Rachel Montgomery was prone to bursts of the dramatic. Whether she was naturally that way, or whether her position on the board of the Washington National

Opera stoked it, was conjecture, and nothing that he particularly cared about.

"Let's take the table," he said.

Gannon was known at the restaurant by its owners, and he and Rachel were led to his favored table in a secluded corner of the smaller of two rooms. Since initiating the affair with the wealthy divorcée four months earlier he'd picked the spots where they would meet with care, nothing in the District unless circumstances demanded it, always across the Potomac, or in suburban Maryland. He'd stressed to her from the beginning the need for discretion, including when she visited him at his Adams Morgan apartment. She was to be sure that no one would see her take the elevator to his floor, and he asked her—no, demanded—that she do everything possible to hide her features, a hat, a scarf, anything to mask her identity. She'd balked at first, but he'd explained that because of his seat in Congress, and because his marriage was falling apart, he didn't want to give his wife ammunition in the inevitable divorce. Their relationship had to be kept secret until he'd given up his seat in the House—which he assured her he planned to do—and until he'd legally separated from his wife and instituted divorce proceedings, which he also swore would be soon.

Gannon's almost full glass of wine had been carried to the table. Rachel had finished hers and ordered a Manhattan.

"We have to talk," she said.

"About what?"

"About us."

"This isn't the time or the place."

"There doesn't seem to be the right time anymore, Hal. I call and get that infernal answering machine. I leave messages, but you don't call back for days. It used to be that—"

Gannon leaned across the table and said in a low voice, "I've been insanely busy, Rachel. You know that."

"So busy you can't pick up a damn phone? I call your office and that bitch Roseann always tells me, 'The congressman is unavailable at the moment.'" She'd adopted a saccharine voice.

"That's right. I've been that busy. Roseann is my chief of staff. She's paid to take my calls."

"Do you sleep with her, too?"

"Maybe we should leave," he said.

She sighed and shook her head. "I'm sorry, Hal, it's just that I—it's just that I love you and want to be with you."

"I know," he said. "I feel the same way. Tell me more about the problems at the opera company."

She guffawed. "You don't give a damn about that."

He leaned forward again. "Look, Rachel, we can hash this out when we're someplace alone."

She started to protest but realized that he was right, and that she was violating the promises she'd made about keeping their affair quiet.

"I'm having the swordfish au poivre," she said.

He gave the waiter Rachel's order and chose duck breast in a raspberry sauce for himself. She had another Manhattan, which bothered him. Alcohol loosened her tongue.

They spent the rest of dinner talking about less contentious things.

"Can I stay with you tonight?" she asked as he signed the credit card slip.

"No, not tonight," he said. "I've got to prepare for a committee meeting tomorrow. But soon."

"Promise?" she said in a little girl's voice that grated on him.

"Promise."

The last time she'd spent the night at his apartment she'd confronted him about a lipstick she'd found in his bathroom.

"Charlene must have left it the last time she was here," he explained, which she accepted. In fact it had been left there by a Dallas-based American Airlines flight attendant he'd met on a flight and with whom he was enjoying an occasional tryst.

He walked her to her car.

"When will you tell your wife you want a divorce?" she asked, her words slurred. She shouldn't drive, he thought, but he wasn't about to suggest that she leave her car and that he would drive her home. It was her problem if she got pulled over for a DUI.

"I'll do it when the time is right," he said. "Charlene isn't well. I can't just walk out on a sick wife."

She wrapped her arms around him and kissed him hard on the mouth. "I love you, Hal."

He disengaged and said, "I love you, too, Rachel. Now get on home. I'll call you in a couple of days."

He watched her drive off and was angry that he'd allowed the affair to progress to the point that it had. He didn't need this complication in his life. The problem was that he wasn't sure how to get rid of her.

4

By late May, Laura Bennett was ensconced in her new life as a congressional intern and loving every minute of it despite the city's fickle weather, hot and humid one day, rainy and chilly the next. Her parents had driven her to Washington from Tampa on April 24 to start her internship with Congressman Hal Gannon. She wasn't due to begin her duties until April 27, but she wanted to get settled in her new digs.

The apartment that Gannon's chief of staff, Roseann Simmons, had secured for Laura was spacious and airy. The furniture, while hardly fashionable, was utilitarian, befitting a space that experienced frequent turnover as twenty thousand young men and women toiling as interns in the nation's center of power came and went. The couch and a pair of cushioned armchairs were covered in green vinyl. A small dining table and four straight-back chairs occupied one corner of the living room. The kitchen was small but usable. It had a dishwasher, a gas stove, and a small refrigerator. The cabinets contained the requisite glassware, plates, silverware, and serving pieces, but Laura prepared and ate few meals there aside from breakfast. She was more interested in exploring the myriad restaurants and bars that dotted the immediate area and beyond, using the credit card her father had provided to pay the tabs.

Her roommate, on the other hand, enjoyed cooking dinner and eating in. Their different approach to meals was but one example of the personality gap that existed.

Reis Ethridge was a studious young woman from a suburb on Long Island who was interning at the Department of Justice. Small and slender, with large glasses and a helmet of tight reddish curls, she was as reserved and shy as Laura was outgoing and gregarious, preferring to stay at home and read on most evenings while Laura immersed herself in the city's abundant nightlife. It didn't take long before their differing lifestyles clashed.

On her first day at work in Gannon's office in the Rayburn House Office Building, one of three buildings housing offices of members of the House, Laura spent her time getting familiar with other interns and staffers, and becoming indoctrinated in how constituent queries and requests were handled. Gannon's unflappable chief of staff, Roseann Simmons, was curt but helpful, and the hours seemed to fly by. At a little after five, Laura asked Roseann to recommend a good place to enjoy a relaxing drink and dinner.

"Depends," was Roseann's reply. "D.C. used to be a joke when it came to good restaurants, but that's changed. The city is loaded with them now. Maybe you'd like to try one of the nearby watering holes that congressional staffers frequent after work. There's Bullfeathers on First Street, the Hawk 'n' Dove—that's on Pennsylvania—and Lounge 201 is popular. That's on Mass Avenue."

"Recommend one?"

Roseann shrugged. "Try Lounge 201. It's on the Senate side of the building. Nice bar, mostly Senate staffers. Their flatbread pizzas are terrific."

Laura poked her head into Gannon's private office to say good night.

"Got through your first day all right?" he asked.

"No sweat," she said, "but this is a busy place."

"Heading home?"

"Heading for a restaurant that Roseann recommended, Lounge 201?"

"Nice place. Did Roseann fill you on bar etiquette in congressional hangouts?"

"No."

"If you're going to complain about me, never mention my name. It's always 'my member.'"

Laura's laugh was risqué. "'Member' like in member of the House of Representatives, or—?"

"No, not *that* member," he said, also laughing.

I'll try and remember your advice," she said, "only I haven't been here long enough to complain about you."

"Give it another couple of days," he said, "and you will." He waved her away. "Enjoy the evening."

As she left the office and headed in the direction of the bar, she kept thinking of Hal Gannon sitting behind his desk, jacket off, tie lowered, looking as attractive as any movie star, and she wondered whether he ever went out for drinks and dinner with his interns. He wouldn't have any reason not to. Going out with people from your office was perfectly acceptable, nothing mysterious about it. She wondered how old Gannon was and whether he ever cheated on his wife. If he didn't, he had a lot of willpower in a city crawling with single women looking to hook up with a powerful man who also happened to be as handsome as sin.

The bar at Lounge 201 was hopping, and she managed to find the only available barstool. Seated next to her was a young man with a heavy five o'clock shadow and a thick mop of black hair. He'd removed his suit jacket and hung it over the back of his stool. A half-consumed mug of beer sat in front of him.

"A cosmopolitan, please," she told the bartender.

"A heavy-duty drinker, huh?" the man next to her said.

"I hold my own," she replied.

"You always drink cosmopolitans?" he asked.

"Sometimes. I like beer, too, and a John Collins now and then."

"What's that?"

"It's a drink like a Tom Collins, only it's made with bourbon instead of gin."

"What are you, a bartender?"

"No, but my father used to be before he became a lawyer."

"My name's Matt. Matt Caruso. Yours?"

For a moment she was taken aback but said, "Laura, Laura Bennett. Caruso? Like the singer?"

"Yeah, but no relation. I'm a big hit on karaoke nights, though."

The bartender delivered her drink, and Laura took a thoughtful sip. She wasn't sure how to proceed, so she asked the easy question. "Do you work on the Hill?"

"Afraid so. You?"

"Yes. I work for Congressman Gannon."

"The right-leaning Democrat."

"He calls himself a Blue Dog."

"He heads up that caucus in the House."

"You? Who do you work for?"

"Senator Jenkins from New York."

"I like her."

"She's the real deal. I'm her White House liaison."

"Interesting job."

"Depends on how you define interesting. Yeah, I suppose it is. Buy you a drink?"

"Thank you."

He touched the rim of his mug to her cosmopolitan. "What'll we drink to?" he asked.

"I don't know, maybe world peace."

"Sure. Why not? Here's to world peace, and all the world's lobbyists. What would we do without them?"

They fell into an easy conversation over more beer for him and her second drink.

"So, it's your first day as an intern," he said. "That demands something special."

"Like what?"

"Dinner at a nice place, my treat. Like Thai food?"

"Yes. We have a good Thai restaurant back home in Tampa."

"Nothing like Basil Thai. It's on Wisconsin. Best steamed dumplings and red duck curry in D.C. Game?"

They drove to the restaurant in Caruso's car, which he retrieved from one of the many parking lots reserved for congressional staffers. Laura had noticed when approaching the red Nissan that the license plate had a blue attachment with white lettering: U.S. SENATE STAFF.

"You have special parking privileges?" she asked.

"It's the least they can do considering how little they pay us. I had a choice of this parking spot or a Metro pass. I took the parking space."

It occurred to Laura that she might learn more about life on the Hill from him than from all the booklets, brochures, and briefings she'd received prior to coming to Washington.

Dinner was as pleasant and easygoing as their conversation at Lounge 201 had been. Caruso was a good storyteller and amused Laura with tales of his family back in New York City, how he managed to be hired by the junior senator from New York, Marcia Jenkins, and the intrigues that Capitol Hill provided, many of them juicy. There was much laughter, fueled by more drinks, and toward the end of the meal the conversation leaned toward the romantic.

When Caruso pulled up in front of Laura's apartment building, he shut off the engine, pulled her to him, and kissed her. She didn't fight the advance. In fact, she returned the kiss with passion.

"Come on," Caruso said, "let's have a nightcap in your place."

"No, I can't."

"Why?"

"I have a roommate."

"Tell her to get lost for a few hours. My roommate and I have an understanding. When one of us is bringing a woman up to the apartment, the other one vacates."

Laura shook her head. "I don't think that Reis—that's her name—would like that. She's from New York, too, Long Island. She's—well, she sort of a sourpuss, not very social."

"Sounds like a real dud."

Laura giggled. "Yes, she is. I really enjoyed the evening, Matt. I hope we can do it again soon."

He kissed her again, and his hand went to her breast.

"No, stop it."

He continued his grip on her breast while he forced his other hand between her legs.

"Please, no," she said, twisting away.

"You ever hear of hormones?" he asked.

"I have to know someone better before I—"

"Okay. I admire that. Sorry. I really am, and I would like to see you again. Tonight was fun. No hard feelings, huh?"

She smiled. "No, no hard feelings, Matt, and I'd like to see you again, too."

"How about tomorrow night?"

"Okay."

She gave him her cell number and the one at Congressman Gannon's office, and he promised to call the following day.

While Matt's sudden aggressiveness had been off-putting, there was something exciting about it, too, and Laura walked into the apartment tingling. Reis was reading a book.

"I met a terrific guy tonight," Laura said, kicking off her shoes and plopping on the couch.

Reis looked up. "Good," she said, and went back to her book.

"Could you put down that book for a few minutes?" Laura suggested. "I want to talk to you about something."

Reis looked at Laura over the top of her glasses.

"Okay," Laura said, "here's the deal. This city is crawling with terrific guys and I'm sure I'll be meeting more of them." She realized that she was suffering the effects of the drinks and worked at speaking clearly. "I met this really nice guy tonight. His name's Matt. He's Senator Jenkins's White House liaison. I wanted to bring him up here but, well, you know, you're here and it would have been, well, awkward. So how about this? If I want to bring a guy up here, it would be great if you found something else to do, somewhere else to go, a movie, have drinks with friends, anything to give me privacy, and I'll do the same for you."

"I'd really be uncomfortable with that," Reis said flatly. "I'm here to learn, not to pick up guys."

She went back to reading.

Laura seethed in her bedroom, not because Reis hadn't agreed, but because she'd been put down by her roommate, portrayed as an empty-brained man chaser not serious about her internship.

Things went downhill from there.

5

Just don't shoot off your mouth," Flo told Brixton.

"Me? Shoot off my mouth? Come on, you know me better than that."

Flo stood with her head cocked and a hand on a hip. "That's why I'm saying it, Robert. I *do* know you. You hate government types and tend to mouth off whenever things aren't going your way. Getting the contract to do background checks will mean a nice steady stream of income for us."

"Yeah, I know. I'll be on my best behavior."

"That's what I'm afraid of."

"You remind me of that mobster and his wife back in Brooklyn, Jimmy Mush," he said.

Flo smiled. "How could I forget him? He was aptly named. His face was all pushed in. He looked like a smashed pumpkin."

"That's a rock group, isn't it?"

"Yes."

"Remember when Jimmy Mush and his wife had that dinner for some of his pals? Everybody's sitting at the dinner table and she's in the kitchen yelling at Jimmy to go out and kill somebody 'cause they need the money."

"And you say that I remind you of her?"

"Not really."

"Well, she was right. They needed the money and so do we." Flo's smile turned into a laugh. "Go kill somebody, Robert, or at least stifle your urge to tell them to go to hell."

"Don't worry. I'll be a pussycat at the meeting."

"As long as you keep your claws in."

Brixton's meeting with officials charged with hiring independent contractors to conduct background checks on potential employees was held in a windowless conference room at Justice. After a half-hour wait, he was ushered into the room, where three men greeted him. Being made to cool his heels did nothing for his mood, but he kept Flo's words in mind as he shook hands and took a chair.

"Good morning, Mr. Brixton," the man in charge said.

One of the others said, "We've reviewed your application and credentials, and frankly, I have a few reservations."

"I'm sorry to hear that," Brixton said. "What seems to be the problem?"

"Well, to be blunt, Mr. Brixton, you've had what might be termed a checkered career in law enforcement."

Brixton smiled. "I suppose you could say that," he said. "I was a cop here in D.C. for four years and with the Savannah PD for twenty. If you mean I've been involved in some controversial cases, you're right. But to me that says that that I've had lots of experience. I assume that's what you're looking for, somebody with knowledge about the way things work here in D.C., somebody who's good at coaxing information out of people."

"That's true, of course," the third man in the room

said, "but these background checks are highly personal. We have to be assured that those conducting them do so with discretion."

"If you're asking whether I have a big mouth, the answer is no, except when my wife and I get into an argument." That he referred to Flo as his wife surprised Brixton, but it was better than calling her his girlfriend. He was too old to have a girlfriend. Paramour? Too French. Significant other? Pretentious.

One of the suits laughed, and Brixton joined him.

The man in charge hadn't found anything amusing in Brixton's comment. He said, "In reviewing your file, we see that you've been the subject of numerous stories in the press."

Brixton sighed. "A few stories have been written about me, but not because I asked for it." He came forward in his chair and said, "Look, I have a PI license here in D.C. because I passed the FBI background check. If the Bureau thinks I'm . . . well, as you put it, *discreet* enough to be licensed, I'd think that should be good enough for you."

The edge in his voice silenced the questioner, but not for long. He tapped the cover of a file folder. "One of your references is Mackensie Smith."

"That's right. Mac Smith and I work together. He used to be a top criminal attorney here in Washington before he became a law professor at GW. He's back in private practice and I do his PI work."

"Mr. Smith is well regarded."

"He sure is."

"You also have an excellent reference from Michael Kogan."

"Mike was my superior when I was on the D.C. MPD. I ended up working for him years later at SITQUAL before it was shut down. That was a private agency State hired to beef up its security."

"We're familiar with SITQUAL and its demise," one of them said.

"Mac Smith and Mike Kogan know I do good work and that I'm . . . *discreet.*"

The three men sat stone-faced, their faces reflecting that they were in the process of making a decision. Brixton sat stoically, wishing he was someplace else. Questioning his discretion was hypocritical, he knew. As far as he was concerned, the Justice Department was one huge leaking boat, its leaks fed to the press on a daily basis, maybe even hourly. Who were they kidding?

It was almost noon. He was tempted to get up, thank them for their time, and head for the nearest bar for a drink and something to eat. But he knew that would be foolish. He wanted the job, needed the work. Nailing down the contract would put the agency on an even keel financially and please Flo, whose tasks included juggling the books and paying the bills.

"When can you start?" one of the men asked Brixton.

"Right away."

"Okay, Mr. Brixton, welcome aboard. There'll be two days of briefings on procedures, protocol, the filing of reports, etc."

"Just tell me where to be and when," Brixton said.

They shook hands and Brixton left. He popped into a restaurant, ordered a drink at the bar, and called Flo with the good news.

"I was on my best behavior," he said proudly. "I told them that if they didn't hire me I'd sic you on them."

"I knew you could do it," she said. "Let's celebrate. Maybe Mac and Annabel would like to join us for dinner."

"Great idea!"

The two couples hooked up for a celebratory dinner at Proof on G Street, where they secured one of two favored booths, table 20, and indulged in a lavish and expensive meal. It turned out to be a romantic evening for both couples. Upon returning home to their Watergate apartment, Mac and Annabel took snifters of cognac to bed with them, toasted all that was good in their lives, and made love.

In the apartment they shared, Robert and Flo didn't bother with cognac. They went directly from the front door into the bedroom, where they continued the evening's celebration in less clothing than they'd worn to Proof.

At Café Papillon on Lee Highway in Arlington, Virginia, Florida Congressman Hal Gannon sat with his intern, Laura Bennett, at the same table he'd recently shared with Rachel Montgomery.

The evening hadn't been planned.

At five that afternoon, Gannon had called Laura into his private office in the Rayburn Building and closed the door.

"What's bugging you?" he asked as he sat with her on the couch.

"Nothing. Why?"

"Come on, Laura, don't kid a kidder. You've been moping around the office all day like you lost your pet dog."

"It's that obvious?"

"Afraid so. Come on, tell Uncle Hal. Get it off your chest." Her response was to well up.

He put his arm around her and left it there until the tears had subsided.

"It's my roommate," Laura said.

"I figured that might be the case," he said. "Your dad mentioned when I was back in Tampa that you were having problems with her. I meant to ask you about it, but it slipped my mind. What does she do, borrow your favorite dress?"

She managed a laugh through her sniffles. He handed her his handkerchief and she dried her eyes.

"It's nothing like that," she said. "It's just that she's such an unpleasant person. I feel like I'm living in a convent."

It was his turn to laugh. "No love life, Laura?"

"How can I, when I'm living with a prude? I've been out with a couple of nice guys, but we have to say good night at the door, as though I'm in high school and still living with my parents."

He gave her another hug. "Tell you what," he said. "I have to meet with Congressman Clarke in fifteen minutes. Shouldn't take more than a half hour. How about we go to dinner, someplace nice? You up for that?"

"Are you sure? I would love it."

He stood. "Good. When I'm finished with my meeting, I'll go to my car." He wrote his parking space number for her on a piece of paper. "It's downstairs under this building. Let me have your cell number. I'll call you and you come down. And look, Laura, don't tell anyone what you're doing or where you're going. I don't need tongues wagging around here."

"My lips are sealed."

"Good girl. See you in an hour or so."

Laura applied fresh makeup and perfume in the lavatory and evaluated what she was wearing. She'd dressed informally that day—tan slacks, a white button-down blouse, and sandals—and debated running home to change into something dressier but decided she didn't have time. She returned to the office and busied herself sorting constituent questions and requests until her cell rang.

"Come on down," Gannon said. "You've seen my car, the red Mercedes convertible."

Ten minutes later, she was in the tan leather passenger seat as he drove away from the Capitol Building complex, the top down, the wind whipping her hair into what she hoped wouldn't end up looking like a bird's nest.

"Where are we going for dinner?" she asked.

"Arlington, a favorite restaurant of mine, Café Papillon. Did I say it right?"

"I think so. I studied Spanish, not French."

"I picked up some Spanish from the Cubans in Tampa. By the way, you look great. *Usted muy bonita.*"

"Gracias." She giggled. "If I knew we were going out to dinner, I would have dressed up."

"You look just fine in what you're wearing. But hell, you'd look good in anything."

His flattering comments pleased her, and she found herself relaxing for the first time that day.

"Drink?" Gannon asked after they'd been seated in the restaurant and Laura had spent time in the ladies' room rearranging her hair and squirting breath freshener from a small aerosol she carried in her purse.

"I'd love one." She told the waiter she wanted a cosmo. Gannon opted for a glass of white wine. He offered a toast: "To Washington's best and most beautiful intern."

"Thank you, kind sir."

"So," he said, "tell me about this dreadful roommate of yours."

Laura proceeded to vent her feelings about Reis Ethridge. "She's just so uptight and judgmental, even nasty sometimes. I hate going home to the apartment because I know she'll be there, reading a book and barely talking to me. I don't think she's left the apartment at night since she arrived. She seems to think that because I enjoy going out and having a good time, I'm some sort of bimbo who doesn't take being an intern seriously."

Gannon's grimace reflected his response to Laura's description of her roommate.

"Your dad offered to rent you an apartment while you're in D.C.," he said, "but I told him that I thought it was better for you to stay within the system."

"I don't want to cause trouble," she said as she finished her drink. "Besides, I think I'm old enough to not have to depend upon my father."

"Another drink?"

"Yes, please."

"I don't want to corrupt you," he said.

"I've already been corrupted," she said. "Four years of college will do that."

"Steady boyfriend?"

She shook her head. "Lots of dates in college but nothing serious. College boys are so . . ."

"Boyish?"

She smiled. "Yes, boyish."

They continued talking after ordering dinner—seafood crêpes for her, steak tartare for him—and a glass of wine for Laura. Gannon's wine had barely been touched.

"I don't think I could ever eat raw hamburger like that," she commented on what he'd ordered.

"You have to pick your place to order it," he said. "It's top-notch here. I know I can trust it. Ever hear about the young man being interviewed for a job over dinner with his prospective employer? He wanted to impress, so when the employer ordered steak tartare, the young guy ordered the same—but added, 'Make mine well-done.'"

It took Laura a moment to get the humor in the story. When she did, she laughed heartily.

"Probably apocryphal," Gannon said.

Laura shifted the focus of the conversation from her to him.

"How did you end up in Tampa?" she asked. "You're originally from Minnesota, aren't you?"

"It's a long story, Laura, but here's the gist of it. I was

within a month of graduating from high school in Minnesota when my dad announced that he was selling the hardware store he owned and they were moving to Tampa. You know, warmer climate, lower cost of living. I was upset by it. I'd been given a track scholarship by the University of Minnesota and was scheduled to begin classes there in September."

"It must have been a blow to you."

"It sure was. Anyway, despite my mother wanting me to apply to colleges in Florida, I convinced them to let me go to Minnesota. The family packed up and headed south and I settled in nicely at the university. I loved it there. I was on the track team in the quarter-mile and broad jump, and even was cast in the leading role in a play." His smile was pleasantly self-effacing. "I hated to leave."

"Why did you?"

I got a call from my mother that spring. Dad had suffered a massive heart attack and was hanging on by a thread in the hospital. My uncle, who lived there too, sent me money for a plane ticket. I arrived a few hours after my father died."

"How sad," she said. "You didn't go back to school in Minnesota?"

"No. My mother and sister really put the pressure on me to stay in Florida and go to school there, but I fought until . . ."

She waited for him to finish. His expression had saddened, but he snapped out of it, grinned, and said, "I decided they were right. I was now the man of the house and they needed me there. Like I said, Laura, a long story that turned out okay. Staying in the Tampa area was the best thing could have happened to me. But enough of my life story, Laura. Another drink?"

What he hadn't included in the tale was that he'd been set to return to Minnesota for his sophomore year when he met Charlene in Florida.

"Does your wife spend much time in Washington?" Laura asked, despite already knowing that his wife spent as little time there as possible.

He became pensive before saying, "No, Charlene has never liked Washington." He chuckled, but it came out more a snort than a laugh. "As a matter of fact, she's never liked that I ran for Congress and won."

"That's—well, that must make it difficult for you."

"It certainly does. We've grown apart since I became a congressman. We live very separate lives these days. She has her art and the kids, and I—I try and make the best of it. She comes to D.C. now and then if I need her on my arm for an event, and she's good about campaigning, but I know she hates it."

"How long have you and Mrs. Gannon been married?" Laura asked.

A small smile crossed his face. "Are you good at keeping secrets?"

"I think so."

"Charlene and I have been married long enough for the bloom to be off the rose. We're heading for a divorce."

His directness startled her, and she didn't know what to say.

"No big deal," he said. "It happens to fifty percent of marriages. The important thing is that we do it honorably and that we all come out of it whole, including the kids, *especially* the kids. Charlene is a terrific woman and we've had a great marriage. But sometimes life gets in the way. Charlene's not well and . . ."

"I'm so sorry," Laura said.

"Nothing life-threatening, but of concern." He reached across the table and placed his hand on hers. "This is just between us, right?"

"Of course."

"Dessert?"

"I don't think so."

"Keeping that gorgeous figure in shape?"

"I try."

"And you've succeeded. Let's go."

As they drove back into the District, Laura was bombarded by a jumble of thoughts. She recalled conversations she'd had with girls in the dorm about their preferences in men. While most disagreed, Laura and a few others supported the view that older men were vastly superior to men their own age as lovers. Not that they had direct knowledge to back up their contention. But the consensus was that older men, including those who were married or had been married, made better lovers because they were experienced and more interested in pleasing the woman than themselves, unlike the young lovers they'd had in college who needed to prove their manhood. Older men had already proved themselves and approached sex from a different prospective.

Those late-night female gabfests, fueled by liquor smuggled into the dorm and punctuated by giggles and four-letter words, were fun. But Laura didn't have any basis for her claim that older men were better in bed. One student claimed to have had a brief sexual relationship with an older professor who, she claimed, was wrinkled and didn't have stamina. Another participant in these discussions, an African-American woman, stated that she would always seek out younger men no matter how old she got.

Yes, those sophomoric conversations were fun.

But as Gannon navigated traffic, Laura couldn't help wondering whether she was getting close to proving her untried thesis that older men were better.

6

Brixton went through his two-day training course to prepare him for conducting background checks on individuals who'd applied for government posts. He was given a dozen files and went to work on the first, a thirty-three-year-old man, William Wilkens, who until recently had been employed by a software company and now sought a job with the Department of Homeland Security. Brixton contacted the five references provided by the job seeker, not expecting to uncover anything damaging. Why give as a reference someone who is likely to say bad things about you?

It was the second phase of the background check that sometimes tripped up people. Brixton canvassed the applicant's neighborhood, questioning those who knew the man. While most had positive things to say, one tenant in his apartment building was less sanguine.

"My name is Robert Brixton," he told an attractive young woman who lived down the hall. He showed her his identification, which seemed to overcome the skepticism she'd exhibited when he knocked on her door. "Your neighbor, Mr. Wilkens, has applied for a job with the federal government and I'm checking out people who know him."

"Oh?"

"I'm sure you know Mr. Wilkens, living so close to him. What sort of guy is he?"

"In what way?"

Brixton gave his best noncommittal shrug and smiled as he replied, "Is he an honest person, pays his rent on time, things like that?"

"I guess he pays his rent because he's still here."

"That makes sense."

She seemed unsure whether to say more.

"How does he get along with his neighbors?" Brixton asked.

"Okay, I suppose." Again, there was hesitation before she added, "Except for—"

"Except for what?"

"Well, I don't like to say bad things about another person, but—"

"But what?" Brixton said, annoyed at her coyness.

"Bill can't be trusted."

Brixton's eyebrows went up. "Why do you say that?"

"Because he doesn't always tell the truth."

"He's lied to you?"

"Oh, you bet he has, plenty of times."

"Care to elaborate?"

"No." A tiny smile crossed her lips. "It's personal."

"Ah, come on," Brixton said, "you can't just drop a bomb like that and not explain."

"As I said, it's personal."

"He owes you money?"

"Let's just say that you can't always believe what Bill says," she said with finality. "Anything else you'd like to know?"

"Not unless *you* have something more to say about him."

"I don't think so."

"Thanks for your time."

"It's okay. Actually, he's kind of a nice guy except for—"

"Except that he's a liar."

"*You* said it."

"Have a good day."

Brixton got in his car and made a note in William Wilkens's file that a neighbor, a young woman, called him a liar, but added that it was his belief that she might have been talking about an affair gone sour. He grinned as he wrote it. If men were disqualified from government work because they lied, especially to women, Washington, D.C., would be a ghost town, including Congress.

He'd learned from one of Wilkens's references that the job applicant was particularly fond of Clyde's on M Street, in Georgetown, one of D.C.'s venerable watering holes. Brixton stopped in at five and found a spot at the bar next to a man busily engaged in enjoying a bowl of chili and a beer. After ordering a martini, Brixton struck up a conversation.

"Has Bill Wilkens been in lately?" he asked nonchalantly.

The man's spoon was halfway to his mouth. He lowered it into the bowl and said, "Haven't seen Bill in the past few days, although he comes in here two, three times a week." He laughed. "You know Bill, a real creature of habit, always has his veggie burger and a glass of Blue Moon Belgian."

"Veggie burger?" Brixton said.

"Don't know how he can eat those things. My motto is if you're goin' to have a burger, have a burger, a real one. Moderation's the key. Not too many burgers, but if you're goin' to have one—"

"My sentiments exactly," said Brixton.

Brixton's bar mate took another spoonful of chili

before saying, "Hope he lands that job he's after with Homeland Security. Course, why anybody would want to work for the government is beyond me, but to each his own. Am I right?"

"You sure are. I always wondered why Bill left his job with the software company."

"Got downsized," was the reply. "Just another word for fired."

Brixton finished his drink, told the man that he enjoyed talking with him, and paid his tab.

"I'll tell Bill you were asking for him," the man said as he used a piece of bread to wipe up the remains in the bowl. "What'd you say your name was?"

"Bill wouldn't remember me," Brixton said. "Good talking to you."

Back in his car, he noted what the man had said about Wilkens being downsized. Wilkens had stated on his employment application: "Resigned current job in order to find more meaningful employment that involves public service." The attempt to verify this with his previous employer resulted in the company giving only Wilkens's dates of employment, which Brixton knew was a common employer response due to fear of being sued for saying negative things about a former employee.

Brixton interviewed four other people who knew Wilkens, none of whom said anything negative about him. His female neighbor had called him a liar, but Brixton chalked that up to a woman scorned. He deleted his comment about her and closed the file by writing: "Background check indicates nothing that would preclude hiring the applicant," although he was tempted to add that Wilkens liked veggie burgers, which Brixton considered a serious character flaw.

Brixton dialed his office number and asked Flo about his calls and e-mails.

"Nothing important," she said. "Oh, you did get a call

from Detective Peterson at MPD regarding the recording you did of the lovely lady who wanted her hubby
killed. He wants to arrange a time for you to come in
and add to the official statement you gave. By the way,
did you read the story about her in today's *Post*?"

"No."

"The judge set bail at a half million. She claims that
she's the victim of entrapment."

"That'll never fly. I'll call Peterson when I get back."

"How did it go with the Wilkens background check?"

"Good. I finished up the interviews."

"Where are you?"

"I just left Clyde's in Georgetown."

"You're supposed to be working, Robert." She'd
slipped into her officious mode.

"I am. I met a guy at the bar who knows Wilkens. He
was helpful. I'm going to swing by that bar in southeast
where Augie hangs out before I come back."

"Why?"

"To make sure he gets the message that if he ever re-
fers anybody to me again as a hit man, I'll kill him."

"Jesus, Robert, that makes as much sense as—"

"Didn't come out right. Anyway, I'll be back as soon
as I see him. Love you."

The bar where Augie often hung out was dark and
dingy, like the neighborhood itself. Brixton was
pleased to see that his former snitch was there, ensconced
at the end of the sticky bar, half hidden behind a gum-
ball machine. Augie considered himself a ladies' man,
which might be true if the lady didn't mind body odor
and a couple of missing teeth. He also had a fertile imagination about who he was. Some days, depending upon
whom he was talking to, he was a descendant of Euro-
pean royalty and liked to be called Count. Other days he

claimed to be the long-lost nephew of Margaret Thatcher, complete with what passed for a British accent. In other words, he was nuts, but charming in his own warped way.

"Brixton, my man," Augie said when Brixton took the stool next to him.

"How've you been, Augie?"

"Couldn't be better, couldn't be better. You're here to pay me a referral fee for sending that knockout of a broad with evil in her heart to you." He furtively looked around at the otherwise empty bar. "How'd it go down?"

"It didn't. She was arrested."

"Her old man's still alive?"

"Very much so, unless he got caught in the compactor on one of his garbage trucks."

"Whew," Augie said. "What happened?"

"Augie," Brixton said, placing his hand on his arm, "it *didn't* happen, because I wore a wire and turned her over to the nice folks at MPD."

"You did *what*?"

"That's why I'm here, Augie, to tell you that if you ever send anybody else to me because you say I'm a hit man, I'll make it the truth and you'll be my first victim."

Augie started to protest, but Brixton quickly added, "And don't ask again about a referral fee. You're lucky I didn't turn you in, too."

Augie fell into a pout. "Geez," he said, "I didn't figure she'd take me seriously. I mean, I didn't tell her that *you* were a hit man, just said that maybe you knew somebody, considering your background and all."

"That's not what she told *me*, Augie."

"Then she's a crazy, lying bitch."

"The point is, Augie, you telling strangers in bars that I hire out to kill people is bad for my image. Understand?"

"Yeah, yeah, Brixton, only don't come down hard on me. I'm not getting any younger, you know, got lots of aches and pains and prostate problems and—I'm just trying to make an honest buck."

"You call arranging for a hit an honest buck?"

Augie gave him a gap-toothed smile and slapped his shoulder. "Hey, pal, no foul, no harm, huh? You say the bitch is in jail. That's where she belongs. Glad her old man is still breathing. Look, pal, can you advance me a few bucks? Things are slow and I'm getting old and—"

Brixton stood. "We'll forget about it, Augie, okay?" He motioned for the bartender, a heavyset, bald man dozing at the far end of the bar. "Hey," Brixton said, "buy my friend here a drink."

He tossed bills on the bar and handed Augie two twenties.

"Thanks, pal."

"Be well, Augie."

7

Laura Bennett looked over at the sleeping Hal Gannon, congressman from Tampa, Florida, who'd scrunched his pillow up beneath his head and snored lightly. It was the second time since they'd had dinner together that she'd spent the night at his apartment. She was giddy with joy.

They'd gone through the mating dance following that dinner in Arlington. She'd accompanied him to the apartment, where he'd poured expensive wine, raised his glass, and said, "Here's to being with the most beautiful intern in the world."

She feigned embarrassment, but his words warmed her as much as the drink.

He'd put a CD on his stereo system, *Timeless Ballads for Timeless Moments,* a compilation of romantic songs performed by various jazz artists. Overhead lights had been left off; the only illumination came from a pair of Tiffany-style lamps. She'd kicked off her sandals and sat on the couch, her bare feet tucked beneath her, the drink held in two hands inches from her mouth. He joined her. He dipped his index finger into his wineglass and touched her lips.

"What are you thinking?" he asked.

"I'm thinking about your wife and the problems you're having in your marriage."

"It happens to the best of couples," he said, "and our marriage was terrific until it started falling apart."

The phone rang.

"The machine will get it," he said. But as his outgoing message was heard from the bedroom, he sprang to his feet and headed in that direction. Before he could reach it and lower the volume, Laura heard a woman's voice say, "Hal, it's Rachel. Why don't you return—?"

He came back into the living room and grinned. "It was nothing," he said as he resumed his spot next to her. "Just congressional business. It can wait until morning. You were saying?"

"I was thinking about your marriage and the problems that you're having. I'm sorry for you."

"Don't be," he said, resting his hand on her knee. "We go through phases in our lives, Laura. My marriage to Charlene has been one phase, and a good one. But it's time to move on. If we don't move on, we stagnate. I suppose it's the old glass half full, half empty concept. My glass is always half full. I wouldn't have it any other way."

She drank. "Have you been—?" she asked.

"Have I been what?"

"Have you been seeing other women since your marriage started to unravel?"

"You're getting personal."

"I'm sorry. I don't mean to pry but—"

"No, no, no, it's okay," he said. "The truth is I have become friendly with a few other women, but it's not what you're thinking. Being alone here in D.C. can get under your skin. I suppose I'm only human needing a sympathetic female to hear my tales of congressional woe. If Charlene were here it might be different, but truth to tell she's never cared about the problems I face as a U.S. congressman. I'm not blaming her. She was happy when I was practicing law back in Tampa and home every night. Different strokes for different folks. I certainly respect her views and opinions, but they just don't match up with mine anymore."

"I understand," she said.

"And I appreciate that." He placed his fingertips under her chin and turned her to him. At first his kiss was gentle, then it became more passionate. His hands went to her breasts, almost causing her to drop her glass and spill the wine.

From that point, the evening was preordained. The couch was abandoned in favor of the bed, covered in a white duvet and with red throw pillows. For Laura it was as though it wasn't happening; there was a dream-like quality to it, no thoughts, only emotions and sensations.

Before they fell asleep, he said, "I don't know what's going on, Laura, but I've never felt this way before."

"How do you feel?" she asked.

"I feel—I feel contented and at ease with myself. You?"

"I feel—I feel contented and at ease with myself," she parroted through a laugh. Thinking back to those late-night dorm discussions about older lovers, she added, "and very, very satisfied."

At six A.M., the alarm went off.

"Good morning," she said, snuggling against him.

"Good morning," he said groggily, rubbing his eyes and sitting up.

"It's early," she said.

"*Too* early. Sleep okay?"

"I slept fine. You?"

"Like a rock."

He swung his legs over the edge of the bed. Naked, he reached for his robe and slipped it on, stood, stretched, and went into the bathroom.

Laura also put on a robe that he'd provided and wondered if it was his wife's. She heard the shower come on and pictured him in it. She went to the window and looked down at the empty street in front of the building. It had been teeming with people the night before, and she'd suggested that they go to any one of a dozen bars that lined the block, but he'd firmly squashed that notion, explaining the need to keep what was developing between them secret and why they had to avoid public places.

"Of course," she'd said. "I understand."

And she did, at least then.

They hadn't spent the entire night together the second time they'd made love at his apartment. He'd gotten them out of bed at three in the morning, spirited her down in the elevator, into his car, and dropped her in front of her building. They made a date for her to visit him again two nights later, and he'd told her that she was to come to the apartment wearing whatever she could to disguise her identity, a scarf, sunglasses, a baseball hat pulled low. "Never answer the phone at my place," he'd told her. "If people ask where you go at night, tell them you go out with friends."

Although she found the instructions amusing, she didn't balk. He was, after all, a married man *and* a leader in the House of Representatives. The stakes were big, as he explained, and she was willing to play the game—because the stakes were big for her, too.

She'd already started to project herself into his life far

beyond their sexual trysts. She pictured herself as the wife of a congressman, attending fancy formal affairs on his arm, helping him make sound legislative decisions, standing proudly at his side at fund-raisers where he spoke of a better future for America. But her projections went beyond even those. Her father had said on more than one occasion that Hal Gannon was possibly cut from future presidential cloth.

"Have you ever thought of running for president?" she'd asked him the second night they were together. He'd ordered in food, and they spent the evening watching TV and making love.

"Sure," he'd replied, "but I'd have to run for another office before that was possible, the Senate, or the governorship of Florida. They don't elect presidents from the House of Representatives."

"Wasn't Gerald Ford a congressman before he became president?"

"True, but he'd been appointed vice president before he went on to the White House. Abe Lincoln had been a congressman, but that was ten years before he became president. The only member of the House who went directly from there to the White House was James Garfield, and look where that got him."

"Where did it get him?"

"Six feet under. He was assassinated, the shortest term as president in history."

"But that's not because he'd been in the House of Representatives," she said.

"No, of course not. The point I was making was—forget it."

"I'd like to take some history courses while I'm here in Washington," she said.

"Why?"

"Oh, I don't know. If we're going to be together it

would be good if I knew more about the government and the presidency and—"

He abruptly got up and went to the kitchen, returning with a plate of cookies made by a constituent. "You don't need a course in history," he said. "It's all pretty dull. Have a cookie."

Laura's roommate, Reis Ethridge, was aware, of course, that Laura spent nights away from their apartment. She didn't ask questions, although her natural curiosity had been raised. It was Laura who initiated a conversation about her comings and goings.

"I'm in love," she told Reis one morning.

"That's good," Reis replied as she mixed her usual breakfast of yogurt, nuts, and berries.

"He's as handsome as any movie star, and he is *very, very* influential."

"Someone you met at work?"

"You might say that," Laura replied, laughing at the little inside joke.

"You stay with him at night?"

"Sometimes, only it will be more frequent. He's—"

She stopped talking. While she was bursting to tell her roommate about her relationship with the congressman— tell anyone, for that matter—she knew it was premature. If word ever got back to him that she'd talked about it, he'd be furious, maybe enough so to break it off. She'd bought into his insistence that discretion was of paramount importance, at least until he'd formally separated from his wife and was free to conduct his new relationship publicly. But it wasn't easy keeping it to herself. She wanted the world to know that she and Hal Gannon were in love and planning a future together. That day couldn't come soon enough.

* * *

Charlene Gannon came to Washington for the better part of a week and stayed at the apartment, which prevented Laura from seeing Hal outside the official confines of his Rayburn Building office. Laura had brought a few items of clothing to leave at his apartment, but he told her to take them away once he knew of his wife's travel plans. This angered Laura; her fantasies about one day becoming Mrs. Harold Gannon were in full bloom, although it was not entirely inner-directed. He'd talked of marrying her once his divorce came through, not in concrete terms but in a what-if context. But as far as she was concerned, he'd already made a commitment, and that belief sustained her during the week that she'd been exiled back to her own place.

When not with Gannon, she went out a few times with Matt Caruso, the young Senate staffer she'd met at Lounge 201 her first day on the job. She mentioned it to Gannon, and to her surprise he encouraged her to see him.

"It'll stave off nosy people asking about your life outside the office," he explained.

"I'll feel funny going out with someone else," she protested.

"It's just for a while, Laura. This is a tricky time for us. We really have to cover our tracks. Charlene will be gone soon and we'll be together again."

She went to dinner with Caruso twice during Charlene's stay in D.C. He continued to try to advance the relationship, but she resisted, and he began to react with anger when she refused to go with him to his apartment.

"There's somebody else in your life?" he asked after again being rebuffed.

"Yes," she lied, "back home in Tampa. But I enjoy your company, Matt. Can't we just see each other like this without having to sleep together?"

"Sure," he said, not meaning it. His calls became less frequent after that conversation, but they did go to dinner occasionally when Gannon was tied up with entertaining his wife or was out of town on government business.

One week slipped by, and then another. Laura spent as much time as possible at Gannon's apartment after Charlene left town—or, to be more accurate, as much time as he allowed. As Washington's oppressive hot and humid summer descended on the city, Gannon seemed—at least it appeared to Laura—to grow more distant. Their sexual passion hadn't abated; in fact, it became more intense and even desperate with each night spent together cooped up in his apartment, food brought in, or an occasional dinner out in a restaurant in Maryland or Virginia, always far from the District where prying eyes might witness them holding hands over a table, or kissing in a parking lot.

It seemed to Laura that Roseann Simmons, Gannon's chief of staff, might have developed an inkling of what was going on between them. She began asking Laura questions, nothing direct or specific, but with enough innuendo for Laura to keep up her guard. She mentioned it to Gannon, who suggested that they take a brief hiatus from their affair.

Laura railed at the term "affair." It represented to her something tawdry and not descriptive of the love she and Gannon shared, and for the first time she took a stand.

"Don't you think it's time that we stopped playing this silly game?" she said, unable to keep the pique from her voice. They'd just made love and now sat at the kitchen table, Chinese take-out containers and chopsticks in front of them.

"Silly game?" he said. "That's a hell of a thing to say."

"But it is a silly game, Hal. It's not like we're having a

one-night stand or anything. It's gone far beyond a roll in the sack."

"I don't know what you're talking about," he said.

"I'm talking about *us*, damn it!" She picked up a chopstick and pointed it at him. "Look, Hal, I love you and I know that you love me. You say that your wife is sick. I saw her every day at the office when she was in town, and she looks fine, the picture of health. You've talked about us getting married once you're divorced, so file the papers and let's get on with it."

He turned from her and tried to keep his anger in check. Although her direct confrontation had caught him off guard, he'd had a vague sense recently that things might be coming to a head.

She continued. "Roseann suspects what's going on between us," she said, "and you know that people are speculating about it around town. You said that life is a series of phases. Fine. Your phase with Charlene is over, and it's time for us to start on *our* new phase."

"I don't like being browbeaten," he said.

"Then do what's right, Hal. If you're worried about getting reelected, you know that's not a problem. My father has always said that you could run for a Senate seat from Florida and win easily. He even talks about you being a great candidate for president someday. Charlene will never help you achieve that but I can. My father—"

"What about your father? Does he know anything about us?"

"No, but—"

"No buts, Laura. He mustn't know until—until we're ready to announce it. I'll be the one to decide when that time is here."

"That time is *now*, Hal."

He got up, went to the living room, and turned on the TV. He seethed inside but managed to shield it from her when she joined him. Any thought of continuing the conversation was lost in the movie they watched. Laura fell asleep toward the end of the film, her head resting on his shoulder. He looked at her, and a wave of disgust consumed him.

One thing he didn't need at this stage of his life was demands from a twenty-two-year-old intern.

She awoke and said, "I'm sorry, Hal. I shouldn't have said what I did."

"It's okay, Laura. I understand."

"Good. I know the pressure you're under, and I don't want to be the source of more pressure. Forgive me?" She smiled and kissed his neck. "I enjoyed the movie, especially the love scenes."

"I enjoyed it, too."

"But we do love scenes better than what was in the movie."

Her hand reached beneath his robe, and minutes later they were in bed.

Laura was right. Hal Gannon *had* been under a lot of pressure recently. His Blue Dog coalition in the House was being attacked by other Democrats who accused him and his caucus of being traitors to the Democratic cause. This was nothing new, but the assault had ramped up in recent weeks.

But he was suffering pressure of a different sort from Rachel Montgomery.

Furious that he'd dumped her, she'd begun sitting in her parked car across from his apartment building in Adams Morgan and observing his comings and goings, particularly the stunning brunette wearing a baseball cap, sunglasses even on the most overcast days, and a scarf wrapped beneath her chin. And she'd done her homework. The mysterious young woman now had a name: Laura Bennett, an intern in Gannon's office.

She'd waylaid Gannon one day as he walked past a pocket park between the Rayburn Building and the Capitol Building and launched into a tirade punctuated with every four-letter word she knew. He managed to extricate himself from that encounter but had to deal with irate phone calls to his apartment until he had the telephone company block all calls from her home and cell numbers. While that proved efficient, he couldn't block her mouth from telling friends of the affair, which, no surprise, quickly found its way into the hyperactive Washington, D.C., gossip mill.

Was Congressman Harold Gannon having an affair with one of his young interns?

If so, he must be mad.

He'd be up for reelection in less than a year.

He was known as a politician with strong moral and family values.

Could it be?

Laura had kept in regular touch with her parents. As the weeks slipped by, it was all she could do to not tell her mother what was happening with Gannon. She knew that her mother would understand her having fallen in love with the handsome congressman, but her understanding would go only so far. On the other hand, her father would come down hard on her, and on Gannon, too. But she had to share it with *someone* close. What was the use of being involved in such a delicious adventure if you couldn't bask in it?

She had talked about it to her mother's sister, Irene, when Laura went to Irene's house in suburban Maryland one evening for dinner. Laura didn't get specific with Aunt Irene, but she knew she'd said enough to allow her to add two and two—she and the congressman were sleeping together. If Irene had been shocked, she didn't show it. She'd been trained as a Freudian shrink; listening without passing judgment was Psychoanalysis 101. But she did swear her aunt to secrecy about the relationship with Gannon.

The next person she confided in was Millie Sparks, a college friend who'd taken part in those late-night gab-fests in the dorm.

Millie had come to Washington to interview for a job and met up with Laura the first night she was in town. They splurged on drinks in the sedate bar at the Four Seasons Hotel in Georgetown, where a pianist played show tunes and conversations were of the hushed variety, a perfect place to share such monumental, shocking news.

"I can't believe this," Millie said after Laura had told her of the relationship. "You and Congressman Gannon are going to be married?"

Laura put her index finger to her lips. "It's got to be kept secret for a while."

"My lips are sealed. How did it happen, Laura? I mean, isn't he your father's friend?"

"My father is a big supporter of Hal."

"But what led to it? I mean, you came here to work as his intern. Did he—did he come on to you, make a pass?"

Laura nodded, sipped her cosmopolitan, and giggled. "Actually, we made a pass at each other. It was like it was meant to be, you know, written in the stars, love at first sight, kindred spirits, all of that, and more."

Millie sipped her gin and tonic while formulating her next question, but Laura continued talking.

"It's a really confusing situation. I mean, like, he's still married, but his marriage is falling apart and he'll be filing for divorce soon." She became conspiratorial, leaning close and grabbing Millie's arm. "Millie," she said, "I think he'll be the president of the United States someday and I'll—" She trembled at the contemplation. "And I'll be first lady. Of course that's far in the future. Right now he has to deal with his divorce and handle the fall-out when word gets around that he's marrying me, *an intern*! You know what I think, Millie? I think that there is something true about fate, about the stars lining up and bringing soul mates together."

"I can't believe all this is happening to you," Millie said.

"I pinch myself every day," said Laura. "Look." She held out her arm, on which was displayed an expensive gold-and-diamond bracelet that Gannon had purchased for her the week before.

"Wow!" said Millie. "He must have plenty of money."

"He does," confirmed Laura, although she was not aware that the bracelet, and other jewelry that Gannon had bestowed upon lovers, were purchased with money from his campaign fund, a violation of the law.

"Has he ever cheated on his wife before?" Millie asked, realizing immediately that it might be an inappropriate question.

Laura confirmed that it was. "It's not cheating when your marriage is coming apart," she said. "There are lots of women in this city after him. There's one old blond hag who's been parking outside our apartment building and calling him every damn hour. To be honest, I think I came along at just the right time and Hal knows it."

A sudden silence ensued.

"I know what you're wondering, Millie, and yes, he's good in bed. He's—he's *sensational* in bed!"

Millie laughed.

So did Laura.

"Strictly between us?" Laura said.

"Strictly between us," Millie confirmed.

* * *

During the fourth week of their relationship, Gannon flew to Dallas for a speaking engagement and told Laura that he'd be back in three days. She'd moped around his office on his first day away, her sullenness observed by the chief of staff Roseann Simmons, who called her into Gannon's office and closed the door.

"Spill it, Laura," Simmons said in her characteristic direct fashion.

"What are you talking about?"

"You and Hal. And don't give me that exaggerated confused expression. I know what's been going on, and I don't like it."

Laura was poised to strike back but didn't.

"This isn't a freaking game, Laura. The rumor about you sleeping with Hal is all over town. Do you know what that could mean for his political career?"

"I don't know what you're talking about," Laura said, crossing her arms defiantly.

"The hell you don't." Simmons softened her tone. "Look, Laura, you're young. I've been around longer than you have and I've seen it all. Getting involved with a married man, and a U.S. congressman, for that matter, is a recipe for disaster."

"Hal's marriage is—"

"Is what? On the rocks? Oh, God, come on, Laura, grow up. Hal Gannon is a handsome guy in a position of power. He's got women all over this town salivating when they think they might have a shot at him. His marriage to Charlene isn't going anywhere. He's not about to walk away from her and the kids. He's a guy who spends lonely time here in Washington and needs a sweetie to cuddle up to, stroke his male ego, and hear his tales of how Congress and all of D.C. are broken."

Laura began to cry, and Roseann put her arm around her. "You listen to me," Roseann said. "Being an intern to a powerful member of the House is something to treasure.

Break off whatever relationship you're having with him, learn the ropes here, and take what you learn into your future life. But for Christ's sake, Laura, use your God-given smarts."

Laura was tempted to ask whether Roseann was doing nothing more than venting her jealousy. Maybe *she* wanted to be Mrs. Harold Gannon and resented Laura for having usurped her. But she didn't say anything as she stood, straightened her skirt, and joined the other interns sorting constituent requests.

The next day in the office she exhibited a more positive and enthusiastic attitude. Gannon would be coming back to D.C. from Dallas the following day, the anticipation of which had buoyed her spirits. She avoided Roseann and was relieved when the chief of staff didn't pursue another conversation. Roseann had no right prying into what was a personal matter. Who did she think she was? It crossed Laura's mind more than once that if she told Hal about the conversation with Roseann, he might be prompted to fire her. It would serve her right, butting in where she didn't belong and taking that phony big-sister approach.

That afternoon she was enjoying a coffee break around a small staff dining table when she heard Roseann tell someone on the phone, "No, the congressman won't be in today. He's not feeling well and is working at his apartment."

That's strange, Laura thought. '*Working at his apartment'? He's not due back until tomorrow.*

She excused herself, went into the hall, and pressed "Hal" on the speed dial of her cell phone. There was no answer. She tried again; the same result. She returned to the office and said she had to run an errand but would be back soon. She hailed a taxi on Independence Avenue and gave the driver Gannon's address. Fifteen minutes later she stood in front of the building and looked up at

Gannon's apartment windows. She saw him pass by. Then a second figure was visible, a woman.

She entered the vestibule and rang his buzzer. There was no response. She rang again, and again, holding the button longer each time. "I know you're there, Hal," she said to the empty space. "I saw you."

Again, the thumb on the buzzer, maintaining the pressure. Suddenly, his voice came through the intercom. "Who is it?" he asked testily.

"It's Laura."

"What do you want? I'm working."

"You said you were coming back tomorrow."

"I got back early. Look, Laura—"

"Who are you *working* with?" She elongated the word to make her point.

"Not now, I'm busy."

The sound of the elevator caught her attention. The lift came to a stop and the doors opened. A stunning brunette carrying an American Airlines tote bag emerged, quickly turned from Laura, and left the building.

"Who are you?" Laura yelled after her.

The woman didn't stop. She walked briskly up the street, with Laura after her.

"Who are you, damn it?"

A taxi pulled up and the woman scrambled in, leaving Laura on the sidewalk, tears running down her face, trembling, fists clenched tightly.

She returned to the vestibule and rang the apartment again.

"Come up," Gannon said angrily.

Laura walked past him into the apartment and went to the bedroom, where the bed had been hastily made up. The aroma of perfume filled her nostrils. The robe he'd given her when she stayed over was tossed on a chair.

Gannon stood in the doorway, arms folded.

"Who was she?"

"Who was *who*?" he said.

"The woman who was here with you."

"Look, Laura. We'd better sit down and come to an understanding."

"I think I do understand, Hal."

"You're upset. Why don't you go home and relax. You've interrupted work I'm doing and—"

She guffawed. "What do they call it, Hal, coitus interrupting or something like that?"

"Get out, Laura!"

"Not until you explain."

"I don't owe you any explanations."

"You don't? How can you say that? We were going to be married."

"Jesus," he muttered, "you've really gone off the deep end, haven't you."

She'd vacillated between crying, gasping for breath, rage, and abject sadness. Then, to her surprise, she experienced a surge of inner strength. She said, "The high and mighty Harold Gannon, U.S. congressman, family man, protector of the weak, champion of the middle class. You know what you really are, Hal? You're a pathetic excuse for a human being and a man. Believe me, Hal, you've deceived the wrong person in Laura Bennett. When people know what you've done, the lies, the deceit—when people back in Tampa know, when my father knows—you'll be lucky to spend the rest of your life rolling cigars in Ybor City."

She stormed from the apartment, her arms tightly holding her stomach to keep the pain in. Outdoors, she leaned against the building and kept shaking her head. A woman who was about to enter the building asked, "Are you all right, miss?"

Laura looked at her through wet eyes.

"Yes, I'm all right," she said. "I'll be fine."

THE
DISAPPEARANCE

8

Gannon went through a series of emotions after Laura left the apartment, her fury wafting in the hallway like strong cologne. Fear was one of them, but that was quickly replaced by anger so intense that it physically shook him. Guilt? No. But disgust with himself for having initiated the affair with a twenty-two-year-old dreamer. "She's nuts," he told himself over and over. "She's mentally unbalanced. Marry her? What does she do, live in a fantasy world?"

A constant companion and complication to his jumbled feelings was Laura's father, Lucas Bennett.

Bennett was a powerful friend, but Gannon knew that the silver-haired, physically imposing attorney, a well-connected member of Tampa's elite, would turn on him if he knew that he'd seduced his daughter. Had he seduced her? Hell, no! *She'd* been the seducer.

Maybe once her anger had abated, she'd chalk it up to an experience and not follow through on her threats to expose the affair. That thought gave Gannon a modicum of comfort, but it lasted only seconds. He'd have to get hold of her, talk to her, make her see that it was just a fling, a rite of passage. Who was she kidding? She hadn't been a virgin. She knew what she was getting into. He hadn't even intended for them to end up in bed. He was being kind taking her to dinner, listening to her complaints about her roommate, counseling, stroking—he'd been a surrogate father. How dare she threaten him?

He was deep into these thoughts when he received a call from Joe Selesky, his Tampa campaign manager.

"How are things?" Selesky asked.

"They've been better."

"Yeah, well, we have to talk, Hal."

"About what?"

"About you and the campaign. I'm flying to D.C. in the morning. Meet me for lunch at that place in Alexandria, Indigo Landing."

"I don't know if I can, Joe. I have a committee meeting and—"

"Screw your committee meeting. Twelve noon. Be there!"

Gannon canceled a date he'd made that night with the VP of a small Maryland bank with whom he'd had an on-again, off-again affair, a situation with which she seemed perfectly comfortable. He stayed in the apartment, jumping each time the phone rang. He'd decided to give Laura plenty of room to cool off before he called her, although the temptation to dial her cell phone was at times almost overwhelming.

He slept fitfully.

The following morning, after spending a few hours closeted in his office—"I don't want to be disturbed," he told Roseann and others—he left the District and drove his red Mercedes convertible across the Fourteenth Street Bridge, took the exit for Reagan National Airport, and continued south on the George Washington Memorial

Parkway to Alexandria, where he parked in a lot near the restaurant. He passed through the dining room to the outdoor deck to see Selesky at a table as far removed from others as possible, a stein of beer in front of him. Selesky was a short, bull-necked man in his late thirties with a shaved head, fuzz on his upper lip that passed for a mustache, and a ruddy complexion, a major player and fund-raiser in Florida Democratic politics who'd managed Gannon's last three runs for reelection. Joe Selesky was known as a take-no-prisoners political manager, as well as for having an amazing capacity for drinking beer and never showing its effects.

A waitress asked if Gannon wanted a drink.

"Just water," he said.

"What the hell is wrong with you?" were Selesky's first words.

Gannon forced a laugh. "Not even a 'Hello, Hal, good to see you, how've you been?'"

"I'm not in the mood for small talk."

"Maybe you could be more specific," said Gannon. He knew how important Selesky was to his political career. At the same time he disliked him personally.

"You know what I'm talking about, Hal. Word's been getting back to Tampa."

"Word? What word?"

"About your overactive libido."

Gannon guffawed. "That's ridiculous."

"Laugh all you want, buddy, but that doesn't blow it away. Besides, it's not just rumor. I *know* that you've been sleeping with women other than your wife."

"Really? How do you know?"

"I've been told by those who know, that's how. There are people who have a lot riding on you getting elected to another term, and maybe a run for the Senate one day. They don't want to see you blow it because you can't keep your pants zippered."

"My House seat is secure and you know it."

"In a pig's ass it is. Pete's Solon's got a lot of friends, plenty of backers. He's putting together a great team, and the money is rolling in."

"He's a Republican, for Christ's sake. The Fourteenth is solid Democrat," Gannon said.

"Not like it used to be, Congressman. You won your last run because you had plenty of Republican crossover voters because—" He shook his head. "Because they're family values voters. They saw you as a straight arrow who shared their views and sided with the House Republicans on issues dear to their hearts. But you know how that works. Some of your Democrat backers are now grousing about how many times you *have* sided with the Republican bloc."

Gannon started to deflect that argument when Selesky held up his hand. "Yeah, I know, Harold Gannon, Mr. Bipartisan. It's not playing the way it used to, Hal. The House is as divided as it can get. The Tea Party whackos want you out no matter how comfy you might be with the Republican leadership. I'm telling you, and you'd better listen to me. I know what I'm talking about."

"Well, *I* don't know what you're talking about."

"Let's start with the stewardess."

"What stewardess? Stewardess? They're called flight attendants."

"Call 'em what you want, Hal. She flies on planes—when she isn't shacked up with the handsome congressman from Tampa."

"All right, so I know this flight attendant. We're friends, close friends, that's all."

"And *she* has close friends."

"Sure."

"And you think she doesn't tell her close friends about sleeping with you? One thing I never thought about you was that you're naïve. She tells her close friends, and they pass the word, and pretty soon the whole freakin' airline knows about it."

Gannon drank water and waved away the waitress. "We're not ready to order yet."

Now Selesky leaned across the table. "An intern, for God's sake?"

Gannon sat back as though punched.

"Yeah, an intern, Lucas Bennett's daughter, no less. Tell me about it, Hal."

"Wait a minute, Joe. Where are you getting this information?"

"It doesn't matter. Let's just say that it came from people who have a lot to lose if you fall on your face this time around."

Gannon looked as though he was trying to find a blackboard with what he needed to say written on it.

"When did you hear about Laura, about the intern?"

"A week, maybe two weeks ago. It doesn't matter. That's why I'm here, Hal." He lowered his voice even farther. "Laura Bennett's father is one of your biggest backers. If he hears that you seduced his daughter, he'll not only drop you like a hot coal, he'll go after your hide."

"I'm not worried about that," Gannon said. "She's basically out of the office, out of my life. She's probably getting ready to go back to Tampa."

"To tell her father?"

"Have you decided yet?" the waitress asked, pointing to the unopened menus.

"Sorry," Selesky said to her, "something's come up. I have to catch a plane. I'll take a check for the beer."

Gannon also elected to skip lunch, and they left together.

"Remember what I said, Hal," Selesky said as he waved down a taxi.

"What?"

"This is about to blow up in your face. Oh, in case I haven't mentioned her, there's that woman who sits on the board of the National Opera."

"Hey, you want a taxi or what?" the cabdriver yelled through his open window.

"In a minute," Selesky said. "Look, Hal, Pete Solon's people have already hired a guy named Wooster to dig up dirt on you here in D.C. He's a private detective. We've hired our own PI to keep tabs on Wooster—and on you. Everybody's scrounging around looking for dirt on Congressman Harold Gannon. Lay low, Hal. Mend your fences. The alternative is to go back to Tampa as a former congressman, see if you can get your wife and kids to forgive you, and try putting your law practice back together. Don't say you haven't been warned."

Selesky scrambled into the cab's backseat. "Reagan National," he told the driver.

Gannon watched the taxi pull away.

Selesky hadn't pulled any punches. If things were as bad as he'd said, something had to be done.

He got in his car and pushed the key for Laura's cell phone. Dead. Nothing. He slammed his palm against the steering wheel. "Bitch!" he yelled. "Bitch!"

9

Brixton finished up conducting background checks on potential government employees. The steady stream of income was welcomed but he found the assignment deadly dull. The men and women who'd applied for the jobs were dull, too, and Brixton knew that unless he had the good fortune to uncover a serial killer or child molester among them, they would all pass muster and become paid members of the D.C. bureaucracy—which would probably lead his employer to think that he hadn't dug deeply enough. Surely one of the candidates for employment had shaved strokes off his golf score, or drank milk straight from the container.

He was sitting in Mac Smith's law office when the attorney took a call.

"Lucas?" Smith said. "This is a pleasant surprise. It's been awhile."

Brixton left and went to where Flo was watering a variety of potted plants she'd recently purchased to brighten up the office.

"Looks like a botanical garden," Brixton commented.

"Aren't they beautiful?" Flo said. "They add color to the place. And they smell so good, too."

"What if a client is allergic to them?" Brixton asked.

"Then he'll have to find another private detective. You finished the interviews?"

"Yeah. Borrrring."

"Luuuucrative," she said. "Mac have anything for you?"

"We just started to talk when he got a call from somebody named Lucas. I'll give him time to finish."

I hear you're back trying cases," Lucas Bennett said to Mac.

"Word gets around, huh? Yeah, I enjoyed teaching, but today's crop of fledgling lawyers lacks something, Lucas. I don't know what it is, maybe not having a true intellectual love of the law, too interested in how much money they'll make when they pass the bar. Then again, maybe I'm getting too old to understand them."

"What are you fifty, fifty-one?" Bennett asked.

"Fifty-two," Smith said, and laughed. "But you didn't call to hear my complaints about the state of jurisprudence. What's up with you? You still Tampa's leading attorney?"

"Things are good, Mac. You remember my daughter, Laura?"

"I certainly do, but it's been a long time since I saw her. A beautiful young woman, and smart, too, as I recall."

"She's both those things, Mac. I thought you might have heard from her."

"Was I supposed to?"

"Not necessarily. She went to Washington to work as an intern for Congressman Gannon in the House."

"Really? She's interested in a career in government service?"

This time Bennett laughed. "God, I hope not. No, she wanted a taste of D.C. and how things work there before she gets on with her life, you know, gets married, has kids. I was all for it. Hal Gannon has been a friend for a number of years, and I've been an active supporter of his from his first run at the seat. Laura volunteered on his last campaign."

"I like that," Smith said, "bright young people getting involved. A lot of them sour after a taste of how things really work here in Washington, especially Congress, but it's a good learning experience."

"I agree. I gave Laura your name and phone number, and urged her to call if she ran into any serious problems."

"What sort of problems?"

"Nothing specific, but you know how young people can make a bad decision now and then. I just thought that knowing there was someone with a mature, level head to talk to would be beneficial. I should have given you a heads-up."

"Well," said Smith, "if she has run into a problem, she hasn't called to tell me about it. Has she raised one with you and Grace?"

"Nothing major. She and her roommate don't get along, but that's not unusual. Mac, the reason I'm calling is that Laura has been good about staying in touch. I can testify that she calls almost every day because I pay her cell phone bill. We haven't heard from her in three days, which *is* unusual."

"You can't reach her?"

"Grace has tried. Laura doesn't have a landline in her apartment, uses only her cell. That seems to be the trend these days."

"No luck raising her on her cell?" Smith asked.

"No. That bothers us, too. We leave voice messages but she doesn't return the calls."

"How about the congressman's office?"

"Grace and I have been reluctant to call there. We don't want to embarrass her by having Mommy and Daddy call where she's working. I've tried Hal's home number, but all I get is his answering machine. I'm sure there's nothing wrong. Laura can be impetuous. She's probably taken a few days off and is hiking somewhere with friends. Still . . ."

Smith said after the pause, "How about if I call Congressman Gannon's office? I'll say that I'm an old friend of her father and want to invite her to dinner. I'm sure she'd enjoy a home-cooked meal that isn't deep fried."

"I'd appreciate that," Bennett said.

Mac checked that he had all of Bennett's contact information and was given Laura's cell number.

"I'll give it a try and let you know if I reach her," he told his friend, whom he hadn't seen in two years.

10

My name is Mackensie Smith. I'm an attorney here in Washington and a friend of Lucas Bennett in Tampa, Florida. Mr. Bennett's daughter, Laura, is an intern in the congressman's office. I'd like to speak with her."

"Please hold a second, Mr. Smith."

A few seconds later, Roseann Simmons introduced herself. "Hello, Mr. Smith, I'm Roseann Simmons, Congressman Gannon's chief of staff. How may I help you?"

Smith repeated his connection with the Bennett family and asked to speak with Laura.

"I'm afraid she's not here."

"Do you expect her back soon?"

"I'm not sure. Laura has taken a few days off. Have you tried her apartment?"

"I'm told she doesn't have a phone there, uses only her cell. Her dad has been trying that number but hasn't been able to reach her. I'm only calling because I thought that she might enjoy a home-cooked meal."

Roseann laughed. "I'm sure she would. I'll leave a message for her."

Smith was distracted by incoming calls before getting back to Luke Bennett in Tampa.

"She's probably decided to take a few days off from whatever it is she's been doing in Hal's office," her father said. "Laura tends to act on the spur of the moment."

"A youthful malady," Smith offered.

"I'm sure she'll surface any time now and return our calls," Bennett said. "It's just that Grace worries about her."

"If she gets back to me, I'll let you and Grace know," Smith said. "I'm sure you're right."

That afternoon Smith did what he always tried to do on Thursdays, take a few hours off to play tennis with friends who shared his love of the game. Despite a bad knee and an occasional pinched nerve in his neck, he played these weekly games with serious intent. It wasn't winning that mattered. Knowing that he'd given it his best was what counted.

Since leaving his teaching position at GW, finding time for tennis proved more difficult. It hadn't taken long for his client base to grow, and blocking out those few hours every Thursday afternoon took some juggling. His wife, Annabel, knowing how much he enjoyed playing, made him promise that he wouldn't give up the weekly ritual. Mac Smith believed in keeping promises, especially those made to Annabel.

The matches were held at various venues, depending upon who was playing. On this Thursday, Mac joined political consultant Fred Mayer at his home in the Sheridan-Kalorama area of the District, an expensive enclave bordered on the north and west by Rock Creek Park. After two terms in the Senate representing Ohio, Mayer had done what too many ex-pols had recently done, at least from Mac Smith's perspective. He'd cashed in on his Washington clout and become a wealthy lobbyist. Smith tended to avoid the lobbying crowd. As far as he was concerned, the lure of easy money had corrupted the electoral and governing process, perhaps beyond repair. But despite those feelings, he'd forged a friendship with Mayer, a former college professor with a keen intellect who hadn't been blinded by his success and whose private views of what the nation's capital had become weren't vastly different from Mac's.

"You know, Mac," Mayer often said, "lobbying in its purest form is a positive thing, helping lawmakers understand the complexities of the industry the lobbyist represents."

"But lobbying isn't practiced anymore in its purest form," Mac would counter. "Too many lobbyists simply buy a legislator's vote in return for the money."

"True, and I wish it weren't so. But all lobbyists aren't the same, Mac." He smiled. "Just as all lawyers aren't money-grubbing, ambulance-chasing manipulators."

That was the last time they'd argued about it. Besides, Mac was well aware that limiting one's tennis partners to those not part of Washington's incestuous insiders' club—government, lobbying, and the media—would reduce the field of possibilities to a precious few. Tennis was a nonpartisan game, maybe the last one in Washington, D.C.

They played on Mayer's recently installed court at his home. His wife, Suzanne, had put out a pitcher of lemonade and home-baked cookies and chatted with Mac and her husband until she sensed that they were eager to get started with their game and disappeared inside the house.

An hour later, after Mayer had eked out a victory in a hard-fought match, they repaired to his study for a glass of lemonade before Mac headed back to his office.

"So they couldn't keep the old warhorse out of the courtroom," Mayer said lightly. "How is it being in the fast lane again?"

"Fast," Mac replied, "but I'm enjoying it. How are things in the passing lane, Fred?"

"Busy. There was a lull for a while, but things are getting active again. I have a new client who's vitally interested in the tax bill that's sure to come up in Congress this session, and I'll be helping shape Pete Solon's run for Hal Gannon's House seat from the Fourteenth in Tampa."

"From what I've read, Gannon has had a lock on that seat ever since he was first elected."

"It seemed that way, but his hold on it has become more tenuous each year. Hell, it should be a solid seat for him. Registered Democrats outnumber Republicans in the Fourteenth by a pretty good margin, and a lot of Republicans have voted for him because of his so-called nonpartisan approach, bedding down with the right wing on many issues. But they don't trust him anymore, especially the Tea Party crowd. For them the only good Democrat is a dead one. Bipartisanship is the old politics, Mac, like fax machines and landlines." He lowered his voice. "And there's the brewing scandal about Gannon's sex life here in D.C. that's filtering back to Tampa. The self-righteous Gannon always runs on being the epitome of a family man, but that pious claim might be ready to blow up in his face. I think Pete Solon has a damn good chance of unseating him."

"The daughter of a friend of mine in Tampa, Luke Bennett, is interning for Gannon."

Mayer laughed. "I hope she packed her chastity belt when she left home," he said. "The rumors about his sexual dalliances are developing legs, Mac."

"Sending e-mails of his *package* to strange women? Frequenting prostitutes?"

"Let's just say that Congressman Gannon has never met a woman he didn't covet. At least that's the scuttlebutt."

"I won't ask for more details."

"And I appreciate that. A refill?"

"Thanks, no. I need to get back to the office."

Smith availed himself of the shower in Mayer's home gym that abutted the tennis court, changed into fresh underwear, socks, and shirt that he'd carried with him in a small tote, and walked with the Mayers to his car.

"If your friend's daughter has anything of interest to say about Gannon, you'll let me know of course," Mayer said.

"Come on, Fred, you know that I won't," Mac replied.

"Forget I said it," Mayer said through a laugh.

"I already have. Good game. I look forward to the rematch. The cookies were good, Suzanne. So was the lemonade."

On the drive back, Smith pondered what Mayer had said about a sexual scandal developing with Congressman Gannon.

He had to smile at the way Mayer had casually dropped it into the conversation. That's the way things worked in the nation's capital. Drop a hint, and anyone who's heard it passes it along as gospel, embellishing the details, putting his or her private spin on it, and using it as currency in the city that's built on a swamp and whose denizens too often act like swamp creatures. Whenever someone wanted to tell Smith something and prefaced it with "just between us," Smith always replied, "Then don't tell me."

Mackensie Smith hated the D.C. rumor game and didn't play it, even with his notoriously close-mouthed wife, Annabel, although he knew that he would tell her what Mayer had said, probably during a moment of pillow talk.

If it weren't for knowing that Luke Bennett's daughter

was interning with Gannon, Mayer's hint that the congressman was behaving badly wouldn't have meant much to Smith. There were plenty of unfaithful husbands in the House and Senate to go around; adding Gannon to the list would hardly be shocking news in a city where scandals were as steamy as the summer weather. It seemed that a day didn't go by where an elected official, a member of the administration, or someone working for an agency wasn't caught with his pants down, or videotaped saying something stupid, offensive, or both.

He and Annabel had once heard a former congressman announce at a town meeting that he was dropping out of politics. "The House of Representatives is aptly named," he'd said. "Every conceivable type of American is truly represented, running the gamut from high-minded do-gooders, attorneys, and businessmen to drunks, wife beaters, and out-and-out thieves. It truly does represent the United States of America." That got a laugh from the small audience, most of whom assumed that he was making a joke. He wasn't.

Mac's thoughts shifted to Laura Bennett and the conversation he'd had with her father.

There was no reason for concern. She wouldn't be the first young person to neglect to stay in touch with family. Luke Bennett had said that she was impetuous, and the fact that her mother was worried was hardly surprising. She was, after all, a mother.

But he made a mental note to follow up with another call to Gannon's office if he didn't hear from Laura in a day or two.

So Republican Pete Solon was about to challenge Gannon for his House seat, Mac thought as he pulled into the parking garage beneath his office building. He didn't know much about Solon, only what he'd read, or heard from talking heads on cable TV.

Solon was the son of a wealthy real estate developer

in the Tampa–St. Pete area and had become a force in local Republican politics when not working in his father's firm. If Solon ran and appeared to be a viable candidate, that would put Lucas Bennett in an uncomfortable position. He'd championed Hal Gannon because of Gannon's penchant for often sliding into the Republican camp on issues that mattered to Bennett, and he'd taken considerable flak from his Republican friends for what they considered an almost traitorous act in backing the "enemy." But if Gannon's reelection bid became tainted by a sexual scandal, it would be difficult—no, make that impossible—for Bennett to continue supporting him.

"Politics," Smith muttered as he parked the car, rode the elevator to his floor, and poked his head into Brixton's office before entering his own. Brixton was behind his desk, feet up on it, reading the paper.

"Catching up on the news?" Smith asked.

"Oh, hi, Mac," Brixton said, dropping the paper on the desk and his feet to the floor. "I was reading about that woman they found in Rock Creek Park."

"I heard on the radio," Smith said. "No suspects yet?"

"No. There's also a piece about that wife who tried to hire me to put a hit on her hubby. The judge granted bail, said she wasn't a flight risk with the big house and her kids."

"No surprise. Are you concerned that she might do something foolish?"

"She already did, trying to hire a hit man."

"What I mean is, do you think she might try something foolish concerning you? She knows who you are and that you set her up."

"Like what?"

"Like hiring somebody else to put a hit on *you.*"

Brixton shook his head. "Nah. That's not going to happen."

"It's happened before," Mac said, "when that psycho

rammed a knife into your arm last year. A few inches to the left and you wouldn't be here. Where's Flo?"

"Shopping. We had a little spat. Whenever we do, she goes shopping."

"You should lock up the credit cards before you argue."

"Good advice from my favorite lawyer. Things good with you?"

"I lost at tennis, but other than that I'm fine. It was close. I'll beat him next time."

"How about I bet on him the next time and you throw the match?" Brixton suggested, laughing.

"Good idea," Mac said, joining in the laughter.

"Check in before you leave," Smith said. "I might have an assignment for you."

Brixton noticed Smith limping as he left the office and went to his own. He knew what a bad knee meant and felt for the counselor. You start wearing out like an old car, he thought, and all the lube changes and new tires and replacement parts didn't make a hell of a lot of difference.

M ac returned a call from Annabel the minute he settled in his office.

"I just want to remind you about Celia St. Claire's party tonight," his wife said.

"I forgot about it because I wanted to," Mac said.

"Then we shouldn't have sent back the RSVP and said that we'd attend."

"A momentary moment of weakness on my part," he said. "What time does it start?"

"Seven."

"I'll be home in time to change clothes. Sure we have to go?"

"Yes, Mackensie, I'm sure."

When Annabel called him Mackensie, he knew she meant it.

Celia St. Claire's soirees seldom had a theme, for which Mac was grateful. He disliked theme parties, especially when it necessitated donning some sort of costume, even a hat, and he and Annabel had an understanding: When an invitation arrived for a theme party, they were busy, or out of town, or deathly ill. But this night's gathering was nothing more than yet another reason for Washington's A-list to dress up and swap gossip about what they'd read that day on Politico's Playbook, or any of the other "insider" political gossip sheets.

Annabel had become friends with Celia St. Claire when they worked together on a charity fund-raiser. Celia was indisputably in the top tier of Washington's social strata. She'd come to D.C. years earlier with her husband, Emile, when he'd been appointed French ambassador to the United States. Emile St. Claire was a wealthy man, having inherited a successful line of department stores in Paris, with satellite stores in other French cities. When his six-year stint in the embassy on Reservoir Road was coming to a close, Celia, who'd become a familiar party giver and had fallen in love with Washington, suggested that they stay. To her surprise— and to the surprise of many, especially family members back in France—Emile agreed, and they put into motion the necessary legalities.

While Celia solidified her position as a favored hostess to the rich and powerful, Emile hooked up with a former high-level member of a previous administration to form a lobbying firm through which they represented numerous companies, many of them French, with a stake in the outcome of congressional legislation and administration foreign policy. Emile's American partner was the face of the firm when it came to registering as a lobbyist, but Emile, suave, handsome, and persuasive, was the one who brought in the business. They worked well together, and the firm prospered.

Emile's beautiful wife's skills included not only planning lavish parties; she possessed a keenly honed sense of whom to invite to ensure mention the following day in the city's most influential media. She'd even launched a blog in which she gushed about her parties and those who'd attended; it was read religiously by the D.C. in-crowd as well as those salivating for acceptance into it.

"Mr. and Mrs. Smith," Emile said when Mac and Annabel entered the palatial home in the posh Hillwood section of the city. "How good to see you again."

"Pleased to be invited," said Mac.

"The gods have looked down at us with the weather," Emile said in his French accent. "Lovely evening. We'll be on the terrace. Please, you know the way there. The bar is open."

As the Smiths were about to step away, another guest arrived and said something to Emile in French, obviously not his native tongue.

"Hah," Emile said, laughing, "and the humor is in the mispronunciation."

The guest laughed along with Emile, but Mac had the feeling that he hadn't found the subtle putdown amusing.

French ditties played by a guitarist, bass player, and accordionist drew the Smiths in the direction of the terrace, large enough to hold sporting events, where at least a hundred people had gathered. Smith found the accordion's sound to be grating unless, of course, accompanying Edith Piaf. But the smile on Annabel's lovely face said that she was enjoying the music, and Mac reminded himself to keep his musical prejudices to himself.

Uniformed waiters circulated through the crowd, deftly balancing large trays with red and white wines and an assortment of canapés. Two bars had been set up on the perimeter of the space for those wanting something stronger. The Smiths had just plucked glasses from a passing tray when the hostess, Celia St. Clair, appeared.

"Annabel darling, how wonderful that you could be here." To Mac: "And with your devilishly handsome husband on your arm. Perfect!"

Mac never knew how to respond to such comments, so he simply smiled.

"A perfect evening for a party," Annabel said. "I love the music."

"So do I," said Celia through a sigh. "Emile and I try not to think about Paris too often, but the music always takes us back."

"Yes, it certainly has a French flair," Mac said.

Celia looked from wineglass to wineglass. "Good," she proclaimed, "you've fortified yourselves. You will excuse me. The dinner buffet will start in an hour. I've hired a new chef, direct from Avignon. He's quite remarkable. Enjoy. Mingle. I'm sure you know many of my guests."

With that, she floated away to other knots of people.

"You didn't know that I was devilishly handsome, did you?" Mac said into Annabel's ear.

Annabel took a step back, looked her husband up and down, and cocked her head, sending her red tresses falling to one side. "Yes," she said with a serious voice, "I quite agree that you are devilishly handsome, Mr. Smith—considering your age."

"Of course. And I find you to be a ravishing beauty—considering—"

"Let's join those people over there," Annabel said as she poked her index finger into his chest.

Celia had been right. The Smiths did know many people at the party. They'd met the new French ambassador and his wife, and stopped to chat with Chris Matthews from the cable channel MSNBC. A senior U.S. senator had gathered around him a half dozen people and, based upon their laughter, was evidently telling amusing stories. Ford's Theatre's resident director gushed over the upcoming season, and a feature writer from *The Washingtonian* buttonholed Mac to request some time with him for an article on presidential appointees to the federal courts whose confirmations were being stonewalled in Congress.

They ended up chatting with two other couples, one of whose husbands taught with Mac at GW, the other man's wife a frequent browser at Annabel's pre-Columbian art gallery in Georgetown.

"Wine?" a waiter asked.

"Yes, please," Annabel said.

"I'm ready for a bourbon," Mac said. "Excuse me."

He got in line at a bar. As he waited his turn, a congressman with whom Mac had served on a panel at GW slapped him on the shoulder.

"Hello, Charles," Mac said.

A man accompanying the congressman extended his hand. "Hal Gannon," he said.

"Oh," Mac said. "Nice meeting you, Congressman. I'm an old friend of a friend of yours, Lucas Bennett in Tampa."

"Are you?"

"Yes," Mac said. "I was just talking to Luke about his daughter, Laura."

He waited for a response. When there wasn't one, he continued.

"I understand that she's interning with you."

Gannon looked beyond Mac as though searching for a savior.

"What? Oh, sorry. Yes, Laura is an intern with me this session. She's a nice young lady."

"Her dad's been trying to reach her," Mac said. "I

called your office and spoke with your chief of staff. She said that Laura had taken a few days off."

"Has she? I can never keep track of my interns."

The congressman was about to pull away when Annabel joined them.

"Annabel, say hello to Congressman Gannon," Mac said.

"It's nice meeting you," Annabel said. "Mac is a friend of the Bennetts in Tampa and—"

"Excuse me," Gannon said. "There's someone I have to catch up with. Great meeting you both. My best to Luke Bennett when you talk to him."

"He was voted the most handsome member of Congress," Annabel commented as she and Mac strolled to a relatively secluded corner of the terrace.

"So I read."

"He is good-looking," she said.

"Yes, I suppose he is."

Annabel took in her husband's serious expression. "Something bothering you?" she asked.

"Congressman Gannon. He didn't seem especially pleased when I brought up Luke Bennett's daughter, Laura."

"He did seem distracted," Annabel said.

"I had the feeling that it was more than that," Mac said, "but maybe I'm wrong. Let's eat. The buffet is open."

The chef that Celia had imported from Avignon was on his game that night, and Mac and Annabel thoroughly enjoyed the meal.

"Time to say our good-byes," Mac suggested.

"Excuse me."

They turned to face a small, wiry man dressed in a white dinner jacket, large red bow tie, and with a red rose in his lapel. *A dandy,* Mac mentally summed up.

"My name's Paul Wooster. I noticed you talking with Congressman Gannon earlier in the evening."

"Right," said Mac.

"I'm from Tampa. The congressman represents my district."

"We have friends in Tampa," Annabel said, "an attorney."

"Really? Anybody I know?"

Mac laughed. "Tampa's a pretty big place, Mr. Wooster. Our friend is Luke Bennett."

"I've met Mr. Bennett a few times," Wooster said. "Don't you hate it when you say you're from someplace and people assume that you know everybody who lives there?"

"Especially if you're from New York City," Annabel said. "What brings you to Washington?"

"Oh, I get up here fairly often. I'm a marketing consultant with a pretty diverse client base. You? Are you in government?"

"No," said Mac. "I'm an attorney. Annabel owns an art gallery in Georgetown."

"Modern art?"

"No, pre-Columbian."

"I don't know much about that. How long have you been friends with Congressman Gannon?"

"We just met tonight," Mac said.

Wooster cast a quick look around before saying, "I hope the rumors about Congressman Gannon aren't true."

Mac had tired of the conversation with this stranger. He said, "It was good meeting you, Mr. Wooster."

"Oh, sure, don't let me hold you up, and forget what I said. It's just that I'm a real fan of Hal Gannon and would hate to see some personal scandal get in the way of all the good work he does here in D.C. A pleasure meeting you."

As Wooster walked away, Annabel asked Mac, "What was *that* all about?"

"I'll tell you when we get home."

Forty-five minutes later, in pajamas and robes, they sat on their terrace nursing snifters of cognac.

"And Fred Mayer told you that there's a sexual scandal brewing with Gannon?" Annabel said.

"That's right. Of course, Fred is about to go to work for Pete Solon, who's going to run against Gannon. He's not an entirely unbiased source."

"Another D.C. congressional scandal," Annabel said, sighing and sipping her cognac. "What is it that makes men think that they're immune from the rules once they get elected?"

Mac laughed. "Maybe it's the hearing aids they start wearing."

"Hearing aids? What does *that* have to do with anything?"

"I was just thinking of what Tom Brokow says when asked about the hearing aids he wears. He claims they're not hearing aids. They're Viagra drips. Maybe elected officials start wearing Viagra drips once they reach Congress."

"If you say so, Mac."

"I say so, Annabel. Time for bed."

11

Paul Wooster had been invited to the party by the chief of staff of a powerful Republican senator with whom he'd become friendly. In Wooster's line of work, becoming friends with people was coin of the realm.

He'd been in Washington for the past three days making contact with people who might have something to offer his client, who was paying him handsomely along with a generous expense account, enabling him to stay in the best hotels and dine in the finest restaurants. On this trip he'd opted for the iconic Willard hotel at Pennsylvania Avenue and Fourteenth Street, a block from the White House and with an illustrious history going back to 1850. It was said that the term "lobbyist" was coined there; people wanting something from the government hung around the opulent rococo lobby hoping to catch the attention of government movers and shakers, including a long line of presidents, to plead their cases. Such bending of an ear in search of a favor seemed quaint compared to today's obscene buying of influence.

For Wooster, the Willard represented the class of establishment to which he was entitled, and he spent freely, capping off each day with drinks in the Round Robin & Scotch bar, where he imagined sitting next to Walt Whitman, Mark Twain, and other notables who'd frequented the hotel, many making it their home for long stretches.

This night, his last in the city for this trip, was special, though, and when he left the St. Claire party he made a beeline for the bar, hoping that she would show up as promised.

He'd been served his first drink when she walked in and surveyed her surroundings. She'd given Wooster a description of herself, detailed enough that he recognized her—blond hair, blue eyes, five feet six inches tall, and wearing a lime green dress. The thought came and went to Wooster that she hadn't mentioned that she was older than he'd expected, or was a woman who obviously had to work hard to keep off the pounds. Appealing in a fleshy way. He could see why Gannon had been attracted to her.

He motioned to her, and she took the barstool next to him.

"Ms. Montgomery?" Wooster said.

"Yes. Mr. Wooster?"

"That's me. Glad you could come. "Drink?"

"A Manhattan," she told the bartender, "and make it with rye, not bourbon. And an extra cherry, please."

"Classy drink, a Manhattan," Wooster said.

"I like it," she said. "What are you drinking?"

"Gin and tonic. So, your friend who put us in touch says you're with the opera. You sing?"

"Heavens no," she said, and laughed. "I'm on the board. Do you like opera, Mr. Wooster?"

"I don't know. I've never been to one. How about we get on a first-name basis? I'm Paul."

"I'm Rachel."

They touched the rims of their glasses.

"My friend tells me that you're a private investigator Mr.—Paul."

"That's right, only it's not like you see on TV or in the movies. I only carry a weapon on special occasions and—"

"Is this a special occasion?"

"It could be, only no guns necessary. So, Rachel, tell me about your relationship with Congressman Gannon."

His words brought a deep frown to her face. Her lips compressed, and her eyes came alive. "Maybe this isn't the place for this conversation," she said. They'd been virtually alone in the bar, but it had begun to fill up.

"Maybe you're right," he said. "We could go to my room, only don't think I'm on the make."

"Why would I think that?"

"Some women would take it that way. It's a nice room. You can see the White House from it. I'll order up food and drinks, and we can have a nice private chat."

She seemed reluctant, which annoyed him. He didn't care whether they went to his room or not, but he wondered whether she was about to back off, suffer a memory lapse, decide not to tell him what he needed to know.

"Suit yourself," he said with deliberate casualness, and drank.

"I just hope I'm doing the right thing," she said.

"That's up to you, Rachel." He twisted on the stool and faced her. "Look, I've been straight with you. I'm working for people in Tampa who don't want to see this hypocrite Gannon get another two years in the House. I don't give a damn about politics, but I sure as hell do care when voters vote for a guy who holds himself up as a bastion of morality and family values and then makes a mockery of it the way he lives." When she didn't respond he added, "Don't you agree?"

She didn't answer his question. Instead she said, "It's just that I'm well known here in D.C. and don't want to be made a fool of."

"Of course."

"And I don't give a damn either about politics or whether Mr. Family Values Harold Gannon gets re-elected or not. I just want to see him hurt the way he hurt me."

"Understandable, Rachel."

She looked as though she might begin to cry, and he hoped she wouldn't, not in a public place.

"I just want that bastard Gannon to get what he deserves, that's all," she said, dry-eyed. And my name doesn't get involved in this. Right?"

"Right. I just need your experience as background."

Whether someone else reveals your story and who you are isn't my problem, he thought.

"A refill?" Wooster asked.

"In your room," she said, finishing her drink and patting her red lips with a cocktail napkin. "Let's go."

B y the time her third Manhattan had been delivered by room service, and over mini–lobster rolls, Rachel Montgomery had recounted for Wooster the affair she'd had with Hal Gannon and the way it had unraveled, every detail of it, how they'd met, what he was like in bed, the need to keep the affair secret above all else, the gifts he'd bought her, and how he'd told her he loved her and was about to divorce his wife.

"He promised to marry you?"

"Yes, of course. Maybe not in so many words, but it was understood. We were a couple, for Christ's sake. I told my closest friends. My God, how he deceived me." Her words were now slightly slurred and moisture clouded her eyes.

The tears came, causing Wooster to wince and to look away. He was well aware that she was the quintessential woman scorned, and he made a mental note not to believe some of the strident claims she made. He'd wanted to make physical notes while she talked, and would have liked to activate the small tape recorder he carried in his briefcase, but he was concerned that doing more than passively listening might turn her off. He'd remember enough of what was said to make notes after she was gone. He was good at that.

She reminded Wooster more than once of the conditions she'd set for telling him about her affair with Gannon—her name would never be used, and Wooster would use her story only to reinforce what he already knew, that Gannon was a womanizer of the first order. It was an empty promise. She'd told her "closest friends" about the affair with Gannon, which meant that they'd told *their* closest friends, who probably told anyone who would listen, close friend or not.

"It must be hard for you to talk about this," he told her when the session was wrapping up.

"Actually," she said, "it feels good, and I hope you and the other candidate use it to good advantage."

"We will," he said. "You can count on it." He took a bite of his lobster roll and asked, "What about other women who've had affairs with Gannon? You mentioned the airline stewardess. Who else?"

"His intern."

"Laura Bennett?"

"Is that her name? You know about her?"

"She's been mentioned to me," Wooster said. "What do you know about her relationship with Gannon?"

"Just what I've been told."

"Who told you?"

"Oh, God, I don't remember. Somebody mentioned

that the rumor was circulating about Gannon and his intern."

"I'll follow up on that," said Wooster. "I really appreciate this, Rachel."

"I have to go."

"Sure. I'll walk you down and get a cab for you."

After getting her into a waiting taxi and paying the driver plenty to cover the fare, he returned to the Willard's bar and enjoyed a leisurely single-malt scotch. The trip to D.C. had been fruitful.

He left the bar and placed a call on his cell phone to Tampa.

"Wooster here. I'm making great progress but need another day or two in D.C. There's an intern I have to look into."

"Stay as long as you need to, Paul."

"Great. Thanks. I'll check in tomorrow."

He ended the call and went to his room, where he made notes of everything Rachel had said, adding it to other notes from his stay in Washington.

Laura Bennett.

Was this intern Laura Bennett related to the Tampa attorney Lucas Bennett? The couple at the party, Mac and Annabel Smith, were Bennett's friends, they'd said.

Mac? Short for what? His wife was beautiful. Annabel? An old-fashioned name. Mac was an attorney, his wife a gallery owner. He wondered if maybe he should make contact with them, plead the need for some legal advice, or pretend to want an education in—what was it that she'd said?—pre-Columbian art? What kind of art was that?

He'd figure it out in the morning.

12

After trying the number for Laura Bennett's cell that he'd gotten from her father, and reaching a dead phone, not even a voice mail prompt, Mac Smith called Brixton into his office and told him what he'd been doing.

"How long has she been out of touch with her family?" Brixton asked.

"Three or four days. I tried Congressman Gannon's office where she's been interning, but she's not there, taking a few days off, they said."

Brixton shrugged. "Pretty young gal away from home for the first time," he said. "Probably fell for some guy and is shacked up with him. It's not something you tell your daddy about."

Smith ignored his investigator's cynical take before saying, "Her father gave me his daughter's address here in Washington. I'll call him again to make sure she still hasn't checked in. If she hasn't, maybe you could run by that address and see if she's there."

"Sure. Happy to."

Mac's call to Lucas Bennett resulted in the same

message: Laura had not checked in with her mother or father, and both parents were now seriously concerned.

"A private investigator who works for me is going to swing by her apartment," Smith told Bennett. "I'll get back to you if he comes up with anything. By the way, Annabel and I ran into Congressman Gannon last night at a party. I mentioned that I'd tried to get in touch with Laura."

"What did Hal have to say?"

"I mentioned that his chief of staff told me that Laura had taken a few days off. The congressman didn't seem to be aware of that. He said that he had trouble keeping track of his interns."

"He didn't seem concerned?"

"No. Let me see what Robert Brixton comes up with. He's the investigator I mentioned. He's top-notch and discreet."

"Thanks, Mac. I need to calm Grace down."

Brixton was glad to have something to do. Business had been slow, although a couple of potential clients had called and scheduled meetings. One was a matrimonial attorney, which meant Brixton would be asked to prove infidelity of a spouse, or maybe find out where a husband was hiding money to keep it out of the divorce proceedings. The other prospective client was a restaurant owner who was convinced that his bartenders were ripping him off. Brixton had been good at those sorts of assignments in Savannah, posing as a customer in some instances, or signing on as a new employee and using that vantage point to build a case against the barroom thief.

He'd always hated getting involved in matrimonial disputes, but a job was a job. Annabel Smith had abandoned her lucrative law practice because she'd become fed up with being in the middle of warring spouses, whose self-serving demands did nothing to help their kids through a difficult period. Brixton admired Annabel for having taken that stance and vowed one day to emulate her—turn down divorce cases. But for the moment, the pile of bills on Flo's desk rendered that a fanciful dream.

He headed for the apartment building on Capitol Hill where Laura Bennett was living during her internship. It occurred to him that if she was there, all he could say to her was, "Call your mother!" His career as a private investigator had come down to this, telling bratty young women to keep in touch with their parents.

He pushed the buzzer in the lobby and waited for a response. When there wasn't one, he buzzed again. No better luck. He'd left the foyer and was on the sidewalk when a short, slender young woman with oversized round glasses and a head framed by red curls approached carrying a grocery bag.

"Hi," Brixton said.

She tossed him a wary glance and continued up the steps.

"Excuse me," Brixton said. "Hate to bother you, but I wonder if you know a woman who lives in this building, Laura Bennett."

"Why do you ask? Who are you?"

"Robert Brixton. I work for an attorney who's a friend of Ms. Bennett's father. They haven't been able to reach her and wondered whether—"

"She's not here."

"Oh? You know her?"

She fixed him in a hard stare, as though sizing up a potential serial rapist.

"Does she have a roommate?" Brixton asked.

"I'm her roommate."

"Oh. Well, I'm a private detective. Ms. Bennett isn't in any sort of trouble. Her parents are worried, that's all."

"Laura isn't here," Reis Ethridge said. "She hasn't been here for days."

"She moved?"

Reis let out a frustrated sigh and looked for a spot to put down the bag.

"Here, I'll take it," Brixton said, extending his hands and offering a smile meant to be reassuring.

She clasped the bag closer to her chest.

"Any chance that I can come up and see where Laura lives?" he asked, certain what the answer would be.

"No!"

"I figured that," Brixton said. "Okay, I know that you're busy and I don't want to take more of your time, but maybe you can give me a clue as to where Ms. Bennett might be."

"Try Congressman Gannon," Reis said.

"My friend already called there."

"I mean try where he lives."

Brixton cocked his head.

"Laura and the congressman are close."

"What do you mean by 'close'?"

"He's her boyfriend. Look, I have to get in before things in this bag melt."

"Sure, of course. Thanks for your time." He handed her his card. "When you see Laura, please tell her to call her folks."

Her smile was sarcastic. "Sure, I'll tell her."

Brixton watched Reis Ethridge enter the building and disappear into the elevator.

Congressman Gannon is her boyfriend?

Brixton had to wait an hour to see Mac Smith because the attorney had a client in with him.

"Where have you been?" Flo asked as Brixton sat in the outer office waiting for Smith's meeting to end.

Brixton recounted his visit to Laura Bennett's building and his conversation with her roommate.

"She said that Congressman Gannon is her boyfriend?" Flo said, stressing the last word.

"Quote, end quote."

"Whew," Flo said. "He's married, has kids."

"That doesn't keep lots of men from having affairs."

"But an *intern*? How old can she be?"

"Old enough to know better. Mac says she's a college grad. Maybe they didn't teach smarts at her school."

"I wonder what Mac will have to say," Flo said.

The door opened and Smith poked his head in. "Any luck?" he asked Brixton.

"Yes and no," Brixton replied as he followed Smith into his office.

Mac wasn't as shocked at what Brixton had been told by Laura's roommate as Flo had been. A look of sadness came over him and he slowly shook his head. "I hope it isn't true," was all he said.

"I'm just telling you what this gal said," Brixton commented. "She's the snippy type. Maybe she doesn't know what she's talking about."

"I'd like to think that's the case," said Mac.

"You have to call her father back?"

"Yes. Of course I won't mention this to him. Could be just another D.C. rumor. But there is cause for concern, Robert. His daughter may have a perfectly good reason to have fallen out of touch with home, but up until now she's been good about calling her folks."

"Anything else I can do?"

"Not at the moment," Smith said, sighing deeply. "I'll make the call and see if there's anything else I can do on this end. What's your day like?"

"Two possible clients coming in."

"Good. Thanks for checking on her."

Mac called Lucas Bennett at his law office in Tampa and reported Brixton's experience.

"I've been telling Grace that Laura is probably off on some adventure," Bennett said. "It's not the first time that she's failed to stay in touch, but never for this long, only a day or two. This has gone far enough, Mac. You say that Hal Gannon's chief of staff said that Laura had taken a few days off. That's not like her. I think the police should be notified."

Smith hated to see it progress to that point but had to agree with Bennett's decision.

"I can ask the police to go to her apartment and look around," Mac said. "Brixton, my investigator, is a former D.C. cop and has connections there. I do, too. I suggest that it be done quietly, Luke."

"Maybe Grace and I should come to D.C."

"Hold off on that until the police have had a chance to check it out. I'll call you the minute I have something to report."

While Brixton met in his office with the bar owner, Smith called a friend at the Metropolitan Police Department, Zeke Borgeldt, who'd recently been promoted to superintendent of detectives. Borgeldt had always accepted Smith's invitation to come to one of his law classes at George Washington University to help educate the fledgling lawyers in the way the department functions, how it *really* functions, and Smith had weighed in on a thorny legal matter that Borgeldt had become involved in. Over the course of the past few years, they'd also developed a social friendship, enjoying dinners out with their spouses.

"What's up?" Borgeldt asked when he came on the line.

Smith explained the situation and asked whether a detective could be sent to Laura's apartment to check on her well-being. "Best that it be kept unofficial," Mac added. "Chances are everything is fine. No sense in raising unnecessary speculation."

"Not a problem," Borgeldt said while jotting down information Mac provided.

"I was also wondering, Zeke, whether my investigator, Robert Brixton, could accompany the detective. He's former MPD and—"

"I know who he is. Sure. I'll have someone go to that address and call you when I've arranged it."

A half hour later, after the restaurant owner had left, Brixton headed back to Laura Bennett's apartment building and waited in front until the detective assigned by Borgeldt, Jay Gibbs, pulled up in an unmarked car. Brixton led them into the foyer and buzzed the apartment.

"Who is it?" Reis Ethridge asked through the intercom.

"It's Robert Brixton again, ma'am," he said. "I'm with Detective Gibbs of the Washington MPD."

"A detective?"

"Yes, ma'am."

Brixton motioned for Gibbs to speak.

"This is Detective Gibbs, ma'am. I need to come up with Mr. Brixton and ask you a few questions about your roommate, Ms. Bennett."

"What's wrong? What's happened?"

"Nothing, ma'am, just a few questions. Please buzz us in."

She did, and they went to the apartment, where she stood in the open doorway. "Do you have some form of ID?" she asked.

"Sure," Gibbs said, flashing his badge.

She looked suspiciously at Brixton before stepping back inside and inviting them to follow.

Brixton and Gibbs stood in the living room and took it in.

"Just the two of you live here?" Gibbs asked.

"Yes."

"You're an intern, too?" Brixton asked.

"That's right. At the Department of Justice."

"And Ms. Bennett interns for Congressman Gannon," Brixton supplied.

Reis turned to Gibbs. "What questions do you have?"

Gibbs took out a notepad and pen and asked a series of questions: when Laura had last been at the apartment;

what, if anything, she told Reis the last time she was there about where she intended to go; whether anyone had come to the apartment with her with whom she might have gone off. Reis's answers were monosyllabic.

"You each have your own bedroom?" Brixton asked.

Reis nodded.

"Can we see your roommate's?" Gibbs asked.

She led them down a short hallway and pointed to one of two rooms.

In it was everything you would expect of a young woman's bedroom. A laptop computer was open on a plank of wood supported by two cheap fiberboard filing cabinets. One of two chairs in the room, a rocker, was more of a repository for discarded clothing than for sitting. Next to the laptop were various brochures from sightseeing sites in the D.C. area. Two suitcases stood in a corner. Brixton picked them up. "Empty," he muttered.

Gibbs sat in the second chair, a small office model on wheels. He touched a key on the laptop, and the screen came to life with a photo of Laura with her mother and father.

"I don't think you should be looking at her computer," said Reis. "That's private."

Gibbs said, "I could get a warrant, but I'm sure you wouldn't want to make me do that." He smiled broadly at her, his teeth white against his African-American skin, and didn't wait for permission to start clicking keys.

Reis left the room.

"There's nothing obvious here," Gibbs told Brixton. "We'll have to get a tech to look at it."

Certain that Reis wasn't within hearing distance, Brixton told Gibbs in a low voice, "When I was here earlier, the roommate said something about this gal, Laura, being a girlfriend of Congressman Gannon, the one she interns with."

Gibbs's eyebrows went up.

"I don't know if it's true," said Brixton, "but that's what she said."

Gibbs quickly leafed through the brochures. There was also a pile of credit card receipts that he perused.

Reis reappeared.

"Thank you for your courtesy," Gibbs said.

"Did you find anything?" she asked.

"No, but we appreciate you letting us look around."

"When's the last time you heard from her?" Brixton asked.

"Days ago."

"She hasn't been back for a change of clothes?"

"Not while I've been here, and I'm here a lot."

"She's never called?"

"No," Reis replied, her tone bordering on nasty. "I've already told you that."

"If you do hear from her, give me a call," Gibbs said, handing her his card.

Outside, Brixton asked Gibbs for his analysis of the situation.

"Nothing to indicate anything bad has happened," the detective said. "There's really nothing we can do unless her parents want to report her as missing. That'd get the ball rolling. This idea that she and the congressman might have been getting it on. Be interesting to talk to *him* about *that*."

"Yeah, it would," Brixton agreed. "Thanks for letting me tag along."

"My pleasure. I'll file a report about the visit and see if the brass wants to follow up."

The visit hadn't turned up anything tangible to report back to Mac Smith. But as Brixton drove away, he had the strong sense that something was wrong—very wrong—in the life of Laura Bennett.

13

Paul Wooster spent the day trying to nail down a tangible romantic link between Hal Gannon and Laura Bennett. He was unsuccessful. As the day wore on, he turned to his original source, a legislative aide to a Republican congressman from Florida's Second Congressional District in Miami, who agreed to meet him for dinner that night at the Willard's iconic Occidental Grill & Seafood restaurant.

Wooster prodded his guest during dinner to provide more than just D.C. gossip about Gannon and Laura Bennett. He wanted to return to Tampa with hard evidence of the affair, the name of someone who knew rather than speculated, have something in hand that Solon's campaign people could use directly against Gannon. Over multiple sidecars, Caesar salads, ten-ounce filet mignons, and crème brûlées, washed down with snifters of the restaurant's most expensive Armagnac, Wooster became more frustrated, which was apparent to his guest.

"Look, Paul," the guest said, "I'd love to come up with what you need, a photo of them playing kissy-face, coming out of a hotel together, an audio- or a videotape of them panting and sweating. But all I have is the scuttlebutt that floats around Congress. My guy has been on committees with Gannon and trusts him only as far as he can throw him."

"But he's sided with Republicans on a lot of issues, hasn't he?" Wooster said.

"Not as many as you think, Paul. He picks the high-visibility ones. It upsets his fellow Democrats, of course, but it plays big back home in his district. Hal Gannon, Mr. Compromiser, the hope and salvation of broken Washington. Tell you what I'll do. I'll spread the rumor and see who confirms it. If somebody does and comes up with the sort of proof you're looking for, I'll pass it along."

"I can't ask for more than that," said Wooster.

Their snifters refilled, Wooster's guest said, "But what's in it for me?"

"What do you mean?"

"I understand that Pete Solon's campaign chest is pretty big."

"I wouldn't know about that."

"I'm sure you don't come cheap, Paul."

"They pay me okay."

"In return for digging up some dirt on Gannon, I'd appreciate having some of Solon's war chest spread around a little between other Florida Republican candidates."

"Like the congressman *you* work for?"

"Yeah. I spend all my days and most of my nights trying to raise money for him. Times are tough, the economy sucks. Solon's got big bucks. If I come up with something on Gannon that helps Solon, he should share the wealth."

Whore, Wooster thought.

"Sounds fair to me," he said. "I'll pass it along."

He was on the first plane back to Tampa the following morning.

B rixton reported to Mac Smith after returning from Laura Bennett's apartment.

"Like I told you, Mac, her roommate's a sourpuss. I'd hate to have to live with her."

"Did she mention again about Ms. Bennett having an affair with the congressman?"

"No, but I told Gibbs, the detective I was with."

"What did he say?"

"He said it would be interesting to question the congressman about it. I'd love to be there if it ever happens. He also said that unless the parents file a missing person report, there isn't much anybody can do."

"Was there anything in the apartment to indicate where she might have gone?"

"No. There were two suitcases, but they were empty. Her clothes were in the closet. Gibbs went through some credit card receipts on her desk, but he evidently didn't see anything of interest. He also took a quick look at her laptop. According to the roommate, Ms. Bennett hasn't been there for a while. Everything was in order except for a couple of pieces of clothing on a chair."

"I'd hate to have her father file a missing person report if it's unnecessary. It could be embarrassing to her, and to her family. On the other hand . . ."

"It's that other hand that I'm thinking about, Mac. I've got a feeling that Ms. Bennett hasn't simply decided to skip town, maybe with some guy, and not call home. My gut tells me that something is wrong. And you know something? I may not be the brightest bulb in the drawer, but my gut never fails me."

* * *

Mac called Lucas Bennett and told him of the visit Brixton and the detective had made to Laura's apartment.

"Her roommate hasn't seen or heard from Laura in days," Mac said. "The detective feels that nothing can be done unless a missing person report is filed."

"Are you suggesting that I do that?" Bennett asked.

Mac hesitated. "Yes," he said. "I think it's reached that point."

"Can you give me the name and number of someone to contact, someone who'll be discreet?"

"Call Zeke Borgeldt. He's superintendent of detectives, a friend. Tell Zeke that we're working together to find Laura."

Fifteen minutes later, Lucas Bennett called Mac to say that he was on his way to Washington on the first available flight and would come directly from the airport to his office.

Mac had intended to leave early to attend an art auction with Annabel, but he canceled in order to be there when Bennett arrived. When Bennett walked in, a small suitcase in hand, Brixton was also in the office going over a deposition of a new client who Mac thought might benefit from the investigator's services.

After introductions, Bennett said, "This is a nightmare."

"I understand," said Mac. "Did you call Zeke Borgeldt?"

"No. I decided to come here first. I haven't even informed Grace of what I'm doing. I told her I was coming on a last-minute business deal. I wanted to get the lay of the land before making her worries worse. She's frantic, Mac. I calmed her down a little by saying that while I was in D.C. I'd be checking into Laura's whereabouts."

"Have you been in touch with Congressman Gannon's office?" Mac asked.

"No. You said you'd called and was told that Laura had taken a few days off."

"Right. His chief of staff told me that. And when I ran into the congressman at a party, he said he wasn't aware of Laura's schedule. I have a suggestion. Now that you're here, and we have Mr. Brixton, let's start making calls. You have Gannon's home number as well as his office?"

"Yes."

"Try and get hold of him. If you do, explain what's going on and tell him we need his help. In the meantime, Robert, you call area hospitals and—"

"Hospitals?" Bennett said.

"To rule out that she's had an accident and isn't capable of speaking, and doesn't have ID with her."

Bennett nodded solemnly. "I've never felt helpless before," he said.

"You aren't," said Mac.

"I feel as though I am. I've spent my adult life taking charge, solving problems, calling the shots, and here I am being told to do what's obvious."

"Perfectly understandable," Mac said. "Here. Use this phone to try to reach Gannon. Robert will use the phone in his office."

"I'll get on it right away," Brixton said.

"I'll call Zeke Borgeldt at MPD on my other line," Mac said. "When I get him, I'll put you on."

Bennett's attempts to reach Hal Gannon at the office and at home failed. He was told that the congressman was away and wouldn't be back for two days. The answering machine at the apartment gave out only a simple, "I'm not here. Leave a message after the beep."

Mac Smith was more successful in connecting with Zeke Borgeldt. The top cop told Mac that a family member would have to physically file the missing person report.

"Will you be there for another hour?" Mac asked.

"Yes, unfortunately," Borgeldt replied. "I'll be waiting for you and Mr. Bennett."

"I want to go to Laura's apartment," Bennett said after being told of Mac's conversation with Borgeldt.

"I suggest you wait until you've filed the report, Luke. The police will dispatch a team and you can join up with them."

"I have to call Grace. It's not right that I'm doing this without her involvement."

"Give her call," Smith said. "I'll check in on how Robert is doing."

Brixton was in his office going down a list of hospitals and clinics in the D.C. area.

"Anything yet?" Smith asked.

"No. I have another three to call."

"I'll leave you alone, but finish up as quickly as possible. Bennett and I are going to MPD to file a report on Laura. I'd like you with us."

"Whatever you say. Flo's gone home. I'll call and tell her I'll be late."

Bennett's call to his wife, Grace, in Tampa was tougher than he'd anticipated. She became hysterical, and it took awhile for her to regain control.

"A missing person report?" she said through tears. "Where is she, Luke? Where can she be? What's happened to her?"

"That's what we're trying to find out."

"I'm coming to Washington."

"No," Bennett said. "Mac Smith has things under control. You stay close to the phone. Chances are she'll surface, and the first place she'll call is home."

"I can't just stay here, Luke."

"You have to. I'll get back to you in a few hours after we file the report. Trust me, Grace. We have to take this in stages, one step at a time."

When he ended the call, Mac suggested, "It might be best if she's here," not adding that he'd come to the conclusion that a phone call to home from Laura was highly unlikely. His gut was in sync with Brixton's. Something nasty had happened to Laura Bennett.

Bennett called the JW Marriott hotel on Pennsylvania Avenue and reserved a room. A few minutes later, he, Mac Smith, and Robert Brixton stopped there for Bennett to check in and leave his bag before going to the Henry J. Daly Building on Indiana Avenue, the Washington MPD headquarters, in the neighborhood known as Judiciary Square. The building had been named for Henry "Hank" Daly, a twenty-eight-year veteran homicide sergeant, who was gunned down inside it in 1994 by Bennie Lee Lawson Jr. A deranged criminal, Lawson carried an assault handgun into the building and killed Daly and two FBI agents.

Smith, Bennett, and Brixton were directed to Zeke Borgeldt's office, where they were told to wait in the anteroom while Borgeldt finished a meeting. Ten minutes later, the door opened and Borgeldt escorted a young man and woman from his office. They were *Washington Post* reporters who'd interviewed the superintendent of detectives about the recent discovery of the body in Rock Creek Park.

"Sorry to keep you waiting," Borgeldt said.

"We appreciate you seeing us last minute," Smith said. "This is Lucas Bennett, my attorney friend from Tampa. You know Robert Brixton."

"The infamous Robert Brixton," Borgeldt said lightly, shaking Brixton's hand.

"Good to see you again," said Brixton.

Borgeldt noticed that the reporters were lingering by the door.

"Anything else I can do for you?" he asked.

"No, thanks, Superintendent," the young woman said. "We're leaving."

Once in Borgeldt's office, Bennett took the lead and gave Borgeldt a capsule account of Laura's disappearance. The superintendent listened closely and made notes.

"Do you have a recent photo of your daughter, Mr. Bennett?"

"Yes. I've brought two with me." He handed them to Borgeldt.

"I'll assemble a team to go to the apartment, Mr. Bennett, and we'll broadcast the missing person alert."

"I'd like to do this as quietly as possible," Bennett said.

"We certainly won't hold a press conference about it," Borgeldt said, "but there's really no way to ensure privacy in these matters."

"I understand," said Bennett.

"Why don't you settle in the waiting room," Borgeldt said, "while I put things in motion."

"We'll want to accompany whoever you send," Smith said.

"Of course. Give me a few minutes."

As Smith, Bennett and, Brixton waited, the two reporters who'd met with Borgeldt had settled in the empty MPD newsroom where press briefings were held.

"That was Mackensie Smith," the man said. "He used to teach at GW, but he's back in private practice."

"I recognized him," his female colleague said. "Who was the man he was with?"

"Lucas Bennett? A lawyer from Tampa? At least that's what I heard Smith tell the superintendent."

"I also recognized the third guy," she said. "Robert Brixton. His picture was all over the papers when he lost a daughter in that terrorist café bombing and shot the congressman's son."

"Right, right. Robert Brixton. Wonder what they're doing here."

She called the paper and asked that a search be done on Lucas Bennett. Ten minutes later, an updated bio on Bennett was e-mailed to her phone. It ended with a note about his daughter, Laura Bennett, interning in the office of U.S. Congressman Harold Gannon.

"So why are these Tampa lawyers Bennett, Mackensie Smith, and Brixton meeting with Superintendent Borgeldt?" he mused. "I wonder if it has to do with the daughter."

She laughed. "Congressman Gannon," she said. "The House's resident Don Juan."

He laughed, too. "One of many. Let's make a couple of calls and see what we can find out."

Borgeldt rejoined Mac and the others in the waiting room.

"I'm sending two detectives to the apartment. Why don't you drive there and wait for them to arrive. One is Detective Gibbs. You were with him earlier, Brixton."

Ten minutes after Mac had parked his car at the curb in front of Laura Bennett's apartment building, the detectives arrived. Along with Detective Gibbs was a lanky older man with thinning hair whose clothing hung loosely on his slender frame. His name was Lars Light.

Gibbs rang the buzzer. No answer.

"Try it again," Light said.

Still no answer.

Light leaned close to the bank of buzzers. "I'll try the super."

"What?" a man's voice said through the intercom.

"Police," Light said. "We need access to an apartment."

"What?"

"We're police," he repeated, louder this time. "We need to get into one of your apartments."

"Police?"

Light looked at the others and shook his head.

"Yes," he shouted, his mouth inches from the microphone. "Police!"

"One minute."

The super, with a shaved bullet head and wearing a sleeveless undershirt and a pair of hearing aids, arrived carrying a large ring filled with keys. "What apartment?"

Lucas Bennett gave him the number.

"You all police?" the super asked.

"Right," Light said, "we're all police." He showed him his badge.

The super opened the inside door and led them into the elevator. He fumbled to find the right key for the apartment. When he did, he opened the door and stepped aside. "What's the problem?" he asked. "Drugs? They seem like nice girls."

Brixton cast a glance at Bennett before saying, "No, no drugs. Thanks. We'll lock up when we leave."

The detectives took in the living room and looked into the kitchen.

"Her bedroom's down the hall," Gibbs said.

The room looked the same as when Brixton had last been there. The suitcases hadn't been moved, and the laptop was in the same spot on the makeshift desk. Light sat and turned it on. Bennett opened the closet door and peered at the clothing. "Damn," he muttered.

Mac Smith went to him. "Is something missing?" he asked.

"No. I don't know. It's just that seeing her clothing and knowing that she might be in trouble is tough to swallow."

Mac patted him on the back and they went to a corner of the room.

"She's neat," Detective Light commented. "Bed's made."

"Yes, she is," her father agreed.

"I wish the roommate was here," Brixton said.

"Your daughter a hiker, Mr. Bennett?" Light asked.

"Yes. She enjoys the outdoors. Why do you ask?"

"She accessed material about Rock Creek Park on her computer, maps, stuff about the mansion. She ride horses?"

"She has," Bennett confirmed.

"There's details here about horseback riding in the park."

"Rock Creek Park?" Brixton said. He was about to mention the recent discovery of another female victim there but caught himself after glancing at Bennett, who sat on the edge of the bed, elbows on his knees, head in his hands.

"We'll take the laptop," Detective Light said. "Let's pack up these papers, too."

"She was always on the computer," Bennett said, "and on her iPad, like everyone her age."

"I don't see an iPad," Gibbs said.

"We'll check the rest of the apartment," said Light. "We'll leave a card and a note for the roommate to call us."

Smith invited Bennett to his apartment for dinner, but the attorney begged off. "I need time alone to sort this out, Mac," he said. "I want to call Grace and have her join me. You were right in suggesting that. Please give my best to Annabel, and I can't thank you and Mr. Brixton enough for what you've done."

"We'll all be thankful when Laura shows up safe and sound," Mac said, as he dropped Bennett at the hotel. "Superintendent Borgeldt said he'd run whatever they come up with through me. We'll stay in close touch."

Mac left Brixton off in front of his apartment building. "What's your take?" he asked.

"My take? Not good, Mac. See you in the morning."

And at the Watergate where Annabel was eager to hear what had happened, Mac told his wife, "I think Luke Bennett had better brace himself for bad news, Annie."

14

Grace Bennett prepared to fly to Washington. She'd gone through a roller-coaster of emotions since speaking with her husband about Laura's disappearance and the plan to have MPD file a missing person report. It had been a sleepless night for the usually well-rested and physically fit woman who applied her knowledge of how the human body worked to her patients at Tampa General Hospital.

She'd called her supervisor at the hospital to say that she needed a few days off.

"Everything okay?" her boss asked.

She was desperate to share her grief but overcame the urge. "Everything is fine," she said, fighting to keep her voice steady. "Luke is in Washington on business and wants me to join him. I'll be back in a couple of days."

"Travel safe, Grace. Enjoy the time off. You deserve it. We'll cover for you with your patients."

She began to cry the minute she hung up the phone.

"Damn it!" she said aloud. "Get hold of yourself."

She was packed hours before the car service arrived to take her to Tampa International Airport and decided to call her sister, Irene, in suburban Maryland. Laura had recently gone to Irene's house for dinner and reported back that she had the feeling that her aunt was analyzing her every move and word.

"That's because she's a shrink, sweetheart."

"I know," Laura had said, "but it's—it's creepy."

They both had a good laugh over it. "I'm just glad that you had a nice home-cooked meal," Grace had said.

"Barbequed ribs, potatoes, and some sort of bread stuffing. It was like getting an injection of cholesterol."

"Fast for a day," her mother had said.

"Fat chance," Laura had said, and they laughed again before ending the call.

Grace and Irene had never been especially close, although there wasn't open hostility between them. Their lives had taken distinctly different paths.

Grace Bennett knew to not comment on her sister's lifestyle, which included overeating and a lack of physical exercise. Irene was a licensed psychologist with a private practice, which she operated from a wing of her home. Her husband had launched a variety of small businesses, all of which failed for one reason or another, and he currently worked as a manager in a Target store. It had been two years since Grace and Irene had seen each other, their relationship limited to phone calls every few weeks and the requisite holiday cards. The tradition of getting together for Thanksgiving and Christmas had fallen by the wayside.

On this day, Grace felt a compelling need to speak with Irene.

"Irene, it's Grace. Is this a bad time?"

"No, not at all. A client just left and I don't have another until late this afternoon. How are you?"

"I'm—" She began to cry.

"Grace, what's wrong? Is Lucas okay? Laura?"

"Oh, God, Irene I—no, things aren't okay. I'm about to leave for Washington."

"To visit Laura? Is she ill?"

"She's—she's missing."

"Missing? What do you mean *missing*?"

Grace explained about Lucas having gone to D.C. and his filing a missing person report. "We haven't heard from her in days. It's uncharacteristic of her to not stay in touch. I'm so fearful that something horrible has happened."

"What about her roommate?" Irene asked. "When Laura came here for dinner, she complained that they weren't getting along."

"I don't know about that, Irene. Maybe Luke has contacted her. I'll know more after I get there."

A silence between them ensued before Irene said, "There's something that you should probably know, Grace. I wouldn't mention it except for what you've just told me."

"What?"

Irene sighed. "I promised Laura that I wouldn't tell you."

"For God's sake, Irene, what is it?"

"When Laura was here she told me that she was— well, she said that she was in love with the congressman she was interning for, Congressman Gannon."

"*In love with him?*"

Irene's soft laugh was meant to comfort. "You know how young women are, Grace. They fall in love with everyone and anyone, especially someone with high visibility. Maybe 'love' is the wrong word. Infatuation is more like it."

"What did she say, Irene? Infatuated with him? In love with him?"

Irene sensed a rising anger in her sister's voice and said, "I really don't think it means anything. Young women of her age go through a series of crushes on older, successful men. I have a few young female clients who—"

"She told you this and you didn't call to tell *me*?" Grace interrupted, pleased that she hadn't said the first thing that came to mind: *Can the psychobabble!*

"She swore me to secrecy, Grace. Besides, I dismissed it as a starstruck young woman having fantasies. I see it all the time in my practice. I told her that she should make sure that it stays just that, a pleasant fantasy, and that if she had any thoughts about turning it into reality, she should think twice."

Grace's voice was now ice-cold. "Did she, Irene, turn it into reality?"

"It's just a fling, Grace. She's twenty-two years old and extremely independent. When I told her that she was asking for trouble getting involved with an older man, and a married one, to boot, she got her back up, said that she was old enough to make decisions. I left it at that. She's very bright, Grace. She'll make the right decisions in her life."

"I can't believe you didn't tell me about this."

"I didn't see any reason to."

"Luke will be furious."

"He doesn't have to know, Grace. I'm sure nothing came of it and—"

"Nothing came of it? She's missing, Irene. *Missing!* If Hal had anything to do with it, I'll—"

"Why don't you talk to him? And Grace, I resent you attacking me. You're way off base."

"I'm not attacking you, Irene. I'm—" Her steely voice melted into sobs again.

"If there's anything I can do."

"I have to go," Grace said.

"I'm sorry about Laura," Irene said. "I'm sure she's all right. You'll stay in touch?"

"Yes, I will. Thank you for the information."

She flew first-class to Washington. Her seatmate was a chatty young man who insisted on telling her of his career plans once he graduated from college. "My dad has plenty of connections in Washington," he'd said, among other things. Grace did her best to ignore him without being rude. Her mind was a jumble of conflicting thoughts and emotions.

Laura involved romantically with Hal Gannon? Preposterous!

Had it been just an infatuation, or had Laura and Gannon actually entered into a romantic relationship?

A sexual one? Each time she pondered that, she waved it away mentally. It couldn't be. It simply couldn't be.

Luke had reserved a car service to bring him to the airport to meet her plane. They embraced but limited their conversation until the driver was no longer privy to what they said. Inside the suite at the Marriott, she broke down, and her husband did his best to comfort her. Once her emotions were under control, he brought her up-to-date on what had transpired over the past twenty-four hours.

"And Mac Smith says that there's been no progress in finding her?" she asked him.

"No. They're analyzing what's on her laptop, tracking down where she might have been recently, people she spent time with, anything to come up with a clue to her whereabouts."

"What do the police *think* happened to her?"

"They're not in the business of speculating, Grace. The superintendent of detectives—a guy named Borgeldt—is a friend of Mac's. He's personally taken charge of the investigation. Everything possible is being done to trace Laura's recent activities."

Room service delivering their dinner interrupted the conversation. When the server was gone, Grace asked, "Have you spoken with Hal Gannon?"

"No. I've tried, but they say he's out of town for a few days."

"You have to get hold of him, Luke. He's the reason she came to Washington in the first place. He must know *something*."

"I'll try his home number again."

He reached the answering machine and swore as he slammed down the receiver.

"Call Charlene in Tampa," she suggested.

Gannon's wife answered.

"Charlene, it's Luke Bennett."

"Hello, Luke. How are you?"

"Not well, Charlene. Does Hal happen to be there?"

"No. He's in Washington."

"No, he's not. There's been no answer at his apartment, and his office says he's away. I thought he might be home with you."

"I haven't spoken to Hal in a few days, Luke. Is there a problem?"

"Yes, there is. Grace and I are in Washington. I'm calling from there. Our daughter, Laura, has gone missing."

"Oh, my goodness. How could that be?"

"That's what we're trying to find out. It's important that I speak with Hal."

"If I hear from him, I'll have him call you right away. You're in Washington?"

He gave her the number of the hotel, their room, and cell phone number.

"Thanks, Charlene," Bennett said.

"How's Grace holding up?"

"As you can imagine, this is a traumatic time for us."

"I imagine. If there's anything I can do, I—"

"Just have Hal call me. Thank you very much."

"She doesn't know where Hal is?" Grace said after Lucas had hung up.

"No."

Grace's expression said that she was grappling with something weighty.

"What are you thinking?" Bennett asked.

"I spoke with Irene this morning."

"How is she?"

"She's fine. Laura had dinner with her one night."

"Sure. I remember you telling me about it."

"She told me something that I think you should know, Luke."

Grace's exposition told that she was struggling with
some unruly

...

...

CHAPTER

15

While Grace Bennett recounted for her husband what her sister had told her about Laura and Hal Gannon, Mac Smith was with Annabel at her Georgetown art gallery admiring two pieces she'd recently purchased, a five-inch-tall solid terra-cotta woman, which Annabel dated back to the Maya culture of 700–900, and a jar in the form of a face, also terra-cotta and dating from a slightly later period.

"You've bought from this doctor before," Mac commented.

"After vetting him carefully," Annabel answered. "He's an avid collector who's getting on in years and wants to pare down his collection. What do you think of them?"

Mac smiled. All he knew about pre-Columbian art was what his wife had taught him since opening the gallery fifteen years ago. They were not objects that he would be drawn to naturally, but their provenance and age couldn't be dismissed.

"I think they're wonderful," he said, not adding that he hoped she could sell them at a profit over what she'd paid the doctor. He also didn't express his wish that his wife not fall too much in love with them—as she had with other pieces in the gallery—and decide that she couldn't part with them. The gallery was, after all, a business.

"Ready to leave?" he asked. "Let's grab a quick bite and head home."

As she prepared to close up, his cell phone sounded.

"Mac, it's Luke Bennett."

"Hello, Luke. Nothing to report yet. As we agreed, my investigator, Robert Brixton, plans to spend time digging up information. He's between assignments right now."

"Whatever you say, Mac, and whatever it costs. I've just learned something from Grace about Laura's relationship with Hal Gannon."

"Relationship?"

"I think they were sleeping together."

Mac immediately thought of what Fred Mayer had said about Gannon's reputation as a womanizer, but he didn't mention it. Instead, he questioned Bennett about the source of this allegation. Bennett told him about Grace's conversation with her sister.

"Sure it's not a young woman's fantasy?" Mac said.

"Grace doesn't think so, at least not based on what Irene said. I've been trying to reach Gannon, without success. I called his wife in Tampa. She hasn't heard from him in a few days. Damn it, Mac, if it's true, it could mean that—"

"Don't jump to conclusions, Luke. I'm sure that Gannon will be back in Washington any day now."

"Grace wants me to tell the police about Gannon."

"That may become inevitable, Luke, but it's premature. Here's what I suggest. I'll have Robert Brixton try and reach the congressman, ask for some time with him, get a sense of what he might know. Brixton has a good antenna."

"Why would Gannon speak to a private investigator?"

"Because talking to a private investigator is better for

the congressman than having detectives arrive at his office. Right now Laura's disappearance hasn't become public, although it's only conjecture how long that will be true. If the congressman brushes Brixton off, we can alert the police about a possible romantic affair between Gannon and Laura. In the meantime, I suggest that you and Grace get some rest. Come by my office first thing in the morning, say eight?"

Mac and Annabel had just pulled up to the curb in front of DISH drinks in the River Inn, not far from the Watergate, when his cell rang again.

"Mackensie Smith?" a woman asked.

"Yes."

"This is Rebecca Paulson. I'm a reporter at *The Washington Post*. Got a minute?"

"Actually, I don't. My wife and I are about to have dinner."

"Sorry to call on your cell, Mr. Smith. I'll make it brief. I've come to learn that your client, an attorney from Tampa, Florida, Lucas Bennett, is in town because his daughter, Laura Bennett, who worked as an intern for Florida congressman Harold Gannon, is missing, and that a missing person report has been filed. I'd like your comment on it," she rattled off.

"Ah, Ms.—"

"Paulson. Rebecca."

"I don't know where you get your information, Ms. Paulson."

"But you did accompany him to see Superintendent Borgeldt at MPD. Besides, I know from a good source that a missing person report has been filed."

A cop with a big mouth, Mac mused.

"Is Mr. Bennett with you?"

"No, he's not, and I have nothing more to say."

"Would you be good enough to tell me how to reach Mr. Bennett?"

"Thank you for the call, Ms. Paulson. Have a wonderful evening."

"What was that all about?" Annabel asked as they entered the restaurant, a popular spot with theatergoers at the nearby Kennedy Center.

"So much for Laura's disappearance being kept quiet. It was a reporter from *The Post*. They've latched on to the story."

"Inevitable."

They'd just been served their usual steak frites when Mac's phone sounded again. It was Brixton.

"Mac, sorry to bother you, but you'll want to know that I got hold of Congressman Gannon, reached him at home. He'd just walked in. He said he knew that there was a question of where Laura Bennett was because he was told by his office, but claims he knows nothing about it."

"*The Post* is about to break the story, Robert, probably in tomorrow's edition. Did he agree to speak with you?"

Brixton laughed. "Yeah, he did. He balked at first, but I told him that the police were involved and it would be better to talk to me first. He didn't agree until I mentioned that you're representing Laura's father. He said he'd met you and knows your reputation, and that he's a close friend of Mr. Bennett. Anyway, I'm going to his apartment first thing in the morning."

"I'm impressed, Robert. He'll want to know how to get in touch with Bennett. Here's the hotel number."

"It was a piece a cake, Mac. I did my best Columbo impression, you know, told him that I knew how busy he was and what a great reputation he had, hemmed and hawed, even said 'shucks' once, I think. He comes off like a nice guy, said he'll do anything to help."

Robert Brixton saying something positive about an elected official? was Mac's unstated thought.

When they ended the conversation, Mac told Annabel about Brixton seeing Gannon in the morning and wondered how the police would respond to it. "Now that they're officially involved, they might get their nose out of joint having a private investigator make the first contact."

"Robert is representing you, and you're representing Luke Bennett," she said.

"I suppose you're right, Annie. I'll be eager to see what Robert comes up with."

Over coffee and a shared piece of key lime cheesecake with raspberry sauce, Mac called Luke Bennett to tell him of Brixton's plan to meet with Gannon.

"I'll go with him," was Bennett's first response.

"Better if Robert goes by himself," Mac said. "I gave him your hotel number. I'm sure Gannon will call you after their meeting."

Bennett didn't sound pleased, but he acquiesced.

"If Gannon had anything to do with Laura's disappearance, I'll—"

Mac understood the frustration he must be feeling. "Let's not jump to conclusions, Luke. See you at my office at eight."

THE SEARCH

16

Brixton arrived at Gannon's apartment in Adams Morgan at eight thirty the following morning. He was buzzed into the foyer and rode the elevator to Gannon's floor, where a young man dressed in a blue suit, white shirt, and red tie waited in an open doorway.

"Mr. Brixton? he asked.

"Right."

He held out his hand. "I'm Cody Watson, Congressman Gannon's press aide. The congressman is on a call but he'll be finished shortly. Come in. Coffee? We have pastries straight from Firehook Bakery on Dupont Circle, juice, too."

Brixton hadn't expected to see anyone other than the congressman, or to receive such a warm welcome. He followed Watson inside and looked around the living room. "Nice place," he said.

"Unfortunately, the congressman doesn't get to use it very often, only when Congress is in session. Sit down, Mr. Brixton. Cream? Sugar?"

"Straight black," Brixton said, perusing a platter of

Danish pastries. He passed them up and took a chair by the window.

Watson placed a steaming-hot black coffee on a table next to Brixton. He'd just taken his first tentative sip when the bedroom door opened and Gannon entered the living room. He went directly to Brixton and shook his hand, a smile on his tanned face. Brixton placed the cup back on the table and tried to stand, but Gannon maintained his grip and said, "No, sit please. Sorry to keep you waiting, but I see that Cody has taken good care of you."

"Yeah, he has, Congressman. Thanks for finding the time to see me this morning."

"I just wish there was a different reason for our getting together. I can't believe that Laura is missing. Let's hope she's simply gone off someplace and will surface safe and sound."

"That's what her folks are hoping for, too. Oh, her father and mother are staying at the Marriott. Here's the phone number and—"

"I know. I just got off the phone with Luke Bennett. He called twenty minutes ago. He and his wife, Grace, are in town hoping to get some word about their daughter. Do you have anything to report?"

"Afraid not. You know that I'm here because Mackensie Smith, an attorney and a friend of Mr. Bennett, asked me to contact you."

"I'm aware of that. I asked Luke—Mr. Bennett about it, and he assures me that we're all playing on the same team, Mr. Smith, you, the Bennetts, and of course me."

Brixton wondered whether Bennett had said anything to Gannon about the rumor that his daughter might have been sleeping with him, but from the congressman's upbeat manner he doubted the subject had been raised.

Gannon took a chair so close to Brixton that their

knees touched. "Now," he said, "let's get down to the nitty-gritty. I know that you're a private investigator working on Luke Bennett's behalf. What have you uncovered so far?"

"Nothing, sir. The reason I'm here is to see what *you* have to offer in the way of help."

Gannon looked at his press aide, who sat on the couch holding a steno pad and pen.

"Me?" Gannon said. "What can I possibly do?" Before Brixton had a chance to respond, Gannon added, "Of course, I'll do anything in my power to find that wonderful young woman."

Wonderful young woman? Brixton mused. *Wonderful as an intern, or in bed?*

"When was the last time you saw Ms. Bennett?" Brixton asked, taking out his own notepad and pen.

"Many days ago."

"At the office?"

Gannon thought before saying, "Yes, I believe that's where I last saw her."

"Did she seem normal to you?"

"Normal?"

"You know, did she seem upset about something, act uptight, look like or say anything that might be weighing on her mind?"

"No, although I must say that I really don't spend much time with the interns working in my office. They're busy with their responsibilities and so am I. My chief of staff, Roseann Simmons, pretty much does all the supervision of interns."

"I'd like to speak with her," said Brixton.

"That's easily arranged."

Brixton wrote her name in his pad and asked, "I don't suppose you know much about Ms. Bennett's life outside the office, men she might have been dating, favorite places she liked to visit, that sort of thing."

"You're right, Mr. Brixton. What my interns—what all interns in Washington—do on their time off is pretty much their own business, unless, of course, they get themselves into trouble."

"Does that happen often?"

"No, of course not, just an occasional foul ball who's away from home for the first time and drinks too much." He flashed a smile. "You know what I mean."

"Feeling his oats."

"Exactly."

"Or her oats."

"Yes, of course."

"Was Ms. Bennett that sort of young woman, you know, away from home and—well, drinking too much?"

"I really didn't know her well enough to make such a judgment."

"Oh? I was told that you were very close to the Bennett family."

"I was. Yes, I am."

"Didn't spend any time with their daughter?"

"Yes, of course I did. No, she never struck me as being immature. Excuse me."

Brixton watched him disappear into the bedroom.

"Did you work with Ms. Bennett?" Brixton asked Cody Watson.

"I knew who she was," Watson responded. "I mean, it's not a big office, but the interns pretty much kept to themselves."

"Interns don't work with press aides?"

"Well, sometimes, but—"

"You don't have an intern working with you?"

"As a matter of fact, I do, but it wasn't Laura Bennett. More coffee?"

"No, thanks."

Gannon reemerged from the bedroom and made a show of checking his watch. "I'm afraid that I'm going to have to end this conversation, Mr. Brixton. I think it's good that Luke Bennett has hired you as a private investigator to help find out what's happened to his daughter, but I'm sure the police will pick it up from this point forward. Luke Bennett has filed a missing person report with the MPD and they're already on the case. I received a call earlier from a detective who wants to talk to me. I suppose they'll go over the same ground that you've covered this morning. I just wish I had more to offer. The Bennett family and my family are close, very close, and I just pray that nothing bad has happened to Laura. It's every parent's worst nightmare."

Tell me about it, Brixton thought as a vision of his daughter Janet being blown up in a café by a female terrorist, flooded his mind.

"Anything else?" Gannon asked.

"Not at the moment, but I'm sure we'll be talking again."

As Brixton stood, a jolt of pain shot through his bad knee. "Ooh," he said.

"Are you all right?" Gannon asked.

"A bum knee," Brixton said, moving his right leg in circles. "It acts up sometimes."

"Maybe you ought to have it replaced," Gannon said.

"Yeah, maybe I should. Well, thanks again for your time, Congressman."

As Brixton walked to the door, he stopped, turned, and asked, "Was Ms. Bennett ever in this apartment."

"No," Gannon said quickly. Then he added, "Well, maybe once, twice at the most, you know, to bring me something from the office that I'm working on. Why do you ask?"

"Just curious, that's all. I don't know much about congressional interns, how close they get to the men they're interning for. I thought maybe you threw dinner parties for them, things like that."

"I don't, and I can't speak for other members of Congress."

Thanks again, Congressman. I'll be in touch."

Cody Watson walked Brixton to the elevator.

"Must keep you busy working for a congressman," Brixton commented as they waited for the car.

"Keeps me on my toes, that's for sure. I remember reading about you. You lost a daughter in that café bombing and—"

"And I shot the congressman's son, who was with the suicide bomber."

"Yes, I remember that. It was big news."

"Was it?"

The doors opened.

"Let me ask you a question," Brixton said, using his hand to keep the doors from closing.

Watson cocked his head.

"How can an intern work in a congressman's office every day and the congressman doesn't know what she does, where she goes, who she sees?"

Watson's laugh was forced, and Brixton knew it. "He's just too busy, that's all," Watson said. "Have a nice day."

"Yeah, you, too. Thanks for the coffee. By the way, I understand that *The Post* is running an article about Ms. Bennett's disappearance."

"I've already read it in this morning's edition. They got a few facts wrong, but it pretty much covers the story. I feel bad for the congressman. He was close to the family. He's really broken up about this."

Congressman Gannon hadn't looked "broken up" to Brixton, but he'd learned years ago not to be too quick to judge anyone's reaction to bad news. He'd testified in murder cases where the prosecuting attorney pointed to a lack of emotion on the part of the accused as proof of guilt. But Brixton knew that everyone grieved differently.

Some wailed in public. Others, stoic in the presence of others, broke down in private.

As Brixton slowly made his way to Smith's office, he couldn't shake what Gannon had said, that losing a child was every parent's worst nightmare.

"Tell me about it," he muttered aloud.

He'd been lured back to Washington to join SITQUAL as a security agent, a civil service job. The mission was to provide protection for the more than 175 foreign embassies, residences, chanceries, and diplomatic missions in D.C.

One day he arranged to meet his daughter Janet after work at an outdoor café near State to discuss a business she wanted to launch with a musician boyfriend. Janet Brixton was a free spirit who sometimes provided her father with sleepless nights, but she also mirrored his shoot-from-the-hip approach to life. Her lip ring and tattoos were anathema to him, but so was much of contemporary society. Little things tended to bother him, including young men who wore baseball caps backward. Didn't they know that the visor was designed to shade the face? And today's music bewildered him. An inveterate jazz lover, Brixton enjoyed quoting the great jazz saxophonist James Moody who, when asked what he thought of rock-and-roll, replied, "You really can't play music while you're jumping up and down."

Despite these misgivings, and a dozen others, Brixton adored his libertine daughter and would have thrown himself under a bus to save her.

They were enjoying drinks and calamari when a young Arabic woman, accompanied into the café by a young

American man who quickly left, detonated a powerful explosive that killed many, including Janet Brixton. Bloodied and in shock, Brixton had followed the young man, cornered him in an alley, and when he pulled out what appeared to be a weapon, Brixton fired, killing him instantly. Brixton's target turned out to be the son of one of the House of Representatives' most powerful members, Mississippi Congressman Walter Skaggs, and Brixton was the only person alive to remember seeing Skaggs's son with the suicide bomber.

Fueled by the need to avenge his daughter's murder and to clear his name, he doggedly pursued the truth, which took him into the world of an Arab-American arms dealer and led him to a charismatic cult leader on the Hawaiian island of Maui, where Brixton was almost killed in his quest for justice. But in the end he managed to clear his name and put an end to a vicious ring of arms dealers providing weapons and explosives to terrorist organizations around the world.

But clearing his name bought little solace. Janet was gone, the victim of a terrorist bomber, leaving a hole in his life too deep and wide to ever be filled.

17

HOUSE INTERN MISSING
by Rebecca Paulson

A missing person report has been filed with the MPD by the parents of Laura Bennett, an intern in the congressional office of Florida congressman Harold "Hal" Gannon. The report was filed by Ms. Bennett's father, Tampa attorney Lucas Bennett, after Ms. Bennett fell out of contact over the past several days.

The missing person report was filed in person at MPD headquarters by Mr. Bennett. He was accompanied by well-known local attorney Mackensie Smith, and Robert Brixton, a Washington, D.C., private investigator.

Congressman Gannon's office released the following statement from the congressman just prior to this story being filed: "This is extremely upsetting, for me and for Ms. Bennett's family. Her father and I have been friends for years, and I only pray that she will soon reappear safe and sound."

"He didn't have anything to offer that could help determine where Laura might be?" Bennett said to Brixton. The Bennetts sat in Smith's office after Brixton had returned from his conversation with Gannon. The morning paper was open to the story of Laura's disappearance.

"No," Brixton said. "He pretty much said the same thing he said in the newspaper, that he hopes she turns up safe."

"What came out of *your* phone conversation with the congressman?" Mac asked Lucas Bennett.

"Nothing more than what Mr. Brixton has just said."

"How about calling me Robert?" Brixton said to Bennett.

"Yes, of course. Bob?"

"I prefer Robert."

"All right, Robert."

"Are you and the congressman planning to get together?" Smith asked Bennett.

"Hal was vague about that. He's been away on business and has a lot of catching up to do at the office. We agreed to make contact later."

Brixton didn't express what his visceral reaction to Congressman Gannon had been during their morning meeting. The congressman came off to him as cool and calculating, his smile practiced and available at a moment's notice, all surface, a quarter inch deep. A politician. The question Brixton had asked Gannon as he was leaving about whether Laura had spent time in the apartment was prompted by what her roommate, Reis Ethridge, had said about their personal relationship. Gannon's answer that she'd been there only a few times to deliver papers rang false to Brixton, nothing specific, just a feeling. And here he was claiming to be too busy at work to get together with his friend and the father of a missing daughter who happened to be his intern.

Hell of a guy.

Did the Bennetts know of the rumors that Gannon and Laura were involved in a relationship that had nothing to do with her duties as an intern? Brixton wondered. If they did, it hadn't come up yet that morning.

"What are the police doing?" Grace Bennett asked.

"They've been given information about Laura, along with names of people to question," Mac replied. "There's her roommate, Ms. Ethridge, names of restaurants she frequented based on the receipts found in her apartment, people she might have met at the health club she belonged to, other interns in Gannon's office. Her small phone book was found in the apartment. Names and numbers in it are being checked out."

"I wish you hadn't given them the photo of Laura that you did," Grace said.

"Why?" her husband asked.

"She looks—well, she looks slutty in that outfit."

"I gave them other pictures, too," he said.

"I just don't like her to come off as cheap," Grace said. "If there's any truth to what Irene told me, I'll—"

"What was that?" Brixton asked, breaking a sudden silence.

"Robert is aware of the rumor about Laura and Congressman Gannon being involved in a more personal relationship," Mac said.

"Where did *you* hear it?" Luke Bennett asked.

Brixton shrugged. "Her roommate mentioned something about it," he said, "and Mac has filled me in."

"It's that widespread?" Grace said. "Oh, my God, it's true, isn't it?"

"Still just a rumor," Mac said. "Let's not jump to conclusions until we have something tangible."

"But if it is true," Grace said, "it could be the reason Laura is missing." Her face and voice turned hard. "Will the police challenge Hal about it? I know that he's a U.S. congressman and all, but—"

"Let's give them time to touch all the bases," Mac said.

"But do the police know?" Grace pressed.

Mac looked to Brixton, who replied, "One of the detectives who came with me to your daughter's apartment is aware of the rumor, Mrs. Bennett."

"I didn't ask Hal about it when we spoke," her husband said.

"If it's true, Hal will only lie," Grace said, struggling to maintain her composure.

"Did your daughter ever say anything to you to indicate that she might be involved in a—well, in a close relationship with the congressman?" Brixton asked the father.

"Not to me, but—"

"My sister," Grace said, interrupting her husband. She told Brixton what Irene had revealed to her.

Smith's assistant, Doris, interrupted the meeting to say that a reporter from *The Washington Post* and someone from WTOP radio had called for Mac.

"I don't want to speak with the media," Mac told her. "Get their contact info and tell them I'll get back to them later." He said to the Bennetts, "I suggest that you maintain a no-comment stance with the press."

But as he said it, he knew that if Laura was to be found it would mean using the press to keep her disappearance in the spotlight. "We may need them," he added, "but not for the moment."

Bennett stood and paced the office. "Mac," he said.

"Yes?"

"You've been incredibly helpful, and Grace and I appreciate it, but I think it's time that we make it official. We'll need legal representation and want you to be our attorney in this matter."

"Of course," Mac said. "May I suggest that you also hire Robert as your investigator."

"If Robert agrees."

"Count me in," Brixton said.

"Why do we need a private investigator?" Grace asked. "Don't you think that the police will do their job?"

"The police will pull out all the stops, Grace," Mac said, "but this isn't the only case on their plate. Robert will have access to some people that the police won't. Besides, he'll be working directly for you."

"All right," she said.

"Good," Mac said. "Now let's get to work finding out what's happened to your daughter."

"I'd like to speak with Laura's roommate," her mother said.

"Let's see if we can arrange that," Smith said.

To Brixton: "You've met her twice, Robert. Why don't you see if you can get hold of her and set up a meeting with Luke and Grace."

"I've got to stay available for when Hal Gannon calls," Luke Bennett said.

"Let's play that by ear," Mac said. "Robert, go back to the hotel with the Bennetts and try to reach Laura's roommate from there."

"Sounds like a plan to me," said Brixton. "Let's go."

While the meeting was taking place in Mac's office, the Washington MPD was in the process of putting together a task force to search for Laura Bennett. Zeke Borgeldt had assembled a team of detectives, including Jay Gibbs.

"According to Brixton, the roommate hinted that Ms. Bennett might be involved with Congressman Gannon," Gibbs told his boss.

"Involved? How?"

"She said that the congressman was Ms. Bennett's 'boyfriend.'"

"Any confirmation on that?"

"Not that I know of."

Other detectives assigned to the squad filtered into the meeting room.

"We've got a missing person," Borgeldt said, "daughter of a prominent lawyer from Tampa, Florida. Name's Laura Bennett." He handed out photos of her that he'd had duplicated, including an artist's sketch of what she would look like with a different hairdo. Accompanying the pictures was a sheet of particulars, her height, weight, age, and other facts. "You've read about it in today's paper," Borgeldt said.

"The twenty-two-year-old in Rock Creek Park?" Borgeldt was asked.

"Negative on that. We have a tentative ID on her. Ms. Bennett came here from Tampa to intern for Florida congressman Harold Gannon."

"There's talk about him," a detective said. "They say he's a real stud."

"I've heard that," said Borgeldt. "I have a call in to his office. I'll talk to him myself. We checked e-mails. Nothing between her and the congressman. We've gone over her laptop, too. She downloaded lots of material about hiking in Rock Creek Park, so we'll start there. A dozen recruits will hook up with you in an hour to start searching the park, focusing on the area around the Klingle Mansion. I want some of you to canvas the restaurants on this sheet. They're places she evidently liked to hang out. Jason, I want you to spend time at the gym where she had a temporary membership, see if you can come up with anybody who got close to her, dated her, had a run-in with her." He said to Jay Gibbs and Jack Morey, "Here are names from her address book. Check 'em out."

"Any theories?" Morey asked.

"The usual," said Borgeldt. "She's either skipped town of her own accord and for her own reasons, committed suicide in some inaccessible place, is wandering around with amnesia, or hooked up with the wrong guy. Let's get moving. We've got a congressman involved, which means the press will be all over it."

The team of recruits and their handlers fanned out around the Klingle Mansion, a Pennsylvania Dutch–style home on Linnaean Hill, built by the horticulturist Joshua Pierce in 1823, who provided the first ornamental plantings to the White House. Located just north of the National Zoo on a hill overlooking a tract of posh homes near a wooded area, it functioned as the administrative center for the park. They searched the nearby woods and areas covered with heavy brush to no avail. Sweaty and disgruntled at the end of the day, they called it quits. If Laura Bennett was somewhere in Rock Creek Park, she wasn't in close proximity to the mansion. They would return the next day and concentrate on those areas of the park in which the two recent female victims had been discovered.

Their activity in the park attracted the attention of the press. Rebecca Paulson and her colleague from *The Post* were dispatched and attempted to interview the detectives in charge, but were rebuffed. The local CNN TV station sent a crew, which returned with footage of the search but no comment from the searchers.

Gibbs and Morey began the slow process of contacting people in Laura Bennett's address book, while others interviewed members of the gym where she worked out, and customers and staff at her favorite restaurants. The few who remembered Laura had little or nothing to offer—"A nice gal." "She'd come in with friends, never a problem." "I recognize her from the photo but never had any direct contact with her." "She came in a few times with a guy, black hair, well built, don't know his name. Oh, yeah, he had one of those five o'clock shadows I guess it's called." "What's the problem? She's missing? Hope you find her."

At the gym, a manager said that Laura didn't use the facilities very often, and when she did she wasn't much into working out, was more interested in socializing with other members. "Sorry to hear what happened to her. Hope some creep didn't grab her. There's more creeps around these days."

At the end of the day it was decided to contact taxi companies and their more than fifteen hundred registered drivers to see whether any of them had picked up Laura Bennett in the days following her last known sighting.

L uke Bennett received a call at the hotel from Hal Gannon.

"Sorry, Luke, but it's been insane around here," Gannon said. "Any word on Laura?"

"No. Hal, I have to talk to you."

"Sure. Are you planning to stay in town for a while?"

"Of course I am. Christ, Hal, Laura is missing. Gone! Grace and I are beside ourselves."

"I know, I know," Gannon said, aware that what he'd said was inappropriate. "I'd be beside myself, too. Look, how about you and I get together tonight, have dinner someplace quiet and away from craziness. The police have called me and want an interview. I told them I had nothing to offer, but I'll have to meet with them. The press has been calling, too. What a mess. Okay, Luke, Dinner tonight?"

"I'll check with Grace and—"

"No, Luke, just you and me."

"Grace will want to—"

"Please, Luke. Just the two of us."

"All right. What time?"

"I'll pick you up at the hotel at six. Be out front. Just you. Six sharp."

* * *

Grace and Brixton had left the hotel fifteen minutes before Gannon called. Reis had answered Brixton's phone call and agreed to see them.

"It may be tough for you to be at the apartment," Brixton told Grace as he drove.

"Yes, I'm sure it will, seeing her things there."

"The police removed some of it. Anytime you want we can cut the interview short."

"I appreciate your concern," she said.

"I know what you're going through," he said.

"How could you possibly?"

"I lost a daughter a year ago," he said, but quickly added, "not that you've lost your daughter. She'll probably turn up soon. Who was it, President Clinton, who said 'I feel your pain'? I mean, I do understand."

"I'm sorry about your daughter," she said, and began to cry.

Keep your mouth shut, Brixton silently chided himself.

"Laura's roommate, Reis Ethridge, is sort of the quiet type," Brixton said as he found a parking space a half block from the building.

"Laura said she didn't like her."

"Yeah, well, sometimes female roommates don't get along," Brixton said, injecting a modicum of levity in his voice. "My two daughters, they—"

There you go again, he told himself as he got out and came around to open Grace's door.

Brixton's introduction of Grace Bennett to Reis Ethridge was awkward. Reis expressed her concern for Laura and said that she was sure that she was all right and had simply gone off for a while.

"Laura wouldn't do that without telling us," Grace said.

"Oh, I'm sure you're right," Reis said. "I just meant that she's okay, not in any trouble. Would you like coffee or tea?"

"No, thank you," Grace said. "Miss Ethridge, surely Laura and you talked about your life as interns here in Washington."

"Not very much," Reis said. "Laura and I were—well, we didn't talk much."

"But you must have discussed your jobs, the people you work with, the things you enjoy doing when you aren't working."

"You mean our lives outside the office?"

"Yes. Was Laura seeing anyone?"

"Dating someone?"

"Yes."

"She—Laura had a very active social life, at least compared to me."

"Men she dated?"

"Yes. No. Laura was never specific, although I knew that she was seeing men."

"Anyone in particular?" Grace asked.

Reis avoided looking at her. "No," she said.

Brixton sat in a chair, taking in the conversation. He was impressed with how Grace had pulled herself together and asked questions in a direct, matter-of-fact manner, and he wondered when she would get around to asking about what Reis had told him, that Gannon was Laura's "boyfriend." He didn't have to wait long.

"Did Laura talk about her relationship with Congressman Gannon?" Grace asked.

"Relationship?"

Don't be coy, Brixton thought.

"Mr. Brixton says that you told him that Congressman Gannon was Laura's boyfriend."

Reis looked angrily at Brixton.

"Did you tell him that?" Grace pressed.

"Because that's what Laura told me."

"She said that?" Grace asked, her voice rising. "She used that term, 'boyfriend'?"

"No. I really don't know what she said, but she did say that she and the congressman were—I don't know, involved, I suppose."

"Did you ever see them together?" Grace asked. Demanded was more apt.

"No."

"Did Laura ever stay with him overnight?"

"She—well, she was gone a lot at night, and I assumed—"

"*You assumed!*"

Reis glared at Grace. "Look, Mrs. Bennett, I don't know anything about your daughter and where she might be. We weren't close. In fact, we didn't get along at all. I've been answering your questions, but unless you have others, I really would prefer that you leave."

The directness of Reis's comment took Grace aback. She straightened before saying, "I don't wonder that you and Laura didn't get along," she said, standing and straightening her skirt. "You are a very unpleasant young woman."

With that, she crossed the room and opened the door. Brixton cocked his head at Reis, smiled, said, "Thanks," and left with Grace.

"Wish it had gone better," Brixton said as they got in his car.

Grace's response was to break down in a torrent of tears and bang her fist on the dashboard.

18

Grace Bennett was angry that she was not invited to accompany her husband to dinner with Hal Gannon. "Why?" she demanded. "Is he afraid to face me?"

"I'll find out when I see him," Luke said. "Look, I'd prefer that the two of us go, but he was adamant. I'll see what he has to say. And don't worry, I'll ask him about the rumors."

"And what do you expect him to say, Luke? He'll fudge the truth, or out-and-out lie."

"I won't let him get away with it, Grace. Mac Smith is right. We're only dealing with rumors. There may be nothing to them. I'll find out the truth, believe me, I will."

His answer didn't appease her and he knew that she would sulk as he left the room and went to the street to wait for Gannon to pull up, which he did ten minutes later.

"How are you, Hal?" Bennett asked as Gannon maneuvered the red Mercedes convertible from the curb and meshed with the traffic on Pennsylvania Avenue.

"Swamped," Gannon replied, "but otherwise okay.

I can only imagine what you and Grace are going through."

"It's a nightmare," Bennett said. "Where are we going to dinner?"

"Restaurant Eve, a favorite place of mine in Alexandria. They have a bistro that's quiet, a good place to talk."

"I don't know why we have to go to dinner to talk," said Bennett.

"I just thought it would be more relaxing, that's all. If you'd rather not we can—"

"No, it's okay, Hal. I'm just not very hungry."

"A drink and some good food is what you need."

They were seated side by side at a red banquette in the restaurant's bistro area that afforded them a modicum of privacy from other diners. Bennett ordered a martini, Gannon white wine.

"Okay," Gannon said after their drinks had been served, "fill me in on what's happening with Laura."

"I was hoping that you could do the filling in, Hal."

"I wish I had something to offer," Gannon said. "The truth is I only know what I've been told by my staff, what I read in the paper, and what some private investigator had to say. This investigator, his name is Brixton. He says that he's working for you and a lawyer named Mackensie Smith."

"That's right."

"Why a private investigator?"

"It was Mac Smith's suggestion."

"The police are the ones who should be handling this."

"They are, but Mac felt that having someone working directly for me might open up some doors. It doesn't matter, Hal. Let's get down to what's really important."

They were interrupted by a waiter bringing them menus.

"Why don't we order?" Gannon suggested as he picked up his menu.

"In a minute," Bennett said. He leaned closer to Gannon. "What's this about you and Laura having an affair?"

Gannon slowly shook his head and leaned back. "I was waiting for that ridiculous rumor to come up."

"Is that all it is, Hal, a rumor? No basis in fact?"

"I should be hurt that you even feel it necessary to ask."

"I have to ask, Hal. There's no truth to it?"

Gannon locked eyes with Bennett. "That's right, Luke, there is absolutely no truth to it."

"Laura's roommate, a Ms. Ethridge, says that you were Laura's boyfriend. That's the term she used, 'boyfriend.'"

A small smile softened Gannon's stern expression. "Do I look like any twenty-two-year-old's boyfriend, Luke? Come on, be serious."

"I am being serious, Hal, and I have every reason to be. Grace's sister, Irene, told Grace that when Laura came to her house for dinner—she lives in Maryland— Laura told her of a relationship she was having with you."

"I feel like I'm a witness at an inquisition," Gannon said.

"That doesn't answer my question."

"I already did answer your question," Gannon snapped back. "Look, Luke, I was hoping that our many years of friendship would suffice, that if I said those rumors weren't true, you'd accept it as fact. What other rumors have you heard? Lay 'em all out so I can defend myself."

Bennett realized that his approach wasn't getting him anywhere. Gannon was responding the way Grace had predicted he would.

At the same time, Gannon was aware that although what his friend was bringing up were only unsubstantiated rumors, he wasn't going to be able to dismiss them with flat denials, wave his hand and see them evaporate.

"I wasn't going to bring this up," Gannon said, "but your refusal to believe me about Laura forces my hand. You want the truth, Luke?"

"Of course I want the truth."

"This might hurt," Gannon said.

"Nothing could hurt more than what's already happened."

"Okay. First of all, nothing matters except getting Laura back. All this nonsense about my having an affair with her is just that, nonsense. Luke, Laura was—is a lovely young woman. She's also typical of women her age, filled with fantasies and dreams, sophomoric flights of fancy, developing crushes on movie stars and rock musicians."

Bennett started to say something, but Gannon held up his hand.

"I told you this might hurt," Gannon said, "but we have to put it to rest. Our friendship is too important to let some goddamn rumors get in its way. The truth is that Laura developed a crush on *me*. She started flirting with me before she ever came to D.C., dropping sly suggestive comments, batting her blue eyes."

"Hal, I—"

"No, Luke, hear me out. Everything was fine the first week after she arrived and started working in my office. But then she started making suggestions—"

"What sort of suggestions?"

"Suggestions that she and I might get close. She kept pressing me to take her to dinner at my favorite places, asked about the state of my marriage, even dropped hints with the other interns that she and I had a thing for each other."

"I don't believe that, Hal."

"You don't seem to want to believe anything I say."

"Laura isn't that sort of girl."

"Hey, I'm not saying she was something evil, Luke. She was just being a typical twenty-two-year-old, her head full of dreams, her imagination running wild. She started coming on to me, which made me damned uncomfortable. I told her in no uncertain terms that it had to stop."

Gannon sipped his wine and allowed what he'd said to sink in. The silence was broken by Bennett. "To say that I'm shocked would be an understatement," he said.

Gannon lightened his tone. "Hey, Luke, Laura is a terrific young woman. What she did was nothing off the wall, nothing to be shocked about. She and I had a long, serious talk. After that things changed. The only problem is that she wanted to share her fantasies with others, like Grace's sister, her roommate, anyone who would listen. I'll tell you this, Luke. Having rumors like this floating around doesn't do my political career any good, to say nothing of the problems it could cause in my marriage."

They shelved the conversation about Laura while they ate dinner. Gannon finished his soft shell crabs; Bennett made a halfhearted attempt to eat his bouillabaisse. It was Bennett who returned the topic to Laura's disappearance. "You say you had a serious conversation with Laura," he said. "Was it an angry conversation?"

Gannon shrugged. "No, I wouldn't say that. She was unhappy, of course, but we had to have that talk. My chief of staff, Roseann, had picked up on what was going on and mentioned it to me. I suppose that was what prompted me to confront Laura."

"I'm just wondering whether her ego and feelings were sufficiently hurt for her to decide to go away and lick her wounds."

"Maybe, Luke. If that's what's happened, I'm sorry for having confronted her, but it couldn't be helped. I'm sure you understand that, might even be grateful that I did."

Bennett said nothing in response. What Gannon had suggested made sense to him, at least for the moment. It was a hopeful contemplation, that Laura, her pride injured, had fled Washington to pull herself together. If that were true, it meant that she was still alive.

But Gannon's claims that Laura had flirted with him, had even tried to seduce him, didn't gibe with what Lucas Bennett knew of his only child.

Gannon sensed the mental maze that Bennett was suffering.

"Luke, what's important is that we have faith that Laura will turn up, hopefully sooner rather than later. All I can say is that I hate what you and Grace are going through. I'll do anything in my power to make it easier. All you have to do is call."

Gannon dropped Bennett in front of the Marriott.

"Remember what I said, Luke. I'm at your disposal, day and night, twenty-four/seven. Be sure that Grace knows that and give her a hug for me."

Bennett stood on the sidewalk and watched Gannon pull away.

Could he believe him?

Could he allow himself to believe him?

And what would Grace say when he recounted the conversation to her?

CHAPTER

19

Anatoly Klimov had come to the United States two years ago from St. Petersburg, Russia. He'd dropped out of high school and started working at the Morskoy Vokzal cruise ship dock hauling the baggage of well-to-do passengers visiting Russia's second-largest city and its cultural and artistic icons, including the famed Hermitage Museum. But at the age of twenty-five, he and his older brother became passengers themselves, using money they'd squirreled away to book passage to New York and a train south. An aunt and uncle in Washington sponsored their immigration and put them up during their early days in the city until they found construction jobs and rented a small apartment close to Rock Creek Park. If they had thought they were escaping backbreaking work for an easier life and riches, they were soon disabused of that dream. When they could find work, their days were long, which didn't seem to bother Anatoly's brother; he was known as "the mule" back home for his seemingly inexhaustible energy and strength. But the slimmer and less physically endowed Anatoly, who had developed back problems while working the

cruise ships in St. Petersburg, increasingly found excuses
to turn down jobs, which angered his brother, who
shouldered the brunt of bringing in money.

Anatoly had always been more of a dreamer than his
brother. He sometimes seemed to fall into a trancelike
state, his eyes focused on things only he could see. There
were times when he heard voices, Russian voices—his
parents, his sister, his bosses at the cruise port. His
brother angrily chastised him when he fell into these
fugue states, which only served to push Anatoly farther
away from the apartment they shared. He became fond
of hiking the myriad trails of the park, having conversations with himself as he soaked in the rugged, natural
beauty of the huge urban green space. He also began to
drink more heavily than usual, carrying a flask of vodka
with him as he whiled away hours in the park.

His brother had met a waitress at the Russian restaurant Mari Vanna, on Connecticut Avenue, and announced that they would marry one day. This news only
heightened Anatoly's depression, and he decided that
what he needed was a woman in his life. There were so
many beautiful young women in Washington, D.C. In
the good weather, they jogged Rock Creek Park's trails,
dressed in skin-tight shorts and T-shirts, seemingly obliv-
ious of the male attention they generated, including
Anatoly's. He made overtures, clumsy, inexperienced attempts to strike up a conversation, but his approaches
were ham-handed, trying to use his spare English to
"chat up a bird," which he'd heard a British actor say.
His rejections only intensified his desire to connect with
a woman, and at times he became physically aggressive,
grabbing a blonde by the arm, or wrapping his arms
around a brunette who stopped to speak with him but
ended up laughing at his stumbling attempt to develop a
relationship—any relationship. When the brunette left
the park that day, she went to police headquarters and

filed a complaint against "the bastard who attacked me in Rock Creek Park." Based upon her complaint, the police accompanied her to the park and brought Anatoly in for questioning. He didn't understand much of what the officer said during the interrogation, only knew that he was being accused of something.

Weeks later, drunk, he manhandled an attractive middle-aged woman strolling with her dog on a leash. Her screams put an end to it; Anatoly backed away, swearing at her. Two men appeared and subdued him while one phoned 911. This time Anatoly faced arraignment, but the woman decided to not press charges, and he was released with a stern warning that if it happened again, he'd end up in jail.

It hadn't happened again, which was why Anatoly was surprised when two officers found him and brought him in for questioning about the most recent female victim in the park—and eventually about the missing congressional intern, Laura Bennett.

"What did she do, Anatoly, slap your face when you tried to have sex with her?"

Anatoly kept shaking his head, hoping it would be a more definitive denial than his fractured English.

"We know that you've had trouble with women in the park before, Anatoly. They teach you that in Russia, grab any pretty woman you see?"

"*Nyet,* no, no," he said, his head continuing to move right and left. "I do not hurt women. I do not."

A detective observing the questioning through a one-way mirror commented to his colleague, "That's the only way he'll ever get laid, knock 'em out. He's an ugly son of a bitch." They both laughed.

The session lasted for three hours. Toward its conclusion, Anatoly was shown a photograph of Laura Bennett. "You know her, Anatoly?"

He gazed blankly at the picture and shook his head.

"I do not know this woman," he said, and repeated it twice more.

"We're going to be watching you, Anatoly," he was warned.

He'd been close to tears, but as he left headquarters, anger welled up inside. They had no right treating him the way they had. He went home to the apartment he shared with his brother and drank himself into a stupor.

20

The call to Brixton's office came from out of the blue.

"Is Mr. Brixton there?"

"Who's calling?" Flo asked.

"My name is—well, I really need to speak to him."

"Can I tell him who wants to speak with him?" Flo said, annoyed.

"Yes, I suppose so. My name is Mildred Sparks. Millie Sparks."

Satisfied that she'd at least elicited a name, Flo asked, "Can I tell Mr. Brixton what this is in reference to?"

"It's about—will he be back shortly?"

"That depends," Flo said, knowing that Brixton was in his office a few feet away.

"I'm a friend of Laura Bennett."

"Hold on a second."

She poked her head into his office, where Brixton had been watching a press conference on TV concerning the missing intern.

"Robert, there's a woman on the line who says she's a friend of Laura Bennett."

"They mentioned me on TV," he said.

"Why?"

"They said that the Bennett family had hired a private investigator to augment what the police are doing."

"They mentioned you by name?"

"Looks like I'm famous again. What's her name?"

"Who?"

"The woman on the phone who says she's a friend of Laura Bennett."

"Sparks. Millie Sparks."

"She sound like a nut job?"

"No."

"All right," he said, and picked up his phone.

"Mr. Brixton?"

"Yes."

"My name is Millie Sparks. I'm a friend of Laura Bennett."

"So I understand. Is she with you?"

"What?"

"Ms. Bennett. She's missing, you know. I thought you might be calling to say that she's with you enjoying a cup of tea and—"

"Mr. Brixton, I know that Laura is missing. That's why I'm calling. I thought you and the family might be interested in something that Laura told me."

"Okay, but before we get started, how do you know Ms. Bennett?"

"I graduated college with her," she said. "We were good friends."

"Where? In Florida?"

"Yes. The University of Southern Florida."

"You were roommates?"

"No, but we lived next door to each other in the dorm."

Brixton gestured to Flo to pick up the extension in the outer office and make notes.

"Go on," he said.

"Well, after Laura came to Washington to become an intern, I interviewed for a job here, at Walter Reed Hospital."

"You're a doctor?"

"No. I work in administration. Mr. Brixton, I'd much rather talk to you in person."

"We can do that. You're here in D.C. now?"

"Yes. I'm at work. When can I see you?"

"Anytime today is fine. You go out to lunch? I'll order in sandwiches. What do you like, roast beef, egg salad—?"

"You don't have to get anything for me," she said. "Tell me where to come."

Millie Sparks walked into the office a few minutes past noon. She was a plain-looking young woman with an openness that Brixton immediately took to, black hair worn in a simple cut that framed her round face, little makeup, and a smile that was genuine. Brixton got her comfortably seated across from him at the desk and asked Flo to bring them two bottles of water.

"Before we get started," Brixton said, "I'd like to ask someone else to join us."

"Who?"

"Mackensie Smith. He's a lawyer and a friend whose office is next to mine. Mac represents Laura Bennett's family. Naturally, he'll be interested in what you have to say."

"A lawyer? Why? Will I be in some sort of trouble?"

Brixton laughed away her concern. "No, of course not," he said, "but having him here will save me having to try and remember what you told me. He's a terrific guy. You'll like him."

She obviously wasn't crazy about the idea but agreed. Moments later Mac walked in, introduced himself, and took a chair next to her.

"Okay, Ms. Sparks, just relax and tell us why you're here," Brixton said.

Millie related the conversation she'd had with Laura one night in the bar at the Four Seasons Hotel. Mac and Brixton listened attentively, interrupting her only to clarify a point. When she'd finished, Mac asked, "And you say that Ms. Bennett actually projected herself as first lady, married to President Gannon?"

"Yes."

Smith and Brixton looked at each other and knew that they were thinking the same thing. It was Brixton who expressed that shared thought.

"How did that strike you, Ms. Sparks? I mean, didn't it strike you as pretty far-fetched, some sort of a dream, like a hallucination?"

Millie laughed softly. "That was Laura, always with big dreams."

"And she claimed that she and Congressman Gannon were going to be married?" Mac said.

"That's what she said, Mr. Smith. She said that he had to work out his divorce before they could make it public and—"

"And she said that he'll be president one day?" Brixton added.

Millie nodded.

"We appreciate you telling us this, Ms. Sparks," Mac said, "but my question is why you think that it might have something to do with Laura's disappearance."

Millie looked at him quizzically. Mac and Brixton waited for an answer.

"I don't know," Millie finally replied. "I just thought that maybe they had some sort of a fight and—well, and maybe he got mad and did something to her, hit her. I mean, maybe it was a daydream on Laura's part, you know, and maybe he was afraid that if word got out that he was divorcing his wife to marry an intern—she's only twenty-two years old—that wouldn't be good for his career—and if it wasn't true that he planned to divorce his wife, that could make for big problems, *really* big problems in his marriage."

Smith shifted the conversation to whether Millie had any idea where Laura might have gone. Did she know of Laura's other friends in Washington, particularly male friends? Where did she like to hang out? Had Laura confided in her any problems she was having with someone, her roommate, people at work, neighbors?

Millie's reply was a blanket no.

"The night that Laura told me these things was the only time I saw her since coming to Washington. I got busy in my new job and she seemed busy, too. I think we spoke on the phone twice, just girl talk, you know, nothing serious."

"Girl talk?" Brixton said. "Laura's boyfriends never came up? She didn't mention her relationship with Congressman Gannon again?"

"Oh, I'm sorry. Yes. I asked her on one of the calls how things were going with the congressman, and she said that everything was fine, that things were progressing smoothly."

Millie checked the clock over Brixton's desk. "I really have to leave," she said. "I'm late already."

"Thank you for coming in," Brixton said.

"Will you let me know if you find Laura?"

"Of course," Brixton said.

"Have you thought of going to the police with what you know about Laura's relationship with Congressman Gannon?" Smith asked.

"The police? I don't want to do that. I've just started my job and wouldn't want to become involved in some sort of scandal. I just thought that you would want to know because you're working for Laura's family."

"What about the media?" Brixton asked.

"I wouldn't want to talk to them either," she said. "You'll keep it between yourselves, won't you?"

Mac Smith wanted to say, "As long as we can," but said instead, "Yes."

When she was gone, Brixton, Flo, and Smith gathered in Smith's office.

"What do you think?" Mac asked Brixton.

"I think Ms. Bennett has delusions of grandeur," Brixton replied.

"You may be right," Mac said. "Then again, maybe the congressman led her to believe what she said, that he was going to get a divorce and marry her."

"From everything I've heard, he's capable of that," Flo offered. "That conversation you had with the private detective from Tampa and what Ms. Sparks just told us. He's a snake in the grass."

"Speaking of that private eye from Tampa," Mac said, "he called here this morning."

"What did he want?" Brixton asked.

"I'm not sure. He started off saying that he was sorry about Laura Bennett having gone missing and that he hoped it wouldn't reflect badly on Gannon. When Annabel and I met him at Celia St. Claire's party, he claimed that he's a Gannon fan who's concerned about the rumors that he's a womanizer."

"Sounds like he has reason to be concerned," said Flo.

"Something doesn't ring right to me about him," Mac said. "I can't get a handle on what he wants from me. He called from Tampa, said he'll be in Washington in a few days. I told him I'd find time to meet with him when he's here, but I'd like to know more about him before I do. Can you check him out, Robert?"

"Sure," Brixton said.

"Mr. and Mrs. Bennett are due here in an hour," Mac said. "They've been inundated with media calls, and I've suggested they hold a joint press conference with the police tomorrow. We'll be discussing it when they arrive. I spoke with Superintendent Borgeldt this morning.

They're still focusing on Rock Creek Park. They're sending an even larger search party tomorrow morning. They
brought in a young Russian man who's been harassing
women in the park."

"And?" Brixton asked.

"No evidence to hold him."

"She could be anywhere," Flo said.

"I can understand why they're making the park their
prime search area," Mac said. "There have been two female victims there in the past few months, and Laura did
a lot of reading about the park on her laptop. But you're
right, Flo. Laura Bennett could be anywhere. I just wish
we knew where."

21

Congressman Hal Gannon had gotten up that morning after a fitful night of nightmarish thoughts and dreams. There had been few unpleasant episodes in his life—losing a track meet, a case of mononucleosis while in college, an auto accident after a night of drinking to celebrate the birth of their first child, and occasionally taking a drubbing in the courtroom.

But nothing compared with this.

He was scheduled to be interviewed by the police for a second time that afternoon. The initial interview had been tense despite the detectives' attempts to put him at ease. Gannon had wanted some of his staff to be present, but the police nixed that. "You can have an attorney present," one of the officers said.

"Attorney?" Gannon said. "Why would I need an attorney?"

"You don't need one, sir. This is just an informal chance for us to ask some questions about your missing intern. We'll be interviewing members of your staff separately."

"I won't have an attorney with me," Gannon said.

"Of course not, sir. As I said, there really isn't any need for one."

They'd met at his apartment. He'd had pastries and fruit delivered in advance of their arrival, which the two detectives passed on. They sat in his living room. The questions were about what Gannon knew of Laura Bennett's life outside the office, his evaluation of her mental stability.

"Are you suggesting that she's mentally unbalanced?" Gannon asked.

"No, not at all, sir, but if she's decided to go off without telling anyone, your office, her family, it could indicate that she wasn't thinking clearly."

"I've known Laura Bennett for many years, ever since she was a little girl," Gannon offered. "I've never seen any sign of mental instability."

"Did she ever give you a hint that she might be considering leaving the D.C. area?"

Gannon scrunched up his face to indicate he was thinking. "No," he said, "nothing that I can remember. I really don't have many conversations with the interns in my office. My chief of staff, Ms. Simmons, has a much closer relationship with them."

"We'll be speaking with Ms. Simmons as soon as we can arrange a mutually convenient time and place," a detective said.

"It's our understanding that you are a close friend of Ms. Bennett's family," said a detective.

"That's right. Her father and I have been friends for years. We had dinner together just recently. We're both attorneys and tried a number of cases together before I ran for Congress."

"We've spoken with Ms. Bennett's mother and father, Congressman. As you know, the family has retained an attorney, Mackensie Smith, and a private investigator, Robert Brixton."

"I've met both of them," Gannon said. "The investigator, Brixton, rubbed me the wrong way."

The detectives laughed. One said, "Brixton does have that ability. Look, Congressman, I know that this is a delicate subject, but we have to ask, based upon rumors that are circulating."

Gannon stared defiantly at them.

"Is there any truth to the rumor that you and the missing intern, Ms. Bennett, had a close personal relationship?"

Gannon allowed a small smile to cross his lips. "Close personal relationship," he repeated slowly. "You mean did Laura Bennett and I ever go to bed together?"

"If you prefer to put it that way, Congressman, yes, did you ever go to bed together?"

Gannon leaned close to the detectives. "Absolutely, positively not!"

"We had to ask, sir."

"I suppose you did, and I won't deny that I consider the question insulting and inappropriate. But I also understand that it's your job is to ask such questions, so no hard feelings. But let me repeat. No, I did not go to bed with Laura Bennett."

One of the detectives thought back to when President Clinton was under the gun about the Monica Lewinsky episode and parsed the meaning of the word "is." Was Gannon doing the same, responding literally to whether he'd gone to bed with Laura Bennett? Maybe they had sex on a couch, on a beach, or in a car. But he was reluctant to press the issue. Both detectives had been warned by Zeke Borgeldt before interviewing the congressman to go easy on the accusations.

"Is there anything else?" Gannon asked. "My wife is arriving in Washington later today, and I have a slew of legislative matters to attend to before she gets in."

"No, sir, that's it. We appreciate you taking the time

for us. If we think of anything else, we'll get back to you."

"Fair enough," said Gannon. "I know you have a tough job to do, and I wish you well in finding Ms. Bennett. My heart goes out to her parents."

The two detectives sat in their car after leaving Gannon's apartment.

"He's smooth, that's for sure," one said.

"Too smooth for my taste. The way he puts it he's never even had a conversation with his interns. I don't buy it."

"Plenty of rumors to back you up," said his partner.

"Let's say this intern *did* have a fling with him. You saw her pictures. Why would a dynamite-looking twenty-two-year-old get involved with an older married guy like him?"

His partner laughed. "Power, my friend. Remember what Henry Kissinger said."

"Who? Oh, yeah, the guy with the funny accent who was big in government. What'd he say?"

"He said that power was the best aphrodisiac."

"He was a powerful guy, must have had plenty of women."

"I wouldn't know. Come on, buy you coffee before we go back and write up what the esteemed congressman said."

With Mac Smith agreeing, the Bennetts offered a $25,000 reward for information leading to the discovery of Laura Bennett and made the offer during a press conference hastily arranged by Mac.

"It is our sincere hope that our beloved daughter, Laura, is alive and well," Lucas Bennett said into the cameras and microphones. "Not knowing her fate has been too much to bear for Laura's mother and me." He pulled Grace Bennett closer and announced, "We are of-

fering twenty-five thousand dollars for information leading to our daughter." He held up two photos of Laura
for the cameras to zoom in on. "We know that she's out
there somewhere, and we are asking for your help—
praying for your help. Thank you."

An announcer replaced the Bennetts at the dais and
told viewers that anyone with information leading to
Laura Bennett's whereabouts should contact two different
phone numbers that flashed on the screen, the MPD, and
the office of the attorney to the Bennett family, Mackensie Smith.

Brixton left the press conference and returned to his
office, where he placed a call to Will Sayers, Washington
editor of the *Savannah Morning News.* Sayers had
worked for the paper in Savannah when Brixton was a
cop there, and they'd become friends. Brixton was unhappy when the paper sent his friend to Washington to
reopen its bureau there, but he found his relocation useful when he became embroiled in the nation's capital in
a case that almost took his life.

Since again returning to D.C., Brixton and Sayers had
drifted somewhat apart, their individual lives keeping
them too busy to reconnect aside from phone conversations during which they promised to get together. Brixton
was calling to arrange that.

"My old friend," Sayers said when he picked up. "I see
that you're famous again, working the mysterious case
of the missing intern."

"I'm on my third fifteen minutes of fame," Brixton
said. "How the hell are you?"

"I am fine, just fine, Robert. What can I do you for?"

"Free for lunch?"

"Of course. I make it a point of always being free for
lunch, or dinner or breakfast, for that matter. In the
mood for good barbeque?"

"Sure."

"See you in an hour at Acre 121, on Irving Street, in Columbia Heights. It's a favorite of mine."

Brixton hung up and smiled. His corpulent friend, Will Sayers, always had a dozen "favorite places" at which to indulge his love of good food and well-made drinks. Before leaving to meet Sayers, Brixton placed a call to a number in Florida for an association whose members were private investigators. The woman who answered didn't seem especially eager to answer Brixton's query about an investigator named Paul Wooster, but he turned on the charm and she agreed to peruse the group's database.

"Sorry," she said, "but there's no Paul Wooster listed."

Brixton was at the bar at Acre 121 when Sayers waddled in. He was dressed in what seemed to be his uniform, baggy chino pants, a striped button-down shirt, wide red suspenders, and a red-and-white railroad handkerchief dangling from his rear pocket. He slapped Brixton on the back and took an adjacent stool.

"You're looking well, Robert," the editor said. "Your lady Flo obviously takes good care of you."

"Despite me being a pain in the butt."

"I was about to add that," Sayers said. "Anything new on your missing intern?"

"No. What do you hear?"

"Me? Not much. Unless a case here in D.C. has some connection to Savannah, I don't pursue it."

"She's still missing," Brixton said, "probably dead."

"Of foul play?"

Brixton shrugged. "Maybe, maybe not. Do you have any connections with private investigators in Tampa?"

"As a matter of fact, I do. Why?"

"I'm trying to run down a guy named Paul Wooster, a private investigator."

"Want me to make a call?"

"Who are you calling?"

"Someone you should remember from your days in Savannah, Joel Callander."

"Callander? He's in Tampa?"

"Right. As I recall, you and Joel had a run-in of sorts when you were competing for clients back in your favorite southern city."

"He cheated me out of one, if that's what you mean. When did he go to Tampa?"

"A few years ago. I've kept in touch. He's not my favorite guy, but he might know of this Wooster character."

Sayers pulled a cell phone from his pants pocket, scrolled through stored numbers, and called one.

"Joel? Will Sayers . . . I've been fine . . . You? . . . Glad to hear that . . . Joel, I'm calling on behalf of a friend of mine. Do you happen to know a PI in Tampa named Wooster, Paul Wooster? . . . You do? . . . Tell me about him."

Brixton listened as Sayers went through a series of grunts to indicate he understood what Callander was saying. "No," Sayers said, "you wouldn't know my friend."

Brixton gave Sayers a thumbs-up.

"Anything else about Mr. Wooster?" Sayers asked.

There evidently wasn't because Sayers thanked Callander and ended the call.

"So what's the scoop on Mr. Wooster?" Brixton asked.

"Seems like he *used* to be a private eye, Robert, but his Florida license was revoked, something to do with bilking clients. But he's still working, only without the benefit of a license."

"How can he do that?"

"According to your old friend Callander, Wooster doesn't bill himself as a PI. He's working for a Republican fund-raising organization in Tampa, does investigative work without having to be licensed."

"Republican?" Brixton said. "When Mac Smith and his wife met Wooster at a party, he claimed to be a big fan of Congressman Gannon—who happens to be a Democrat."

"With right-wing leanings as I understand it," said Sayers.

"Wooster also mentioned to Mac and Annabel that he was concerned about rumors concerning the congressman's healthy libido, hoped it wouldn't impact his re-election chances."

"Who can figure politicians, Robert? Let's order. The big barbeque platter is terrific, sausages, chicken ribs, pork, the works."

"To share?"

"Hell, no. I'm a growing boy. Order what you want. The po'boy sandwiches are top-notch, same with the grits."

"You know I don't eat grits," Brixton said, making a face to reinforce what he'd said. "Hate 'em."

"You rebel against anything southern," Sayers said through a laugh.

And so Brixton and Sayers ordered their meals, accompanied by mugs of beer, and said little—until Brixton's cell phone rang.

"Hello?"

"Robert, it's Mac Smith. Where are you?"

"At a restaurant having lunch with Will Sayers. What's up?"

"A lot. They've found Laura Bennett."

Brixton sat back in his chair, his eyes wide. "Where? When?"

"An hour ago. The Congressional Cemetery. How soon can you get back to the office?"

"Fifteen minutes."

"What's up?" Sayers asked.

"The missing intern, Laura Bennett. She's not missing anymore."

THE DISCOVERY

CHAPTER

22

Cheryl Randolph had lived in Washington, D.C., her entire life. She loved the city, even the silly circus that its major industry, politics, had become. She proudly proclaimed herself an equal-opportunity political junkie; her TV set was seldom turned off, the remote getting a workout as she switched from MSNBC to Fox News, to CNN, and to any other channel on which politics was covered. She basked in the power of the city's leading political lights and developed a crush on a variety of elected officials as they came and went, hanging on every word of their speeches and reveling in any gossip surrounding them.

She was divorced. She'd met her now ex-husband when he came to town from Kansas to work for the Department of Agriculture, and it didn't take long for the bloom on the rose to fade and wither. Three years after tying the proverbial knot, they divorced, and he hightailed it back to Topeka, where the last she heard he'd remarried, had three kids, and operated a dairy farm. Good riddance was the way Cheryl viewed it. Spending the day wallowing in cow manure was what he deserved.

Fifty-eight years old, she lived in a two-bedroom apartment on a quiet street in the city's Southeast Quadrant. Her father's death shortly after her divorce, and the money he left his only daughter, enabled Cheryl to quit her job at a real estate firm and spend her days volunteering at favorite charities and landmarks, and enjoying the company of her dogs, the latest named Jessie, a shepherd-Lab she'd adopted from a shelter, the joy of her life.

Her favorite volunteer experience was the Congressional Cemetery, located on the west bank of the Anacostia River, two blocks from her home. She was one of five hundred volunteers who worked to maintain the almost two-hundred-year-old cemetery for those visiting the more than sixty-five thousand individuals buried or memorialized there. Among the underground residents were one vice president; one Supreme Court justice; six former cabinet members; nineteen senators; seventy-one representatives, one of whom was a Speaker of the House; John Philip Sousa; and the first director of the FBI, J. Edgar Hoover. There were days when Cheryl could almost hear them speaking from their graves.

But while she loved the national historic landmark's rich history, the main attraction was being able to walk Jessie off-leash in its fenced-in thirty acres. Volunteering for the Association for the Preservation of Historic Congressional Cemetery (APHCC) enabled Cheryl to join the cemetery's K-9 Corps, made up of volunteers who also owned dogs and had special dog-walking privileges, for a fee, of course. In the early days, the cemetery had fallen into serious disrepair, and the area became overrun with drug dealers and prostitutes. But the introduction of the K-9 Corps, dozens of dogs running off-leash around the cemetery, coupled with an infusion of federal money, drove the unsavory element away; the fees paid by members for the right to walk their dogs now provided twenty percent of the APHCC's operating income. The dogs and their owners were welcomed with open arms, and coffers.

On this day she left the apartment at noon and took Jessie to the cemetery for her daily romp. It was overcast, and the humidity had risen to an uncomfortable level. Rain was in the air, which prompted Cheryl to bring along an umbrella for her and a yellow dog slicker for Jessie.

The threat of inclement weather had kept most dog lovers away from the cemetery, which pleased Cheryl as she entered through the E Street entrance. She enjoyed the way Jessie and other dogs played, but there had been a few times when another dog recoiled at Jessie's rambunctious nature and a fight almost ensued. On this muggy day, Cheryl and Jessie had the cemetery virtually to themselves.

She unhooked Jessie's leash and laughed as she scooted away, zigging and zagging, nose to the ground as she picked up on the myriad scents, disappearing behind monuments, burial vaults, and tombstones, then reappearing as she continued her quest for the source of the scents, basking in her freedom but frequently stopping to be sure that Cheryl was following. The grass had recently been trimmed, thanks to one hundred goats that had been trucked in from a Maryland farm to take the place of mechanical mowers; Eco-Goats they were called. This unusual approach to grounds maintenance had generated widespread media attention across the country. "They cost less than a grounds crew and don't pollute the air the way gasoline mowers do," the administrative head of APHCC had said when announcing the goat project. Then, with a smile he added, "And besides, they do a pretty good job of laying down fertilizer."

Cheryl carried a pocketful of dog treats, and Jessie occasionally returned to her side in anticipation of receiving one, sitting smartly, tail wagging, and with an expression on her tan-and-black muzzle that Cheryl was certain was a satisfied smile.

As the sky continued to darken, Cheryl wondered whether they had better cut Jessie's romp short. They'd passed through a cluster of cenotaphs, Aquia sandstones painted white as monuments to those buried elsewhere but who'd passed through the cemetery before being transported to their final resting places. Some had been stored in the Public Vault, a partially subterranean vault constructed in 1834—three U.S. presidents had resided in it: John Quincy Adams, William Henry Harrison, and Zachary Taylor. President Harrison had stayed there for three months, three times longer than he'd been president. And First Lady Dolley Madison was a guest in the vault for two years while funds were being raised for her reinterment at Montpelier. Cheryl had always been particularly fascinated by the vault and its history. Had Lewis Powell, pursued for his role in the assassination of Abraham Lincoln, actually hid in it for a night? Cheryl liked to think so.

She saw that Jessie had reached the vault and stood at attention, her attention focused on its wrought-iron doors, PUBLIC VAULT spelled out on them by a series of vent holes.

"Jessie, come on, girl," Cheryl called.

The dog didn't move. She slowly approached the doors, and Cheryl heard a low growl come from her.

She closed the distance between them and was now fifteen feet from the entrance to the vault. It was then that she noticed that the doors were slightly ajar. *Strange,* she thought, as she took a few steps closer. She knew that the vault had fallen out of use many years earlier. Had a visitor decided to peek inside? As far as she knew, the doors were locked shut—or so she assumed. It had never occurred to her to think otherwise.

She grabbed Jessie's collar and attached the leash.

"Time to go home, baby," she said.

But the dog resisted Cheryl's pull. Her growl grew louder, and she yanked Cheryl closer to the doors.

Jessie's growl turned into a whine as Cheryl tentatively reached to open one of the doors. As she did, the rain began to fall. Cheryl peered into the vault's dim, musty interior and blinked rapidly. At first she wasn't sure what she was seeing. But as her vision penetrated the gloom, it became obvious that there was a person lying on the vault's cold, hard floor.

A woman.

Cheryl turned, and with Jessie running at her side, raced toward the cemetery's entrance yelling, "Help! Help!"

23

Cheryl, who didn't believe in cell phones and didn't own one, ran up to the first person she saw on the street, a man on his way to work.

"There's a dead woman in the vault," she sputtered.

"What vault. What dead woman?"

"In the cemetery. My dog—her name is Jessie—found her. She's dead."

Jessie tried to jump up on the man, but Cheryl held her back.

"Please, call someone. Call nine-one-one."

The man did as requested and told the operator who answered that a body had been discovered. "What?" he said. He said to Cheryl, "Where's this vault?"

"In there," she said, pointing.

"In the Congressional Cemetery," he said into his phone. "A vault."

"The Public Vault," Cheryl said.

"The Public Vault she said . . . What? . . . I'm with the woman who said she discovered the body. We're on E Street Southeast, by the entrance to the cemetery."

The man grumbled about being late to work but

stayed with Cheryl and Jessie until the first police units arrived in marked squad cars, four uniformed officers. One, a beefy young man with freckles, asked who had made the call.

"I did," the man said. "This is the woman who told me that she had discovered a body."

"Will you please show us where you found this body," Cheryl was told.

"I have to get to work," the man said.

"Take his info," an officer said.

"Do I have to?" Cheryl asked. "It's in the Public Vault."

"It's a pretty big cemetery, ma'am."

Jessie barked at the officer.

"Keep him on the leash," he told Cheryl.

"It's a female," Cheryl said. "She isn't vicious."

"Ma'am, please take us to this vault."

"All right," Cheryl said, "but can I bring Jessie home first? I only live two blocks from here and—"

"After you show us, ma'am."

The rain had waned and was now a fine mist. Cheryl put the yellow rain slicker on Jessie, and with her umbrella popped open led three of the officers into the cemetery. The ground had become spongy; one of the officers muttered a four-letter word as a shoe sank into a particularly soft patch. When they reached the vault, Cheryl and Jessie hung back as the officers approached the partially opened door. One aimed a flashlight into the dark, dank space. "It's a woman," he announced. "Better call for the ME and backup."

Soon, the area surrounding the Public Vault, the temporary resting place of a who's who of bygone days in the nation's capital, was filled with a variety of officers and civilian employees. The D.C. medical examiner had arrived with an assistant, and they huddled inside the vault conducting a visual exam of the body. A police photographer was summoned and took pictures of the deceased from as many angles as the cramped space allowed. The activity outside the cemetery's entrance had attracted dozens of passers-by who'd followed the crowd and stood en masse on a slight rise overlooking the vault. They spoke to each other in hushed tones as officers kept them from getting closer. Eventually, two EMTs replaced the ME and his assistant in the vault, and they emerged with the body on a stretcher, which they lowered to the ground beneath trees surrounding the area. A tech placed a clear plastic tarp over it and used a large golf umbrella to further protect it from the elements.

Superintendent of Detectives Zeke Borgeldt received a call at headquarters from one of the detectives at the cemetery.

"Looks like the missing intern has been found," the detective said.

"It's Laura Bennett?" Borgeldt said.

"Yes, sir."

"No doubts?"

"No, sir. She has ID on her."

"And she's in some vault at the cemetery?"

"Right. A woman walking her dog discovered the body."

"What's your read on it?"

"Homicide. The ME said something about blunt force trauma to the head."

Before leaving to go to the scene, Borgeldt called Mac Smith. "We've found Laura Bennett," he said, and told the Bennett family attorney what he'd learned. "You'd better tell the family."

Brixton had left Sayers with the lunch bill and raced back to his office, where Mac was still on the phone with Borgeldt.

"Brixton just arrived," Mac told Borgeldt. "Hold on." He filled Brixton in on what had transpired. "Why don't you run over to the cemetery, Robert, and let me know what's going on there."

Mac told Borgeldt, "Brixton's on his way to the cemetery. I'll wait to hear from him before making that call."

Brixton arrived just as the body was being brought from the vault.

"It's Laura Bennett?" Brixton asked Borgeldt.

Borgeldt nodded.

"Mac Smith said you'd called."

Another nod from Borgeldt.

"How'd they make the ID?" Brixton asked.

"She had it on her. There's an iPad, too. She put a label on it with her name."

Borgeldt walked to the two detectives and the ME who stood near the body.

"No doubt on the ID?" he said.

"No," was the answer. "The parents will have to confirm it, but it's her, Chief. Laura Bennett."

Borgeldt moved closer to the stretcher and peered down into Laura's face. The corneas of her once lively eyes were milky. He cocked his head to better see the side of her head where a blow of some sort had created a depression in her temple; dried blood covered it and had expanded into her copper-tinted hair. Her lips were twisted into what might have been considered a smile under other circumstances.

She wore an orange blouse, black slacks, and sneakers, one of which had fallen off. Her face was bloated, its skin waxy.

"Any guess when she died?" Borgeldt asked the ME.

"Wasn't yesterday, that's for sure. Couple of days, maybe a week. I'll know more after the autopsy."

"Looks like somebody got mad and whacked her in the side of the head."

"Not a bad first guess, Superintendent," said the ME. "Are we cleared to remove her?"

"If you've done what you need to do, sure, go ahead."

A clean white sheet was placed over the body and tucked beneath her. Two EMTs lifted the stretcher and began their trek back to the cemetery's entrance where their ambulance awaited, uniformed cops leading the way.

"What's it look like to you?" Brixton asked Borgeldt when the superintendent rejoined him.

"If you mean is it a homicide, you could get rich betting on that, Brixton. Tell Mac and the Bennetts that I'll be available all afternoon."

Brixton called Mac on his cell. Before he could report on what he'd learned, Smith said, "Luke Bennett just called. It's already on TV. He and his wife are on their way here."

"Hell of a way to hear about it," Brixton said.

"Have they removed the body?"

"A few minutes ago. Looks like somebody hit her in the head pretty hard. Borgeldt was there."

"I know. Anything said about a press conference?"

"Not that I heard. I'm heading back."

"I'll be here."

Smith had no sooner hung up when Annabel called from her Georgetown gallery.

"I just saw on TV that they've found Laura Bennett," she said. "They said she'd been killed."

"That's the way it looks, Annie. The Bennetts are on their way from the hotel."

"Want me to come?"

"That'd be good, Annie. Grace will need all the support we can muster."

"I'll close up and be there as soon as I can."

Mac told Doris to expect the Bennetts at any minute. He retreated into his office, poured himself a shot of bourbon, and leaned back in his chair. He dreaded facing the Bennetts. He knew what it was like to lose a child. As he thought about that fateful night when his first wife and son were killed on the Beltway, and the intense, intractable pain the grim phone call had caused, he also thought of Robert Brixton, who had lost one of his daughters in the café bombing a year ago. "Damn!" he muttered. Three young lives taken by others—a drunk driver, a crazed terrorist, and now someone for whom Laura Bennett's life wasn't as important as what had prompted her killer to take her life.

"Damn!" he repeated as the door opened and Doris said, "The Bennetts are here."

Hal Gannon learned about the discovery of Laura Bennett's body the same way her mother and father had, from a TV news bulletin.

He was at the apartment with his wife, Charlene, who'd arrived in D.C. the previous evening. It had been a frosty reunion.

Laura's disappearance had become national news, with newspapers in Tampa and Washington giving it front-page status. Adding to Charlene's awareness that Laura was missing had been the call from Luke Bennett. Now, nursing a glass of orange juice in her husband's Adams Morgan living room, she'd been absently watching TV news when the announcement came that Laura was no longer a missing person.

"She's been murdered," Charlene blurted out as she leaped from the couch and turned up the volume.

"What?" Gannon called from the kitchen, where he'd been filling the dishwasher.

"Laura Bennett. They've found her in some cemetery. She was murdered."

"Oh, no," he said as he came from the kitchen, wiping his hands on a towel.

They watched as an update was broadcast, including an on-camera statement by Superintendent Zeke Borgeldt at the cemetery: "We are confident that the body discovered today in the Public Vault of the Congressional Cemetery is the intern who has been missing, Ms. Laura Bennett. Until official identification has been established, an autopsy has been performed, and we have had a chance to analyze existing evidence, we will have no further comment." He ignored shouted reporters' questions and walked away.

"How dreadful," Charlene said. "My God, who could do such a thing?"

"There's a lot of bad people out there, Charlene."

She followed him into the kitchen. "Hal, we have to talk."

"Sure," he said, putting the final pieces of silverware in the dishwasher. "Jesus, Laura murdered. It's inconceivable, it's crazy. Why would anyone want to snuff out the life of an innocent young woman?"

"We have to talk about what's happened to Laura Bennett," Charlene said sharply.

"What's to talk about?" he said, his back to her, "except to tell Luke and Grace how sorry we are, and to be there for them."

"The rumors," Charlene said.

Gannon turned. "Rumors? What rumors?"

"The ones about you and other women."

He dropped the towel on the counter, leaned against it, and smiled. "Charlene, you know that this town is fueled by rumors. The damned media looks for every little scrap of dirt on anyone in the government and then blows it up to sell newspapers and drive ratings."

"Those rumors are circulating in Tampa, too, Hal."

"And why do you think that is?" he asked.

"You tell me."

"Look, Charlene, I know that politics isn't your cup of tea, and I don't blame you. But you are aware that Pete Solon has announced that he's running against me for my congressional seat."

"Yes."

"And where do you think these kinds of rumors emanate? Politics is rough-and-tumble, a dirty business. The Solon people will stoop to anything to take me down. It shouldn't be that way, but it is. That's reality."

"I don't need a lecture on politics, Hal."

"Maybe you do need a lecture about what I do," he said, crossing the kitchen and placing his hands on her shoulders. "Look, I know that you were never pleased with my decision to run for Congress, and I also know that you find politics to be distasteful. So do I at times. You're happy to be home with the kids and your studio, and I respect that, always have. Do I wish that you took a more active role in my career here in Washington? Sure I do, and I think about it a lot. But the fact that you don't want to share in it is the primary reason these stupid, slanderous rumors get started in the first place. The media ghouls zero in on someone like me, a congressman whose wife stays home in Tampa. He's got to be up to no good. Right? That's the way they view it. They're whores, Charlene. Nothing but liars and cheats and whores."

Charlene moved away from him and went into the living room. She stared out the window. The mist had turned to a harder rain again. People scurried along the sidewalks, umbrellas raised, or the day's newspaper held over their heads. The weather matched Charlene's mood. She wanted to believe her husband—desperately wanted to—but something inside told her that he wasn't being truthful.

Gannon's campaign manager in Tampa, Joe Selesky, had come to the house one day—"Purely a social call," he'd said—and during the course of the conversation he'd suggested that she make a point of spending more time with her husband in D.C., at least during the campaign. She hadn't thought much of the request—a politician running for reelection with his wife standing proudly at his side, which she'd done at campaign events in Tampa—and told Selesky that she would consider increasing her time spent in Washington. But then she asked whether a problem had arisen.

He responded, "Some people who would like to see Hal lose reelection are questioning whether your marriage is stable." He laughed to soften his message. "You know, handsome congressman alone in big, bad D.C. with all those available females running around. Washington has the highest ratio of women to men in the country."

The possible meaning behind what he'd said sank in.

"What are you suggesting, Joe?" she asked.

"I'm not suggesting anything. I just want to nip any rumor in the bud, that's all. The best way to do that is for you and Hal to be a couple in D.C."

When Charlene didn't say anything, he added, "I know how much you enjoy being in your studio turning out Picassos, Charlene, but think about it. That's all I ask."

"Sometimes you can be so damn patronizing," she said, venom in her words.

She did think about it, but not for very long . . . until one day when a talk-show host on the conservative radio station WWBA suggested that voters question Hal Gannon's claim to be a family man with Christian values. "Based upon what we're hearing, the congressman has more on his mind than passing legislation, with plenty of attractive female company to help him pass the time while away from his wife and kids back here in Tampa."

The offhand comment had angered Charlene and fueled the questions and doubts that had begun to fester. She decided to dismiss the comment by the radio host and chalk it up to just a political smear. Which it was, of course, a story planted with the talk show by an operative in Republican Pete Solon's campaign.

But now that she was in Washington, D.C., with her husband, the doubts that she'd managed to suppress emerged front and center.

Was there any truth to those rumors?

She continued to peer out at the street scene below the apartment. She didn't want to cry, but it took every ounce of willpower to keep the tears from flowing.

When Hal returned to the living room, Charlene asked whether he'd been questioned by the Washington police about Laura's disappearance.

"Twice," he said, "but I wouldn't use the term 'questioned.' There's no need to question me. They just wanted to find out whether I knew anything about her life here in D.C. aside from the office. Naturally, I had nothing to offer in that regard. Laura's folks have hired an attorney, Mackensie Smith, and a private investigator, a guy named Brixton, Robert Brixton. I did some checking into his credentials. He's a real foul ball, got himself in a mess of trouble twice, a year or so ago and even back farther than that."

Another update on the discovery of Laura Bennett's body filled the TV screen.

"Credible sources tell us that the police now believe that the missing intern, Laura Bennett, is a homicide victim, and a special unit has been established within the MPD to investigate."

The ringing phone caused Gannon to turn down the volume.

"Hello?"

He held his hand over the phone and said to Charlene, "My press aide, Cody Watson. Have to take this."

He disappeared into the bedroom with the wireless phone and closed the door.

"I have nothing to say to the police," he said into the phone. "They've already questioned me twice . . . What? . . . No, Cody, no press conference, no media interviews . . . Yeah, all right, issue a statement from me but make damn sure you run it past me first . . . I'll be here at the apartment for another hour . . . Charlene and I will be having dinner at Cafe Milano . . . Let a few of your contacts in the press know where we'll be . . . I know, I know, some of them may want a statement, and I'll give them one if I have to . . . I want to take advantage of having Charlene here . . . Yes, that'll be fine. Get back to me."

"Sorry," Gannon said when he returned to the living room. "Always something. Anything new on TV about Laura Bennett?"

"No," she replied. "You said that the police had interviewed you twice about Laura."

"Right, about her disappearance. Now that she's no longer a missing person, it'll be a homicide investigation, which will have nothing to do with me. I've made dinner reservations for us at Cafe Milano. You'll like it. The murals on the walls are all hand painted, including a portrait of Placido Domingo. The food is great and—"

"I've read about the restaurant, Hal. It sounds very nice, but I'm really not in the mood for some fancy place."

"Nonsense. I'm so damn happy that you're here. I've missed you terribly." He put his arms around her and tried to kiss her, but she moved her head. He stepped back and said, "I won't take no for an answer. We're going to Cafe Milano and that's that. Put on something pretty. Use the bedroom. I have some calls to make and then I'll be free. We'll enjoy a night out." He grinned. "Let's call it a date night, just the two of us."

Cody Watson, press aide to Congressman Hal Gannon, busied himself drafting a statement to come from Gannon regarding the discovery of Laura Bennett's body. He filled it with what he knew his boss would want it to say: The congressman was as shocked as the rest of Washington with the tragic news . . . he couldn't begin to imagine what the Bennett family was suffering, and his prayers, and those of his wife, were with them . . . his office would do anything it could to help the police identify and bring the killer to justice . . . anyone with any information should contact the Metropolitan Police Department immediately.

He called Gannon at the apartment and read it to him.

"Sounds good," Gannon said. "What do you think about Charlene and me going to the Congressional Cemetery to visit where Laura's body was found?"

"It'll come off as grandstanding," Cody said.

"Yeah, maybe you're right."

He'd no sooner hung up than Superintendent Zeke Borgeldt called.

"Sorry to bother you, Congressman, but I'm sure you've heard about Ms. Bennett."

"Yes, on TV of, all places. I would have expected a call from you."

"The media trumped us," Borgeldt said, keeping pique from his voice. "Congressman, I know this is an imposition, but we need to talk to you again."

"Again? Why? I'm suddenly feeling as though you view me as a suspect, or what you call 'a person of interest.'"

Borgeldt's laugh was forced but sounded sincere. "Nothing could be farther from the truth, Congressman.

But as you now know, we've got a homicide on our hands and need all the help we can get."

"My office is just now issuing a statement," Gannon said, "including a pledge to be help. Sure, I'll be happy to speak with your people again. I'm tied up for the next few days but maybe later we can—"

"Whatever fits into your busy schedule, Congressman. I'll get back to you in a day or two."

Borgeldt ended the call and looked across his desk at Detectives Gibbs and Morey.

"He balked at another round of questioning?" Gibbs asked.

"No," Borgeldt said, "but he isn't happy." He tapped a sheet of paper on his desk on which he'd made notes during a previous conversation that day with Robert Brixton. Let's go over this again," he said.

B rixton had met with Borgeldt at Mac Smith's urging. It came about because of a conversation Mac and Brixton had had concerning the visit from Millie Sparks and what she'd related to them regarding Laura and Gannon.

"You believe her?" Smith had asked Brixton.

"Yeah, I do. She has no reason to make it up."

"The question is whether we pass it along to the police," Smith said.

"I'd hate to drag her in like that," Brixton said. "She was really concerned that the police and the media not be involved. I don't blame her."

"I can understand that," Smith said, "and if Laura were still missing I'd tend to agree with you. But it's a homicide now. Not telling the police about a possible—and I stress *possible*—affair between the congressman and Laura could be construed as withholding evidence."

"Can you do it without naming Ms. Sparks?"

"For the moment, yes, but if anything develops as a result, it won't be possible to keep her identity unknown. Tell you what, Robert. You were here and heard what she alleges. It would be best if you were to fill Zeke Borgeldt in on it."

B orgeldt listened passively as Brixton related what Millie had told him and Mac. When he was finished, Borgeldt said, "It's just hearsay, Brixton."

"I know that, but the kid has no reason to lie. She and Laura Bennett were close friends in college."

"I'm not saying that this friend is lying, but it sure as hell seems to me that Ms. Bennett was off on a wild flight of fancy where it involves Congressman Gannon."

Brixton didn't argue the point with the superintendent of detectives, but he did say, "Look, maybe Ms. Bennett was projecting some fantasy to her friend. Maybe she took what was a romantic fling and built it up in her mind to something far beyond what it really was. But you're as aware as I am, and as lots of people in this town are, that *something* was going on between the congressman and his intern. I've talked to Gannon, and you know what I think? I think he's a liar. Can I prove it? Not at the moment. But the guy has a lot to lose if shacking up with a twenty-two-year-old intern—who also happens to be the daughter of one of his best friends and biggest supporters—goes public. Good-bye wife and kids and your cushy job in Congress."

Borgeldt made a few notes before Brixton continued.

"The possibility that Gannon was sleeping with the intern is getting more and more likely, Zeke. There's this gal, Ms. Bennett's college buddy, who Ms. Bennett confided in about her affair with Gannon. The roommate here in D.C. says that Gannon was Laura Bennett's 'boyfriend.' Laura goes for dinner to her aunt's house in Maryland and tells her the same thing, only according to her it's gone beyond the boyfriend stage. According to Mac Smith, Gannon's love of the ladies is big in the rumor mill."

Borgeldt made another note before saying, "Let's say it's true that the congressman and his intern were engaged in a sexual relationship. Let's say that Gannon is everything you and the rumor mill say he is, a lecher, adulterer, liar, cheat, all-around bad guy, the sort that makes your skin crawl if you have any sense of decency. But how does that translate into him being her killer?"

"He sure as hell had a motive," Brixton countered.

"What motive? She wasn't good in bed?"

"Come on, Zeke, don't play games with me. Let's say the congressman gets tired of having to make conversation after a roll in the sack with a twenty-two-year-old. Great sex, maybe, but vapid talk. He dumps her. She gets mad and threatens to tell Mommy and Daddy and the rest of the world that he's a dirty old man. It flashes before his eyes—his downfall, disgrace, losing his seat in Congress. His kids hate him, his wife writes a tell-all book about the lying bastard, and he becomes a homeless alcoholic living on Skid Row. Is that motive enough to get mad at his Lolita and smack her upside the head?"

Borgeldt laughed. "Jesus, Brixton you do have a vivid imagination."

"But what I said could be true. No?"

"Could be, but when's the last time somebody was arrested and accused of murder because a PI has an imagination?"

"Yeah, yeah, I know," said Brixton, "but right now I have to assume that you have Gannon on your list of suspects."

Borgeldt's lack of response told Brixton what he needed to know. It was true.

"Can we make a deal?" Brixton asked.

"What sort of a deal?"

"You give me access to what you come up with in your investigation and I won't release anything I uncover without running it past you first."

"You're doing your own investigation?"

"Of course I am. I'm on the Bennetts' payroll now, along with their attorney, Mac Smith. They expect me to do some digging, which I intend to do. Believe me, Zeke, anything I turn up comes to you first. If it helps solve the case, you get all the accolades. Seems like a no-brainer to me. You're up to your necks with more cases than this one. Me? Just consider me an extra hand."

Borgeldt grunted.

"Look at it this way, Zeke. I used to work here at MPD. I put in twenty, most of it as a detective in Savannah. And I'm a licensed PI. *Plus* I intend to do everything I can to help my client, the Bennett family, find out who killed their daughter whether we work together or not. I don't want to butt heads with you and your guys, that's all."

"Strictly off-the-record?" Borgeldt said.

"Strictly off-the-record."

"Strictly between us? No media leaks?"

"You got it."

"What do you want, Brixton?"

"Access to her address book and information you get off her laptop. She had an iPad with her in that vault. Fill me in on what your people take off that."

Borgeldt agreed, but added the caveat, "If you so much as mention it to anyone, even your wife, I'll arrange for your public hanging on the Mall."

Brixton winced, smiled, and said, "I've been strung up before and didn't like it. Not to worry, Superintendent."

"And anything you do regarding Congressman Gannon is on you. You're on your own."

"Understood. Now, about that address book."

After leaving MPD with names from the address book, and a short list of programmed numbers from her cell phone, Brixton returned to his office and perused the information. Millie Sparks's name popped out at him and he dialed her cell number.

"Ms. Sparks, it's Robert Brixton, the private investigator working for the Bennett family."

"I just heard," she said. "Is it true? Laura is dead?"

"I'm afraid so. I'm very sorry." He waited for her to compose herself. "Let me ask you a question. Aside from everything Ms. Bennett told you about her relationship with Congressman Gannon, did she talk about other men in her life?"

He heard her blow her nose. "Sure. She said she'd been dating another fellow but that it wasn't serious."

"Remember his name?"

"Only because of the way she told me. She sort of sang his name because it's Caruso, like the famous opera singer."

"I see. Anyone else?"

"No, I can't think of anyone. Mr. Brixton, do the police know who killed Laura?"

"If they do, they haven't told me. Thanks for the info. Hope I haven't interrupted anything important."

"I'm at work, but nothing seems important, does it, now that Laura has been found dead, murdered!"

She sniffed back tears, and Brixton ended the call with, "I know that Laura was your good friend, Ms. Sparks. I'm sorry that you've lost her."

He called the number in Laura's address book for Matt Caruso, who answered the call on his cell in New York senator Jenkins's office. Brixton introduced himself and asked if they could arrange to get together.

"Yeah, I heard about Laura on TV," Caruso said. "Terrible."

"Can we meet?" Brixton repeated.

"Why? Why are you calling *me*?"

"Because I know that you and the victim had a relationship."

Caruso's laugh was more of a snort. "I wouldn't exactly call it that. We knew each other, that's all."

"You and Laura dated?"

"We went out a few times."

"Just casual dates?"

"Yeah. Look, you said that you're a private investigator working for Laura's family. That's fine, but why talk to me? I don't know anything about what happened."

"I'm not saying you did. But Laura is a homicide victim. The police are working to find the murderer and so am I. Buy you a drink after work, a cup of coffee?"

"I have nothing to say except that I'm sorry what happened to Laura."

"Suit yourself, Mr. Caruso. I'm sure the police won't be as flexible as I am."

The click in his ear caused Brixton to hold the phone at a distance.

His next call was to Gannon's chief of staff, Roseann Simmons. After going through his usual introduction, he said, "I spoke with the congressman at his apartment and told him that I wanted to meet with you."

"Who are you again?"

"Robert Brixton, investigator for Laura Bennett's family. The congressman said that you had a close relationship with the interns in your office. Since Ms. Bennett was an intern, it makes sense for me to ask you questions about her life both in and out of the office."

"The police have contacted me for an interview."

"I'm sure they have, but that doesn't pose a problem. The police know that I'm also investigating Ms. Bennett's death and it's fine with them. Can we meet, Ms. Simmons?"

"Yes, all right. I just got back last night from Tampa and I'm a little behind at the office. Can you come here, and can we make it quick?"

"Sure, we'll make it quick, and anytime you say."

"In an hour?"

"I'll see you then."

Brixton met with Mac Smith and told him of his calls to Matt Caruso and Roseann Simmons.

"Caruso wasn't cooperative?" Mac asked.

"Not at all. Makes you wonder. Ms. Simmons seems nice enough. I'm meeting her at the congressman's office in an hour."

Brixton also filled Mac in on the deal he'd struck with Superintendent Borgeldt.

"I'm not surprised that he'd cooperate with us," Smith said. "Zeke Borgeldt gives all cops a good name."

Brixton handed Mac the information he'd taken with him from MPD headquarters.

"I'll go through these," Mac said.

"Where are the Bennetts?" Brixton asked.

"At the hotel, but Grace will be going back to Tampa

for a few days. There's nothing she can do here. She wants to meet with Congressman Gannon. She's convinced that he knows something about her daughter's death.

"She's right," Brixton said flatly.

"About Gannon?"

"Yeah. As far as I'm concerned, he knows what happened to her."

"That's a pretty serious charge, Robert, without something to back it up."

"And that's what I intend to do, Mac, back it up. I'd better head over to Gannon's office. I'll check in with you when I get back."

Brixton expected Roseann Simmons to be older than she appeared to be. He pegged her in her midthirties, taller than the average woman, attractively slim, her blond hair shoulder length and with lots of sheen, and a nicely formed face anchored by a lovely smile—when she chose to display it. She led him through an outer office where a dozen people worked. Gannon's press aide, Cody Watson, was one of them and gave Brixton a casual wave of the hand. They went into a small conference room. Roseann shut the door and they took seats at the oblong table.

"I must admit that I've never met a private investigator before," she said.

"Your lucky day, huh?" Brixton said. "I really appreciate you finding time for me."

"It's the least I can do to help. I couldn't believe it when I heard that Laura was dead, had been murdered."

"That's the preliminary finding, only there doesn't seem to be any doubt. She was found in what's called the Public Vault at the Congressional Cemetery. I never even heard of it."

"She was murdered there?"

"Hard to say. If I were guessing I'd say she was killed somewhere else and her killer took her there to hide the body, which means that whoever did it knew that cemetery pretty well. Ever been there?"

She hesitated before saying, "Once or twice. Went for a walk through it. How can I help?"

"Well, according to Congressman Gannon, you were the person here in the office closest to the interns, and I assume that includes Laura Bennett."

"I knew Laura as well as I knew the others, which doesn't mean that we were close. Interns come and go. Some stay in Washington in governmental jobs, but they're a minority. I don't think that Laura had aspirations to stay once her internship was over. She came to work in the morning, did her job, and left in the evening."

"What did she do in the evening?"

Simmons laughed. "I haven't the slightest idea," she said.

"No idea at all?" Brixton said.

She shook her head.

"Never went out for a drink with her, dinner, that sort of thing?"

"No. Do you find that strange?"

"Yeah, I do. People who work together usually get together after work, down a few drinks, get to know each other better on a personal level."

"That may be true in other offices, but it doesn't apply here. Next?"

That she'd gotten her back up wasn't lost on him.

"Okay," he said, "so you didn't spend time after hours with her, but what about when you both were here working? She never said anything about what she did the night before, who she saw, you know, some terrific guy she met?"

Another shake of the head. "We're very busy here, Mr. Brixton. Congressman Gannon keeps a hectic schedule that has everyone on their toes. There isn't time during the day for office gossip, if that's what you're referring to."

"No water cooler rumors being passed."

"Exactly."

"You say that the police will be interviewing you."

"That's right. We're in the process of setting up a time and place."

"Anybody here in the office have a problem with Ms. Bennett?"

"A problem?"

"You know, someone she didn't get along with, who had a grudge against her."

"No."

She cast a furtive glance at her watch.

"Just a couple more questions, Ms. Simmons. This is a little sensitive, but I'm sure you'll understand why I have to ask it. There are rumors around town that Ms. Bennett and the congressman might have been having an affair."

She stared at him.

"Have you heard those rumors?"

"Yes, I have, but those rumors are generated by the congressman's enemies who want to see him become a *former* congressman." Her face hardened as she leaned across the table. "If you are insinuating that Congressman Gannon might have had anything to do with Laura Bennett's death—anything!—then I suggest that this little get-together is over."

"Hey," Brixton said, holding up a hand as a shield against her words, "I'm not even suggesting that they did have an affair. But this young woman has been murdered and dumped in some vault to rot. The congressman seems like a nice guy and all, but every avenue has to be followed, no matter how upsetting it might be. And if you don't think that the police are going to be asking these same questions, you're very mistaken."

She backed off a bit. "It's just that the notion that Congressman Gannon would become involved with an intern in his office is simply unthinkable. You do know that her parents are close friends of the congressman."

"I know that, Ms. Simmons. Thanks for your time, ma'am. If anything develops that causes me to want to talk to you again, I'll call."

"That will be fine."

He followed her from the conference room and through the work area to the entrance to the office. As they shook hands and said their good-byes, Brixton saw Cody Watson get up from his desk and headed in their direction. Brixton went through the door into the hallway and paused. Seconds later the door opened and Watson came through it.

"Mr. Brixton," the press aide said.

"Yeah."

"I knew that you were having a meeting with Roseann," Watson said.

"We had a nice chat," Brixton said.

"I wondered if we could find some time to get together."

"Sure. You name it."

"Don't misunderstand. It's just that—"

The door opened and Roseann Simmons stood there. "Did you forget something, Mr. Brixton?" she asked.

"No."

"Back in a minute," Watson told Roseann as he headed for a door with the sign MEN.

Brixton started walking in the opposite direction toward the elevators. He glanced back, saw that Roseann had returned into Gannon's office complex, turned and entered the men's room, where Watson stood at a urinal.

"Figured I'd go before I hit the road," Brixton said brightly. "My mother always told me not to wait when there was a men's room handy."

"I'd like to talk to you," Watson said.

"Sure. Anytime. What's it about?"

"About Laura Bennett."

"How about right now?" Brixton said.

"It's not a good time," Watson said.

Or place, Brixton thought.

Brixton handed him his business card. "Give me a call," he said. "I'll meet with you any time and place you say."

Watson kept glancing at the door.

Brixton washed his hands. "Another thing my mother always made sure I did," he said. "I had an uncle who washed his hands before *and* after. He went to some Ivy League school and—"

"I'll call you," Watson said, and was gone.

26

Brixton wished that he and Cody Watson could have had their conversation then and there. The press aide had said that he wanted to talk about Laura Bennett. What a tease. Brixton's initial reaction to Watson when they'd met at Gannon's apartment was predicated on Brixton's visceral feelings about press aides and all PR people in general. Cody's job was to make the congressman look good even when he was doing bad things. Was that why he wanted to talk to Brixton, lay on him a list of achievements his boss had accomplished on behalf of the American people? If so, Brixton wasn't interested.

But did he know about any personal relationship Laura might have had with the congressman, and would he share it? Maybe Watson had a bone to pick with Gannon, had been slighted or abused in some way and was looking to get even. In that case, Brixton was all ears.

Flo was reading that day's edition of *The Washington Post* when Brixton returned to the office.

"Look," she said, pointing to an open page on her desk. In *The Post*'s gossip section was a photograph of Hal and Charlene Gannon leaving Cafe Milano. His arm was around her and both smiled broadly. The caption read: "Beleaguered congressman Hal Gannon and wife, Charlene, enjoyed a dinner together at Cafe Milano. The rumors that the Florida congressman might have had an affair with his intern, Laura Bennett, a murder victim, prompted Gannon to say upon leaving the iconic restaurant in response to a question, 'Don't be ridiculous. There's not an ounce of truth to it and I resent the question.'"

"Out on the town with his sweetie," Brixton grumbled. "How nice."

"You really have it in for him, don't you?" Flo said.

"I don't believe the guy, that's all. I had an interesting few moments with his press aide after I left the meeting with Gannon's chief of staff.

"Oh? What did he say?"

"Just that he wants to talk to me about Laura Bennett."

"Any idea why?"

"No, but I'm hoping that it concerns a relationship she might have had with the congressman. I gave him my card. If he calls, put him right through. Is Mac in?"

"He has Mr. Bennett in with him. Mrs. Bennett has gone back to Tampa. By the way, that other private investigator is dropping by later."

"Which other private investigator?"

She consulted a note on her desk. "Paul Wooster, from Tampa."

"*Former* private investigator. They lifted his Florida license."

"How do you know that?"

"Through my superior investigatory skill."

Brixton knocked on Smith's door.

Smith and Bennett sat on the couch with file folders on their laps.

"I understand that Mrs. Bennett has gone home," Brixton said.

"She had to be persuaded," Bennett replied. "I didn't see any sense in her staying here and being subjected to the media circus. Her sister, Irene, and a brother from New York will be with her. We can't make funeral arrangements for Laura because the medical examiner won't release her body as long as it's an ongoing homicide investigation."

"Have you spoken with Congressman Gannon again?" Brixton asked.

"No, but I did see the photo in the paper this morning. Frankly, it sickened me, having dinner in a trendy restaurant with his wife, big smile and all. I'm afraid I might have been terribly wrong about Hal Gannon."

Brixton took Bennett's comment as an opening to express his own thoughts about the congressman. After he had, Bennett got to his feet and paced the office. "To think that I championed him in his runs for Congress, entertained him and his wife countless times in our home. You know what he told me when we had dinner together? He said that Laura had come on to him, flirted with him, wanted to instigate an affair. I'd like to wring his neck."

Mac quickly jumped into the conversation. "Let's put this in perspective," he said. "These rumors about Congressman Gannon having had an inappropriate relationship with your daughter are just that—rumors. Other information about it has come from people who claim that Laura confided in them."

"Are you suggesting that Laura lied to her aunt and to her college friend?"

"Of course not," said Mac, taken aback by the vehemence in Bennett's voice, yet understanding the emotional strain he was under. "But we don't know for certain that Gannon and your daughter had an affair, and we certainly don't know if Gannon has any information about, or had anything to do with, her murder."

"The thought of them being intimate is hard to take, Mac."

"I understand." Mac turned to Brixton. "Anything new on your end, Robert?"

Brixton decided on the spot to not mention his interview with Roseann Simmons or the overture made by Cody Watson. It would only feed Bennett's anger, which would accomplish nothing at that stage. He was pleased when Bennett announced that he was due at police headquarters to give whatever additional information about Laura he could to the investigators.

When he was gone, Brixton filled Smith in on his experience at Gannon's office.

"No idea what this Watson fellow wants to tell you?"

"No, but he did say it was about Laura. Ms. Simmons is a tough cookie. I'm sure she runs that office with an iron fist. I also don't believe that she knows nothing about Laura's private life outside the office."

"What about this guy Caruso?" Smith asked.

"I'm going to call him again."

"Good. I don't want us focusing on Congressman Gannon to the exclusion of everyone else she might have had a relationship with, maybe even a stranger. It's logical to look first at people close to her, but the answer doesn't necessarily rest with them."

"Gotcha," Brixton said.

Doris interrupted to inform Mac that Mr. Wooster was there.

"Ask him to wait a few minutes," Mac told her. He said to Brixton, "This is the PI from Tampa I told you about. Did you come up with anything about him?"

"I forgot to tell you. He's not a licensed investigator anymore. Will Sayers checked on him for me. He works for some Republican fund-raising group in Tampa. Want me to leave?"

"No, I'd like you to stay. I have no idea what he wants. He said something about being interested in Annabel's gallery, and having some legal matter to discuss with me."

Doris showed Wooster into Mac's office. The short, slender man wore a tight double-breasted blazer over a blue-and-white shirt and bright red tie. Smith introduced him to Brixton and they settled around a small round table. "What can I do for you?" Smith asked.

Wooster glanced at Brixton as though asking why he was there.

"Robert is a private investigator who works for me," Smith said. "I thought you two could talk shop, but if you'd rather he leave, I'm sure that—"

"No, no, no, that's fine," said Wooster. "I've read about you, Mr. Brixton. You're helping investigate Laura Bennett's death."

"Right," Brixton confirmed.

"I can't believe what's happened to that poor young woman," Wooster said. "When I met you and your lovely wife, Mr. Smith, she was missing, and we all hoped and prayed that she would be found safe."

Mac waited a beat before asking, "Are you here to discuss Ms. Bennett's death?"

"That wasn't my intention, but it seems that's all anybody is talking about these days. Actually, I just wanted to follow up on the brief conversation we had at Celia St. Claire's party."

"About Congressman Gannon?"

"That, and to learn more about your wife's art gallery. I've done some reading about pre-Columbian art since we met. It's a fascinating subject."

"It certainly is," said Mac. "My wife isn't here. I suggest that you stop in her gallery—it's on Wisconsin Avenue in Georgetown—and I'm sure she'll be happy to show you around and answer any questions you might have."

"I'll do that," Wooster said. "I'll make a point of it. Is there anything new in the investigation of Ms. Bennett's murder?"

Smith and Brixton looked at each other before Mac said, "You said you had a legal question, Mr. Wooster. I'm running short on time. Robert can leave and you can run this legal question past me. Otherwise—"

"Oh, my petty little legal query can wait," Wooster said.

"Why don't you run, Mac," Brixton suggested. "I'd enjoy talking some more with Mr. Wooster. We can compare war stories."

"Good idea," Mac said, standing. "Nice seeing you again, Mr. Wooster. Wish I had more time."

With Smith gone from the office, Brixton said, "How about we grab a cup of coffee or a drink?"

"That sounds like a good idea," Wooster said.

"In fact, let's make it lunch," Brixton suggested.

Ten minutes later they were settled at the bar at Tune Inn, an unpretentious dive bar and restaurant known for its beer-batter burgers and large drinks.

"Interesting place," Wooster said as he surveyed the restaurant's interior.

"'Interesting,' like when you go backstage to see a friend who's been in a play and you say it was interesting because you don't want to say how lousy it was?"

Wooster laughed. "No, I mean interesting like, ah— well, interesting. You come here often?"

"My favorite pickup line. I come whenever I feel like taking in a thousand calories at a clip."

A draft beer for Brixton, a glass of red wine for Wooster.

"So, tell me about being a private eye in Tampa, Florida."

"No different than being one here in Washington, D.C."

"Yeah, except I'm involved with the murder of a congressional intern. You ever been involved in a murder case?"

"No, I can't say that I have. I also know something about you from previous years."

"You Google me?"

"Of course. I'm sorry about the daughter you lost in that terrorist bombing."

"Thanks. Let's level with each other. What's your real reason for wanting to see Mac Smith?"

"Cut to the chase?"

Brixton nodded.

"That works two ways."

"Fair enough."

"I'm interested in the investigation into Ms. Bennett's murder and how it relates to Congressman Harold Gannon."

"Interested personally or professionally?"

"Professionally. You see, Mr. Brixton—"

"It's Robert. I'll call you Paul."

"Good. It's already working two ways. Have you Googled *me*?"

"In a manner of speaking. I know that you lost your Florida PI license and that you work for a Republican fund-raising outfit."

Wooster tasted his wine. "Not bad," he proclaimed. "Yes, I lost my license. I was set up."

Being set up wasn't anything new to Brixton.

"I've been working for Pete Solon's election committee."

"The Republican after Gannon's congressional seat."

"One and the same."

"Mac Smith told me that when he and his wife met you at that party, you said that you were a big Gannon fan. How does that square with working for his opponent."

"It's a paycheck."

"*That* I understand," said Brixton.

"I don't care about politics and politicians," Wooster said. "It's true that before I got involved in Solon's campaign I liked Gannon, appreciated his willingness to reach across the aisle, as they say. But as far as I'm concerned, every politician is corrupt. You see that recent poll that has members of Congress lower in the public's estimation than hemorrhoids?"

"No argument from me. But how does this jibe with Laura Bennett's murder?"

"I've been asking around Washington about Gannon's extracurricular sex life."

"He evidently has one."

"Big-time."

"You come up with anything that directly links him to Laura Bennett, proves that they had an affair?" Brixton asked.

"Good testimony."

"Testimony?"

"A very credible woman who had a fling with the congressman."

"She is?"

"I promised I wouldn't reveal her identity. But she's no bimbo. She's on the board of a major arts group here in D.C."

"But how does that link up Gannon and Laura Bennett?"

"She knows that Gannon and his intern had an affair."

Brixton sighed and took a drink.

"I know what you're thinking," said Wooster. "It's all hearsay."

"That's exactly what I'm thinking. It also occurs to me that you and this Solon guy you're working for have a lot to gain by pegging Gannon as Laura Bennett's murderer."

"True, but that doesn't mean that I'd—we'd—concoct something in order to do that. Think about it, Robert. Just being able to prove that Gannon is a womanizer and adulterer and world-class hypocrite would be enough to see him lose reelection. Adding murder to that list would be icing on the cake."

While listening to what Wooster was saying, Brixton's mind was working on a parallel channel. The Tampa PI seemed straightforward enough. He wasn't trying to put a spin on why he was digging into Gannon's background, and the fact that he was reluctant to reveal the name of the woman who claimed an affair with the congressman was a point in his favor. Still . . .

They ordered—a burger and fries for Brixton, a salad for Wooster.

"I'd hate to see your arteries," Wooster quipped.

"I doubt if you ever will," said Brixton.

"I showed you mine," Wooster said. "I mentioned the woman who slept with Gannon. What do you have?"

"No doubt that Gannon has been sleeping around. I interviewed a young woman who Laura Bennett confided in."

"Who is she?"

Brixton laughed. "Her name stays with me the way your lady's name stays with you."

"Maybe we should agree to be more forthcoming, Robert."

"Depends. What do you want out of it?"

"Information I can bring back to my employer, information that proves that Hal Gannon is what the rumors say he is, a cad."

"A nice old-fashioned word," Brixton said.

"And what do *you* want out of it?" Wooster asked.

"Proof that Gannon killed Laura Bennett."

"You're convinced that he did?"

"I *think* that he did, and I'm out to prove it."

"If you succeed, you help me and my client."

"Which is not why I'm doing it, but if that's how it ends up, so be it."

"Then we're on the same page, after the same thing," Wooster said. "By the way, there's also an airline flight attendant alleged to have shared the congressman's bed."

"Know who she is?"

"No, but I'm working on it."

"Let me know how you make out."

"I'll do that. Eat your burger before it gets cold."

"Eat your salad before it gets warm. I think we have a lot more to talk about."

27

Upon returning to his office, Brixton was told by Mac Smith that an interview had been granted to the *Post*'s Rebecca Paulson, the reporter heading up the paper's coverage of the Laura Bennett murder.

"What brought that about?" Brixton asked.

"Luke feels that the more press coverage, the better the chances that Laura's killer will be caught. He's pressing the MPD to ask Gannon to take a lie detector test and wants the media to help put the pressure on him."

"You agree with him?" Brixton asked.

"Not my call, Robert. The interview will take place at five today, here in my office. The reporter has asked that you and I be present to answer some questions. Luke will be heading back to Tampa after the interview. He needs to be with Grace and get out from under all the scrutiny here. You comfortable with being in on the interview?"

"Yeah, I guess so."

"It's important that whatever we say, we not step on anybody's toes over at MPD."

"No problem."

"How was your get-together with Wooster?"

"It went okay. He claims to have met a woman here in D.C. who had an affair with Gannon."

"Another one?"

"Gannon ought to do ads for Viagra. Anyway, Wooster would only say that she's on the board of some arts agency. Oh, and he also says there's an airline flight attendant who was cozy with the congressman."

Smith shook his head. "Sounds like Gannon has an insatiable appetite for the opposite sex. What's Wooster's story?"

"Strictly professional where Gannon is concerned. The guy who's after Gannon's seat in the House comes up a big winner if they can show Gannon as a liar and hypocrite. Like Wooster says, if Gannon ends up involved in Laura Bennett's murder, that's icing on the cake."

"If *that* turns out to be true, Gannon loses more than just his seat in Congress."

Luke Bennett walked in at four thirty rolling his suitcase. "I'll head for the airport right after the interview," he said. "Any news?"

"No," Smith said. "Robert and I will sit in on the interview as the reporter requested, but we'll withhold comments unless directly asked."

Bennett said to Brixton, "Based upon what you've said about Hal Gannon, maybe you should tell the reporter your feelings."

"No, I don't think that would be appropriate, Luke," Smith said. "Robert's view isn't backed up by known facts."

"The only fact that matters to me is that Hal Gannon is a liar, and Lord knows what else."

A few minutes later, Rebecca Paulson arrived, along with a photographer. After some discussion about where in the office the interview should take place, they settled on pulling a low table in front of the couch. Bennett sat with the reporter, with Smith and Brixton taking chairs to either side.

"First of all, I'm so sorry for the loss of your daughter," Paulson said as she opened a steno pad and uncapped a pen. "I realize how difficult this is for you, and I really appreciate you giving me an opportunity to ask some questions."

The photographer's strobe light flashed a few times, causing Bennett to blink.

"Hold off, John, until we're into the interview," Paulson suggested.

As the questioning commenced, Smith and Brixton were impressed with Paulson's professional demeanor. She put Bennett at ease almost immediately, and he gave a series of full, thoughtful answers. She was in the midst of getting background information on how Laura decided to become an intern in Congressman Gannon's office when the door opened and Flo stuck her head in. She held a hand up to her ear to indicate to Brixton that he had a phone call.

"Excuse me," he said, and joined her in the reception area.

"Cody Watson is on the phone," Flo told him. "I wouldn't have barged in, but you said to put him right through."

"I'll take it."

"Mr. Watson, Brixton here."

"Can we get together?"

"Sure. You name the place and time."

"Tonight, eight o'clock, the bar and lounge at the Lombardy hotel on Pennsylvania Ave."

Brixton rejoined Mac and the others. Smith had just given a statement to the reporter regarding a new reward that Luke Bennett was offering for information leading to the apprehension and conviction of his daughter's murderer.

"I spoke with Superintendent Borgeldt this morning," Paulson said. "He couldn't say much because of the on-going nature of the investigation, but when I asked whether Congressman Gannon was a person of interest, he didn't deny it."

"Did you bring up the rumors that the congressman and Laura Bennett might have had an affair?" Brixton asked.

All eyes went to Luke Bennett for a reaction.

"If those rumors are true," Bennett said, "Hal Gannon has to be at the top of the suspect list."

"He's on the top of *my* list," Brixton threw out.

Now all eyes turned to him.

"I mean, it makes sense, doesn't it?" Brixton said.

"Robert—Mr. Brixton—is working with Mac Smith and has been digging into whether Congressman Gannon might know something about Laura's disappearance and death," Bennett told the reporter.

Paulson scribbled notes furiously and motioned for the photographer to get shots of Brixton and Smith.

"Let's not have any misunderstanding," Smith said. "The police are in charge of the investigation, but Robert is using his background as a private investigator to seek information that could prove valuable to them. If Congressman Gannon is ruled out as a person of interest, then Robert has done both the MPD and the Bennett family a service."

"Is that what you're doing, Mr. Brixton, trying to rule out Congressman Gannon?" Paulson asked.

"I suppose you could say that."

The interview ended at six. After Paulson and her photographer had left, and Bennett had also departed, Brixton told Smith about his scheduled meeting with Gannon's press aide, Cody Watson.

"No idea what he wants to say," Mac said flatly.

"Just that it's about Laura Bennett."

"I was a little uneasy during the interview, Robert."

"About what?"

"About you. I know how fixated you are on the congressman, but unless—and until—you come up with a piece of hard evidence, I think it best to temper your comments about him."

"You're right, Mac. Sorry. Will you and Annabel be home this evening?"

"That's the plan."

"I'll give you a call after I meet with Watson."

It was a lovely evening, cooler than previous days, and with a gentle breeze. Brixton and Flo drove to Pennsylvania Avenue between Twentieth and Twenty-first Streets where they found a legal parking space just a short walk to the Hotel Lombardy, a charming landmark boutique hotel across from a small manicured park.

They sat on one of the park's benches. Brixton leaned back, closed his eyes, and sighed.

"This is the most relaxed I've seen you all day," Flo commented.

"Makes me think that when this business with Laura Bennett is over, we should get away, maybe take a cruise someplace, do nothing but lay back and smell those roses."

"Do you mean that?"

He came forward. "Of course I mean it. Hey, you know me. My word is gold."

She pressed against him and said, "Maybe we should leave Washington and settle in a place without so much tension, you know, like a Caribbean island or somewhere in the desert, Arizona or New Mexico."

"We'd get bored," he said.

"Getting bored is appealing," she said.

"Everything's appealing compared to Washington. Know what I think?"

"Tell me."

"I think that Gannon knows what happened to Laura, and unless I can prove it he's going to slide right by and get away with it."

"Members of Congress get away with things every day."

"Yeah, I know, but wouldn't it be nice if this congressman didn't? Let's grab something to eat."

"In the hotel?"

"Yeah. I understand the restaurant and café are good."

"I shouldn't be there when Watson walks in."

"Doesn't matter. I'll introduce you as my partner in the agency. If it looks like he's about to bail, you can leave, take the car, and I'll grab a cab when we're finished."

"Sure?"

"Sure. Let's go."

Brixton's immediate impression of the hushed, sedate bar in the hotel was that it would be the perfect rendezvous for a mole reporting to his handler. He and Flo were the only two customers, at least for the moment. They took a small table in a secluded nook, and over drinks and snacks discussed the meeting that would soon take place between Brixton and Cody Watson.

"I have an idea," Brixton said. "I know what he looks like. When he comes in, I'll go to him and shake his hand. You snap off a picture or two of us with your cell phone."

"Why?"

"So I have some proof that we met. Just be sure to do it fast so he doesn't see you, and make sure your flash is off."

"Is there enough light in here?" she asked.

"Probably. That's a fancy phone you have. Anyway, let's give it a shot."

"And then what do I do?"

"It probably is best if you split. I'll tell him that you're

my date, say good-bye to you, kiss you on the cheek, and
you take off. I'll see you at home."

"I liked it better when you said I'd be your business
partner."

They lingered over desert and second drinks until, at
a few minutes before eight, Watson came through the
door. Brixton waved and got to his feet. As he approached Watson, his hand outstretched, a large, heavyset middle-aged man with salt-and-pepper hair pulled
into a ponytail also entered the room. He excused himself and skirted Watson as he went to the bar and took a
stool.

"Right on time," Brixton said.

Watson shook the hand and looked nervously about.

"I had dinner with a date," Brixton said, indicating
Flo. "She's just leaving. Let me say good-bye. We can take
the same table, nice and quiet."

For a moment Brixton thought that Watson might
change his mind and leave. But he didn't as Brixton returned to the table, took Flo's hand, kissed her lightly on
the lips, and said in a voice loud enough for Watson to
hear, "Sorry, hon, but business is business."

"That's okay," she said sweetly, returning the kiss. As
she passed Watson, she said over her shoulder, "Call me
when you get a chance."

"Shall do," Brixton said.

Watson came to the table, hesitated, and took the seat
vacated by Flo.

"What are you drinking?" Brixton asked.

"A Rob Roy," Watson said.

"Nice drink," said Brixton. He ordered a martini. "So,
I'm glad we have this chance to meet. We didn't have
much time to talk at the congressman's apartment."

"I couldn't talk there anyway."

"I understand."

Brixton took in Watson. He was nicely dressed in a

foppish sort of way, his yellow bow tie long and floppy, his double-breasted blazer festooned with large gold buttons on the wrists. He hadn't noticed when he'd first met him that his mousy-brown hair was lank and parted in the middle, an old-fashioned look. He also noted that his perfectly manicured fingernails were covered with clear gloss. Brixton had never had a manicure and was distrustful of men who did and who used nail polish. Just one of the private investigator's many quirks.

Brixton raised his glass. "Here's to meeting you."

Their attention went to the door, where a couple entered and were shown to a table in the opposite corner.

"Maybe we ought to have our talk before the place fills up," Brixton suggested.

"A good idea," Watson said. "Is there anything new in the investigation of Laura's death?"

"Not a hell of a lot, I'm afraid. The police have a special unit assigned to the case, and I've been following what leads I come up with. What about you, Mr. Watson? You said that you wanted to speak to me about Laura."

Watson had appeared nervous when he entered the room, and it hadn't abated. His blue eyes behind his glasses darted back and forth as though searching for a safe spot to land.

"I couldn't believe when I heard that Laura had disappeared, and then to learn that she'd been murdered," Watson said. "It was surreal, something out of a bad movie."

"It sure was for her folks."

"I keep thinking about her. She was a really nice young woman, always laughing, ready to pitch in whenever you needed something. She was also—well, I think she was a little naïve."

"In what way?"

"Oh, I don't know, not very worldly, I suppose, is a

better way to put it. She was someone who could easily be taken advantage of."

"And was she?"

"Taken advantage of?" He nodded and sipped his drink.

Brixton sipped, too. As he did, he glanced at the bar where the heavyset man was looking at them. Aware of Brixton's interest, he turned, motioned for the bartender, and said, "Check."

Brixton returned his attention to Watson as the man at the bar paid and left.

"You know that I had a meeting with Ms. Simmons," Brixton said.

"Did she have anything to say that helped in your investigation?"

"No, but I didn't expect some startling piece of information to come out of it. How long have you worked for Congressman Gannon?"

"Three years."

"You have a little bit of a southern accent. You from Tampa?"

"I'm originally from Georgia. I moved to Tampa to work for a newspaper and wrote some pieces that Hal liked. When his press aide left, he offered me the job."

"That's a pretty big jump, isn't it, from being a newspaper reporter to being a U.S. congressman's spokesman?"

"Not as big as you think. While I try to get media attention for things Hal does as a congressman that are positive, I also have to keep other aspects of his life out of the media."

Brixton debated before asking, "Like screwing interns?"

Brixton's directness hit Watson like a punch. A burst of air came from his lips, and he drummed his fingertips on the table.

"Look," said Brixton, "I know that the congressman's alleged relationship with Laura Bennett is just that, alleged. But I'm convinced that it's true, and if so he had every motive to keep her from spreading the word about their affair. I don't give a damn what becomes of the congressman, whether he keeps his seat in Congress or not. But Laura Bennett's parents deserve closure on this. If that means the congressman submitting to a lie detector test, so be it. If he has nothing to hide or lie about, he should welcome the chance to clear his name."

"He'd fail," was Watson's terse response.

"Fail a lie detector test?"

"Yes. He had an affair with Laura, but she wasn't the only one." He managed a wry smile. "I thought I'd be working with a congressman who was doing great things for the country. Don't get me wrong. Hal *has* done some good things for the American people. But lately my only job seems to be covering up for him and his women."

"Does one of those women sit on the board of an arts agency here in D.C.? Is there an airline flight attendant, too?"

"You know about them."

"I'm surprised all of D.C. doesn't know. There're plenty of rumors about it, and I imagine it doesn't stop with those two."

"It really doesn't matter, does it?" Watson said, his voice tinged with sadness.

"How many women the congressman had bedded? No, it doesn't matter. What *does* matter is Laura Bennett. How did their affair start?"

Watson was less nervous now, maybe the effect of the drink. He shrugged, sipped, and finished what was in his glass. Brixton suggested another round, which Watson agreed to.

"How did their affair start? I don't know."

"Soon after she started working as an intern?"

"It seems that way. I noticed that she flirted with Hal right after she arrived, nothing overt or distasteful, but I picked up on it. I really didn't have much interaction with Laura. Roseann had her working on constituent requests and problems. That's where most interns get their feet wet."

"What about Ms. Simmons? Did she pick up on the flirtation, too?"

"Sure." He snorted. "Roseann picks up on everything. She runs the office like a mother hen, all-seeing, like a matron in a sorority house."

"She doesn't look matronly to me," Brixton said.

"No, she doesn't, does she? She's a beautiful woman."

"A beautiful woman running an office for an inveterate woman chaser. Did the congressman ever hit on her? Did they ever have an affair?"

"Not that I know of. Roseann is a strange woman, Mr. Brixton. She's very rich, you know."

"I didn't know."

Her father was a big-time mover and shaker in Tampa, owned half the farmland on the Gulf Coast, auto dealerships, anything that generated money. When he died, he left everything to his only daughter, Roseann."

"She talks about this?"

"No. You'd never hear it from her. I ran across the story when I was working in Tampa for the newspaper. People I talked to said her father was a ruthless guy, left bodies buried all over Florida. Roseann disappeared from Tampa before I got there, came to D.C., where she went to work for another member of the House."

"Interesting story," Brixton said. "The obvious question is why, if she's so rich, does she work for anybody?"

"You'll have to ask her, only don't expect an answer. Her background is strictly off-limits. You don't go there."

"She never married?"

"Not that I'm aware of."

"Where does she live?"

"On N Street in Georgetown, a really fancy Federal-style house. Number three thousand. Got to be worth millions. No one from the office has ever been invited to visit, except the congressman, of course. She hosts fund-raising parties for him there but strictly off-limits to staff."

"A real mystery lady."

"A *tough* mystery lady," Watson added.

"You said you think that Ms. Simmons was aware of the flirtation between Laura Bennett and the congressman. Did she ever say anything about it?"

"Not to me, but there were plenty of subtle clues. It was obvious—at least it was to me—that Roseann didn't like Laura."

"Because she flirted with the congressman?"

"Maybe, maybe not. She never expressed it in so many words."

"You hungry?" Brixton asked.

"I had dinner before I came here."

"Let me ask you this. You work for Congressman Gannon, a pretty important job. What you're telling me could play a role in his losing his seat in Congress, and you losing your job. Why are you doing it?"

Watson's pause was long and meaningful. It was obvious to Brixton that he was having trouble deciding whether to answer the question, and how to phrase it. Finally he said, "I'm gay, Mr. Brixton."

That possibility had crossed Brixton's mind.

"So?" Brixton said, not adding what he was also thinking, that maybe Congressman Gannon was interested in women *and* men. Had Watson and his boss had an affair that went sour?

"Let me explain," Watson said.

"Please do."

"When Hal hired me, he didn't know that I was gay.

I'd stayed in the closet while working as a reporter in Tampa and after coming here to Washington to work for him. There's a lot to be admired about Hal. He's signed on to some important legislation that benefits a lot of people. He can be kind, too, to certain people. Things were okay as long as I played the game and helped him cover up his affairs." He face turned hard. "You ever meet his wife, Charlene?"

"No."

"She's a terrific lady, really classy. He's got great kids, too. But he's got this need to prove that he's macho, a stud."

Where was this leading? Brixton wondered. Was Watson about to reveal that Congressman Harold Gannon was a bisexual who bedded women to cover up his homosexual tendencies?

Wrong.

"I got tired of covering for Hal," Watson explained. "I resented how he used Charlene to perpetuate his image as a devoted family man. It disgusted me."

"Why didn't you quit?" Brixton asked.

"Because it's a good job otherwise. Hal is generous. The benefits are top-notch like they are for anyone who works on the Hill. Hal knew how I'd covered for him and he tossed some money my way, not a lot, but enough to make leaving difficult."

"So what's changed?" Brixton asked.

"Me," Watson said. "I developed a relationship with a fellow I met here in D.C. He works for another congressman. I don't know how, but Hal got wind of our relationship and reamed me out, told me that he couldn't have a fag working for him—that's what he said, called me a fag, a sissy-boy. He told me to find another job."

"But you didn't."

"No. My partner—his name is Roy—told me to stand my ground with Hal and not let him push me out because

I'm gay. I took that stance, and Hal backed off, not because he'd changed his view of my sexual orientation but because of what I knew about his own extracurricular sex life."

"And here you are telling me about it," said Brixton.

"Only because of Laura Bennett's murder. I think that Hal killed her to keep their affair quiet."

"Got anything to back that up?"

"No."

"I appreciate you coming forward like this, Mr. Watson. Would you be willing to tell the police the same things you've told me?"

"I'd rather not. That's why I've contacted you instead of the police. As you've said, I have nothing to substantiate what I'm claiming. But I thought you ought to know."

Brixton appreciated Watson coming forward as he had. His reasons for doing so were irrelevant. What was important was that he'd added another witness to Gannon having had a sexual relationship with Laura Bennett.

But the meeting hadn't provided any tangible evidence of the affair, and unless those with tales to tell were willing to go to the police and give a sworn statement, the word "alleged" prevailed. There was Laura's college chum, Millie Sparks, who'd been told about the affair. Paul Wooster had pointed to an unnamed woman as having been intimate with the congressman and also cited an unnamed airline flight attendant. Laura had spoken of the relationship with Grace Bennett's sister, Irene. And now Gannon's press aide was alleging—there was that word again, "alleging"—that he knew of the relationship between his boss and the murdered intern.

"If you change your mind about making a statement to the police," Brixton said, "let me know. I'm working with a top attorney, Mackensie Smith, who I'm sure will do everything he can to protect your interests."

"Like find me another job on the Hill?"

"Sounds to me that you aren't long for that job anyway, Mr. Watson. But it's your call."

Brixton motioned for the check.

"I'll think about going to the police," Watson said. "If I decide to, I'll let you know first."

"It's a deal," Brixton said as Watson got up, shook hands, and left.

28

The following morning at ten, Brixton met with Mac Smith in his law office. Brixton had called Smith at his Watergate apartment the minute he arrived home from his meeting with Cody Watson and replayed for him what had been discussed. Now they went over again what Brixton had said on the phone the night before.

"Watson left it that if he decided to talk to the police, he'd contact me first."

"We can't depend upon him to do that," Smith said. "I've had a slew of phone calls this morning, including one from Zeke Borgeldt. They've interviewed Grace Bennett's sister, Irene, about what Laura had told her of her fling with Gannon. He wants the names of others we've uncovered who know something about it."

"I hate to sell them out, Mac. They came forward willingly with the understanding that their names wouldn't be involved."

"But this has gone beyond protecting these people. Millie Sparks and now Cody Watson have to be urged to give voluntary statements to the authorities. There's also Paul Wooster, who told you about the woman here in D.C. and some anonymous airline flight attendant. Luke Bennett wants Gannon to take a lie detector test. If these individuals, who have information about the affair, no matter how tangential, tell their stories to the police, it will give the MPD the ammunition to pressure Gannon. On top of that, we are guilty of withholding information."

"You're right, I know, Mac. Want me to call Watson?"

"No. Call Millie Sparks, explain the situation to her, and see if she'll agree to accompany you to headquarters to give her statement. If she declines, tell her that I'll come with her, too. She might feel more comfortable having an attorney present. I'll call Wooster to see if he'll give me the name of the woman here in D.C. and the flight attendant."

The phone continued to ring during their conversation.

"The press," Smith grunted. "It's a national story now. There's been a half dozen calls from media this morning. Doris has been fielding them. Go call Ms. Sparks and let me know how you do."

Millie Sparks was not happy with Brixton's call, but when he explained that she wasn't in any trouble, was helping a murder investigation of her college friend, and would have the Bennett attorney, Mackensie Smith, with her, she agreed to provide a sworn statement to the police.

Mac's call to Paul Wooster didn't go that easily.

"Brixton told you about our conversation?" he barked into the phone. "What I told him was off-the-record, strictly confidential."

"That may be, Mr. Wooster, but there's no confidentiality clause in the law for conversations between private investigators. More important, this is a homicide investigation. If you have any information that might be useful to the authorities in their investigation, you have an obligation to come forward."

"Let them subpoena me."

"Which I'm sure they'll be delighted to do. But here's what I don't understand. Robert Brixton tells me that you work for the Republican who is trying to take Congressman Gannon's seat in the House of Representatives away from him. If the information you have is legitimate, it will taint Congressman Gannon and help your guy."

"That may be true," Wooster said, "but I sort of promised the woman I talked with that her name wouldn't be made known."

"Sort of promised?"

"It was understood."

"I'm sure she'd understand that there's a murder of a young woman to be solved. She didn't have any problem telling her tale to you."

"No, she didn't."

"It doesn't do any good for you to be sitting on it. Tell you what. Give me her name. When I contact her I won't mention where I got it."

"She'll know."

"Oh, come on, Mr. Wooster. I'm sure you're not the only person she confided in. She's probably told a dozen friends. Word gets around, like the rumor that Congressman Gannon had a number of affairs. But it's your decision."

There was a long pause on Wooster's end. Finally he said, "Her name is Rachel Montgomery. She's involved with the Washington Opera, on the board, something like that. Satisfied?"

"Appreciative. What about the flight attendant?"

"I haven't the slightest idea who she is. I wish I knew."

"Thanks," Smith said. "The Bennett family appreciates your candor."

Brixton and Smith compared notes after their respective phone calls.

"Millie Sparks says she'll do it," Brixton said.

"The woman Wooster talked to is Rachel Montgomery. She's involved in some capacity with the Washington Opera. Get hold of her."

"Shall do."

Mac's private line lit up.

"What's up, Annie?" Smith asked.

"Do you have the TV on?"

"No. Why?"

"There was just a brief item about a murder, Congressman Gannon's press aide, Cody Watson."

29

I can't believe it," Brixton muttered. "I was with the guy only last night."

"Did he say anything to indicate that his life might be in danger?" Smith asked.

"No, nothing."

"Annabel says that the TV report indicated only that he was found in his apartment, the victim of an assault. Did he say he was going directly home after meeting with you?"

"No. That never came up."

"Ms. Sparks is on the phone," Flo announced.

"When can we set up a time for her to give a statement to the police?" Brixton asked Mac.

"I'll call Zeke Borgeldt now," Smith answered. A minute later he interrupted Brixton's conversation with Millie. "Can she be at my office at five?" he asked.

Brixton relayed the question to her and nodded to Smith.

"Have you contacted Rachel Montgomery?" Smith asked after they'd returned to his office.

"I'll get on it right away," Brixton said, and headed back to his suite. Flo joined him.

"Hey," Brixton said, "did the picture you took last night come out?"

"I never even looked," she said. "I managed to get off two."

She pulled her cell phone from her purse and scrolled to the shots she'd taken at the Hotel Lombardy. Although the photos had been taken in dim light, the figures were clear enough to be identifiable, including the second shot that included the heavyset man who'd come into the restaurant on Watson's heels.

"Good job," Brixton said, tapping her rear end as she turned to leave.

He pulled up the home phone number for Rachel Montgomery and the number of the Washington Opera's offices. He tried the office first and reached her. After introducing himself, he said, "Ms. Montgomery, I have information that you and Congressman Hal Gannon had once been engaged in a close relationship."

"You say you work for the Bennett family?'

"Yes, ma'am, that's right. You're aware of course that Congressman Gannon's intern, Laura Bennett, was murdered."

"Of course. But why are you calling me?"

"Because the police need all the help they can get to solve Ms. Bennett's murder. The fact that you and the congressman had an affair and—"

"I can't talk to you here at the office."

"Tell me where to call," he said.

"I'll call you back. Give me your number."

"Okay, but don't disappoint me. It'll be better for you to voluntarily give a statement than for the authorities to subpoena you. I'll be here for the next fifteen minutes."

She called back five minutes later. She was obviously on the street; Brixton heard traffic sounds.

"I don't want to be made to look like a fool," she said.

"No reason for you to be," Brixton replied.

"Who told you about Hal and me?"

"It doesn't matter. Rumors about his affairs are all over town."

"It won't be in the papers, will it?"

"If it is, it won't come from me. The Bennetts' lawyer's office at six tonight?" Brixton suggested, counting on whoever was there from the MPD to take Millie Sparks's five o'clock statement would be happy to take another.

"All right," she said.

He gave her the address and confirmed her promise that she'd show up.

When he returned to Mac's office, the attorney had the TV on.

"Anything new on Watson?" Brixton asked.

"Gannon was just on. They waylaid him coming out of his apartment with his wife."

"What did he have to say?"

"Nothing unusual, how shocked he was to hear about his press aide, characterized him as an outstanding young man, hopes his killer will be brought to justice quickly. Reporters brought up the fact that both his intern and his press aide have now been murdered."

"What did he say to that?"

"He said that someone is obviously out to get him through members of his staff. After that he cut off further questioning."

"His wife was with him?"

"Right."

"Standing by her man. Why do women do that when their man is a dirtball like Gannon?"

"You'll have to ask her, Robert. While I was on the phone with Borgeldt, I asked about the guy you spoke to, Caruso, who'd dated Laura. Borgeldt says that they interviewed him. He said that he's an arrogant young guy and although they have no reason to suspect him of her disappearance and murder, they're not ruling him out. Oh, I also told him that you were with Watson last night. He wants to talk to you. You might be the last person to have seen him alive."

"Which probably tosses me into the suspect pool."

"Nonsense. But if you want, I'll come with you."

"Not necessary, Mac. I'm happy to oblige the superintendent. What I'd like to do is see where Watson was killed."

"I'll ask Borgeldt to arrange that," said Smith. "And while you're there, you can fill Borgeldt and his people in on what Watson told you about Gannon's affair with Laura Bennett."

"How many more testimonies do they need to know that the rumors of an affair are true?" Brixton grumbled as he headed out.

W hen Brixton arrived at police headquarters, Borgeldt was out of the office. But Detectives Gibbs and Morey took Brixton into an interview room, where he told them of his meeting with Cody Watson and the press aide's claim that he knew of an affair between the congressman and his intern.

"I wonder if the congressman knew that his trusted aide was selling him out?" Morey said.

Brixton further explained Watson's reasons for telling tales of the congressman's life, his disgust with Gannon's posturing as a devoted family man, and the fact that Watson's sexual orientation had been demeaned by his boss.

"Did Watson live alone?" Brixton asked.

"No, he had a roommate," Morey said.

"Gay?" Brixton asked.

"We don't know," Gibbs replied. "He was out of town. He works for a computer-consulting firm. He's just arrived back. There's another team working the Watson case, but we're coordinating with them because of the Laura Bennett murder. We're heading over there once we finish up here with you.

"Zeke said you're to have access to the crime scene," Gibbs said. "He must be a fan of yours."

"He's a fan of Mac Smith," Brixton said. Let's go."

Cody Watson lived on the second floor of a well-maintained row house in the Capitol Hill area. Yellow crime scene tape had been strung across the entrance, and a uniformed officer stood guard to keep gawkers, and the media that had descended on the scene, at bay. When Brixton and the other detectives arrived, the tenants of the downstairs apartment were outside complaining about their loss of access. The officer, who'd been on the receiving end of their complaints, referred them to one of two detectives who'd been at the scene since the murder had been discovered.

"We'll try to finish our crime scene investigation by evening," he told the tenants, "and you'll be able to return to your home, but there'll be an officer outside the building all night."

That seemed to placate the tenants, a young couple, who'd been questioned about whether they'd heard anything the previous night that would indicate a struggle. They'd heard nothing. When asked about Cody Watson and his roommate, they'd said only that he and his roommate had been quiet neighbors. They were aware of Watson's job as press aide to Congressman Gannon because he occasionally appeared on TV, but other than that they knew little about him.

Gibbs, Morey, and Brixton were allowed to pass the perimeter tape and went up the stairs to the victim's apartment, where a tech was dusting for fingerprints and a police photographer snapped shots of the living room in which the body had been found. The second detective assigned to the investigation greeted them.

"He died here in the living room?" Gibbs asked.

"Yup," was the answer. "Right there." He pointed the crude outline of a body created by strips of red tape.

"Fully dressed?"

"Yup."

"Blue blazer. Yellow bow tie?" Brixton asked.

The detective looked at him curiously.

"I was with him last night," Brixton explained. "That's what he was wearing."

"How did the attacker get in?" Morey asked.

"Lock wasn't broken. The vic must have let him in."

"Can we see his bedroom?" Gibbs asked.

The detective led the way down a long, narrow hall lined with modern art prints to a room at the rear of the apartment. Brixton noted how immaculate it was, nothing out of place, no clothing draped over chairs, the bed made, a circular Oriental rug perfectly centered on the floor. One wall contained framed photographs of Watson with recognizable members of Congress and local media types, perks of his job. Another wall held photos of a more personal nature, Watson running the rapids in an unidentified place, about to go up in a hot-air balloon, and a series of framed pictures of Watson with what Brixton assumed were family members at various celebratory gatherings.

"The victim worked for Congressman Gannon," Brixton said, "and met with me to say that the intern who was murdered, Laura Bennett, had been having an affair with the congressman. I'd like to take a look at his desk."

"I don't know, I—"

"It's okay," said Gibbs. "He's working private for the intern's family. We're working with him. Superintendent Borgeldt has cleared him."

"Techs will be taking the laptop and other stuff from the desk."

"I won't disturb anything," Brixton assured him. "Just want to look."

He didn't wait for further protestations before sitting at the desk and taking in what was on it. He had no idea what he was looking for, except that maybe there was something that provided proof of what Watson had alleged, that his boss was bedding down his intern. He was tired of rumors and allegations and hearsay. He wanted—needed—something tangible. There was nothing overtly visible, and he realized that he was just going through the motions.

"The neighbors didn't see anyone who shouldn't have been here last night?" Gibbs asked the detective on duty.

"We talked to the downstairs neighbors. Nothing from them. They'd gone out to dinner, came home, and watched a movie before going to bed."

"He told me last night when we met that he had a partner, a boyfriend. I think he said his name was Roy."

"He's already been here," the detective on the scene said. "He's down at headquarters being questioned."

Brixton wandered downstairs to the street. He kept replaying in his mind the conversation he'd had with Watson last night, trying to come up with something the press aide said that would have bearing on his murder, but came up empty. But one thought kept intruding. He'd been obsessed with the theory that Laura Bennett had been killed because of the affair she'd had with Hal Gannon. Now, less than twenty-four hours later, another person associated with the congressman who'd known of the affair was dead, the second victim of a vicious blow to the head.

It looked like Watson had admitted his attacker, which pointed to their having known each other. Watson's roommate was ruled out; he wasn't even in town when the murder occurred. Watson's new friend, Roy, was always a possibility—a homosexual partnership gone awry? Had Watson been in contact with Roy after leaving the Lombardy?

No, Brixton decided as he stood on the sidewalk and wished he still smoked. Watson's death had to be linked to Laura Bennett's, and her affair with Gannon was undoubtedly at the root of it.

He rode back to headquarters with Morey and Gibbs.

"Thanks for taking me along," he told them.

"No problem, Brixton."

"Say hello to Borgeldt for me."

Brixton got into his car and drove back to the office. When he arrived, he interrupted a meeting that Mac Smith was having with a man Brixton pegged as a lawyer before even being introduced. His name was Richard Nichols, and he had been retained by Hal Gannon as his attorney. Mac explained Brixton's role, and Nichols didn't have a problem with him sitting in on the meeting.

"As I was saying," Nichols said, "Congressman Gannon is amenable to taking a lie detector test, but only with a licensed lie detector expert of our choosing."

"That's short-sighted, isn't it," Smith said. "If the congressman passes it, the public will view such results with skepticism. I strongly urge that he consider being tested by someone cleared by the MPD and prosecutor's office."

Nichols, who sounded as though there was an obstruction in his nasal passages, shook his head. "I know that your clients, the Bennetts, have been pressing my client to take the test, and we're cooperating. They should appreciate that. Congressman Gannon has willingly given multiple interviews to the authorities and has agreed to this lie detector test."

"Frankly, they're not in the frame of mind to appreciate anything the congressman does," Smith said. "What about the MPD's request that he give a DNA sample?"

"That's an unnecessary intrusion into his privacy," said Nichols.

"Laura Bennett's murder was an unnecessary intrusion into *her* privacy," Smith countered. "She hasn't had a say into whether *her* DNA could be taken, which it has. Now there's the apparent murder of Congressman Gannon's press aide. Robert was with him last night. Why don't you tell Mr. Nichols what Cody Watson told you, Robert."

Brixton recounted what Watson had said about Gannon's affair with Laura Bennett.

"That's at least four, maybe five individuals who'll testify to an affair having taken place," Smith said.

Nichols guffawed. "All hearsay," he said. "As far as Mr. Watson is concerned, the congressman has told me that he was on the verge of being fired, and had badmouthed the congressman to others on the staff, including the chief of staff, Ms. Simmons. As for other women coming forth to claim having had an affair with Mr. Gannon, their motives, to say nothing of their moral character, are certainly in question."

"*Moral character?*" Smith said, incredulous. "Sounds to me as though you're admitting that they willingly entered into a relationship with Gannon, a married man. Is that what you mean by their 'moral character'?"

"What I'm saying, Mr. Smith, is that Congressman Gannon denies having had an affair with Ms. Bennett, or with anyone else, for that matter. Unless someone comes forward with irrefutable proof to demonstrate otherwise, the congressman's word is good. He is, after all, an

elected member of the United States House of Representatives."

Nichols delivered that last line with exaggerated grav-
ity, and Brixton turned his head to shield his smile.

The meeting ended with the two attorneys agreeing to
talk after Nichols had again posed the question of his
client taking a police-arranged lie detector test. "I already know the answer," he said on his way out the door,
"but I will pass it by him."

With Nichols was gone, Brixton said, "Did I detect a
little pomposity, Mac?"

Smith laughed. "He does come off that way, but he's a
good attorney who's represented some heavy hitters.
What did you come up with at Watson's apartment?"

"Not much. Flo says I've had a half dozen calls from
the press."

"Join the celebrity crowd, Robert. Doris also has a
long list of calls."

"I want to talk to Gannon's chief of staff again," Brixton said, "find out whether what this attorney Nichols,
said is true, that Gannon was about to fire him. I didn't
get that impression from Watson."

"What about Gannon's wife?" Smith mused.

"What about her?"

"She must know that the rumors about her husband's
sexual escapades are more than just rumors. I wonder if
there's some way to get to her."

"She was standing tall with him on TV," Brixton
said.

"But she may get sick of playing that role," said Smith.
"Let's think about it."

"The Bennetts are friends with her," Brixton said.
"Maybe one of them can get her to open up."

"I'll raise that with Luke when we talk."

Brixton went to his office and called Gannon's office,
asked for Roseann Simmons.

"Ms. Simmons is out of town," he was told.

"When do you expect her back?" Brixton asked.

"I don't know," was the response, which struck Brixton as odd. A congressman's chief of staff is out of town and the office doesn't know when she'll return? Gannon would probably know, but Brixton didn't suffer any illusions that the congressman would agree to speak with him again.

Brixton stayed for the two interviews held in Smith's office, Millie Sparks and Rachel Montgomery. He felt sorry for Montgomery. She seemed like a nice woman who fell for Gannon's masculine charms and in the process bought herself a few months of misguided belief that the relationship would go beyond Gannon's self-serving romp in the sack. *She wasn't a kid; she should have known better,* was the conclusion to which he came.

That night Brixton and Flo ordered in a pizza and hibernated in the apartment. They watched a movie, but Brixton kept switching to TV newscasts to see the latest on the Watson and Bennett murders. When the film ended, he said, "When I talked to Gannon's chief of staff, she said she'd just gotten back from Tampa. Maybe that's where she is now."

"Are you thinking of going there?"

"Yeah."

"To hunt for her? Tampa's not a small place."

"No, not to hunt for her, Flo. I'd like to catch up again with the private investigator, Paul Wooster. We got along okay. Hell, it's to his benefit and to the people he works for to help nail Gannon. As far as I know he's still looking for proof that Gannon is an adulterer and, more important, that he might be a murderer. Wooster gave me the name of the woman who was interviewed at Mac's office, didn't fight it."

"When will you go?"

"Hopefully tomorrow. I'll run it past Mac."

"I'll miss you."

"I'll miss you, too. I'll only be a few days. I'll call Wooster first to make sure he'll be there."

They were about to go to bed when the phone rang. It was Brixton's ex-wife, Marylee.

"Robert, we have to talk," she said in a tone he remembered and was glad to be free of.

"About what?"

"Can you come here tomorrow?"

"Is Jill okay?"

"She's fine. I need to see you."

"I'm leaving town tomorrow, but I can make time in the morning. Ten o'clock all right?"

"That's acceptable," she said.

Brixton smiled. *How nice that ten o'clock was "acceptable" to his former spouse.*

"I hear that Tampa is nice," Flo said as they cuddled in bed.

"I'll find out. I know that they're big on cigars there."

"So?"

"Maybe I'll buy some and start smoking again."

"You do and I'm outta here."

"Cigars give a man a certain status. Big shots smoke them."

"You want to be a big shot?"

"Sure, why not?"

"But you already are," she said sweetly, "in my eyes."

Her comment melted him, and a half hour later, sweaty and sated, they fell asleep.

30

Marylee Greene Lashka lived in a spacious tract home in suburban Maryland. Her mother, now deceased—who Brixton often said had cornered the market on pomposity and self-righteousness—had purchased the house for her daughter when she and Robert divorced after a rocky four years of marriage. Brixton had met the blond, gushy Marylee while working as a uniformed cop in D.C., and it didn't take long for the hormonal rush to be replaced by two infant daughters and Mrs. Greene's constant criticism of her only child's decision to marry a cop. Marylee's father had been a successful businessman. When he died, he left his widow a sizable fortune. She bought the house, had a large wing added for her, and lived there until the day she died.

Brixton pulled up into the driveway at ten sharp. He hoped that his ex-wife's new husband, a smarmy lawyer named Miles Lashka, wouldn't be there, and was relieved when Marylee appeared at the door by herself. She led him into the kitchen, where the aroma of freshly baked chocolate chip cookies filled the air.

"I didn't that know you baked," Brixton said.

"There's a lot you don't know about me," she replied tartly as she pulled a cookie rack from the oven and placed it on a folded towel on the counter.

Had he responded, it would have been an opening for a tart exchange. He didn't. Instead he said, "I'm here because you asked me to be. What's up?"

"Coffee?" she asked.

"You still drink instant?"

"There's nothing wrong with instant coffee."

"Maybe not, but I still have standards. No on the coffee."

She made herself a cup and sat at the kitchen table. He continued standing.

"I called you, Robert, because I'm going to write a book about Janet's death."

He pulled out a chair and joined her. "You're right, Marylee," he said. "There are things about you I don't know. Since when did you become a writer?"

"I have a friend who is a literary agent in Washington."

"Not Robert Barnett."

"Of course not. I'm sure he wouldn't be interested in representing me."

"And I'm sure you're right. So who is this agent?"

"That doesn't matter at this moment," she said. "The point is that the book will include what happened to you after the terrorist bombing that killed Janet."

"Me? You want to write about that? About me?"

"You're part of the story, although the emphasis will be on Janet. She deserves to have her life celebrated in a book."

Brixton grunted. "Does this agent know that you've never written a book before?"

"Yes. He says that he can pair me up with one of the seasoned writers he represents."

"A ghostwriter."

"I suppose you could call it that."

"What else would you call it?" Brixton said. "All I can say is that I wish you well."

"I need more than your good wishes, Robert. The agent says that for the book to be what it should, it will have to have your input."

"Oh, I see. You want me to write it with you and this—this ghostwriter."

"Not write it with me, Robert, but agree to let the writer interview you about what you did following the bombing, shooting the congressman's son, your adventure in Hawaii with the gunrunners, the sort of stories that make the book a best seller. The agent says he can smell a future motion picture deal."

"He has a large nose?"

"Oh, stop it, Robert."

"Well, Marylee, like I said, I wish you all the best, but it won't include me. I've got other things to do."

Her face morphed into a pout, an expression he didn't miss. "You owe it to Janet," she said angrily.

"What I owe our daughter is to love her and miss her every day, which I do. I'd better get going. You're aware that I'm working on the intern murder, Laura Bennett. It's been on the news."

"Yes, I saw."

"Good luck with the book, Marylee," he said. "Mind if I have a cookie for the road? They smell good."

She said nothing.

He plucked one from the rack, left, got into his car, and drove away. He'd been right. It was delicious.

As for Marylee's proposed book, Brixton hadn't been forthcoming with her. His friend, newspaperman Will Sayers, was in the process of writing a book proposal about illegal arms sales throughout the world and had mined Brixton's experiences following the café bombing.

* * *

His flight to Tampa was scheduled to depart Reagan National Airport at three. He'd run taking the trip past Mac Smith, who'd readily agreed. A call to Paul Wooster accomplished what Brixton had wanted, a commitment by the Tampa private eye to meet with him.

That their relationship was a quid pro quo was a given. Both wanted to dig into Congressman Hal Gannon's life and the role he might have played in Laura Bennett's death, but they came at it from different directions. Wooster was out to hurt Gannon to the extent that he became a *former* member of Congress. For Brixton, it was a matter of fairness. Gannon's affair with his intern and his hypocrisy should be made public. At the same time, if Gannon had had anything to do with Laura's disappearance and murder, Brixton was determined that he wouldn't get away with it, wouldn't walk free. Had he become obsessed with Gannon? Sure, he had.

He called Mac Smith from his car phone to check on new developments.

"I spoke with Superintendent Borgeldt a few minutes ago," Smith said. "Watson's lover, Roy Ulano, had an alibi for the time that Watson was killed."

"I'd like to talk to him," Brixton said. "Did Borgeldt mention whether Ulano was aware that Watson had told me about Gannon's affair with Laura Bennett?"

"He didn't say."

"Got a number for Ulano?"

"Hang on and I'll get it for you."

After his conversation with Mac, Brixton called the number for Roy Ulano, who answered on the first ring. Brixton explained who he was and asked if he could swing by, or treat the young man to a fast lunch.

"I've already been questioned by the police," Ulano said.

"I know that, but I'm interested in things they might

not have covered with you. I was with Cody the night he died."

"What?"

"We met at the Hotel Lombardy. He wanted to tell me about Congressman Gannon's relationship with the murdered intern, Laura Bennett."

"He told *you* about that?"

"Right, and I assume that he also told you. Like I said, I work for the family of Ms. Bennett, and I would really appreciate hearing what Cody told you."

"I told him to be careful," Ulano said.

"Careful about what?"

"About telling people what he thought of Congressman Gannon. I didn't want to see him lose his job. It was a good one."

"Cody told me that you also work on the Hill."

"That's true."

"You're right about Cody's job being a good one. I imagine that there are plenty of people who'd want it."

Brixton heard a concerted effort to stifle tears on the other end.

"You there, Mr. Ulano?"

"Yes. Sorry. The impact of Cody being killed is just now hitting home."

"I understand. Did Cody ever show you anything that might be considered evidence that the congressman and Ms. Bennett had an affair, a note from one of them, something Ms. Bennett might have said to you, a lovey-dovey card one sent the other?"

"No. I never even met Ms. Bennett."

"But Cody did confirm to you that an affair was going on."

"Many times. He hated the hypocrisy that Congressman Gannon represented."

"Well, thanks for your time, Mr. Ulano, and I'm sorry for your loss."

"It's true, isn't it? Cody is dead."

"I'm afraid so. I'll be in touch again."

Brixton hated flying, and he boarded the plane to Tampa with trepidation. Because he'd booked late, he was wedged in between a heavyset woman who dominated the armrest on her side, and an older man with either terminal sinus problems or one hell of a head cold. Brixton was glad that he'd brought along a dog-eared paperback into which he could bury his face during the flight. He declined to purchase a bag of mixed nuts for three dollars but did pay for two miniature martinis with his credit card, which came with a package of stale multicolored chips. Ah, for the good old *Coffee, Tea or Me?* days of air travel.

He'd reserved a rental car and a room at the Tampa Airport Marriott. His meeting with Wooster was scheduled for eight o'clock at a restaurant and sports bar called Lee Roy Selmon's, on Boy Scout Boulevard. Selmon, Brixton knew, had been the Tampa Bay Buccaneers' very first draft pick and had gone on to become an NFL Hall of Famer. Whether the food served at his namesake restaurant matched his exploits on the gridiron remained to be seen.

Before leaving the hotel, Brixton called Luke Bennett, which he'd promised Mac Smith he would do while in Tampa.

"I understand that Gannon has agreed to take a lie detector test," Bennett said, "but only one that he arranges."

"That's the latest word."

"He's afraid to take one administered by an impartial examiner."

"A fair assumption," said Brixton.

"I spoke with Mac earlier in the day," Bennett said.

"He told me you were coming to Tampa to meet with another private investigator."

Brixton confirmed it and explained Paul Wooster's connection with the campaign of the Republican Pete Solon.

"Do you think he can prove that Gannon and my daughter had an affair?"

"Proof is hard to come by, Luke, but Wooster has been doing some serious digging into Gannon's personal life. I just thought it might be useful to compare notes."

"I'd like to join you when you meet with him."

"I don't think that's a good idea," Brixton said, "but I'll be sure to let you know what comes out of it."

"What about the murder of Gannon's press secretary?" Bennett asked. "Has any link been established between that and Laura's death?"

"Not that I know of. Mac is keeping tabs on what's being done at the MPD."

"I saw a news report an hour ago that said that you spent time with Gannon's aide the night he was killed."

Brixton hadn't wanted to subject Bennett to yet another claim that his daughter had been intimate with Congressman Gannon. He could only put himself in Bennett's shoes; every claim had to hit the Tampa attorney hard in the gut. At the same time he knew that he hadn't the right to withhold information from a paying client.

"Gannon's press aide confirmed to me that Laura and Gannon had been in a relationship," Brixton said. "I also spoke with Watson's partner—Watson was gay—who said that Watson had told him on numerous occasions about the affair."

"Damn him!" Bennett growled.

"The problem is, Mr. Bennett, that unless Gannon admits it—and if he does he puts himself at the top of the suspect list in Laura's murder—we only have hearsay."

"What the hell are the police doing? Why aren't they putting pressure on Gannon to acknowledge the—acknowledge that he seduced Laura?"

Brixton wasn't sure that Laura's father's analysis of how the affair commenced was entirely accurate, but he wasn't about to debate it.

"The police are pulling out all the stops, Mr. Bennett. Mac is riding herd on them, and I have an in with their investigators. Have you been in touch with Gannon again?"

"No. What's the use? The man is a liar through and through. God, how could I have been so blind all these years?"

"It happens to the best of us," Brixton said. "What about Mrs. Gannon?"

"She's in Washington with him, isn't she? That's what I gather from the news."

"Tough position she's in."

"She must know the truth."

"But it looks like she's standing by her husband. I have to run to meet the investigator. I'll check in with you again before I leave Tampa."

Brixton plugged 4302 West Boy Scout Boulevard into his rented car's GPS and headed for the restaurant, following the woman's recorded directions coming through the speaker. It wasn't far south of the Tampa Airport, and he pulled into the parking lot twenty minutes early. The lot was full and so was the restaurant. Multiple TV sets hung up high carried myriad sporting events. The noise level was high, and Brixton questioned having this as a meeting place.

He found the only available seat at the bar and ordered a beer. He was watching a game when he felt a pat on his shoulder.

"Hello," he told Wooster.

"Come on," Wooster said, "let's grab a table."

Brixton paid his bar tab and they found a vacant table at the front of the place. Wooster ordered a gin and tonic from the attractive waitress. "Good flight?" he asked Brixton.

"If you like that sort of thing. I felt like I was part of a cattle drive."

"Not like it used to be, huh? I hate flying these days."

"I swore after nine/eleven that I'd never get on a plane again," Brixton said.

"But here you are in Tampa, Florida, home of the Buccaneers, former center of cigar making, and the domain of the esteemed Congressman Harold Gannon. What's new with the investigation? Or I should say investigations now that there's been another murder of someone close to him?"

"I got hold of Rachel Montgomery. She was interviewed by the police along with a college friend of Laura Bennett who'd been told about the affair."

"You told her that I was the source?"

"No, never did. She seems like a nice lady. Pretty, too."

"Anything new and startling come out of it?"

"No. How about you? Have you unearthed another Gannon paramour?"

"No, but frankly I'm not as interested in his extracurricular sexual life as I am now with whether he's a murderer."

"That'd be a first, wouldn't it?" Brixton said. "A member of Congress convicted of murder. Then again, a lot of what they've done has killed plenty of innocent people, sending off young people to get killed in stupid wars, cutting off food for the hungry, you name it. What are they, *legal* murders?"

They munched on sports bar staples, wings and sliders, while debating the state of politics.

"Do you know people here in Tampa who work on Gannon's campaign," Brixton asked.

"Sure. His campaign manager is Joe Selesky, a tough guy, won't take losing as an answer."

"You know him pretty good?"

Wooster laughed. "I've met him a few times, only I'm persona non grata with Selesky and his people. I work for the enemy."

"I thought while I was in Tampa I might try and meet him."

"Lotsa luck, Brixton. Word's around that you and the lawyer Luke Bennett hired are out to get Gannon. But hell, give him a call. You never know."

"We're not out to get anybody," Brixton said defensively. "Just doing our job."

The words sounded good but didn't accurately reflect the reality, at least from Brixton's perspective.

"What about his chief of staff up in D.C.?" Brixton asked.

"Roseann Simmons? I've met her. Tampa's a small town when it comes to politics. She's a cold cookie. She's from here, you know."

"So I've heard. Cody Watson, Gannon's press aide— *former* press aide—had a few things to say about her."

"Negative?"

"Not necessarily. He painted her as kind of a mystery woman, has lots of money, comes from a wealthy and controversial family here in Tampa."

"All true. Why do you ask?"

"I spent a little time with her and asked about Laura's life outside the office. She claimed to know nothing about it, which I don't buy."

"She's a zealot when it comes to protecting her boss."

"Gannon's office says that she's out of town, and when I spoke with her she'd just gotten back from Tampa. I wonder if she's here again."

"I wouldn't know," said Wooster. "Like I said, I'm not exactly welcome at Gannon headquarters."

"I'll swing by there tomorrow before heading back."

They split the check and shook hands outside the restaurant.

"You come up with anything, you fill me in. Right?" Wooster said.

"It works two ways."

"You got it, pal. We're a team."

Brixton wasn't sure that he wanted to be a teammate of Paul Wooster, but it had been copacetic so far. It wasn't so much that Wooster worked for a political organization that bothered Brixton. It was more that Wooster didn't share Brixton's fever to show Gannon up for what he was, and to solve the murder of a young woman who didn't deserve to die. For Wooster, it was a payday, which Brixton couldn't dismiss as an unreasonable motive. He'd taken on plenty of distasteful assignments himself in order to keep the lights on in his office and to avoid being evicted and consigned to the curb. He also couldn't help but wonder about the case that caused Wooster to lose his Florida PI license. Ronald Reagan's words came back to him as he drove in the direction of his hotel: "Trust but verify."

It was early when Brixton left the sports bar, and he was not ready for bed. Had he been in a more cosmopolitan city, he would have headed for a club that featured live jazz, like Blues Alley in D.C., the Blue Note in New York City, or Yoshi's in San Francisco, caught a set or two, and let the music buoy his spirits. But he doubted Tampa had any jazz clubs, or clubs featuring what they considered good old American jazz, more likely bluegrass and country and western and fiddlers' jam sessions. So he returned to the hotel, had a drink at the bar, ordered a second, which he carried to his room, and called Flo.

"How's it going, hon?" she asked.

"Okay." He filled her in on his meeting with Wooster,

which he realized hadn't accomplished anything except to keep the contact alive.

"I'm going to see if I can connect tomorrow with Gannon's campaign manager here in Tampa, a guy named Selesky."

"Why?"

"A shot in the dark, I guess. I figure it can't hurt as long as I'm here. What's new at the office?"

"Nothing much. Can I ask you something and not make you mad?"

"Me? Get mad?"

"Yes, you. Robert, do you think that you're too obsessed with Gannon and the intern's murder?"

It was more of a snort than a laugh from him. "Funny you should ask that," he said. "I've been thinking the same thing lately."

"Did you come to a conclusion?"

"No. All I know, Flo, is that I feel like I've been spinning my wheels, and I need to talk to someone, anyone, who can link Gannon to what happened to Laura Bennett. And now there's Cody Watson, his press aide or whatever he's called. Press secretary? Mouthpiece? Spin doctor? Yeah, I am obsessed, but you know that's in my genes. Remember the Watkins case back in Savannah? Talk about obsessed. I damn near got killed because of my obsession."

"I just hate to see you end up in a funk, that's all," she said.

"I'll do my best," he said. "I'll be back tomorrow night."

"I'll be waiting."

He took his drink to go out on the small balcony. The sound of jets taking off was much louder outside the room, and he could see the lights on the planes as they came in and took off. Every time he watched the planes, he tried to imagine who was on them, passengers going someplace on business or to visit family and friends, men, women, little kids driving everyone crazy, old people who needed a wheelchair to navigate the airport and Jetway. Him someday. He sipped his drink and again wished that he still smoked. He'd quit in Savannah shortly before leaving there, and the urge, while having lessened, had never truly disappeared.

He recognized that he was slipping into depression. Being depressed wasn't anything new to Brixton. People subjected to his moods either chalked his behavior up to being a skeptic, a cynic, or someone who simply had become curmudgeonly before his time. The truth was that depression was never far from him, and he often had to give himself a pep talk to shift moods.

It didn't take much to depress Robert Brixton.

A story about the mistreatment of four-legged animals would do it.

The realization that an elected member of Congress put his or her own self-interests before the good of the nation was guaranteed to send him into a funk, usually short-lived because he knew that he, or anyone else, couldn't and wouldn't change it.

Becoming involved in the Laura Bennett case through Mac Smith hadn't triggered depression in Brixton. He liked being involved, and the case's momentum—her disappearance, finding her body in the Congressional Cemetery, and now the murder of Cody Watson—had focused his mind on doing what he did best, investigate.

But being alone on the balcony of the Marriott in Tampa, Florida, his morose set of genes kicked in. That horrible moment in the café when a terrorist suicide bomber had taken his daughter's life and the lives of other innocents flooded him and he welled up. His daughter's face occupied his vision, laughing, making fun of his quirks, basking in the joyous anticipation of her life and where it would lead.

But then he saw Laura Bennett on his imaginary screen, also young, vivacious, a thousand-watt smile, the future hers to grasp, and anger began to displace the depression. He'd risked his own life to bring to justice those who had taken Janet from him, and now he was determined to do the same for the young woman he'd never met but whose photos told him who she was and why her life was precious.

He swallowed the remains of his drink, went back into the room, stripped naked, and climbed beneath the sheets.

Snap out of it, Brixton, he told himself before sleep came. *You've got work to do.*

31

Congressman Harold Gannon's campaign headquarters was in a storefront on busy North Tampa Street, flanked by a bookstore and a luncheonette. Brixton stood in front and took in the campaign posters, huge blow-ups of Gannon (some with his wife and kids), and piles of literature in the window. He looked beyond the displays and saw a dozen desks manned by fresh-faced young men and women who were either on the phone or stuffing envelopes.

He walked in and was immediately greeted by a middle-aged man dressed in a brightly colored Hawaiian shirt, tan slacks, and sandals. He wore a large VOTE FOR GANNON button on his chest.

"Hello there," he said through a large smile. "Welcome to Gannon Land."

"Gannon Land?" Brixton repeated.

The man laughed. "That's what we call it around here. Has a nice ring to it, don't you think?"

"I suppose so."

"Are you a Gannon supporter, or on the fence? If you're on the fence, we have some material that I think you'll find very interesting. Congressman Gannon is one of those rare politicians who truly reaches across the aisle in the interest of getting things done for the American people. With all the lies and double-dealing in Washington, having someone of Hal Gannon's character and devotion to rock-ribbed American virtues and beliefs is something we can't afford to lose. Come with me. I have some reading material and—"

"Before we do that," Brixton said, "I was wondering if Mr. Selesky is in."

"Joe? Do you have an appointment?"

"No, but I'm sure he'll want to speak with me."

"He's up to his neck these days, as you can imagine. Congressman Gannon's opponents will stoop to anything to deny him another term. The lies they tell are outrageous."

The man looked beyond Brixton, and his eyes indicated that he'd seen something of interest. Brixton turned and saw a stocky, bald, red-faced man with a small mustache emerge from an office. He looked all business with his tie lowered and collar unbuttoned, the sleeves of his white shirt rolled up to reveal thick forearms.

"That's Joe," the man told Brixton.

"Thanks."

"Mr. Selesky," Brixton said as he approached.

Selesky stopped and stared at him.

"Robert Brixton," Brixton said, extending his hand.

"Yeah, hello," Selesky said, accepting the gesture. "You're—?"

"I work for the Bennett family. You know, their daughter Laura was murdered and—"

"Yeah, yeah, I know who you are. The private investigator."

"One and the same," Brixton said pleasantly.

Selesky looked around the large central room as though to see whether anyone else was interested in his exchange with Brixton. No one seemed to be except for the man who'd greeted Brixton when he entered.

"What can I do for you?" Selesky asked.

"A few minutes of your time," said Brixton.

"This is a busy day," Selesky said. "I'm up to my eyeballs with work and—"

"I think you ought to talk to me," Brixton said. "Since you know who I am, you also know that I've been working as a PI for the Bennett family to prove that the congressman had an inappropriate relationship with his intern, Ms. Bennett."

"Jesus," Selesky muttered.

"I don't think he'd be much help here," Brixton said. "Let's go where we can have a private chat. I promise not to take too much time from your busy schedule."

"Come in my office," Selesky said grumpily, and led Brixton through the door.

The campaign manager's office defined cluttered. Campaign materials were everywhere, multiple boxes of campaign buttons with Gannon's smiling face on them, thin booklets extolling the congressman's legislative achievements, posters and flyers, everything in red, white, and blue, plenty of stars and stripes, boxes of small American flags piled high on the desk.

"Looks like the campaign is in full gear," Brixton commented.

"What do you want?" Selesky asked, leaning against a wall, arms folded across his barrel chest.

Until that point Brixton hadn't decided what he would say or ask for once he was in Selesky's company. "What do I want?" he said to buy think time. "What I want, Mr. Selesky, is to know what role Congressman Gannon's affair with his intern, Laura Bennett, played in her disappearance and murder."

"In the first place," Selesky said, "Congressman Gannon did not have an affair with Ms. Bennett. Once you get that through your skull, the rest of your comment is just plain stupid."

"You know about Gannon's press aide being murdered."

"Of course."

"I was with him the night someone bashed his head in. He told me about the affair. Laura Bennett told her roommate about it, and did the same with her aunt. A college friend was also taken into her confidence."

"All part of the Washington rumor mill, generated by Congressman Gannon's political enemies." Selesky said it firmly, no room for debate.

"You aren't denying that the congressman has had a series of extramarital affairs, are you?"

"You bet I am. If you came here to get my response to these scurrilous charges by an emotionally fragile young woman, you've gotten what you wanted. Anything else? I have other more realistic things to do today."

"What about the other women?"

"As far as I know—and I follow the news carefully—there's never been a woman to come out publicly and claim to have had an affair with Congressman Gannon."

"I'm working on it, Mr. Selesky."

"Why? What the hell are you getting out of it except money? What kind of an American are you? This nation needs the Hal Gannons of the world. He's a stand-up guy in a Congress filled with namby-pambies, weak sisters who don't have a bone of conviction in their bodies. Hal Gannon also happens to be a human being."

"What do you mean by that? That it's only human for him to cheat on his wife?"

"What I mean is that—"

"Not that I disagree, Mr. Selesky. Sure, elected officials are human beings, and some cheat on their spouses. But they don't prey on twenty-two-year-old interns. What did Ms. Bennett do, threaten to expose your guy? Show him to the world and the voters for what he really is?"

"Your time is up, Mr. Brixton."

"Gannon's time is up, too, if I have anything to say about it. Take this to the bank, Mr. Selesky. The truth about Congressman Harold Gannon will come out, and I'll raise a glass to having made sure that it does."

Selesky's already reddened face turned crimson. His mouth was clamped tight, and there was fire in his eyes. Brixton wondered whether he was about to be attacked by the campaign manager and braced himself. But Selesky, as much as he would have liked to scramble Brixton's brain, held himself in check. "Get out and take your cockeyed notions with you."

"Thanks for your time," Brixton said, giving him what passed for a salute. "And good luck in your next job after Gannon leaves D.C. with his tail between his legs."

Brixton walked out of the office leaving Selesky steaming. He stood in the midst of the central office area where volunteers for Gannon's reelection continued to answer phones and lick envelopes. He was tempted to climb up on a desk and shout that they'd been hoodwinked, that they were investing their time and energy—and probably hard-earned money—in a fraud.

He didn't, of course. The man who'd greeted him intercepted him on the way to the front door and said, "Ready to make a donation to ensuring that the nation has Congressman Gannon for another two years?"

Brixton reached into his pocket and handed the man a five-dollar bill. "Buy yourself a beer to drown your sorrows when Gannon is kicked out of Congress," he said.

He left the man open-mouthed as he went through the door, stood on the sidewalk, and took a series of deep breaths. He wished that Selesky had taken a swing at him. He would have fought back and discharged the tension that had built up during their exchange.

A few more breaths helped him calm down and he started to walk to his rental car. He came around to the driver's side and unlocked the door. As he did, a taxi pulled up a few car lengths behind. Brixton turned at the sound of the door being opened and closed. It was Roseann Simmons, Gannon's chief of staff. He was poised to say something, but she quickly walked from the cab and entered Gannon headquarters.

He decided to linger awhile. Across the street was a bar and restaurant. He checked his watch. Eleven o'clock. Too early for the bar to open? He crossed against the traffic and opened the door. It was empty except for staff getting ready for the lunch crowd. Brixton asked the bartender whether he was serving yet. "Sure," the young man replied.

Brixton took a seat at the bar that afforded him a view of the entrance to Gannon headquarters and slowly sipped a Bloody Mary. He didn't have a plan. He simply wanted to see where Roseann went next. Then, ten minutes later, he did a double take as another cab pulled up and Paul Wooster got out and entered Gannon's campaign headquarters. "What the hell?" Brixton muttered. Wooster had told him that he wasn't welcome at Gannon headquarters, but here he was with Roseann Simmons going in, undoubtedly to meet with Gannon's manager, Selesky.

Brixton's stomach sank. He'd been snookered by Wooster.

It was another ten minutes before Simmons and Wooster emerged from the headquarters and waved down a passing taxi into which they climbed and sped away.

Brixton placed a cell call to his airline to see whether they had an earlier flight back to Washington than he was scheduled for. They did, and for an additional fee he made the change in booking. The airlines seemed to have a fee for everything—he'd read in that day's paper that an airline in Europe was considering charging to use the lavatories, so much per minute of use—and he silently cursed as he paid his tab and left.

When he crossed the street and was about to enter his rented car, he had a vague, uncomfortable feeling that someone was interested in him. He looked left and right but saw nothing; no one was looking his way. He got in, strapped himself in, started the engine, and navigated the traffic flow.

As he did, a man who'd been sitting in a booth at the luncheonette next to Gannon headquarters paid his bill and stepped outside. He'd followed Brixton from his hotel to the storefront and had waited for him to emerge. While Brixton sat in the bar watching the campaign headquarters, the man had been watching him. He hailed a taxi and told the driver, "Please follow that car," adding a touch of politeness to the standard grade-B movie line.

When Brixton returned his car to the rental lot and boarded the shuttle bus to his terminal, the man placed a call on his cell phone: "He's getting on a plane. I assume he's coming back to Washington."

To the driver he said, "Thank you, sir. Please take me back to where you picked me up."

32

While Brixton was bouncing around Tampa in search of something tangible to pin on Gannon, Mac and Annabel Smith had been busy in Washington.

Annabel was knee-deep in preparing a show at her gallery due to open in two weeks. She'd brought in a number of pre-Columbian pieces on consignment and was hopeful that their sale would generate enough income to expand the gallery's space. She was in her small office at the rear of the gallery writing descriptions of one of the pieces to be offered during the show when the phone rang. She'd been expecting a call from Mac and said as she picked up, "Hi. How's it going?"

"Mrs. Smith?" the male voice said.

"Yes."

"Lay off Congressman Gannon."

"What?"

"You heard me. Tell your husband to back off on Congressman Gannon."

"Who is this?"

"Just do the smart thing, that's all. You've been warned."

The line went dead.

Annabel stared at the phone before replacing it in its cradle. She called Mac at his office and told him of the message.

"No idea who it was?" he said.

"No. I didn't recognize the voice."

"Was he specific in his threat?"

"No. He just told me to tell you to lay off Gannon. It was chilling."

"Of course it was. I'll call Zeke Borgeldt and report it. Maybe you should close up and come here."

"Oh, no, I don't think that's necessary, Mac. I'll be fine."

"Keep the door locked."

"If I do that, I might as well close the gallery. I just wanted you to know."

"I'll call Zeke now," he said. "Stay in touch."

Smith had been informed by Gannon's attorney, Richard Nichols, that his client would be taking the lie detector test administered by a former FBI expert now in private practice. Smith knew that asking to be present during the test was a long shot but called Nichols anyway to make the request.

"That's out of the question," Nichols said.

"I can't imagine why," Smith said. "I simply want to observe. Having a representative of the Bennett family would go a long way to deflecting any charges that the test was, in some way, slanted in your client's direction."

"You aren't suggesting that I would be a party to that, are you?" Nichols asked, his tone pleasant.

"Of course not," Mac responded, "but you know how people put a spin on things. If Gannon passes the test, which I'm sure you're counting on, his enemies, including the man running for his seat in Congress, will accuse the tester of being biased. I'm not saying that he is, or that you would be putting pressure on him. But why not head off that sort of interpretation before it starts?

"I understand where you're coming from, Mac, but I've assured Congressman Gannon that only he, the tester, and I will be present. He isn't crazy about taking the test in the first instance. It took some persuasion on my part to convince him to do it."

Gannon's reluctance to be tested for his veracity said to Mac that he was afraid of flunking. So much depended upon the tester's questions and how they were worded. Would Gannon be questioned only about Laura's murder? Would the most recent murder of his press aide be part of the questioning? What about his relationship with Laura Bennett? Would the tester probe the possibility that Gannon and his intern had been intimate? Submitting to a lie detector test without any transparency into the test itself proved nothing. Of course, Mac was well aware that the result of any lie detector test was inadmissible in court. But this test wasn't for the purpose of a court proceeding. If the script was followed, Gannon would pass the test and that result, however skewed, would be the basis for a PR blitz heralding his innocence of anything having to do with either murder, and even of having been involved in an illicit affair with his twenty-two-year-old intern.

The conversation with Nichols concluded, Mac leaned back in his tan leather office chair, closed his eyes, and sighed.

Having become involved with the Laura Bennett case and its ramifications had cut deeply into his professional time. He'd had to decline taking on other clients because of it, and as he sat there he wondered whether anything concrete, anything worthwhile would come of it.

He'd been around D.C. long enough to know that rumors about an elected official's sex life often didn't punish that politician at the polls. The voting public had a short attention span and an even shorter memory. With enough money to mount a TV onslaught—and there was always plenty of that from lobbyists with deep pockets and agendas of their own—a sitting congressman or senator whose reputation had been sullied could overcome negative rumors and effectively smear the opposition. In Gannon's case, there hadn't been one shred of tangible evidence to prove that the rumors were true. What Laura Bennett told her roommate and her college chum was pure hearsay. Rachel Montgomery's sworn statement to the police would probably be viewed as the bitchy complaint of the proverbial woman scorned. How dare she libel a sitting U.S. congressman, a man with a fine family and a solid voting record in the House of Representatives? Everyone knew that politics was a dirty, cutthroat business. Had she been paid by Gannon's opposition to dirty his reputation? There was his beautiful wife standing proudly at his side.

What more did a voter need to know?

Of course, Gannon's extracurricular sex life would be rendered the least of his problems if a link could be made between him and the murders of Laura Bennett and his press aide, Cody Watson. But was that likely? As far as Smith knew, there wasn't an iota of evidence to make that connection. Brixton's belief that the congressman was involved in some way with Laura's murder was just that, his personal belief, nothing more. Try making a case in court based upon *that*.

Smith got up and paced the office. He had a prospective client coming in and knew that he'd better prepare for that meeting. He'd returned to his desk when Flo Combes, Brixton's "friend" and receptionist—Brixton would rail at her being labeled his girlfriend—knocked and entered.

"What's up, Flo?" Smith asked.

"I just got a phone call from a woman who wanted to speak with Robert."

Mac cocked his head. "And?"

"She says she knows something about Laura Bennett's murder."

Mac sat up straight. "Who is she?"

"She wouldn't tell me, Mac. She says that she'll only talk to Robert."

"When is he due back?"

"Soon. He called to tell me that he's taking an earlier flight. He should be landing within the hour."

"How did you leave it with this woman?"

"I asked how Robert could reach her when he returns, but she wouldn't give me a number, said she'll call again."

"Then we'll just have to see if she does."

"Do you think—?"

"That it might be another Gannon sweetie?" Mac laughed. "If it is, he could hold a hell of a reunion. I'll be with a prospective client for a while." He checked his watch. "He should be here momentarily. Let me know when Robert arrives."

The lawsuit the client wanted Mac to bring on his behalf struck the attorney as ill-advised and a loser as well. Smith was up front with the client and told him he'd have to find another attorney, which seemed to anger the would-be client. Based upon their conversation, Mac was glad that the suit was without merit. He'd taken an almost immediate dislike to the man and was happy to see him leave.

Annabel's call had concerned him, and he was considering calling her back and insisting she leave the gallery when Brixton walked in.

"Welcome back," Mac said. "Successful trip?"

"It turned out to be at the last minute. I met with Wooster, the PI, and we got along great. But then I stopped in to talk with Gannon's campaign manager, a guy named Selesky, who was not happy to see me, damn near threw me out bodily. So I go across the street for a Bloody Mary and to see who comes and goes at the headquarters. Who do I see? Gannon's chief of staff, the lovely Roseann Simmons. That's okay. No reason for her not to be there. But then who else shows up? Paul Wooster himself, and he goes inside. A few minutes later, Simmons and Wooster come out and get in a cab together."

"I thought Wooster worked for Gannon's opponent, Pete Solon."

"So did I. But he's obviously a lot cozier with the Gannon people than he let on to me."

"And told me," Mac added.

"The question is, what's he up to? I feel like I've been taken, Mac, and I don't like being taken."

"It sounds to me like he's working you for dirt on Gannon, which he can then report back to Gannon's own people, and maybe to Solon, too."

"Playing both sides," Brixton muttered. "I'm glad he lost his license."

"Better keep a closed mouth with him from now on."

"Or *hit* him in the mouth. What's new here?"

"Nothing, aside from Gannon taking his lie detector test."

Flo popped in. "That woman's on the phone," she said.

"What woman?" Brixton asked.

"She wants to talk to you. She says she knows something about Laura Bennett's murder."

Brixton took the call in his office. "Robert Brixton here."

"Mr. Brixton, my name is Peggy Talbot."

"Yes?"

"I'm—I was an airline flight attendant."

Could this be the flight attendant Gannon was rumored to have had an affair with? Brixton wondered.

"I'm calling about the intern who was killed."

"Laura Bennett?"

"Yes."

"What do you know about her?"

Smith had followed Brixton to his office, and Brixton motioned for him to pick up the extension on Flo's desk.

"I saw her picture in the paper and knew she was the same one who threatened Hal—Congressman Gannon."

"Threatened him? How?"

"I was—oh, I might as well be straightforward. I'd been with Hal in the apartment in the afternoon. I'd worked a flight to Washington that he was on and we—well, we were intimate. It wasn't the first time we were together. We'd been seeing each other on and off. I live in Dallas and was based there. We met on a flight and—"

"You say you no longer work as a stewardess—as a flight attendant."

"I worked my final flight four days ago."

"Go on."

"As I was saying, I was with Hal one afternoon when someone rang his buzzer. He ignored it, but this person kept buzzing, buzzing, buzzing, and shouting curses into the intercom. She was really out of her mind, had gone ballistic."

"What did the congressman do?"

"He tried to talk sense to her, but she was beyond being reasoned with. I knew that I'd better leave, and I did. When I got off the elevator on the ground floor, this young woman was there. She was crying, yelling. She followed me out of the building and kept screaming at me, wanted to know who I was. I got in a taxi and left."

"I assume that this young woman was Laura Bennett, the murdered intern," Brixton said.

"Yes. When I saw her picture in the paper—that's how I learned about you—I recognized her immediately. What a horrible way to die, and so young. She was really pretty."

Brixton checked Mac Smith before he continued. "It's a good thing that you called," he said, "but I have to ask why. You told my receptionist that you knew something about Ms. Bennett's murder."

"Oh, I'm sorry," she said. "I don't know anything about how she died, nothing like that, but I thought that I had a duty to call and tell someone what I knew about her and Congressman Gannon. I don't think I could live with myself if I didn't."

"I admire you for making the call, Ms. Talbot. Tell me about Congressman Gannon. How did he react when Ms. Bennett was acting irrationally in the lobby, pushing the buzzer and cursing, that sort of thing?"

"He was furious, Mr. Brixton. He was red in the face and swearing at the woman."

"And you say she threatened him?"

"Yes. I mean, not physically. She didn't say she'd kill him or anything but—"

"Was he mad enough to want to physically harm her?"

"You mean—?"

"Yeah, that's what I mean. Was he mad enough to kill?"

"Oh, my God, I know what you're saying. No, I could never say that about Hal. Kill her? That can't be."

"Look, Ms. Talbot, would you be willing to give a statement to the police?"

"About—?"

"About what you've told me. Do you still see the congressman, I mean personally?"

"Like sleep together? No. I know that you're probably thinking poorly of me, seeing a married man. I knew he was married, but his marriage was about to end and—"

"He told you that."

"Yes. He lied to me."

"Happens every day, Ms. Talbot. About giving a statement . . ."

"Yes, I would."

"You're in Dallas?"

"Yes. I live with my fiancé."

"He knows about you and the congressman?"

It was her first laugh since coming on the phone. "Of course. We have an open relationship."

Brixton shook his head at Smith, who smiled and shrugged.

They concluded the call with Talbot agreeing to give a statement to a Washington detective over the phone. It ended with Brixton asking, "How come you quit flying?"

"Have you flown lately, Mr. Brixton?"

"Today, as a matter of fact."

"Then you know it's no fun. I got tired of passengers being angry and taking it out on me. We're on the plane to ensure safety, not to take abuse."

"So I've heard. Thanks for calling, Ms. Talbot. I'll put my associate, Ms. Combes, on, and she'll get contact information for you. You have a good day."

Brixton followed Mac into the attorney's office.

"Annabel called earlier," Smith said, and told Brixton about the threatening call that she'd received.

"Sounds like somebody in Gannon's camp is getting serious," Brixton commented.

"And I don't like it," said Mac. "Gannon's walking a tightrope. The stakes for him are big. He's proved himself to be a serial liar as well as a serial adulterer. There's no telling what lengths someone like him, with so much to lose, will go to."

"We have this Ms. Talbot who just called," Brixton said. "It's the first example of a direct confrontation between Gannon and Laura Bennett, and an angry one, at that. Seems to me that once she gives her statement, it should be enough for Borgeldt to haul him in for another round of questioning."

"I'll suggest that to Zeke."

Brixton handled some paperwork while Mac called the superintendent of detectives about the call from the former flight attendant. He came into Brixton's office and said, "Got some free time?"

"Sure."

"Borgeldt wants to see us. He's available now."

"Let's go," said Brixton.

On their way to police headquarters on Indiana Avenue, Brixton asked, "You and Annabel been on a plane lately?"

"No, but we're due to take a vacation once this Gannon business is resolved. Why do you ask?"

"I see why this Ms. Talbot quit. The stewardesses working the plane I was on—I still call them stewardesses—were a grumpy bunch, and who can blame them? Every passenger was grumpy, too. The seats are designed for dwarfs, they nickel-and-dime you for everything, and even the expensive bags of peanuts are stale."

Smith laughed. "In other words you had a wonderful flight."

Brixton laughed, too. "Yeah, it was the highlight of my life. Let's hope Zeke decides to bring Gannon in for more questioning. *That* would really be a highlight."

33

Congressman Harold Gannon arrived at the office of the polygraph examiner with mixed emotions.

On the one hand, he viewed the test as confirmation that he was considered a suspect in the murders of Laura Bennett and Cody Watson, and he initially refused to participate. But he eventually acquiesced to his attorney's insistence that taking and passing the test would put to rest any speculation about his involvement in the killings, at least in the general public's mind.

Nichols prudently pointed out to his client that passing the test would not prove to the authorities that he was innocent of any wrongdoing. The use of polygraph test results in courts is banned in many states; in those states in which it is admissible, juries were told that its results weren't always accurate. It was estimated that as few as sixty percent of polygraph tests were valid. But taking the test was a good PR move that could go a long way toward tamping down the scuttlebutt that had arisen about Gannon's possible connection to the disappearance and murder of Laura Bennett and the more recent slaying of Cody Watson.

The test would take upward of four hours, including the preliminary questioning by the polygrapher, who would ascertain whether Gannon had any physical or psychological problems that would preclude his participating. He would also ask the subject questions about the crime in question to establish a baseline of answers before hooking him up to the polygraph machine. He would then provide the questions that would be asked during the test so that the subject wouldn't be blindsided, which could taint the result. And then Gannon would be attached to the machine's leads, and changes to his cardiovascular activity, respiratory activity, and galvanic skin reflexes (sweat) would be recorded on the moving chart, the squiggly lines to be interpreted by the examiner. There were only three possible results: truthful, lying, or inconclusive.

Gannon's attorney had provided the examiner with most of the questions to be asked. Standard procedure prohibited questioning about more than one crime at a time, so the session was limited to Laura Bennett's disappearance and murder. Nothing else was to be probed, including—and especially—rumors of Gannon's affair with Laura, or with other women outside his marriage.

Charlene Gannon had returned to Tampa the night before the test, which pleased her husband. Their time together in D.C. had been tense, a gross understatement, and he was nervous enough about the test without her probing the rumors of his infidelity. He'd managed to coax her into accompanying him on various public appearances, but she soon tired of putting on a false happy face and refused to continue. Their final night together had turned nasty, and he'd slept on the couch. A car service picked her up the following morning and took her to Reagan National Airport for her flight home.

As he walked her to the limo, he said, "Joe has some events lined up in Tampa that he wants you to attend on my behalf."

"Tell your Mr. Selesky to shove it," she snapped.

"We can get through this, Charlene," he said. "It's worth doing."

She glared at him. "I don't intend to be made a fool of, Hal. You say that none of what's being said about you is true. Well, when you prove it, then we can talk. In the meantime, the kids need me and that's where my efforts will be directed, them and my art. Good luck with the polygraph."

She got in the vehicle, slammed the door, and didn't look back as the driver pulled away.

At the end of the polygraph, the examiner told Nichols and Gannon that he would have a final evaluation of the answers within the hour. But he added, "Based upon my preliminary reading, I'd say that the congressman was being truthful."

Four hours later, Roseann Simmons conducted a hastily convened press conference.

"Under ordinary circumstances," she said from a makeshift dais, "Cody Watson would have stood here. But these are not ordinary circumstances. As you all know, Cody was the victim of a senseless, brutal attack, as was Laura Bennett. Because both victims were connected with Congressman Gannon's congressional office, a spate of vicious rumors have circulated regarding the congressman and his relationship with these individuals. While we mourn the deaths of two exemplary young people, we also must make sure that the truly guilty party or parties be brought to justice, and that scurrilous charges leveled in the heat of a political battle be exposed for what they are—lies, blatant lies. I'm here today to announce that Congressman Gannon has taken a polygraph test and the results are rock-solid. It has exonerated Congressman Gannon from every aspect of these tragic events. With this phase of the investigation completed, he is now free to do what the people of Tampa, Florida, have sent him here to do, legislate for the good of the American people. I'll take a few questions."

Simmons deflected any queries about the details of the polygraph except to name the examiner and to laud his credentials as a retired FBI special agent. "The examiner has said without a shadow of a doubt that Congressman Gannon told the truth when answering every question he'd posed. Those who have done everything possible to sully Congressman Gannon's good name had better look for someone else to attack."

Smith and Brixton's visit to Superintendent of Detectives Zeke Borgeldt, prompted by the call from former flight attendant Peggy Talbot, resulted in more than they'd expected.

After Brixton had recounted for the superintendent what Ms. Talbot had said, Borgeldt assigned a detective to contact her and arrange for a Dallas detective to take her statement. "Better it be done in person," he said, to which Mac agreed.

"Seems to me," Brixton said, "that this is the first evidence of a direct confrontation between Gannon and Ms. Bennett."

"Still doesn't prove anything," Borgeldt said, "but I agree with you. "It justifies our requesting another interview with the congressman."

"Requesting an interview?" Brixton said. "Since when is a prime suspect in a murder case *requested* to give an interview?"

"Back off, Brixton," Borgeldt said. "Gannon is still an elected member of Congress."

"So what?" said Brixton. "That doesn't give him immunity from banging interns and killing them to keep their mouths shut."

Borgeldt looked to Mac Smith. "Maybe you ought to inform your compatriot, Mac, about being innocent until *proved* guilty."

"Robert knows that, Zeke. But it does seem that Gannon has to be at the top of your list of possible suspects. He's lied repeatedly about not having had an affair with Laura Bennett, and now we know that they had a heated exchange."

"Based upon what some airline flight attendant says."

"And Laura Bennett's college friend, and her roommate here in D.C., and what she told her aunt," Brixton said. "Oh, and there's Rachel Montgomery, who knew about Gannon having had an affair with his intern. Yeah, yeah, I know that none of what they say nails Gannon as having killed Laura Bennett, but he sure as hell had one great big motive to see that she never lived to talk about the fling they had. Screwing a twenty-two-year-old intern isn't a vote getter."

Borgeldt shifted conversational gears. "We brought in the Russian kid we questioned earlier about the two female victims in Rock Creek Park," he said. "He's still high on our list with those murders, but he had nothing to do with Ms. Bennett's death. Our initial analysis was that she was killed somewhere else and taken to that vault in the Congressional Cemetery. We've changed our mind. We're now going on the theory that she was killed there, not in the vault, but in its vicinity, and placed inside it."

"Which probably means that she agreed to meet someone there," Smith said.

"Like what, a stranger?" Brixton said.

"Why would she agree to meet a stranger?" Borgeldt said.

"The Congressional Cemetery," Brixton said, "close to the Capitol Building, home of the House of Representatives, which happens to be where Congressman Gannon plies his dubious trade."

Borgeldt checked the clock on the wall. "I have to run," he said.

"We appreciate the time," Smith said.

"What are those pictures?" Brixton asked, pointing to a pile of eight-by-ten color photographs on Borgeldt's desk. He'd been going through them when Mac and Brixton arrived.

"Photos taken off Ms. Bennett's cell phone camera," Borgeldt explained.

"Mind if I take a look?" Brixton asked.

"I suppose it's all right."

"I'll take responsibility for them," Smith said.

"Give them to Officer Sims outside."

"Shall do," Smith said.

Borgeldt left the office, and Brixton and Mac slowly perused the photos. Some were selfies, pictures taken of herself by Laura while holding the phone at arm's length and catching herself making funny faces.

"She sure was pretty," Brixton commented.

"Very," Mac agreed.

There was a picture of Laura, Roseann Simmons, Cody Watson, and other members of Gannon's staff posing in front of the Capitol Building. Laura had taken a few shots of scenes around Washington, and she'd snapped off a picture of two squirrels wrestling while she was on a hike. But the majority of the photos appeared to have been taken in bars and restaurants where Laura had gathered with friends. Everyone in the pictures seemed in a festive mood, broad smiles everywhere, tankards of beer raised, couples hugging. There was one shot of Laura with a young man with a heavy five o'clock shadow who had his arm around her. Another young man had donned a funny hat and mugged for the camera.

"Makes you realize how precious life is," Mac muttered as he tossed the last of the photos on the desk. "One minute you're having a party with friends, the next you're dead in a cold, damp vault in a famous cemetery."

Brixton thought of his daughter Janet and pressed his lips together to keep them from trembling. "Let's go," he said.

"I have to give these photos to the officer outside," Mac said as he scooped them up. He and Brixton were about to leave when Brixton said, "Mind if I take another fast look at those?"

"Go ahead," Smith said.

Brixton discarded the ones that hadn't been taken in bars and restaurants and focused on the rest, bringing them closer to his face and squinting.

"Damn," he said into the air.

"What?" Smith asked.

"See if they have a magnifying glass," Brixton said.

Smith went to the bullpen outside Borgeldt's office and asked, and was immediately handed one, which he brought back to Brixton. Brixton used it to enhance the image of the photograph that had captured his attention.

"Look," Brixton said, handing the glass to Mac, who also used it examine the picture.

"What?" Smith asked.

"That man at the bar behind Laura Bennett and her friends."

Mac looked again. "Yes, I see him. What about him?"

"I've seen him before," Brixton said.

"Where?"

"At the bar in the Hotel Lombardy, the night I met with Cody Watson. He walked in right after Watson."

Smith handed the glass back to Brixton.

"How about that?" Brixton said. "He shows up where Laura Bennett is enjoying a night out. He shows up the night Cody Watson had a drink with me and tells me about Gannon's affair with Laura. Laura Bennett is dead, murdered. Cody Watson is also dead, murdered. And this guy has been hanging around both of them."

Smith didn't need Brixton's analysis of the situation. He'd thought the same thing.

"Know who he is?" Smith asked.

"No, but I think we'd better find out."

"Is there any way to identify the bar the picture was taken in?" Smith asked.

"We can go back and ask some of the people we know palled around with Laura," Brixton said. "There's that guy, Caruso, who dated her and blew me off when I called. The police questioned him. Let's see what they have on him. Maybe he can identify the joint."

"What about when he came into the bar at the Lombardy?" Smith said. "Did he pay with a credit card?"

"Easy enough to check," said Brixton.

"Could be just a coincidence," Smith said.

"Maybe, but I doubt it," Brixton said, grabbing the photo. "Let's see if Zeke is still in the building."

They found Borgeldt, who'd been meeting with two members of the Laura Bennett case team. Smith explained what Brixton had seen in the photograph.

"I thought that one of the guys in the picture could tell us what bar it was," Brixton said.

"Morey's working the case," Borgeldt said, nodding toward the detective who'd been in the meeting. Brixton handed him the photo.

"That's Caruso," Morey said without hesitation.

"The guy I talked to on the phone," Brixton said.

"I interviewed him," Morey said. "He went out with the victim a few times, said she told him that she was seeing somebody else and wouldn't go to bed with him."

"Must have made him mad," Brixton said.

"He didn't seem that way," Morey said.

"He can tell us what bar this photo was taken in," Smith said.

"Let's ask him," Brixton said, handing the picture to Borgeldt. "Can I get a copy of this?"

Ten minutes later, Brixton and Smith thanked the superintendent, left headquarters, and drove back to the office, where Brixton placed a call to Caruso.

"We talked before," Brixton told the Senate staffer, "about Laura Bennett's disappearance and murder. Remember?"

"Sure, I remember. What do you want? I already talked to the police."

"I know that. I have a photograph that was taken with you and Laura at some local bar. I need to know what bar it was."

Caruso snorted. "We went to a couple of bars."

"Yeah, I'm sure you did, but maybe something in the picture would help you identify where it was taken. I'll meet you anywhere you say."

"Now? I'm real busy now."

"Is that so? Well, Mr. Caruso, I think the police will want to talk to you again, probably more than once, when I tell them how uncooperative you are. I'm working closely with the police on this case, and they gave me the photo. If you'd prefer, I can have them bring you in to ask about it. By the way, Mr. Caruso, you're still a suspect."

"I don't believe I'm hearing this," Caruso said.

"Believe it, Mr. Caruso. This is not a game. Where can we meet in a half hour?"

There was an angry silence on Caruso's end, and Brixton heard him mumble curses under his breath. Finally, he said, "All right. How about A BAR on Pennsylvania? You know it?"

"I'll find it. A half hour. Don't be late, Mr. Caruso. I really get upset with people who are late."

After telling Smith where he was going, Brixton looked up the address for A BAR and headed for it. His evaluation of Caruso as an arrogant guy after their first phone conversation hadn't changed, and he would have enjoyed seeing the police put pressure on him and take him down a peg. But that wasn't at the top of his priority list. If Caruso recognized the bar in which the photo was taken, it might help track down the identity of the man with the ponytail.

Brixton knew the minute he stepped inside A BAR that it wasn't his kind of watering hole. It was sleek and modern, and featured wine and small plates, tapas as they were called in Spanish restaurants. He took a stool at the bar and ordered red wine: when in Rome. A few minutes later Caruso arrived and sat next to him.

Brixton wasted no time with greetings and small talk. He laid the photograph on the bar and said, "Recognize the place?"

Caruso picked it up and scrutinized it.

"Yes," Caruso said. "Laura and I went there a few times. She liked it."

"I'm listening."

"The Capitol Lounge on Capitol Hill."

"Sure?"

"Yeah, I'm sure."

"Okay," Brixton said. "What night was it taken?"

"What night? How the hell would I know? Like I said, we went there a few times."

"Take another look," Brixton said. "Maybe this was a

special night, a party or something, some kind of celebration."

Caruso didn't bother taking another look. "No," he
said, "there was nothing special. We were just having fun."

"Did Ms. Bennett drink a lot?" Brixton asked.

Caruso laughed. "She drank some. Look, I told you
I'm busy. You know what bar it was now. See ya."

Brixton put his hand on Caruso's arm. "Take another
look at the picture, Mr. Caruso. See the man sitting at
the bar behind you and Laura, the guy with the ponytail?"

Caruso looked. "The old guy?" he said.

"He's not so old."

"He's old to me."

"Yeah, I suppose he would be. Who is he?"

Caruso shrugged. "Beats me."

"You didn't talk to him?"

"No. Why would I talk to him? I didn't know him."

"Did he talk to Laura?"

"I don't think so, but from the picture, I'd say I was
pretty wasted."

"You didn't see him pay any attention to her?"

"What are you getting at? Who is this guy?"

"I was hoping you'd tell me."

"Well, you wasted your time—and mine. But I will tell
you something. Laura was a tease, and I'm not surprised
that some guy got mad at her."

Brixton fixed him in a hard stare. "What are you
suggesting, Caruso, that she brought her murder on
herself?"

"Maybe not in so many words, but she played a game
with guys."

"Guys like you?"

"Yeah, and plenty of others, I'm sure."

"You know what, Caruso, Laura deserved better than

you. I'm going to give you ten seconds to be out of here. One second more and I'll go outside with you and trounce your sorry ass."

"Who do you think you are?"

"Ten, nine, eight—"

Caruso got up and headed for the door.

"Seven, six, five—"

Brixton stopped counting and smiled. Would he have gone outside and taken on Caruso physically? He would have, although he was glad that he hadn't needed to follow through on his threat. Beating up a law-abiding citizen, especially one who worked for a U.S. senator, no matter how obnoxious, didn't sit well with those in government who renew private investigators' licenses. Besides, Caruso looked like he could take a punch and throw a few.

He was glad that it had ended as it had. He'd gotten what he wanted, the name of the bar in which Caruso and Laura had frolicked one night. With any luck someone at that bar would know who the man in the ponytail was. It was a long shot, but you had to start someplace.

34

Brixton swung by the Capitol Lounge on his way back to the office and showed the photograph to the day bartender.

"That's Mark," he told Brixton, recognizing the bartender on duty that night from the photo. "He won't be in until this evening."

"I'll come back," Brixton said. "You happen to recognize the guy with the ponytail at the bar?"

The bartender shook his head. "Never saw him before, and I remember my customers."

Assuming that he would be faced with the same response from whoever was on duty that afternoon at the bar at the Hotel Lombardy, Brixton decided to make the rounds once the sun had set and the nighttime crews were plying their trade.

"You had a call from a Dick Sheridan," Flo said, when Brixton got back to the office. "He says he's an old friend from New York, a musician. He's playing tonight at Blues Alley and wants you to come."

"Dick Sheridan," Brixton said, smiling. "Good guy

and a hell of a drummer, played with every big name. He leave a number?"

She gave it to him.

"How did it go with Caruso?" she asked.

"Arrogant bastard," was Brixton's reply, "but he told me what I needed to know. It was the Capitol Lounge in the picture. I have to go back when the night guy is on. Same with the Lombardy hotel."

"Let's make a night of it," Flo suggested. "We haven't been out in ages. I'll go with you while you check out the bars, and you can catch up with your old friend and we can hear some good music."

"I like the way you think," Brixton said. "You're on."

Flo ran back to the apartment to dress for the evening while Brixton stayed at the office to catch up on e-mails and other tedium. But first he returned the call to his old friend Dick Sheridan, and they spent almost a half hour catching up on each other's lives. Brixton fondly remembered when he would catch the last set at Manhattan's tony Café Carlyle where Sheridan played with the popular pianist and singer Bobby Short for twelve years. The drummer raved about the pianist and bass player he was bringing with him into Blues Alley, and when they'd finished their conversation, Brixton's mood had improved considerably.

He'd been in an angry funk for the past few weeks, a situation with which he was only too familiar, and was glad to feel his spirits rise. Lately he'd been short with Flo, even brusque at times, and he didn't want to suffer a repeat of when his glum, cynical mood had caused their breakup after returning to New York from Savannah. He knew that she deserved better, if only in return for putting up with his sometimes dumb antics. It was good that she'd suggested a night on the town. It was much needed.

Their first stop was the Capitol Lounge, where the

night bartender had arrived. No, he didn't know who the man with the ponytail was, had never seen him before that one night. He did remember serving him, however. "He asked for what he called a stabilizer, half port wine and half brandy, served in a snifter."

"You ever make that drink before?" Brixton asked.

"No. It was a first for me."

"How did he pay?"

"Cash. I'm sure of that. He paid cash and tipped big, as I recall."

They left the Capitol Lounge and headed for the Hotel Lombardy, where Brixton recognized the bartender as having been on duty the night he'd met there with Cody Watson.

"That guy I was with," Brixton explained, "was the press aide to Congressman Harold Gannon."

"The one who was murdered?"

"Right. The night we were here, a man came in right after Watson, middle-aged, salt-and-pepper hair pulled into a small ponytail." He laid the photograph on the bar.

"Sure, I remember him."

"Got a name for him?"

"No. It was the only time I'd ever seen him in here. He ordered a drink I'm seldom asked for."

"Half port, half brandy?"

The bartender laughed. "You know more about him than you let on," he said.

"Another bartender at another place just told us about the drink."

"I remember thinking that he must have had an upset stomach. The drink's called the stabilizer because it stabilizes a bad gut. The cruise lines all offer it on their bar menus for passengers who get seasick. I've never tried it, but people say it's like a miracle medicine when you have a bellyache."

"He pay cash?" Brixton asked.

The bartender nodded.

"I was hoping he used a credit card," Brixton said.

"Sorry. Can I make you two a drink?"

"Thanks, but no," Flo said. "We're on our way to Blues Alley to hear some jazz. We'll eat there."

It had been overcast when they entered the bar at the Hotel Lombardy. Now, as they left, it had started to drizzle and they picked up their pace as they walked to the car.

"We struck out in both places," Brixton said as they headed for Wisconsin Avenue in Georgetown where the jazz club was located. "I still don't know who that guy is."

"And you really don't know whether he had anything to do with Laura Bennett's death."

"True, but there's an easy way to find out. Find him and ask."

They parked at Canal Square and walked quickly to the club, where Sheridan had reserved two spots for the eight o'clock show. They were seated at a prime table affording them a perfect sightline to the small stage. After drinks were served, Brixton looked at Flo, smiled, and took her hand in his. "I feel like the world has disappeared," he said, looking around the crowded room with its brick walls that had all the trappings of a speakeasy. "This is the oldest continuous jazz club in the country," he said.

"So you've said."

"Strange that it's in Washington."

"Why?"

"Washington doesn't deserve a great club like this."

"That's silly," she said, squeezing his hand. But she knew that he meant it.

Brixton's disdain for the nation's capital was deeply etched. He enjoyed concerts at the Kennedy Center and

liked visiting the Air and Space Museum and the Smith-
sonian, but these were nonpolitical venues. Every run-in
he'd had with Washington's political establishment—
which meant everyone, it seemed—had proved disap-
pointing at best, more often disastrous. He was fond of
something that Mark Twain once said: "If we got one-
tenth of what was promised in those State of the Union
addresses, there wouldn't be any inducement to go to
heaven."

Of course Brixton wasn't the only person with a jaded
view of the nation's capital. Mac and Annabel Smith,
who might be considered a part of the Washington establishment, held their own cynical views, which went a
long way to cementing the bond Brixton had developed
with the erudite attorney and his gorgeous redheaded
wife. Having been accepted into their lives was one of
the best things that had ever happened to him.

They ordered from the Creole menu—Sarah Vaughan's
Filet Mignon for him, Dizzy Gillespie's Jambalaya for
her. Sheridan joined them at the table while they were
on dessert, and they chatted until it was eight o'clock
and time for the first set of the evening. Robert and Flo
basked in the music, the trio a tight-knit unit that played
standards—"On Green Dolphin Street," "Lover, Come
Back to Me," the ballad "But Beautiful," and an original
by Sheridan, "Bonnie's Blues." The house was full, every
spot at the bar was occupied, and Brixton and Flo joined
the crowd in applauding each musician's improvisations
on the themes.

"I'm really glad that we did this," Brixton told Flo after they'd paid their tab and had arranged to get together with Sheridan the following day. "Good for the
soul."

"Your face is more relaxed than I've seen it in a long
time," Flo said.

"It's that evident, huh?"

"It certainly is."

They joined the throng on the way out of the club to make room for those attending the ten o'clock set, who were lined up at the door. The drizzle had turned to a steady rain now, and they cursed not having brought umbrellas.

"Want me to go get the car?" Brixton asked.

"No. I don't melt in the rain," she said. "Come on, we can make a run for it."

Wisconsin Avenue was bustling with people coming out of shops, some with newspapers over their heads, others having been forward looking enough to tote umbrellas. Vehicular traffic was fairly light, and Brixton and Flo decided to take advantage of a break in it and run across the avenue. He grabbed her hand. They looked right and left, then stepped off the sidewalk and headed for the opposite side. A nondescript gray sedan that had been parked at the curb with its engine running suddenly jerked forward and headed directly at them, its lights off. Flo didn't see it, but Brixton did out of the corner of his eye. He forged forward to the safety of the sidewalk, dragging Flo with him, but he wasn't fast enough. The car missed him, but its right fender clipped Flo, sending her sprawling on to the wet roadway.

Bystanders who'd witnessed the accident screamed. A few hurled curses at the fleeing car. Brixton turned and fell to his knees, his hands all over Flo. "Hey, you okay?" he managed.

She moaned.

"Son of a bitch," he said as he looked at the people lining the sidewalk. "Get an ambulance," he barked. "Get a cop."

As Flo was loaded into an ambulance, Brixton asked two men who'd witnessed the hit-and-run whether they saw the driver or got a plate number.

"Negative on the second," one replied. "But I got a

quick look at the driver in the light from a streetlamp, just a second or two. It was a kid."

"A kid? A teenager?" Brixton said.

"Yeah, I guess that's what he was. He had a ponytail. That's all I noticed."

An hour later, Brixton sat with Flo in the emergency room at Georgetown University Hospital. She'd been sedated to alleviate the pain from her battered right leg. It was swollen and raw where the pavement had roughed up the flesh, ripping it open in spots. But it was her knee that was of primary concern. The emergency room physician on duty said that it might be broken and had scheduled an X-ray.

When Flo was returned to the ER, the doctor said that the X-ray didn't show any broken bones; the knee was badly bruised, and she would be placed in a brace to allow it to heal.

"You're lucky you're alive," Brixton said, using his fingertips to push away hair from her forehead.

"Thanks to you."

"I should have pulled harder."

"You pulled hard enough."

Because Flo had also hit her head on the pavement, the doctors insisted that she remain in the hospital overnight to check for any signs of concussion. They were discussing that decision—Flo wanted to go home but Brixton was adamant that she stay—when Mac and Annabel walked in. Brixton had called Mac once the ambulance had delivered Flo to the ER.

"How are you doing?" Annabel asked Flo as she came to her bedside and placed her hand on her arm.

"I'll be okay," Flo said. "Thanks for coming."

"It was a hit-and-run?" Mac asked.

"Yeah," Brixton confirmed.

"No one got a plate number?"

"No, but someone caught a brief glimpse of the driver."

"Oh?"

"He has a ponytail."

Mac and Annabel looked at each other.

"That's right," Brixton said. "This aging hippie was close to Laura Bennett and Cody Watson before they were killed. Looks like he's got me on his list, too."

35

Brixton, Mac, and Annabel met with the emergency room doctor in the hall after having accompanied Flo to the room in which she would spend the night.

"You think she'll be okay?" Brixton said.

"We'll evaluate her overnight to make sure there aren't concussion symptoms."

"She hit her head pretty hard on the pavement," Brixton said. "It was a real thud." He forced a laugh. "But she's got a pretty hard head."

The doctor, who Brixton judged to be in his thirties, didn't smile.

"Take good care of her," Brixton said.

"She'll be fine, Mr. Brixton. Are you sure you're okay?"

"Me? I'm fine."

"Sometimes a trauma like this catches up with you later," Annabel offered.

"No, no, no, I'm okay."

The doctor walked away.

"How about coming back to our place?" Annabel

suggested. "Spend the night. You can get out of those soggy, wrinkled clothes and relax."

"Thanks, but I want to get back to my own place. Why don't you two come with me. I'll make some coffee, and we have dynamite lemon wafers that Flo likes and keeps in the house."

A half hour later they were settled in Brixton's kitchen, where coffee brewed.

"You and Flo are lucky you're alive," Annabel said, as she arranged the wafers on a serving plate.

"I guess we are," Brixton said. He'd taken a fast hot shower and was now dressed in gray sweatpants and a blue sweatshirt.

"So the driver had a ponytail," Smith said bluntly.

"According to one eyewitness."

"Which means it could have been the man in the photograph with Laura Bennett and in the picture that Flo took at the Lombardy."

"*Could* have been?" Brixton repeated. "It *had* to have been him."

"I'm not arguing with you, Robert," Smith said. "Chances are it was the same man. What did the cop who took your statement at the hospital have to say?"

Brixton snickered. "I told him that I thought I knew who drove the car, but he didn't buy it. He made a big deal out of us crossing Wisconsin in the middle of the street, said that we were jaywalking. He pointed out that it was nighttime and raining, hard for the driver to see. He also debated whether it was a hit-and-run, said the driver probably didn't even know that he'd hit anybody."

"The problem," Mac said, "is that we don't know who the man with the ponytail is."

"Why not run it past Zeke Borgeldt?" Annabel suggested. "You have two photos in which he appears. Can't they can do a search of their databases based on the description?"

"Good idea," Mac said. "I'll give Zeke a call in the morning and we'll arrange to meet with him."

"I hope Flo is okay," Brixton said. "It happened so fast. No doubt about it, that creep with the ponytail was aiming for us."

Mac had fallen silent.

"You okay?" Annabel asked.

"What? Yeah, I'm fine. I was just thinking that if this guy is responsible for Laura Bennett and Cody Watson's murders, and has now targeted Robert, we have a psychopathic killer on our hands."

"That's for sure," Brixton said. "Let's say he did kill Watson and Laura. Why? What was his connection with them? None as far as I can see. Now he tries to run me down. It has to go back to Gannon and the affair he had with Laura. She was a threat to him. His own press aide knew about the affair and talked to me about it. And let's face it, I've been in the papers as someone working on behalf of the Bennett family, and I haven't exactly been what you'd call discreet about my belief that Gannon's behind it."

"So you're speculating that this man killed Laura and Cody Watson on behalf of Congressman Gannon," Annabel said.

"Yeah," said Brixton, "on behalf of, or on direct orders from him."

"If you're right," Mac said, "you're about to unleash one of the biggest political scandals this city has ever seen."

With that thought lingering in the air, Mac and Annabel said good night.

"I'll call Zeke first thing in the morning and tell him what happened, ask that we can get together to show him the photos," Smith said.

"I'm not sure what time I'll be bringing Flo home," Brixton said, "assuming she is coming home."

"Call me after you get her settled in," Mac said.

"Shall do," said Brixton. "Thanks for coming to the hospital and for being here for me."

"We'll always be here for you, Robert," Annabel said as she kissed his cheek.

The rain had stopped. Brixton poured himself a snifter of brandy and took it out to the small terrace, where he dried off a chair. He'd started to second-guess his decision to leave Flo alone at the hospital but decided that she was in good hands. Besides, what Annabel had said about feeling the effects of a traumatic experience was true. He'd begun to ache, starting with his legs and progressing up to his shoulders and arms. As he shifted position in the chair against the pain, a succession of faces appeared before him: Congressman Hal Gannon—his chief of staff Roseann Simmons—Laura Bennett, that lovely young woman whose life was snuffed out . . . Cody Watson, Gannon's press aide, who wanted to do the right thing and died in the process . . . Gannon's campaign manager, Joe Selesky, arrogant and obnoxious . . . the double-dealing private eye Paul Wooster . . . Millie Sparks, Rachel Montgomery, and Peggy Talbot, the airline flight attendant, three women who'd been seduced by Gannon's good looks, suave demeanor, and position of power . . . everyone he'd come into contact with since becoming involved with the Laura Bennett case.

But they faded from his consciousness as quickly as they'd appeared.

Now the only face that remained was an unnamed man, middle-aged, salt-and-pepper hair, who tied what was left of his hair into a tight ponytail, a cold-blooded murderer. Brixton retrieved the two photographs he had of the man and stared at them, memorizing every facet of his face. As he did, the anger that coursed through him was so intense that he dropped his glass to the concrete floor of the terrace, where it smashed into pieces.

"I'll get you, you bastard," he said aloud as he headed for the kitchen to get a broom and dustpan. "I'll find out who you are and I'll get you. You can count on that."

36

The subject of Robert Brixton's wrath sat in the bar
at his hotel near Reagan National Airport. He'd
changed hotels frequently since coming to Washington,
using different names that appeared on multiple IDs in
his wallet. The young bartender, a recent graduate of a
bartenders' course at a community college, had never
heard of a stabilizer and couldn't find the recipe in the
guide that was kept behind the bar. He asked the customer to explain.

"It's quite simple," the customer said, smiling. "Take a
snifter, pour in a jigger of port wine, then add a jigger of
brandy, and stir. Any brand will do."

"Thanks," the bartender said, and managed to find a
bottle of rarely requested port.

The customer, who wore a green sport jacket of the
type frequently seen at golf tourneys at exclusive clubs,
and a crisp butter-colored button-down shirt, tasted his
drink. "Perfect," he announced.

The woman seated next to him asked about it.

"Something I learned years ago from my father," he
said pleasantly.

Which wasn't true. While being blessed with good genes and an imposing physique—as well as suffering very few physical maladies over the course of his fifty years—he'd been cursed with a sour stomach since childhood that demanded constant attention. There was a large ulcer, and he suffered from almost nonstop acid reflux that he tried to keep under control by popping countless Tums each day. He'd learned about the medicinal properties of the stabilizer during a stay at a hotel in John o' Groats on the barren northern coast of Scotland after an especially rough trip on a small ferry coming back from the Orkney Islands.

The woman glanced at his left ring finger in search of a wedding ring. There wasn't one.

"Buy you a drink?" he asked.

"All right."

She drank bourbon and soda.

"If you're buying me a drink, I should know your name," she said.

"John," he said.

"Just John?"

"John Mitchell."

"Thank you for the drink, John Mitchell. My name is Lila Franco."

She was taken with John Mitchell. He was a handsome man by any standard, nicely dressed and well-groomed, with deep-set blue eyes and a well-modulated voice that conveyed his obvious intelligence. He was certainly polite; if he was on the make, he was classy in the way he approached it. That he pulled his hair back into a ponytail was somewhat off-putting, but she chalked it up to wanting to appear younger, or at least to indicate that he wasn't behind the times.

He'd showed interest in her, offering to buy her a drink, but she didn't know, couldn't know that he had no interest in her beyond passing the time with some pleasant conversation. Not that he didn't like women. He'd been married twice. The first, entered into at a very early age, lasted only a year. The second ended with the tragic murder of his wife. She'd been battered to death in a secluded wooded area near where they lived. He was considered the prime suspect, but without evidence the DA declined to prosecute. There had been many women since then, but they came and went, one-night stands, some prostitutes, no one for whom he felt anything except lust and a vehicle for a quick release of his passion.

"Are you in Washington on business?" she asked.

"Yes."

"What do you do, if you don't mind my asking?"

"I'm a consultant," he said.

"Oh? For the government?"

"Sometimes. I consult for a variety of companies and agencies. And you?"

"I work for a real estate firm in Crystal City."

"Is the real estate market here strong?" he asked.

"Very. People are always coming and going in Washington, selling their houses and buying new ones. It's the government. Always new people arriving and leaving."

"Sounds like an interesting career," he said, glancing at his watch. "I've certainly enjoyed meeting you, Ms. Franco, and having this pleasant chat. I'm afraid I must be going."

She was disappointed.

"You're staying here at the hotel?" she asked.

"Just for the night," he said. "I have a business appointment to go to."

She found it strange to be off to a "business appointment" at ten o'clock at night but, of course, didn't express it. He paid the tab, nodded as he got off the barstool, almost bowed to her, and left.

A strange man, she thought. *I would like to have gotten to know him better.*

He left the hotel and got into his black SUV, which he'd rented after returning the gray sedan to the rental company at the airport. He'd checked the sedan to make sure that there wasn't any sign of having hit a pedestrian before turning it in, explaining that he needed to move some things and needed a larger vehicle.

He listened to an all-news radio station as he drove to a street on the fringe of Georgetown, where he parked at a meter, turned off the lights and engine, and trained his eyes on a bar and restaurant across the street. He opened an expensive black alligator briefcase that sat on the passenger seat and removed a file folder with a name handwritten on the tab. Inside the folder were three photographs of a middle-aged man, and a sheet of paper on which information about the man was written.

As he waited, he thought of the woman he'd met at the hotel bar. There were so many women at bars in Washington, lonely women, women with a drinking problem or harboring anger at lives misspent, women with their makeup just so, hair coiffed perfectly, looking for someone, searching for a man to make them feel whole. He felt sorry for them. They wouldn't find what they were looking for in Washington, D.C., not in a city crawling with spineless bureaucrats, dishonest men with large egos, men without values. That's what set him apart, he was sure. He had values, core values. He was a man of action.

At fifteen minutes before eleven, he got out of his car and walked to an alley that separated the restaurant from another building. He casually stood and waited, his eyes on the front door, the long, needlelike knife concealed in his hand. This was the part of his job that Bruce McGinnis hated most, the waiting.

The front door opened a few minutes past eleven, and the restaurant's staff came through it, laughing, kidding, complaining about the tips they'd received, and comparing notes about certain patrons who'd acted stupid. After they'd dispersed, McGinnis went to the door. Shades had been drawn, but there were gaps through which he could peer inside. The man whose picture he had had studied in the car was seated alone at the bar with his back to the door, a glass of amber whiskey in front of him, a pile of cash next to it. McGinnis had been told that the man was careless about not locking the door after his staff had left and that he relaxed over a drink while counting the night's cash receipts. McGinnis was also informed that the restaurant owner possessed a handgun but kept it in a small office at the rear of the restaurant. His routine, according to the men who'd hired McGinnis, was to spend fifteen or twenty minutes drinking and counting before taking the cash to a safe in his office, turning out the lights, activating the alarm, and leaving for home. Fifteen or twenty minutes—more than enough time.

McGinnis slowly turned the door's knob. It opened silently. He stepped inside and closed the door behind him. His presence alerted the man, who turned, a quizzical expression on his round Hispanic face.

"We're closed," he said.

"I know," McGinnis said, quickly closing the gap between them. The man started to get up, but McGinnis rammed the needlelike knife blade into his back. It went in easily, came out easily, and went back in again.

The man slumped to the floor.

McGinnis turned and was out the door within seconds. He drove to the hotel, parked the SUV, and went to his room, where he turned on television, drew the drapes, and swallowed a half dozen Tums to ease the acidic pain that erupted from his gut to his mouth. That was the downside to what he did for a living. Killing people always brought on the worst symptoms.

Before retiring for the night, McGinnis took one of the

folders from his briefcase. Written on it was *Brixton, Robert*. In it were two newspaper photos of Brixton and notes taken from articles written about him over the years. His address was written on a sheet of paper that also included pertinent information about him, his career, and a description of the woman with whom he was involved, Flo Combes. With any luck, McGinnis would be able to accomplish this next Washington, D.C., assignment and return to his home and his fishing dragger on the Gulf coast of Florida.

37

Brixton arrived at the hospital the following morning at eight and sat with Flo in her room until she received final approval to be released. They chatted about many things, but the conversation kept coming back to what had happened on that rainy night on Wisconsin Avenue, and Brixton's conviction that the driver had been the man with the ponytail.

"He was aiming for me," he said.

"Thank God you saw him and reacted the way you did."

"Sometimes you get lucky," he said. "How are you feeling?"

"Like I was hit by a car. My knee is killing me."

"They give you painkillers?"

"Yes, but I hate to take them. Make me woozy."

"I talked to the doc when I arrived. He says you have to wear that brace for at least two weeks and stay off your leg as much as possible."

"Easy for him to say."

"Hey, you listen to what he says, Flo. You have great legs. That's what attracted me to you."

"My legs? That's all?"

"There were a few other attributes. Good you don't have a concussion."

"The doctor told me that you said I had a hard head."

"I was kidding."

"You'd better be. What's new with the man with the ponytail?"

"Mac and I are meeting with Zeke Borgeldt later today. We'll show him the two pictures of the guy and explain what happened after we left the jazz club. They'll go through their databases and see if they can ID the bastard."

"Good luck," she said as the doctor entered and had her sign a few forms.

"Thanks for the good care," Flo told him.

"That's what we're here for," he said. "Safe home."

It took some maneuvering to get Flo into the passenger seat of their car because of her leg brace, but once she was strapped in, Brixton drove them to their apartment, where he got her settled on the couch, pillows stuffed behind her head and one under her leg, and a cup of hot tea and a plate of lemon wafers within reach.

"I don't need to be treated like an invalid," she said, "but you're sweet to do it."

"That's me, Sweet Robert. You'll be okay for a few hours?"

"I'll watch a movie and fill my face with these cookies. You go catch up with Mac. Give me a call after you've met with Borgeldt."

Brixton met Smith at Borgeldt's office at four.

"This is becoming a habit," the superintendent said.

"Sorry to take up your time again," Brixton said, "but I don't like becoming a target of a psycho, who, by the way, killed Laura Bennett and Cody Watson. Find this guy and you solve both cases. It'll make you a star around here."

"I already am a star," Borgeldt countered. He started to say something else, but Brixton added, "And no need for a parade or a dinner to honor me for breaking those cases. I'm still just a humble guy."

"I'll cancel the parade," Borgeldt said, casting an exasperated look at Smith.

"What we need," said Smith, "is for you to have someone go through your databases to see if this man with the ponytail crops up. You have the two original photos— the one from Laura Bennett's cell phone camera and the one Robert's friend took at the Hotel Lombardy. Now this same man has tried to run Robert down. Fortunately, he failed. If you can identify him, you'll obviously want to bring him in for questioning."

"Why didn't I think of that?" Borgeldt said wearily, and rubbed his eyes.

"I just thought that—" Smith started to say.

"I know, I know, Mac. Don't take anything I say seriously. It's been a long day following a long night. How's your lady friend?" he asked Brixton.

"Sore, banged up, but she's okay. She has great legs. Hate to see one of them go through a meat grinder."

"You're a leg man. You don't have anything else about this guy with the ponytail except the pictures?" Borgeldt asked.

"That's it," Brixton said. "I figure that somebody who goes around killing people must have a rap sheet, maybe not for murder but for some other offense over the years."

"Do you think he's from here in the D.C. area?" Borgeldt asked.

Brixton shrugged.

"If he's not," Mac said, "it could mean that he's staying at a hotel in the area. Can you have some of your people canvass hotels with the photos?"

"That takes manpower, Mac. You might have read that we're fighting budget and staffing problems."

"I seem to have heard that somewhere," Mac said, tongue-in-cheek. "We're not asking that you drop everything to go after this guy, Zeke. But now that he's evidently out to kill Robert, I'm sure you don't want another dead body on your hands."

"I'll see what I can do," Borgeldt said.

"Can't ask for more than that," Mac said. "Thanks. Let me know if you come up with anything."

Brixton missed seeing Flo sitting at the front desk as he and Mac walked into their office suite. He called her. "How're you doing?" he asked.

"Okay," she said. "Watched a bad movie and kept dozing off. Tell me about Borgeldt."

Brixton filled her in on the meeting. "What do you feel like for dinner? I'll bring something home with me."

"Pizza. I have this overwhelming urge for pizza with pepperoni and sausage."

"Consider it done," he said. "I've got some catching up here at the office, should be home in a couple of hours."

"Take your time," she said. "Wish I was there to help. I'll come in tomorrow."

"The hell you will. You're staying home with your gorgeous leg propped up on a soft pillow." She started to protest, but he added, "Don't argue with me. You know I become irrational when anybody argues with me."

That issue settled, Brixton ensconced himself behind his desk and caught up on what seemed to be a never-ending flow of paperwork. He was immersed in it when Mac poked his head in. "I just got a call from Gannon's attorney, Richard Nichols. It was a sort of heads-up call to let me know that Gannon has agreed to do a live interview with CNN."

"Why would he do that?" Brixton asked.

"According to Nichols, all the negative press has eaten into his support back home in Tampa. Nichols has convinced him to do the interview as a way to clear the air. It's strictly a PR move."

"When?"

"The interview is scheduled for tomorrow afternoon. They'll air it tomorrow night."

"Must-see TV," Brixton said. "Why did Nichols think it was necessary to give you a heads-up?"

"He wants the Bennett family to know it from me before they learn about it on the news. You have to give it to Gannon. It's a gutsy move on his part, but I suppose the pressure is on back home. He's been on the receiving end of some pretty tough media exposure, editorials accusing him of stonewalling the investigation, not being truthful with authorities, falsely denying that he had a sexual relationship with Laura Bennett. It's a story that won't go away. I spoke with Luke Bennett. He says that media types have been parked outside his door ever since Laura went missing."

"Sounds to me like a Hail Mary approach from Gannon," Brixton said. "Who's doing the interview?"

"Donna Lewis."

"They're bringing in the heavy artillery," Brixton commented. "She's good."

Donna Lewis was a beautiful, vivacious young African-American CNN reporter whose interviewing technique had been on display recently while questioning controversial lawmakers. Nichols had lobbied for someone else, but the CNN brass insisted on using Lewis.

"She has a pleasant persona but asks tough questions. Should be interesting."

"That's for sure. I'd better get home and play nurse to my patient," Brixton said. "She has a craving for pizza for dinner."

"Love from Annabel and me," Mac said. "And you take care, Robert. Annabel and I are on alert after that threatening phone call she received at the gallery, and you know there's a guy with a ponytail on your case."

As Brixton left the office and headed for a pizza parlor near the apartment, Hal Gannon was huddled in a hotel suite with his attorney, Richard Nichols; his chief of staff, Roseann Simmons; two other members of his congressional staff; his campaign manager from Tampa, Joe Selesky; and a woman, Candy Tresh, whose PR firm had been hired to prep the congressman on how to handle himself during the CNN interview. She'd prepared a list of questions that she thought Donna Lewis might throw at him, and played the role of the inquisitor while Gannon struggled with the answers. It was not going well.

"I don't like this, Dick," Gannon said to his attorney during a break.

"You can't avoid it, Hal," Nichols said. He turned to Selesky. "Am I right, Joe?"

Selesky's mood was even gruffer than usual. Polls in the Tampa area showed that Gannon's lead in the race had eroded by a startling amount. The prevailing attitude on the part of voters was that Gannon was being evasive and uncooperative with the authorities; many who were questioned wondered whether he knew why Laura Bennett had disappeared and might even know something about why she was killed, and by whom. Selesky had urged Nichols to arrange for the CNN interview and to hire the PR woman, and he'd made a last-minute trip to D.C. to oversee it.

"We don't know what she'll ask," Gannon protested. "You know the media, it wants the juiciest stuff. She'll ask whether Laura and I ever had an affair."

"Simple," Selesky said. "You just say that you aren't about to sully the reputation of this lovely young woman who blah, blah, blah. Talk about her wonderful family, how she came here to D.C. to begin her career in public service, and how some insane person snuffed out her life at such a young age. Come on, Hal, get with it. Your goddamn career, not only in the House but beyond that, is at stake. The Bennett family has been injured by the loss of their beloved daughter, but you've been injured, too. You hear me, Hal? You've been injured, too! Play the injured man. Talk about Charlene and the kids, for Christ's sake."

"I would have preferred that Congressman Gannon have his wife at his side during the interview," Candy Tresh said.

"Yeah, well, that didn't work out," Selesky growled.

Gannon had called Charlene and tried to convince her to come to Washington to participate in the interview, but she'd adamantly refused.

The PR woman said to Gannon, "Look, Congressman, it doesn't matter what Ms. Lewis asks. You have to know what it is you want to say and twist the question around to allow you to make your points. Let's assume that she'll ask whether you ever had an affair with Ms. Bennett. Mr. Selesky is right. You launch right in to what a wonderful family the Bennetts are, how you treasure your friendship with them, and you'll be damned if you'll soil Laura's name by violating her privacy and yours, not in those words necessarily but along those lines. Let's start again."

And so it went for three hours, the participants fortified with trays of food and bottles of liquor from room service as they went through the mock interview that would become a reality the following day.

Gannon had been convinced to stay in the suite overnight to shield him from media that might be waiting at his apartment building. The others left, with the exception of Roseann Simmons, who tidied up the living room in anticipation of the meal carts being removed.

"Level with me," Gannon said. "How bad did it go?"

Simmons had been standing at the window looking out over the city. She turned and said, "It went very well, Hal, very well. You just have to believe in yourself and do what Candy Tresh said, know what you want to say and say it regardless of what Lewis asks."

"I just wonder if I'm coming off too defensive," he said.

"That's exactly the point," Roseann said, joining him on the couch. "Don't *be* defensive. Dismiss those who want to taint you for political reasons. Attack them for their motives. Mourn the death of Laura Bennett and Cody. Condemn those who are behind their deaths. Play up the polygraph test you passed. There's so much positive for you to be proud of, Hal."

"I'm disappointed in Charlene," he said. "Having her with me would go a long way to convincing whoever's watching the interview that what people are saying about me is wrong."

"I'm disappointed in her, too, Hal," Roseann said, "but you can't let it throw you. You must keep one thing uppermost in mind during the interview, and that's the fact that this country needs you. This will pass, Hal. The voters will chalk it up to what it really is, a witch hunt by those who would bring you down. There is such a wonderful future awaiting you. All you have to do is keep your eye on that future and don't let anything or anyone stand in your way of achieving it."

Gannon went to hug her as she left, but she pulled away and kissed him on the cheek. "Everything will work out fine, Hal," she said. "Trust me."

The mock interview had been exhausting, and Gannon flopped on the bed still wearing his clothes. *How could this be happening to me?* he mused as he lay there, eyes wide open, lights from outside casting playful shards of brightness on the ceiling.

He knew the answer, of course. He'd succumbed to

what had always been a weakness, a driving need to conquer women and to prove his manhood, if only to himself. He felt terribly fragile at that moment.

But then Roseann's inspiring words kicked in.

He got up, went to the living room, and poured himself a drink from one of the bottles on the room service cart. She was right. He had great things ahead of him and would not allow this detour to take him permanently off the road to his destiny. The CNN interview would set things straight, and he could put this nasty episode behind him. After he'd been vindicated, Charlene would come around to see again that she'd married someone with drive and ambition, a man for whom thousands of voters had cast their votes of confidence, and for whom millions more would one day do the same.

F ollowing the run-through, Joe Selesky stopped by his hotel to pick up some papers before taking a taxi to a Georgetown town house where a half dozen men awaited his arrival. One of them, Arturo Casson, an African-American member of Tampa's City Council, had flown to D.C. earlier in the day. A tall, imposing man, Casson's mother had been Cuban, his father an African from Angola. They'd fled to Florida from Cuba after Castro's takeover and had settled in the Tampa area. Arturo excelled in school and graduated from the University of Southern Florida with top honors, and then went on to obtain his law degree from the University of Miami. His law practice thrived, and he became active in Democratic politics, running for the City Council and winning handily in District Four. He chaired the council's Barrio Latino Commission, charged with preserving the architectural character of Ybor City and its rich history. Married with two children, Arturo occupied a position of leadership in Florida's Fourteenth Congressional District, represented by Harold Gannon in the U.S. House of Representatives.

"How does it look?" a man at the late-night meeting asked Selesky.

"Not good," Gannon's campaign manager replied. "Gannon has this interview with CNN tomorrow and hopes he can sway enough people to put his reelection back on track. You want my professional judgment? I don't think the interview, or anything else he does, will accomplish a damn thing. I think Hal Gannon is dead meat."

"But he's not about to drop out of the race, is he?" Casson asked.

"Not without a push from me and the rest of you, and it's a push we have to make. Democrats have held this House seat for a long time, and I'll be damned if I'll see it go to a Republican."

All attention went to Casson as he shifted in his chair and rested his chin on his fist, a man deep in thought.

"If Joe is right," someone said, "we have to act fast to replace him on the ballot. What about it, Arturo? We need a commitment from you if Gannon is persuaded to drop out of the race."

"I've always liked Hal Gannon," Casson said in a deep baritone. "A very pleasant fellow."

"And a world-class screwup," Selesky said. "If you take his place and run, Arturo, you have a damn good chance of winning."

"That's nice to know," Casson said, "but Hal is still the candidate."

"But maybe not for long," Selesky said. "Let's cut to the chase. If Gannon resigns his seat in Congress, are you willing to run?"

The large Afro-Cuban, dressed immaculately in a blue suit, white shirt, and tie, pursed his lips. "Yes," he said. "I am willing to run."

38

The scheduled airing of Gannon's CNN interview with Donna Lewis was the topic of conversation across Washington the following day.

The interview itself took place in the same suite in which the mock run-through had been held. Gannon's attorney, Richard Nichols, had laid down strict rules as to who could be present. Ms. Lewis was accompanied by a producer, the director, and the all-news channel's technical crew, whose members had to pledge that they would not talk about it until it had been aired that evening. Gannon's entourage consisted of Roseann Simmons, another member of Gannon's staff who'd taken the place of the murdered Cody Watson, Nichols, and Candy Tresh, the PR consultant. Included in the CNN crew was a makeup artist, who made Gannon look good for the camera, taking the sheen off his skin and working with his hair to tame errant strands. Two armchairs had been positioned facing each other, and Cody Watson's replacement acted as the congressman's stand-in while the lighting director made adjustments.

Gannon's makeup had been applied in the bedroom. He emerged into the living room and huddled with Roseanne and Candy Tresh in a corner.

"How do I look?" he asked.

"As handsome as ever," Roseann said.

"You look relaxed, Congressman," Tresh said. "I'm glad to see that."

"I feel pretty good," Gannon said. He looked across the room, where Lewis was going over notes on a clipboard with the producer. Gannon and Lewis had been introduced earlier before they went their separate ways to get ready. "I feel comfortable with her doing the interview," he said. "She has a nice way about her."

"But she's a pro," Simmons said. "Don't get suckered in and become complacent. Just keep remembering those points you need to make no matter what she asks."

"Yes, Boss," Gannon said, smiling and tossing her a salute.

"We set to go?" the producer asked in a loud voice.

Gannon and Lewis settled in their respective chairs, the soundman positioned their microphones, the two cameras rolled, and the interview with Hal Gannon was under way.

That same morning, Brixton stayed home with Flo as she recuperated from the hit-and-run that almost took both their lives. She'd slept soundly, helped by painkillers that she'd been prescribed and reluctantly agreed to take. Brixton, however, tossed and turned all night, unable to shut down his overactive brain. Crossing Wisconsin Avenue in the rain that night, and coming close to being killed, kept running over and over in his mind like a video loop. He'd come close to death more than once during his career as a cop in D.C. and in Savannah,

Georgia, and working as a private investigator in the nation's capital had spawned other near misses at the hands those hell-bent on snuffing out his life.

But this time it had involved the love of his life, Flo Combes, who'd almost died for no reason other than that she was with him. Wrong time, wrong place, wrong company.

"Today's the day that Gannon is being interviewed by CNN," Flo said as they sat at their small kitchen table, her braced leg propped on a pillow on a chair. "It's supposed to air tonight."

"I hope he falls on his face," said Brixton. "I can't imagine it'll do him any good. "He'll have to lie through his teeth, and people pick up on when somebody's lying."

"And maybe people won't care," Flo said. "I remember when the mayor of Boston was reelected while he was in jail. And lots of people in Toronto loved that buffoon of a mayor no matter what he did."

"Go figure. If you're feeling okay, I'll get to the office. There's cold cuts, bread, and some chicken salad in the fridge."

"I'm coming with you," she said.

"No you're not. The doctor said—"

"The doctor said to stay off my leg as much as possible. Sitting at a desk in the office doesn't violate that instruction. Hand me my crutch. I'll be back in a minute."

He watched her hobble to the bathroom and had to smile. There was no sense in trying to argue her out of her decision. He'd learned early in his relationship with Flo Combes that once she made up her mind about something, there was no dissuading her. An hour later he was helping her from the car and steadying her as they walked into the office.

Mac Smith was in conference with a client. When it broke up, he came to Brixton's small suite. He was surprised to see Flo there. "Can't keep a good woman down, huh?" he said.

"I have to keep Robert on the straight and narrow," she said.

"Lots of luck with that," Mac said as he joined Brixton in his office.

"Hear anything from Borgeldt?" Brixton asked.

"Yes, I did. Nothing came up in their database, but he took our suggestion and has dispatched a couple of detectives to area hotels armed with copies of the photographs. Maybe that'll turn up something."

"I hope so. As long as this guy is out there, Mac, I have to look over my shoulder, and that's no way to live. He almost killed Flo, too, and it was probably the same guy who delivered that threatening message to Annabel. I feel like one of those cartoon characters who goes through life with a cloud over his head."

"We'll get him, Robert. He'll make a mistake, take a wrong turn, and he'll pay for it."

Smith left. Brixton appreciated his vote of confidence and was certain he was right.

"The Ponytail Killer," as Brixton had named him, had already made one mistake, attempting to run over Brixton and Flo. Until that moment, the only reason Brixton was convinced that Mr. Ponytail had killed Laura Bennett and Cody Watson was that he'd been in situations in which both victims were present, hardly the sort of evidence that would make a prosecutor's heart trip with enthusiasm.

But the incident on Wisconsin Avenue was tangible. Thanks to an eyewitness, Brixton knew that the driver of the car had sported the telltale ponytail. That was enough for Brixton, and he'd not wavered in his conviction that this was the killer. At the same time, he felt helpless. If Zeke Borgeldt and his detectives didn't find the guy, there was nothing he could do but look over his shoulder and hope that he was quicker on the draw than Mr. Ponytail.

D etectives Jack Morey and Jason Ewing had been assigned by Borgeldt to canvass hotels to see if any-
one remembered the man in the photos. It was the sort of assignment that both veterans tried to avoid. It meant getting in and out of the car countless times and hoping—*hoping*—that someone at the check-in desk would remember the man. By noon they had visited eleven hotels. Borgeldt, assuming that the subject of the search would not be the type to spend big money at fancy places, had instructed them to focus on lesser ho-tel chains. He'd also suggested that they begin their search at hotels close to Reagan National Airport, on the theory that if he was from out of town he would opt to stay within close proximity to a way to leave quickly.

The detectives decided to try one more hotel before taking a lunch break. They entered the lobby and waited until a line at the counter had dissipated to approach a young uniformed woman with a huge smile. Morey dis-played his ID and placed the two photos on the coun-ter. "Has this man recently been a guest here at the hotel?" Ewing asked.

She looked closely at the pictures. "He doesn't look familiar to me," she said, "but let me get my associates. They're off duty for lunch. Be right back."

A man and woman emerged from a room behind the desk. Morey explained their visit and showed them the photos.

"I remember this man," the male clerk said.

"When was he here?" Ewing asked.

"I'm not sure, maybe last night, the night before that."

"Remember his name?"

"No. What I remember was what I was thinking when

I checked him in. I thought the ponytail was a little—well, a little silly I suppose, because of his age. Not that he was old."

"How old do you figure?" Morey asked.

The clerk shrugged. "I'm not good at ages," he said. "Fifty, maybe. Maybe fifty-five. Like I said, I'm not good at guessing somebody's age."

"Think you could go through your records for the last couple of nights and come up with a name for us?"

The clerks looked at each other before the woman said, "We have so many guests. I don't see how we could do that."

"I understand," said Morey. "Do you remember how he paid?"

"We didn't check him out," they said in unison, "but we always ask for a credit card for incidental expenses when they check in."

"Even if they pay cash?" Ewing asked.

"Yes, but if someone insists on only using cash, we drop the request for a credit card. Some guests give us a cash deposit above and beyond the room rate to cover incidentals. What isn't used is returned to them when they check out."

"He gave you a cash deposit?"

"Yes. A hundred dollars."

"Know whether he ate in the restaurant, had a drink at the bar?"

"No idea. If you come back later, you can check with the restaurant and bar staff."

"Yeah, we'll have to do that," Morey said, not sounding happy about it.

They decided to have a sandwich in the hotel's dining room. After they'd been seated, Morey showed the waitress the photos and asked whether the man in them was familiar.

"No," she said, "I don't remember ever seeing him."

"I'll check out the bartender," Morey told his partner.

"Don't bother," said Ewing. "If the guy hung out at the bar, it'd be at night."

"Worth a shot," Morey said, and went to the bar, where the bartender was going through his ablutions to get ready for customers. Morey showed his ID and displayed the photos. "Does the man in these photos ring a bell?" he asked.

The bartender, who looked to Morey to be too young to be serving drinks, looked at the pictures and laughed.

"Funny?"

"No, it's just that I do recognize the guy. I usually work nights, but they called me in today for the early shift. Sure, I remember him. That's the Stabilizer."

"Huh?"

"The Stabilizer. That's what I call him. It's the name of a crazy drink he ordered, half port wine, half brandy. He had to tell me how to make it."

"When was he here?"

The bartender screwed up his face in thought. "A night or two ago. He was hitting on a woman at the bar. I figured they'd leave together, but he split and she stayed."

"How did he pay?"

"Cash. He tipped good, too. Some customers stiff you."

"You didn't happen to hear the woman he was hitting on say his name, did you?"

"No. Wait a minute. I think he told her his name was John."

"John *what?*"

A shrug from the bartender.

"John Doe, huh?"

Another laugh from the young man. "I guess so," he said.

The detectives drank iced tea with their lunch.

"What about that restaurant owner in Georgetown who was killed?" Ewing asked.

"Sounded like a professional hit."

"He was in heavy to the loan sharks," Ewing said. "At least that's what Zeke said at the briefing."

"He should have gone to a bank," Morey said. "I'd better call Zeke and tell him what we've got so far."

"What'd he say?" Ewing asked after Morey and Borgeldt had spoken.

"He wants us to stay here and show those pictures to everybody who works here at the hotel. The bartender says he thinks the guy's name was John. They can go through their records and pinpoint any guy named John who checked in over the past couple of days and paid cash."

The hotel's manager was cooperative, and within an hour a guest named John, who'd paid cash, was identified as John Mitchell. The same desk clerk with whom the detectives had spoken earlier was summoned to join the manager. He looked at the photos again and said, "Like I said, I remember the ponytail." He laughed. "It looked kind of cool with his tan."

"He had a tan?" Ewing said. "You didn't mention that."

"I guess I forgot."

"Oh."

"Had he made an advance reservation?" Morey asked. "Maybe through a travel agent?"

No," the clerk replied. "I do remember him saying he'd just arrived in town at the last minute, some sort of meeting I think."

"Anything else you now remember?" Ewing asked, not bothering to mask his annoyance at the clerk's renewed memory.

"I don't think so."

"What did he give as his home address?"

The manager gave Ewing the address that the man known as John Mitchell had provided, a street number in

Clearwater, Florida. Morey called into headquarters and had someone there run a reverse check on the address.

"It doesn't exist," he told his partner after the call was ended.

"This John Mitchell, how did he pay when he checked in?" Ewing asked.

The manager referred to a printout. "Cash, and he gave us a hundred-dollar deposit against charges he might run up while staying here."

"Did he run up any charges?"

The manager took another look at the printout. "No," he said. "The hundred dollars was returned to him."

"Anything else you remember about the man when you checked him in?" Ewing asked the clerk.

"Come to think of it," the young man replied, "he was well-spoken, sounded sort of cultured. He might have had an accent."

"Accent? What kind of accent?"

The clerk shrugged. "Not really an accent," he said. "You know, sort of like a—oh, maybe he was British or something."

"He had a British accent?" Morey said.

"Not really a *British* accent," said the clerk. "As I said, he was well-spoken."

"Thanks for your help," Morey told the clerk and the manager. "We appreciate it."

The manager walked them through the lobby and outside. "Mind if I ask what this is all about?"

"We can't say more," Ewing said, "because this case is ongoing. Thanks again."

On the drive back to headquarters, Ewing said, "I'm thinking about the phony address the guy used, Clearwater, Florida. I've got family in St. Pete, Florida. It's close to Tampa, where the congressman's from. So was the intern who was murdered. Maybe there's a connection. The clerk—nice guy, by the way, but it took him a while to remember things—said this John Mitchell guy had a tan, so maybe he *is* from Florida.

"We'll mention it to Zeke. You going to watch the interview with Gannon tonight on CNN?"

"Yeah, sure. The whole city'll be watching."

"I don't figure where this guy, John Mitchell, with the ponytail and the so-called British accent, comes in," Morey said. "Brixton, the PI, and the attorney Smith think that Gannon killed the intern."

"This guy Mitchell was at parties or something where the intern was, too, and according to Brixton tried to run him down. Maybe he and the congressman got together."

"I know one thing for sure," Morey said.

"What's that?"

"Whatever the congressman says tonight will mean squat. He's a politician. He'll lie."

39

Mac and Annabel Smith watched the Gannon interview at their Watergate apartment. It struck Mac
that Gannon was nervous and unsure of himself. As he
said to Annabel, "It reminds me of Nixon during his debate with JFK. Gannon's sweating the way Nixon did."

Annabel agreed. "He sounds as though he's full of bra-
vado, but his face says something else."

Gannon had put into play what he'd been instructed
to do by his handlers, including the PR woman, Roseann Simmons, and his attorney, Richard Nichols: Say
what you want to say regardless of what you're asked.

LEWIS: You're aware, Congressman, that there are numerous rumors that you and your murdered intern, Laura
Bennett, were engaged in a sexual affair.

GANNON: Yes, I'm aware of them, and it breaks my heart to
hear them. Ms. Bennett was a fine, decent young woman
from an upstanding family, and to see her name dragged
through the mud by those with political motives is atro-
cious.

LEWIS: But did you and Ms. Bennett have an affair?

GANNON: No disrespect, Ms. Lewis, but the media's love of anything salacious, no matter how inaccurate—and especially when an elected official is involved—distorts the truth.

Lewis tried to elaborate on her question, but Gannon cut her off.

GANNON: Not only does it distort the truth, it focuses the public's attention away from the important issues facing the nation . . .

And so it went, Lewis probing and Gannon deflecting, back and forth, the interviewer's frustration held in check, the congressman's annoyance, as well as his building anxiety, in plain view to the millions across the country and around the world watching it unfold on their TV sets.

Laura's parents, Lucas and Grace Bennett, watched at their Tampa home.

"He's a goddamn liar," Luke barked at the TV screen. "Tell the truth, damn it!"

Brixton and Flo sat said by side on the couch in their apartment, their attention fixed on their TV, a bowl of popcorn in Brixton's lap.

"Look how he avoids answering any of the questions," Brixton grumbled. "He must have been prepped up to the gills by his people."

"Have you ever heard a politician who *didn't* avoid answering a direct question?" Flo said, popping a puffed kernel into her mouth.

When the interview ended, Brixton called Mac Smith.

"What did you think, Mac?"

"The same thing you thought," the attorney replied. "He got through it, but he sure looked uncomfortable."

"As he should be," said Brixton. "Did you see how he played up his polygraph test, how he passed it with flying colors?"

"That's why he took the test, so he could crow about it. Any word from your friend with the ponytail?"

"No. How about you and Annabel. She receive any more calls?"

"No." Smith's other line rang. "I'll call you back, Robert," he said.

Twenty minutes later Brixton's phone rang again.

"It's Mac," Smith said. "That other call was from Zeke Borgeldt. His detectives had some success in tracking down your assailant." He gave Brixton a rundown on what Detectives Morey and Ewing had learned from the hotel staff.

"He said his name was John Mitchell?"

"Right. A phony name. He also gave a phony address in Clearwater, Florida."

"But he's from out of town," Brixton said. "No doubt about that. He checked out of that hotel?"

"Yes, and there's no telling where he went next," Smith said. "For all we know, he's left D.C."

"I wouldn't count on that," Brixton said. "He's got unfinished business here—me."

"Zeke is sending the same two detectives to other hotels with the photos."

"Borgeldt's a good guy."

"No argument from me. You and Flo enjoy the rest of your evening. I'll see you at the office in the morning."

Donna Lewis was not happy as she rode back to CNN from the hotel.

"I couldn't move him off his damn prepared statements," she said to her director.

"You did fine, Donna," the director said. "You had

him squirming. His body language and facial expressions showed him to be a liar, no matter what words he used."

"That may be true," she said, "but it'll work for him. Look."

She displayed her iPhone for him on which tweets to CNN from listeners had been forwarded to her. Those viewers who bought what Gannon had said ran three to one over those who considered his performance disingenuous. She read one of the tweets aloud: " 'It was disgusting the way the interviewer kept badgering Congressman Gannon. The man told the truth. Leave him alone!' "

The director laughed. "Never overestimate the average voter's intelligence," he said.

"He lied every minute we were on the air," Lewis said. "He'll come out of this unscathed."

"Welcome to the nation's capital, Donna."

Bruce McGinnis had watched the interview in his motel room in Bethesda, Maryland.

After having killed the Georgetown restaurant owner the previous night, he'd driven to Maryland and checked into a small, individually owned motel away from the bustling downtown area.

He'd wanted to leave Washington, but his assignments kept him there. The restaurant owner, who'd also dealt drugs and had run afoul of other dealers to whom he'd owed money, was assigned to McGinnis as a target, and he'd fulfilled his contract with the swiftness and assuredness that he was known for.

He'd left the motel only once that day, to drive a different rental car into the District's Southeast to collect the second half of his fee from the dealer who'd put out the hit on the restaurant owner. He'd carried a handgun with him in the event the dealer balked at turning over the second payment, but it hadn't been necessary to use it. The money was handed over, and McGinnis returned to the motel, where he lolled by the small pool and read a historical murder mystery, his favorite genre.

While watching the Gannon interview, McGinnis perused the material in his briefcase that related to his final mission in Washington, D.C.—to get rid of a private investigator who had made it very plain that he viewed Congressman Harold Gannon as the man behind the disappearance and killing of his intern, Laura Bennett, and the murder of his press aide, Cody Watson.

He was sorry that he'd agreed to take on this final assignment. He'd had enough of Washington and yearned to return home. His stomach was acting up, worse than it had ever been, and the contemplation of yet another killing only exacerbated the pain. Maybe it was time to give up this lucrative but stressful line of work. He'd been doing it for years, and it had provided a sizable nest egg. People retired, didn't they? He was fifty-eight, in excellent physical shape aside from the problems in his gut. How many lives had he taken since leaving the army, where he'd been trained in the art of taking another's life? Nine? A dozen? The number didn't matter. What counted was that he'd been the best at what he did for a living, and he took pride in that.

Robert Brixton.

McGinnis had Brixton's home and office addresses, photos, a rundown of his daily activities, the name of the woman with whom he lived and worked, and his close friends, Mackensie and Annabel Reed-Smith.

As the final minutes of the Gannon interview played on the TV, McGinnis, aka John Mitchell and other aliases, decided to wrap up this assignment as quickly as possible. He called and made a reservation for a flight to Atlanta leaving Reagan National at eight A.M. the day after tomorrow. Booking flights that didn't take him directly to Florida was part of his planning wherever and whenever he traveled on an assignment. It was always a flight to another city in the event he was being watched, and then connecting to a final leg back home. You couldn't be too careful in his business.

40

Before returning to Tampa from Washington after having secured Arturo Casson's commitment to run for Hal Gannon's House seat—provided Gannon could be convinced to resign—Joe Selesky met with leaders of the House Democratic Caucus in an apartment maintained by the DNC as a secure location. There were six in the room besides Selesky, five men and one woman.

"He's got to go," one of the men said. "I like Hal personally, but his behavior has made every elected official the butt of jokes. Letterman cracked a few last night, and let me tell you, my wife didn't appreciate the message behind those jokes, that we're all philanderers and skirt chasers."

"What did you think of his appearance on CNN, Joe?" Selesky was asked.

"Candidly? He bombed. Look, as long as the murders of his intern and press aide go unsolved, the spotlight is squarely on Hal Gannon. Our polls in Tampa–St. Pete show his support fading fast. Not only is he now thought of as a liar who cheats on his wife, his voting pattern has finally hit home with Democrats. He's gotten too damn cozy with Republicans for their taste. He made that work in his favor for a while, but it doesn't play anymore."

"Have you discussed with Hal the possibility of stepping down?" Selesky was asked.

"That would seem the next logical step," someone else said.

"He won't buy it from me," Selesky said.

"What about his family? We hear that his wife and he are on the outs over this."

"Charlene Gannon was never happy with Hal running and winning his House seat. That's why you seldom see her here in D.C. She used to show up at some of his appearances, but from what I can tell she wants nothing more to do with his campaign."

"Have you spoken with Roseann Simmons?" the lone female in the room asked. "She's been with Hal since the very beginning. She has clout with him."

Selesky guffawed. "Roseann? She'd lay down her life for him. Christ, Hal Gannon is her reason for existence. We should all have somebody that loyal in our corner. Look, all this conversation is nice, but we're running out of time. It's too late for a primary, and even if it weren't, it would only drive a wedge in our core base. Casson has agreed to run providing Hal is persuaded to step down. Arturo will make a hell of a good candidate. He'll have the backing of the Cuban-American community, and he's on the progressive side of the issues that matter with the core. But like I said, we've got to move fast to make Hal see the light and drop out. He can take the high road, say he's doing it to spend more time with his family, the usual BS, wants to clear the decks for a true progressive like Arturo, and get back to practicing law. At the same time he can make the point again that he wants whoever killed his intern and press aide brought to swift justice."

"Let me ask a tough question," one of the men said to Selesky.

"Shoot."

"Do you think that Hal Gannon had anything to do with what happened to his intern and press aide?"

"What does it matter what I think?" Selesky countered. "He says he didn't, and that's good enough for me."

His answer didn't necessarily reflect his true feeling, that he wouldn't be surprised if Gannon had had, in some way, a hand in those.

"You have to make the case with him to drop out," Selesky was told.

"Me? Fat chance. It's the people in this room who have to make him see the light, put the pressure on him, threaten to strip him of committee assignments, whatever you have to do to get it done." He checked his watch. "I have to catch a plane. Buttonhole Gannon and lay down the law. Threaten to withhold your support for his run. Do whatever you have to do—but do it fast!"

Brixton brought Flo to the office that morning and got her settled behind the desk, her injured leg in a comfortable horizontal position. He checked in with Mac Smith, who informed him that the Russian immigrant, Anatoly Klimov, had been arrested and charged in the murders of the two young women in Rock Creek Park.

"Any link to the Laura Bennett case?" Brixton asked. "He was considered a suspect."

"Not according to Borgeldt. No connection at all. Luke Bennett called to vent about the Gannon interview on CNN. He's flying to Washington to see if he can help put pressure on the congressman."

"Pressure to do what?"

"Come clean about having slept with his daughter and to fess up what he knows about her disappearance and death."

"He's wasting his time," Brixton said. "The one who knows about Gannon's involvement is my pal with the ponytail. The way I figure it, Gannon hired this guy to make sure that Laura Bennett never talked about their affair."

"And Cody Watson, the congressman's press aide?"

"Same thing. Killing somebody—actually taking somebody's life—isn't Gannon's style. Too messy, would get his hands dirty. But hiring it out isn't hard. Look at the sicko wife who was willing to pay me forty grand to bump off her husband. Life's cheap to lots of people, Mac, plenty of guys, and women, too, available to kill somebody for a buck. Gannon had a lot to lose."

Brixton spoke the truth, Mac knew.

"What's on your agenda today, Robert?"

"I'm going to have coffee with my old pal from New York, Dick Sheridan, the drummer that Flo and I caught at Blues Alley the night we got run down. He's leaving later to go on tour with his trio. And I'm having lunch with Will Sayers."

"Give him our best. He introduced us to you."

"For which I've thanked him many times. I'll check in later."

Brixton met up with Dick Sheridan at a Georgetown coffee shop.

"I still can't believe what happened to you and your girlfriend," Sheridan said.

Brixton explained the circumstances surrounding the Laura Bennett case and his conviction that the driver of the car probably had a hand in her murder.

"You should get into a different business," Sheridan said.

"Too late to learn to play the sax," Brixton said.

"Never too late. If you ever do, I'll hire you, turn the trio into a quartet."

"It's a deal," Brixton said.

They hugged on the street before Sheridan got into a taxi, and Brixton knew that they might never see each other again. The thought saddened him, and he was glad that he and Flo had caught his performance. Old friends were hard to come by.

Sayers was in his usual expansive mood when they had lunch at Martin's Tavern. Sayers had followed all the media coverage of the Gannon story but was not aware of the man with the ponytail.

"And he actually tried to run you and Flo down?" Sayers said.

"He sure as hell did. I've put together the pieces. Gannon hires this guy, whoever he is, to snuff out his intern to keep word of their affair from getting around and blowing up his phony family man façade. He finds out that his press aide is telling me tales out of school and sics the aging hippie on him for the same reason. Me, with my big mouth, goes around telling people, including the media, that I'm sure that Gannon was behind the murders. That adds me to the list of people that Gannon needs to get rid of."

Brixton also told Sayers that he'd spent time with the PI, Paul Wooster, who Sayers had checked on.

"A charming fellow, I'm sure," Sayers said.

"I'm not sure I'd use that word," Brixton said. "I think he's a guy who's comfortable playing both sides against the middle."

"Is he involved in any way in this scenario you're painting?"

"I can't see how. He works for the Republican running against Gannon but seems cozy with some of Gannon's people, too. Like I said, he's a double-dipper."

Sayers indulged in his usual large lunch while Brixton

contented himself with a chef salad with chicken. Flo had been on a healthy eating kick lately, and Brixton felt as though she was looking over his shoulder.

Sayers's healthy appetite always amazed Brixton. The corpulent former newspaper editor would duplicate at dinner what he'd had for lunch, with a few extra helpings tossed in, and Brixton always wondered whether he'd be attending his friend's premature funeral one day soon. He hoped not.

They were on coffee—with a slice of blueberry pie for Sayers—when Brixton's cell rang.

"Sorry to interrupt your lunch, Robert," Mac Smith said, "but I just got a call from Zeke Borgeldt. He has some additional information about the guy with the ponytail. Seems that a woman, a regular at the bar where the bartender told the detectives he'd seen him, had stopped back in and got talking to that bartender. He told her that the authorities were looking for the man that she'd struck up a conversation with, which prompted her to contact the police."

"Did she get his name?"

"Just the one we know was false. But she described him as having what she termed a 'cultured way of speaking,' almost an accent, like British or Scottish."

Brixton sighed. "I was hoping that they'd come up with more than that."

"It's more than we had a few hours ago," Mac said. "Oh, she also said that he left the bar at about ten that night to go to a business meeting."

"Maybe he's a vampire."

"If he is, I suggest that you start wearing turtlenecks."

"I'll ask Flo to buy me some. Thanks, Mac. I'll be back in a half hour."

Sayers picked up the lunch tab. A family member with whom he hadn't been particularly close had died and left a portion of her sizable estate to him, which he'd graciously accepted.

"She must have thought a lot of you," Brixton said as they prepared to part outside Martin's.

"She found me amusing," was the journalist's comment. "Aunt Monique—her real name was Emma but she found that too pedestrian—was the quintessential free spirit, many lovers, never a husband, a house filled with cats and even a baby alligator that she kept in the bathtub. She loved the fact that I was a journalist, a calling she considered akin to sainthood. Anyway, her will was read, and to the chagrin of others I was named as a beneficiary. Life takes funny turns, huh?"

"Screw those others who lost out," Brixton said. "Your aunt Monique, or whatever her name was, did what made her happy. Enjoy the money, my friend, and thanks for lunch."

B rixton had appointments after lunch, and by the time he returned to his office it was almost six. Flo wasn't happy.

"Sorry," he said, kissing her cheek. "I got tied up."

"Sounds perverted," she said.

"Nothing that enjoyable," he said.

"When are you going to write that proposal for the man in Virginia?" she asked. "He called again while you were out being *tied up.*"

"I'll get around to it one of these days."

"You keep putting it off, Robert, and you'll blow this job. The guy owns a defense-contacting company and is willing to spend big money to solve his security problem. It's a win-win situation. All you have to do is come up with a plan for him to keep tabs on employees who he's convinced are stealing from him. He pays you for the plan and you keep collecting to implement it."

"I know, I know. It's just that this situation with Gannon is all-consuming."

"That's understandable. But why not write the proposal and put it behind us? You've already figured out his problem. All you have to do is put it on paper. Tell you what. Let's bring in food for dinner and get it done. You can dictate it to me."

"I'll think about it," he said, and disappeared into his office, where he spent the next half hour sorting through piles of paper on his desk. When he emerged, he said that he had to run back to the apartment to pick up the file on the Virginia defense contractor that he'd forgotten to bring with him that morning. "You're right about the proposal," he told Flo. "We'll get takeout when I come back—I'm in the mood for Chinese—and we'll get it done."

He drove from their reserved space beneath the office building to the apartment, where he found what he was looking for, and stayed a few extra minutes to nibble on leftover lemon wafers. The salad at lunch had been good but not filling. He rode the elevator down to the ground floor and walked to the semilegal parking spot he'd found a half block from the building. Since the incident on Wisconsin Avenue that had almost taken their lives, he'd become especially aware of his surroundings, and looked up and down the darkening street before getting into his car. No tan man with a ponytail in sight.

But Bruce McGinnis *was* there, parked a block away, on the other side of the cross street, far enough away to not be seen but close enough to keep his eye on Brixton's car. He eased into traffic and maintained a safe distance to avoid being spotted by Brixton in his rearview mirror.

When McGinnis had followed Brixton from the office

and saw that he'd gone inside his apartment building, he considered confronting Brixton there. But there were too many people coming and going, and he decided to wait for a more opportune moment. What he knew for certain was that it had to be done that night before his flight back to Tampa. He was eager to get home.

He found a parking place a dozen spots from Brixton's office building, turned off the engine, put on earphones attached to his iPod, listened to classical music he'd downloaded, and formulated his plan for the rest of the day and evening.

If Brixton remained in his office after others had closed, he'd go there and get it over with. If he left the office, he would follow him, hoping that an opportunity would present itself on the street. And if Brixton returned to his apartment for the night, it would have to be accomplished there.

Of course Brixton's lady friend, Flo Combes, presented a complication. The assignment did not include her, and ideally he could corner Brixton when he was alone. But her presence hadn't stopped him from aiming his rented car at both of them when they'd exited Blues Alley. Sometimes the innocent became victims, too; the military termed it collateral damage. He knew that she'd been injured—he'd seen Brixton help her into the apartment building the day he'd brought her back from the hospital, her leg swathed in bandages and encased in a large, cumbersome brace. He'd missed following Brixton the first day that he'd brought Flo to the office, having gotten tied up in a traffic jam, and had also missed him this morning when he'd overslept. But as far as he knew she was confined to the apartment and couldn't pose a problem should he kill Brixton in his office or on the street.

* * *

B rixton and Flo were about to start preparing the proposal for the Virginia defense contractor when Mac Smith interrupted.

"Robert, I'm meeting with a client, who it turns out could make good use of your talents. Come on in and meet her. She has an interesting story, and case."

Brixton shrugged and said to Flo, "Back in a jif, hon, and we'll wrap up the proposal."

He returned an hour later. "Sorry," he said, "but Mac was right. I think I've got a fascinating new case. This new client of his is a—"

"The proposal," Flo said flatly.

"Oh, right, the proposal," Brixton said. "I started to write something the other day. It's in this file I grabbed from the apartment. Start inputting it. You've got to be hungry. I know I am. Mac's working late, too. I'll see if he wants some Chinese and run to that little take-out joint behind the building. The usual? General Tso's chicken? Shrimp fried rice? Maybe some steamed dumplings with peanut sauce?"

"Just as long as it's quick," she said.

Smith put in his bid for beef with snow peas and a container of hot-and-sour soup. Brixton phoned in the order and left the office. When he stepped out of the elevator in the underground parking garage, he realized that he hadn't locked the office door on his way out. Since learning that he was a target in the Bennett case, he and Flo had made it a habit to lock up, although they didn't always remember to do it. Should he call Flo and ask her to do it? He decided against having her haul her braced leg from the comfort of her desk. Run back up? He'd only be away a few minutes. The food order had already been phoned in and would be waiting for him. He quickened his pace and went through a rear door.

* * *

McGinnis surveyed the windows in the office building. Many lights had been extinguished. In one office suite he saw a cleaning crew doing its job. He didn't know whether Brixton's office faced front or overlooked the rear, but it didn't matter. The private investigator had entered and hadn't left. The flow of people in and out of the lobby had waned to just an occasional few. This was as good a time as any, he reasoned. He took off his earphones and checked the pockets of his sport jacket to be sure his knife with its pencil-thin blade was where it should be. He reached down and patted his ankle holster in which his Glock 29SF semiautomatic handgun was nestled. He preferred to not use the weapon—too loud. He also satisfied himself that the leather pouch filled with lead was readily available. That was what he'd used on Laura Bennett and Cody Watson.

Killing her had been one of the most difficult assignments he'd fulfilled in recent days. He hated smashing in such a pretty head. On top of that, his instructions had been to not only silence her; he also was to dispose of the body in such a way as to delay its discovery. He'd followed her into the Congressional Cemetery where she'd gone for a jog and attacked her close to the vault, a perfect place to stash her. From the looks of things, no one ever went inside it.

He got out of his car and approached the building's entrance. He'd reconnoitered it earlier and knew that the man at the front desk, through which all visitors had to pass, went off duty at six. He stepped into the marble lobby and went to the directory, where he saw that Robert Brixton's suite was on the second floor, directly across from the elevator. He also took note that the attorney, Mackensie Smith, had a suite that, based upon its number, was adjacent to Brixton's.

* * *

As McGinnis pushed the button for the elevator, Brixton was sipping a glass of rice wine that the owner of the Chinese take-out shop had insisted he accept. Brixton was a familiar face there, and the owner often offered him a drink on the house, calling Brixton his *péngyôu*, his friend. To which Brixton always replied in the only Chinese he knew, *xie xie*, thanking the owner for his generosity.

McGinnis reached the second floor, stepped from the elevator into the carpeted hallway, and cocked his head, searching for sounds. The whir of a vacuum cleaner could be heard in the distance, and music coming from an office a floor above reached his ears, some rock-and-roll song of the type he despised.

He went to the door bearing Brixton's suite number and paused. Brixton, a private investigator, was undoubtedly armed. McGinnis pulled the Glock from his ankle holster, drew a breath, and tried the door. He knew that it might possibly be locked and was surprised, and pleased, when the knob turned and the door opened.

Flo Combes was at her desk typing in things that Brixton had written in longhand, her back to McGinnis. He took the few steps to close the gap between them and clamped his hand over her mouth, the Glock pointed at her neck. "Quiet," he whispered into her ear. "Make any move and I'll kill you."

He looked at the open doorway into Brixton's office.

"He's in there?" he whispered again.

His large hand over her mouth kept her from speaking, but she managed to shake her head.

"He's not there?" McGinnis repeated, his tone mirroring his surprise.

Flo shook her head again.

"Where is he?"

She tried to answer but her words came out garbled, a series of grunts.

He eased his grip on her and said, "One word from you, one scream, and you are a very dead young lady."

"I won't—I—who are you?"

As she looked at him she answered her own question. His ponytail said it all.

"Why do you—?"

He put his finger to his lips. "Where is he? When is he coming back?"

"He went out to get dinner. He's—"

"Dinner? What dinner? Where?"

She started to say that he was bringing back Chinese food but stopped herself. It sounded as though he thought that he'd gone to a restaurant and wouldn't be back for a while. Let him think that.

McGinnis looked at the door leading to Mac Smith's office, the Glock still leveled at Flo's head. While Smith and Brixton's offices had separate entrances off the hallway, the large suite that had been carved up to accommodate both men contained an inner door that provided easy back-and-forth access.

Smith had stayed late to redraft a document for a client. He'd told Doris that she needn't stay, that she could prepare the final version the next day. As he often did when alone in the office, he'd put on a CD, this evening a compilation album of familiar Broadway melodies performed by the National Symphony Orchestra. The faint strains of "Some Enchanted Evening" could be heard.

"Who's in there?" McGinnis asked Flo.

"A lawyer, Mac—"

Brixton would be walking in at any moment, she knew, and wished that she were able to call him, to warn him to stay away. She was consumed with that thought when the door to Smith's office opened and he stepped through it, the louder music following. McGinnis turned the Glock on Mac, who froze.

"What the hell is going on?" Smith blurted, although

he knew the answer before the words came out. He was face-to-face with the man with the ponytail.

"Over there!" McGinnis commanded, indicating with his head that he wanted Smith to move to a corner of the reception area. "Move! Move!"

Brixton left the Chinese restaurant carrying a large plastic bag with the dinners in it. He realized that he'd taken more time than he'd intended and quickly crossed the street and headed for the rear door to the parking garage. He entered and crossed the large space, his footsteps reverberating on the concrete floor. He stood in front of the elevator and saw on the display above the door that the car was stopped at the second floor. He pushed the button and the car slowly descended, bypassing the lobby level and coming to the garage. He stepped in and rode up. As the doors opened and he stepped from the car, a tickle in his throat that had been bothering him all day caused him to cough.

Flo heard the elevator arrive. And then the cough.

Brixton's hand on the doorknob made a noise. The knob turned. As the door opened, Flo shouted, "No! Don't!"

McGinnis leveled the Glock and squeezed off a shot. It struck the take-out bag, sending Chinese food flying into the air. Brixton was stunned. He stumbled back, his hand on the knob, slamming the door closed. He righted himself and pressed his back against the wall, simultaneously grabbing his revolver from the holster beneath his left arm. It had all happened fast, but in the few seconds it took for the door to have opened and the shot fired, he'd seen Flo and Mac—and the shooter, the man with the ponytail.

There was silence from inside Brixton's reception area, where Flo and Mac Smith waited for McGinnis to make his next move. The door leading to Smith's office was ajar; the sound of the National Symphony playing "Night and Day" came through the opening. McGinnis appeared to be flustered. His eyes shifted back and forth between Flo, Mac Smith, and the door to the hallway where Brixton lurked, his weapon at the ready as he tried to formulate *his* next move. He slipped his cell phone from his pocket and dialed 911. When the operator came on the line, he said softly, "Armed standoff taking place." He gave the address on Pennsylvania Avenue. "Second floor. Killer in an office holding hostages. Need police here fast!"

He repeated the message. The operator told him to stay out of the fray and that police had been notified and were responding.

As the standoff continued, Smith tried to analyze the situation from his perspective. The man in the ponytail had seemed to be calm and focused. But he could now see an expression of panic on his square, tanned face. McGinnis looked back into Brixton's empty office, and Smith thought that if he retreated there they might have an opportunity to slam the door shut and contain him. Although neither Smith nor Flo knew whether Brixton had called for help, they assumed that he had. If so, it was a matter of waiting it out—provided that McGinnis didn't decide to leave carnage in his wake and kill them both.

The silence in the room was broken when Brixton shouted, "Give it up in there. Lay down the gun and come out."

His message prompted McGinnis to stiffen, and Smith wondered whether he was about to try and shoot his way out. He approached the hall door, his weapon leveled at it. Was Brixton directly behind it? If he was, a shot into the door would strike him. McGinnis locked the door and stepped back.

Sirens sounded outside the building.

McGinnis heard them and muttered under his breath.

The final strains of "Night and Day" were replaced by the beginning of "On a Clear Day."

In the hall, a contingent of uniformed police poured from the elevator to where Brixton stood to the side of the office door. Seeing the weapon in his hand caused some of the officers to draw theirs, but Brixton shook his head and held his handgun up in the air. He told the first officer off the elevator, "I'm Robert Brixton, a PI. That's my office in there. The guy who killed Congressman Gannon's intern and his press aide is in there. He's armed and holding the attorney, Mac Smith, and a woman at gunpoint."

Other officers came bounding up the stairs; one held a shield, the other a battering ram.

Brixton holstered his gun and repeated what he'd told the others. As he did, a ranking officer arrived and took Brixton aside. Brixton gave him a fuller explanation than he'd provided the others. "Call Zeke Borgeldt," Brixton said. "He'll confirm everything I've said."

The officer did as Brixton requested. "He's sending a hostage negotiator," he said after ending the call.

"He fired once at me when I came back from getting take-out dinners," Brixton said, pointing to the mess of food scattered over the hallway floor.

The ranking officer was handed a bullhorn.

"This is the police," he barked. "The building is surrounded by armed officers. There is no way for you to escape. Put down any weapons you possess and come out with your hands high."

There was no response from inside the office.

"You say there's a woman in there?" Brixton was asked.

"That's right. She's my—she's my fiancée and my partner in the agency. Name's Flo Combes. She's got a brace on her leg. This same guy with the gun in there tried to run us down the other night."

"What is he, a psycho?"

"Not a bad guess," said Brixton. "What do you suggest?"

"We wait for the hostage negotiator to arrive."

"He's liable to kill them both while we wait."

"And he's liable to kill them if we try to break in," was the officer's reply. "We wait."

Brixton knew that was the right call. While a police officer in D.C. for four years, and during his longer tenure with the Savannah PD, he'd been involved in a number of hostage situations. Patience was always the operative policy, although there had been times when patience had backfired and the hostage or hostages were killed. It was a delicate situation, and he'd developed a lot of respect for trained negotiators.

It seemed hours, although only a few minutes had passed before the negotiator arrived, a veteran FBI agent working under a contract with the Washington MPD. Brixton was asked to fill him in, which he did in as much detail as the negotiator seemed to want.

"What's the phone number in there?" Brixton was asked.

He gave it to him.

Using a cell phone, the negotiator called the number. It wasn't answered.

"Are there windows in there?" he asked Brixton.

"In my office, at the rear of the suite. The reception area where I last saw them doesn't have any."

He pictured Flo with her leg in a brace and a gun to her head, and a knot formed in his stomach. She didn't deserve this. Why hadn't he locked the door before he left to pick up the food? She should have stayed home nursing her injury. Maybe he shouldn't have been so public in his conviction that Gannon was behind the murders of Laura Bennett and Cody Watson. He'd created the situation that brought the ponytailed killer to his office and threatened the lives of the woman he loved and the attorney who'd become one of the best friends he'd ever had.

Shoulda, coulda.

The negotiator walked away, leaving Brixton to deal with his frustration and concerns about Flo and Mac. He moved down the hall until he was in front of the entrance to Smith's suite and thought of the door separating their offices. That Smith was in the reception area with Flo probably meant that he'd used that door. Had he closed it behind him? Probably not. He seldom did. But how open was it? Fully? Partially?

He reached down and tried the knob to Smith's door. It opened. He held it slightly ajar and listened to the music being played on Smith's stereo system, "Maria" from *West Side Story*.

Brixton opened the door just enough to slip through, and gently, quietly closed it behind him. The door linking the suites was halfway open. The only illumination in the room came from a pair of halogen desk lamps that pooled their bright white light on Smith's desk. Brixton was glad that the music played. It covered any noise he might make.

He hugged the wall, his Smith & Wesson in his hand, and slowly, deliberately made his way toward the door between the suites. He held his breath to hear more acutely. Mac was speaking to McGinnis, trying to convince him to give up.

"Shut up!" McGinnis snapped.

"He's right," Flo said. "The police are everywhere. You can't—"

Brixton heard a dull thud, followed by Flo's anguished, painful scream. He was about to enter the reception area when McGinnis suddenly pushed the door fully open and peered into Smith's office. Brixton was shrouded in shadow against the wall, but McGinnis stood out as a vivid silhouette, backlit by lights from the reception area. It took a moment for him to acclimate to the darkness of Mac's office. When he had, he became aware of Brixton.

Brixton didn't hesitate. He fired off two shots in rapid succession. One struck McGinnis in the right shoulder, causing his weapon to spiral into the air and land in the middle of the room. The second shot passed cleanly through the right side of his abdomen. Brixton pounced on McGinnis, who'd fallen face-first. Smith ran in and helped Brixton, who was having trouble keeping McGinnis pinned to the floor despite his wounds.

"Get the police in here," Brixton shouted.

Flo hobbled to the door, unlocked it, and the officers rushed in.

"Good job, Robert," Smith said as he got to his feet.

"Sorry about the blood on your new carpet," Brixton said.

Flo joined them and hugged Brixton.

"You move pretty good for a cripple," he told her.

He saw the welt on her cheek. "He hit you," he said.

"I'm just glad we're alive," she said.

"Me, too," he said. "Just wish he hadn't shot up the Chinese food. I'm starving."

41

Smith, Brixton, and Flo watched as EMTs placed Mc-Ginnis on a gurney. They'd stemmed his bleeding and stabilized his condition. He wouldn't die, at least not from Brixton's shots. The police had manacled his ankles and wrists. A white sheet covered him up to his neck. Mac had never seen such cold eyes, and looked away. Brixton's thoughts went from wanting to shoot him again to wondering what was going through his mind or, more accurately, what sort of mind would lead a man to such senseless killing.

Large red stains on the gray carpet in Mac's office gave testimony to what had just occurred there.

Zeke Borgeldt had arrived after being alerted. He was accompanied by two other detectives, who'd emptied McGinnis's pockets before he was taken away. His wallet contained multiple false IDs and two bogus credit cards. Other items gave his address in Clearwater, Florida. There was also a business card indicating that he owned and operated a fishing charter service.

He had two sets of keys, one containing what appeared to be personal keys, the other from the car rental agency on which the agency's name and phone number were printed, along with a paper tag with the vehicle's license plate number.

"He must have parked somewhere close to here," Brixton said.

Borgeldt dispatched officers to search for the car on surrounding streets. They reported back within fifteen minutes that they'd located it.

Brixton accompanied Borgeldt and the detectives to the car. Borgeldt donned a pair of gloves and opened the door. Seeing nothing of interest, he opened the trunk.

"Fancy briefcase," Brixton said of the black alligator case Borgeldt extracted.

"Get this hauled to the vehicle yard," Borgeldt ordered. "I want a top-to-bottom sweep of it."

They returned to Brixton's office, where Annabel had just arrived after receiving a call from Mac. "Thank God you're all okay," she said as she stood with Mac's arm around her.

"Fortunately, Robert's a good shot," Mac said.

"Not good enough to have killed the bastard," Brixton said.

"It's good that you didn't," Borgeldt said as he sat at Flo's desk and opened the briefcase. "We need a lot of answers from him."

"I'd like to go home," Flo said from where she sat on a small couch, her battered leg stretched out.

"I'm all for that," Brixton said. He looked over Borgeldt's shoulder at items that he'd pulled from the briefcase. "Anything of interest?"

"There's this notebook, an address book, and his airline tickets. That's about it. Look at this," he said, handing Brixton the notebook, its pages containing handwritten jottings.

Brixton went through some of the pages and stopped

at one. "Listen to this," he told everyone. "He has this entry: 'LB 35,000. CW 35,000. RB 45,000.'"

"Initials," Smith said.

"Laura Bennett's initials," Brixton said. "Cody Watson's, too. And guess who RB is."

"What do you figure?" Mac said. "That the numbers are how much he was being paid for each hit?"

"Sounds right to me," said Brixton. His laugh was ironic. "I should be flattered. He was getting more for me than the others."

"The question is, who was paying him?" Borgeldt said.

"Who else?" Brixton said. "Our friend Congressman Gannon."

"You have proof of that?" Borgeldt asked.

"No," Brixton said. "But wait a minute."

"What?" Annabel said.

"Look at this notation at the bottom of the page."

He showed it to Borgeldt.

"It's an address," Borgeldt said.

"N Street Northwest," Brixton said.

"That's in Georgetown," Annabel said.

"Three thousand," Mac said. "Mean anything to anyone?"

No one responded.

Brixton handed the notebook back. The others looked at him as his face reflected the thought process he was going through. "I know that address," he said. "When I met with Cody Watson at the Hotel Lombardy, he said that Gannon's chief of staff, Roseann Simmons, lived there."

"You're sure," Flo said.

"Yeah, I'm sure."

"What say we swing by there and see why her address is in a killer's notebook," Brixton suggested.

"I intend to do that," Borgeldt said, "but without you. This is a police matter."

"You really know how to hurt a guy," Brixton said, placing his hands over his heart. "Come on, Zeke. You've got your killer because I put myself on the line. The least you can do is let me tag along. I've been bird-dogging this case right alongside you and your people. I'll stay out of your way, but you owe me."

"He has a point," said Mac. "It can't hurt having Robert with you. Annabel and I will take Flo back to our place at the Watergate. That okay with you, Flo? Robert?"

Brixton nodded. He went to Flo, kissed her, and said, "I really need to be there, babe, but if you really want me to—"

"No," she said, "you go. You'll be a wreck every minute if you don't follow through. I'll be fine. Mac and Annabel run a first-class rehab center. Besides, he makes a dynamite Manhattan." She returned the kiss and said to Annabel, "Let's go."

Borgeldt acquiesced and told Brixton he could accompany them, but to stay in the background.

"Count on it," Brixton said. He took a final look at the bloodstained rug on the other side of the open door and said, "Get some new carpet, Mac. It's on me."

42

Borgeldt had considered calling Roseann Simmons but decided against it. Better to simply show up and catch her off guard. Not that he'd decided that she was guilty of anything. The only reason they were going to her home was that her address was in McGinnis's notebook. But he also knew that Brixton had been right to question why a U.S. congressman's chief of staff's address would even be there. Just to be certain that he had all his bases covered, he dispatched two detectives to the area, with the instruction to stay out of sight unless needed.

Borgeldt, Detective Morey, a female plainclothes detective, and Brixton rode to the address in Borgeldt's unmarked sedan. They made a slow pass of the house. Lights were on. Two cars were parked in a cramped cutout in front of a small garage, a silver Lexus and a red Mercedes convertible. They turned at the end of the street and drove back, parking across the street.

"She has good taste in cars," Brixton commented. He'd told the detectives on the way what Cody Watson had told him, that Roseann came from a wealthy family in Tampa, its money from questionable sources.

Borgeldt led the way to the front door and rang the bell. It took awhile for Roseann to answer. She wore a white bathrobe and slippers. She looked past Borgeldt and recognized Brixton.

"Superintendent Borgeldt," the detective said, showing her his identification. "We have some questions."

She ignored him and asked, "What's *he* doing here?" looking at Brixton.

"You were expecting someone else?" Brixton said snidely.

"May we come in, Ms. Simmons?" Borgeldt said.

"I have company."

"If you'd like, Ms. Simmons, I can get a warrant," Borgeldt said, "but I suggest it would be a lot easier for you if you allow us to come in and ask you some questions." He sounded friendly, but there was steel behind his words.

Brixton looked past him into the interior of the house, where someone walked quickly from one room to another. Although he had only a momentary glance, he was sure it was Gannon.

"This is an outrageous intrusion," she said. "Maybe you'd better get a warrant. Good evening."

She tried to close the door, but Borgeldt's foot was faster. "Last chance, Ms. Simmons," he said. "You either invite us in or I summon the troops. Having a dozen patrol cars with lights flashing and sirens wailing should draw some press interest, wouldn't you say?"

She stood frozen, conflict written on her pretty face. Then, before she had a chance to respond, Gannon appeared behind her.

"Good evening, Congressman," Borgeldt said, and went through the introduction again and the presenting of his ID.

"Let them in, Roseann," Gannon said. He was dressed

in slacks, a blue dress shirt that wasn't tucked in his pants, and loafers.

"Hal, they have no right to barge in like this."

"They'll get in one way or the other," Gannon said. "You heard him. He'll get a warrant and turn it into a circus. I don't need another circus."

She muttered a curse and stepped back, allowing Borgeldt and the others to enter the expansive foyer that was an art gallery, its walls covered with dozens of what looked to Brixton like original oil paintings—not that he was an art connoisseur. There were a few prints and even an occasional original in the apartment he shared with Flo, a jazz-themed painting by James Vann that Brixton treasured, a Haitian oil that he'd been given in Savannah to pay a debt, some Picasso prints, and an oil painting hanging over the fireplace that he'd picked up for $150 at a yard sale and that he was certain was worth millions if he brought it to *Antiques Roadshow*. Flo wasn't so sure about that.

"I was just leaving," Gannon said, tucking his shirt into his pants and slipping on a sport jacket.

"Maybe you ought to hang around," Brixton said.

"Why is he here?" Roseann demanded, pointing again at Brixton. "He isn't the police."

"No, ma'am, he isn't," Borgeldt said, "but he's got a pretty big stake in what's been happening."

Brixton had brought with him the notebook found in McGinnis's briefcase. "Care to take a look?" he asked Roseann.

"What is it?"

"A notebook belonging to the guy who tried to kill me tonight. Name's McGinnis, although he goes by a few other names. Here. Check out what's written on this page." He handed it to her.

"I don't see why I would be interested in this," she said.

"That's your address, isn't it?" Borgeldt said.

"It appears to be, but so what?"

"See those initials and the numbers next to them?" Brixton said. "LB." He turned to Gannon. "Laura Bennett, maybe?"

"Roseann," Gannon said, "why is your address here?"

"How would I know?" she said. "This is ridiculous."

"If you'll excuse me," Gannon said.

"CW," Brixton said. "Cody Watson?"

Despite announcing that he was leaving, Gannon didn't move. He said to his chief of staff, "What does this mean, Roseann?"

"See those third initials?" Brixton said. "RB. That's me. You wouldn't happen to have forty-five thousand bucks laying around, would you, Ms. Simmons? The guy you were going to pay for getting rid of me won't be dropping by for his payment. He's in the hospital with two bullets in him."

"We didn't expect to find you here, Congressman," Borgeldt said, "but since you are, maybe you can fill us in on Ms. Simmons's involvement with this."

"I haven't the slightest idea what you're talking about," Gannon said.

"I find that hard to believe," Brixton said.

"I don't need your snide remarks, Mr. Brixton," Gannon said. He turned to Roseann. "Tell me what's going on here. There's obviously been a big mistake that these officers are making. Why *is* your address in that notebook? What do those initials and numbers mean?"

"Oh, God, Hal, for someone as bright as you, you can sometimes be so dumb."

Her comment hung in the air like a stench, causing everyone to fall silent and look at her. Finally, she said, "Did it ever occur to you, Hal, that you were about to be professionally and personally buried because of your inability to keep your pants zippered?"

"Your chief of staff is pretty loyal," Brixton said. "Everybody should have someone that loyal."

If this were a cartoon, a lightbulb would be shown coming on over Gannon's head. Whether it was a true revelation, or some good acting, wasn't clear. He said, "I hope what I'm taking from this conversation isn't true, Roseann."

She looked at him with a mixture of pity and scorn. "You didn't have the guts to take care of it yourself, did you? You didn't have the fortitude to dig out of the hole you dug for yourself."

"Roseann," he said, "I think it's best if you stop talking and call your lawyer. These people are not your friends."

"You heard him," she said to Borgeldt. "Our conversation is over."

Borgeldt radioed for the backup team to come to the front door. He said to Roseann, "We're taking you in, Ms. Simmons."

"On what charge?"

"Suspicion of conspiracy to murder. I can come up with a few other charges if that will satisfy you."

"I'm not dressed," Roseann said.

"Detective Quinto will accompany you to your bedroom and you can change clothes."

Without another word, she headed for the stairs, with the female detective close behind.

"I don't believe this," Gannon said. "Yes, Roseann is loyal, but it's inconceivable that she would have gotten involved in what happened to Laura and Cody."

"We'll get it all sorted out," Borgeldt said.

"Well," said Gannon, "I hope that you're not thinking that *I* had any knowledge of what was going on."

"That'll get sorted out, too," Brixton said.

"Believe me," Gannon said, "this all comes as a complete shock to me. To think that my chief of staff would—"

"Can it, Congressman," Brixton said. "Your words might work with voters, but they don't work for me."

Ten minutes later Roseann descended the stairs along with Detective Quinto. She'd put on a teal jumpsuit that showed off her figure nicely, and she'd done something with her hair and applied makeup.

"Whatever happens," Gannon said, "we'll fight it. I'll be with you every step of the way."

She gave him a sardonic smile. "Despite being a fool, Hal, you'll always be a man who I look up to. I've always believed in what you could do to help this country, and still do. Oh, and by the way, I love you!"

CHAPTER

43

Bruce McGinnis didn't try to deny his involvement in the murders of Laura Bennett and Cody Watson. He willingly gave a long, detailed written statement to the police, a portion of which was leaked to *The Washington Post*. The excerpts gave its readers a chilling look into a man for whom human life was there to be taken away. It read in part:

... And so I've made a very nice living cleaning up messes that others create. Given a choice I would prefer to simply operate my fishing boat for well-heeled cretins who wouldn't know a fishing rod from a rake, but that business never gave me the financial stability I aspire to. I must admit that killing that lovely young woman, the intern to Congressman Gannon, was difficult, and my gastrointestinal condition, which I've suffered from since a child, reflected my displeasure at having to do it. But a deal is a deal, and a contract must be fulfilled. Ms. Simmons, to whom I was introduced in Tampa by a mutual friend, paid handsomely for my services, and deserved results ...

As far as the young man who worked for Congressman Gannon as a press aide, I'd followed him to the Hotel Lombardy, where he'd met with the private investigator, Robert Brixton. Ms. Simmons had learned that Mr. Watson was telling people, including Brixton, about the congressman's affair with his intern, and wanted him stopped. When Mr. Watson left the hotel, he went into a gay bar. I'm not a homosexual, but I joined him there, struck up a conversation, and was invited back to his apartment to listen to selections from what he said was a sizable CD collection. I stayed only ten minutes. When I left, he was dead. Mission accomplished . . .

As for what happened with Brixton, the private investigator, I must admit that I got sloppy, which isn't like me. I should have acted quicker when he arrived at his office door carrying food, but my stomach was acting up again (sometimes the pain is unbearable), and I wasn't thinking clearly. So, here I am, facing my fate, and not the least bit concerned about it. We live and we die. I just wish I'd been able to carry through on my obligation to kill Brixton. He seemed like a disagreeable sort to me . . .

Ms. Simmons is a nice lady and I'm sorry she'll have to face the same fate that I do. I admire her staunch defense of Congressman Gannon. She said that with the proper handling he could have become president of the United States one day, and that she intended to be at his side. I don't know whether she was right or not, nor do I care . . .

I have already given you the names of others I have killed, including my second wife. If anyone deserved to die, it was her. Hopefully, this will avoid having innocent people charged with those crimes. I have always believed in fairness and justice.

That is all I have to say.

Congressman Harold Gannon was never charged in the Laura Bennett or Cody Watson murders, nor was he linked to the attempt on Brixton's life. Roseann Simmons vehemently denied his involvement, as did he. The funny thing was that Brixton came to believe him.

Not that Brixton's view of the congressman had changed in other ways. He still considered him a dirtbag, and the voters in Florida's Fourteenth Congressional District evidently agreed. Gannon's refusal to step aside despite pressure from his Democratic colleagues precluded an opportunity for Arturo Casson to take his place on the ballot, and Pete Solon, the Republican, won handily.

Roseann Simmons eventually confessed to having contracted with Bruce McGinnis to silence Laura Bennett and Cody Watson—and by extension Robert Brixton. Her initial denials were undercut by McGinnis, who was a strong witness against her.

A month later, Brixton and Flo were at the Smiths' apartment enjoying a Sunday brunch.

"McGinnis is an intelligent guy," Brixton said.

"Native intelligence, maybe," Annabel said, "but put to the wrong use. He's morally bankrupt."

"Anybody know what's happened with Gannon?" Mac asked.

"I heard on a talk show that he's in Miami practicing law," Annabel said. "His wife filed for divorce."

"A guy like him will ride it out," Mac said. "He'll get married again to a woman who feels he's been unfairly smeared, and he'll make a living, probably a better one than being a U.S. congressman."

Brixton said, "I was wrong about Gannon." He held up his hand. "Not about him being a smarmy guy, but that he was behind the killings. He created the situation with his womanizing but didn't know how to get out of it. His chief of staff thought she had the answer in hiring McGinnis."

"It was a bad answer," Mac said.

"A very bad answer," Annabel chimed in.

"Washington is full of bad answers," Brixton said.

"Luke and Grace Bennett stopped by," Mac said. "Luke wanted me to thank you for all you did for him."

"Tough what they went through," Flo said.

"Luke didn't look well," Annabel said. "Laura's murder seems to have sucked all the energy out of him."

Brixton understood. Losing his daughter in a terrorist bombing had taken something out of him, too.

"Is your former wife going ahead with the book she wants to write?" Mac asked.

Brixton shrugged. "If she does, it won't be with my help," he said.

"Well," Annabel said, "with all this behind us, maybe we can get back to normal."

"Normal?" Brixton said. "I'm not sure what normal is. If you mean getting on with our lives, you're right, including enjoying a Sunday brunch with friends. You have any more quiche, Annabel? It's really good."

Read on for a preview of

MARGARET TRUMAN'S

DEADLY MEDICINE

A CAPITAL CRIMES NOVEL

▸ DONALD BAIN ◂

Available in June 2016
from Tom Doherty Associates

A FORGE BOOK

1

Flo's Fashions was located on upper Wisconsin Avenue, at the tail end of Georgetown's main commercial drag. Flo Combes, lady friend of Robert "Don't Call Me Bobby" Brixton, had opened the women's clothing boutique six months ago and all signs pointed to it becoming a success. Word had gotten around that the lines of American-made clothing she featured combined casualness with a touch of flair, and business had been brisk. She'd owned a similar shop in Savannah, Georgia, when she and Brixton had lived together in that genteel southern city and before they ended up in Washington, D.C.—after a brief detour to their native Brooklyn—and it was in a retail setting that Flo felt most comfortable.

Although Brixton was proud of Flo and her determination to open the shop, he had mixed emotions, which he managed to keep to himself—for the most part. Since returning to D.C. and establishing his private detective agency in a small suite adjacent to the law offices of Mackensie Smith, Brixton's patron saint in the nation's capital, Flo had been his decorator, confidante, painter, booster, lover, and receptionist/secretary. Her decision to

strike out on her own and open the boutique had sent
Brixton into a funk that negatively impacted the investigative work he did, and it had taken pep talks from Smith
and his wife, Annabel, as well as some gentle soothing
of his ruffled feathers by Flo, before he snapped out of it
and accepted the fact that she was no longer in his outer
office greeting clients with her infectious smile. Flo had
personally chosen her replacement, Eloise Warden, aptly
named as far as Brixton was concerned, a stern, no-
nonsense middle-aged woman with a headful of tight
graying curls who was every bit as efficient as Flo had
been, but who lacked her beauty and outgoing personality. Had Flo deliberately picked Ms. Warden from the
roster of women who had applied for the job, most of
them young and sexy, to head off competition for Brixton's affection? Flo had flared when he'd raised that possibility and he'd wisely not brought it up again.

On this lovely spring day Brixton stood across the
street from the boutique and admired a new green-and-
white awning that had been installed above the large window and door. He'd just returned to the city from time
spent following a young Department of Agriculture
bureaucrat whose wife was convinced that he spent his
lunch hours visiting a lover. Brixton followed the guy
from the Department of Agriculture building to a Virginia
town where he entered a one-story building in which
customers raced miniature cars around a large, elaborate
track using a joystick to control the cars' speed. Brixton
figured that as long as he was there he might as well sign
up for a session, too, rather than sit outside in a hot car
waiting for his target to emerge. He ended up racing the
man he'd been following, a pleasant way to spend the
afternoon although he lost every race.

"You come here often?" Brixton asked casually, realizing that he sounding like a guy using the oldest icebreaker
in the world to chat up a woman at a bar.

"Every chance I get," the man said. He was short,

chubby, prematurely balding, and wore thick glasses that rendered his eyes twice their normal size. Hardly the lothario type.

"I really enjoy this place," the man said after winning their fourth race. "My wife won't let me race real cars so I come here. It's an addiction I suppose."

"Like sex?" Brixton asked as he positioned his small yellow race car at the starting line in preparation for the fifth race.

"Sex? Addiction? I wouldn't know. You have that problem?"

"Me? No. But I can see how this can get in your blood. It's my first time."

"You'll get the hang of it. Ready, set, go!"

They shook hands as they left the racing hobbyists' emporium.

"A pleasure meeting you Harold," the alleged cheater said, using the name Brixton had assumed. "What do you do for a living?"

"Ah, I'm self-employed. Finance."

"Well, hope to see you here again. Have a nice night."

Brixton surreptitiously followed the guy home until he pulled into his driveway. On his way back to the District Brixton could only laugh at what he would consider writing in his report to the suspicious wife: "Husband skipped out of work and spent the afternoon being aroused while playing with his joystick." *Nah. Don't be a wise guy Robert. Make the wife happy by reporting that her husband's passion wasn't another woman, just little model cars going around in circles.*

He dodged traffic as he crossed Wisconsin Avenue and stepped into the shop where Flo was busy with a customer. She waved and flashed him a smile. "Robert," she called, "I want you to meet someone."

Brixton circumnavigated clothing racks and went to where Flo stood with a strikingly beautiful woman who was admiring her image in a full-length mirror.

"Jayla," Flo said, "this is the Robert I've been telling you about."

The woman with the unusual name smiled at Brixton. That she had African American blood in her genetic makeup was obvious from the rich cinnamon sheen of her face and hands. Her features were what writers termed "classic," a thin nose in perfect proportion to her facial architecture, somewhat angular, a lovely set of lips above a proud chin, all of it framed by ebony hair that glistened in the shop's overhead lighting. Brixton recognized the tan fitted dress she wore. Flo had shown that model to him when the shipment had arrived two months ago from the San Francisco designer with whom she'd forged a close working relationship.

"Hi," Jayla said, extending long, slender hands tipped in red to match her lipstick. "Flo is always talking about you."

"Probably better that I not know what she says about me," Brixton said through a grin.

"Would I ever say anything bad about you, Robert?" Flo asked, feigning hurt.

"Probably, but then I suppose I deserve it." He kissed Flo on the cheek and said to the customer, "I see you're wearing one of Flo's creations, Ms. . . ."

"King, but please call me Jayla."

"I don't create it," Flo protested. "Jason in San Francisco creates it. I just sell it."

"But you have a very good eye for what looks good," Jayla said.

"I'll accept that," Flo said.

"I second it," Brixton threw in. "Nice name, Jayla King."

"I obviously didn't choose it," Jayla said. She turned to Flo. "I really like this dress."

She disappeared into one of three fitting rooms at the rear of the boutique.

"A knockout of a woman," Brixton commented.

"Isn't she beautiful? She's a scientist."

"A beautiful scientist," Brixton said reverentially.

"She does medical research for a company in Bethesda."

"Maybe she can give me something for my bald spot," Brixton said. "It's getting bigger."

"It's supposed to. You're a man. Get a testosterone shot."

"Bad for the prostate."

"I wouldn't know about that."

Jayla emerged from the dressing room wearing the new dress. "I love it," she announced, doing a pirouette in front of the mirror. As she did, her cell phone, which rested on a small table next to her purse, sounded. She picked it up and said, "Hello? . . . Yes, this is Jayla . . . Eugene? . . . Is something wrong? . . . Oh, no . . ."

She sat heavily in one of two tan barrel chairs near the dressing rooms.

"How, Eugene? . . . When? . . . Oh, my God . . . Yes, of course I'll come . . . As soon as I can . . . What? . . . The lab? . . . Why? . . . I know, I know, I'll know soon enough . . . Thank you for calling, Eugene . . . Yes, good-bye."

"Something wrong?" Flo asked her.

She slumped in the chair, her face a portrait of despair. "That was my father's lab assistant. He's been killed."

"The lab assistant?" Brixton asked.

"No, my father. He's been murdered." Her fingers trembled as she brushed a hand through her hair.

Brixton and Flo expressed their dismay at the news and asked if they could do anything.

"Thank you, no," Jayla said. "I have to get home and pack, book a flight." She realized that she was wearing a dress that she hadn't purchased. "I love it but—"

"I'll put it aside for you," Flo said. "Please, Jayla, let us know if there's anything we can do."

Jayla changed back into her own clothes, gave Flo a brief hug, and shook Brixton's hand. "It was good to meet you," she said. "I have to run."

"Travel safe," Brixton said. "Sorry for the reason for your trip."

After Jayla had left, and the shop was empty aside from Brixton and Flo, Brixton took a bag of trash to a dumpster in the alley behind the shop. He returned, made sure that the back door was securely locked, and rejoined Flo. "Her father was murdered, huh?" he said. "Where's she from?"

"New Guinea. Papua New Guinea."

"Where's that? In Africa?"

"Somewhere near Australia. I feel terrible for her. She's a terrific person and a good customer. Let's turn out the lights and go home. It's been a busy day."

2

PAPUA NEW GUINEA

Jayla King caught the last flight that evening from Washington to Los Angeles where she would connect with a Qantas flight to Sydney, Australia. It had been a mad scramble to make the flight. She'd raced home to haphazardly pack a carry-on bag, and called Renewal Pharmaceuticals' CEO and president Walt Milkin, to tell him that she wouldn't be at work the following day due to a family emergency.

"Your father was *murdered*?" he said, his voice mirroring his shock. "You take all the time you need, Jayla."

She called a car service to rush her to Dulles Airport where she boarded the United flight a little after nine. It was fourteen hours earlier in Papua New Guinea, seven o'clock in the morning. It had been three A.M. there when her father's assistant, Eugene Waksit, had called her cell to deliver the devastating news.

Because she'd booked the flight at the last minute she ended up in a middle seat, between a middle-aged woman with a seemingly endless supply of chocolate-covered fruit candies and who obviously wanted to engage in conversation, and a heavyset man with a perpetual scowl who opened his laptop computer immediately upon sitting and made a show of angling it away from Jayla, who wasn't the least bit interested in what was on his screen. As she tried to get comfortable in the hard, narrow coach seat she wished that she'd been born shorter. The back of the seat belonging to the passenger in front almost touched her knees; with any luck he wouldn't decide to recline once they'd taken off.

Jayla King stood three inches shorter than six feet thanks to her father, a lanky man who seemed always to be leaning slightly forward. "You have a socialite's slouch," a colleague used to say, which amused her father. His untamable shock of white hair also elicited the comment, "You have the look of a mad scientist," which also brought forth a hearty laugh. Dr. Preston King's laugh was always at the ready, and Jayla heard his laugh as though he was there with her as the flight attendants closed the aircraft's doors and the recorded preflight instructions came through the speakers.

There hadn't been time to cry between the moment she'd received the bad news and boarded the 767 to Los Angeles. Now strapped in the metal tube that would wing her on the first leg of her trip, the tears came softly, quietly. She did her best to keep her sorrow to herself, not wanting others to be aware of her sadness. It was hers alone to suffer.

Once the plane was airborne, the passenger in the seat in front of her reclined his seatback as far as it would go, and Jayla wished that she was wealthy enough to have booked a first-class seat, assuming one had been available. While well paid at her job at the Renewal Pharmaceutical Company in Bethesda, whose financing came mostly from venture capitalists, she knew that she would never be rich. Not that she aspired to riches, aside from when forced to squeeze into a torturous airline seat.

She'd achieved her lifelong dream in 2010 of earning her PhD in molecular biology from the Australian

National University in Canberra. Landing a job as a re-searcher in the United States with Renewal Pharmaceuti-cals added to her joy and sense of accomplishment. The memory of her father beaming at the ceremony when she was awarded her doctorate brought more silent tears as she maneuvered her body to shield her emotions from her seatmates. She'd managed politely to fend off attempts at conversation by the woman next to her, who eventually fell asleep. Jayla wanted to sleep, too, but each time she closed her eyes her father's smiling face roused her: "Just remember, Jayla," he'd often said, "medical research is controlled by those with money, big money. Never let their money corrupt you. Always be true to yourself."

Her sudden audible burst of tears captured the atten-tion of her male seatmate, who looked up quizzically. "Just relax," he said. "These planes don't go down." He went back to his laptop, and Jayla managed a grim smile. He'd thought she was afraid of flying. At least he hadn't grabbed her hand to offer comfort. Her only concern about flying was whether she would arrive in Los Angeles in time to catch the Qantas flight that left a few minutes before midnight. On other trips to Sydney she'd broken up the long, tiring trip with a layover in L.A, but this time was different, of course. Her only thought was to get to her hometown of Port Moresby, Papua New Guinea, as quickly as possible.

He's dead? Murdered?
How could it be?

Headwinds from west to east had thankfully been light, and the flight arrived at LAX a few minutes early. She raced through the terminal with her small carry-on bag, made it through the second layer of Security with-out incident, and was the last passenger to board the Qantas 747 before its doors closed. This time she had a row to herself and managed to doze off, awakening when the cabin crew served meals, and when the cap-tain announced that they were approaching Sydney where, he happily reported, the weather was sunny and pleasant.

Her nap on the flight had served only to contribute to her grogginess as she deplaned at Terminal One in Sydney's Kingsford Smith International Airport. She passed through Customs and headed in the direction of the Air Niugini desk where she was told that the next flight to Port Moresby would depart in two hours. She purchased a ticket, found the nearest restaurant, and took a chair in an exterior section that jutted out into the terminal, affording a view of the multitude of passengers scurrying to and from their flights. She'd sat in that same outdoor café with her father during a previous trip home.

He'd flown to Sydney from Port Moresby to meet his daughter and only child and they'd spent a glorious four days together, taking in shows, dining in good restaurants, and catching up on their respective lives. She hadn't accompanied him back to Port Moresby that time—her vacation days were few—and now wished that she had. While her father was unfailingly pleasant and at times even gregarious, it was in Papua New Guinea (PNG) that his good nature and belief in his work truly emerged.

Dr. Preston King had trained to become a physician in Sydney and had begun his medical practice at the Royal North Shore Hospital in that city, where he advanced through the ranks to become the youngest doctor in the hospital's history to be named head of a department, in this case the bustling emergency room. He was revered by staff and patients alike, although he could be harsh on those who didn't live up to his high standards. Medicine was his life; he hadn't married by the age of forty although he'd had affairs and was considered a prize

catch by the many single women with whom he inter-
acted, professionally and otherwise.

But Preston King had another passion besides medicine,
and that was anthropology, particularly the indigenous
tribes of New Guinea, the world's second largest island,
trailing only Greenland. He devoured books by anthro-
pologists, and began making trips to the island to learn
firsthand about its myriad tribes. It was during one of
those trips in 1982 that he developed a powerful sense
of mission to bring an improved health system to the
island's people. Upon his return he made a shocking announcement to his superiors at the Sydney hospital: "I am
resigning and moving to Papua New Guinea."

A year after settling in Port Moresby and opening his
clinic, King fell in love with Lanisha, one of his nurses, a
stately, sensuous black woman whose Melanesian heri-
tage traced back thousands of years to one of hundreds
of primitive tribes. Eyes were invariably raised over the
marriage between the fair-skinned Australian physician
and his ebony wife, which cut into their social life. It
meant little to King. He'd become immersed in his work,
both as a clinician, and in the laboratory he'd built as an
addition to their modest house.

A year later Lanisha gave birth to a daughter, Jayla,
whose arrival filled them with unimaginable pride and
joy. For Lanisha that ecstasy was short-lived. She died of
pneumonia when Jayla was three, leaving Dr. King with
the task of being both mother and father to the child.

When Jayla was sixteen, her father left her at home in
Port Moresby while he traveled to the jungles of the Sepik
River where he was privileged to witness the coming of
manhood in native boys. They were initiated by having
their backs, chests, and thighs sliced open with a bamboo
razor, one cut after another until, despite having ingested
a drink made from coconut leaves to dull the pain, they
passed out. Ash was then worked into the gaping wounds
to create what resembled the backs of crocodiles, and

the wounds were rubbed with clay. The young men then waited together for days in a special hut until they were told by tribal elders that they were now men and could rejoin the world, having been "ingested" by the mighty crocodile and emerging with the power of those powerful, mystic reptiles that ply the waters of Papua New Guinea. Those with the most grievous wounds were considered especially attractive to the tribe's females.

"A brutal rite of manhood," Dr. King told Jayla after he'd returned and had recounted his firsthand look at the practice, "but with important meaning for the tribes. Despite the cruel nature of the initiation, they are peaceful, kind people, and treated me with respect."

By the time King's wife had died he'd purchased acreage in the Sepik River region, a remote area of the island on its northwest corner named after the winding river, where many of Papua New Guinea's primitive tribes still lived. He didn't buy the tract as a land speculator. He'd become infatuated with the need to develop more effective pain medications after treating patients with intractable suffering, and it was in his lab that he'd begun experimenting with natural herbs and plants grown in his four-acre plot in search of a more potent medicine without the addictive qualities of the day's popular prescribed painkillers. To say that he was dedicated to that goal was not an overstatement.

Jayla was so consumed with memories of her father and of growing up in Port Moresby that she almost failed to hear the boarding call for her Air Niugini flight and had to run to the gate.

She was going to what had been her home, but it would not be the same without him. She handed her ticket to the gate agent and prepared for the final four-hour leg of her sorrowful journey to Papua New Guinea, seventeen hundred miles away—a million miles away in her heart.